KINGDOMS ON FIRE

CARLY STEVENS

For my readers

May it rain hope always

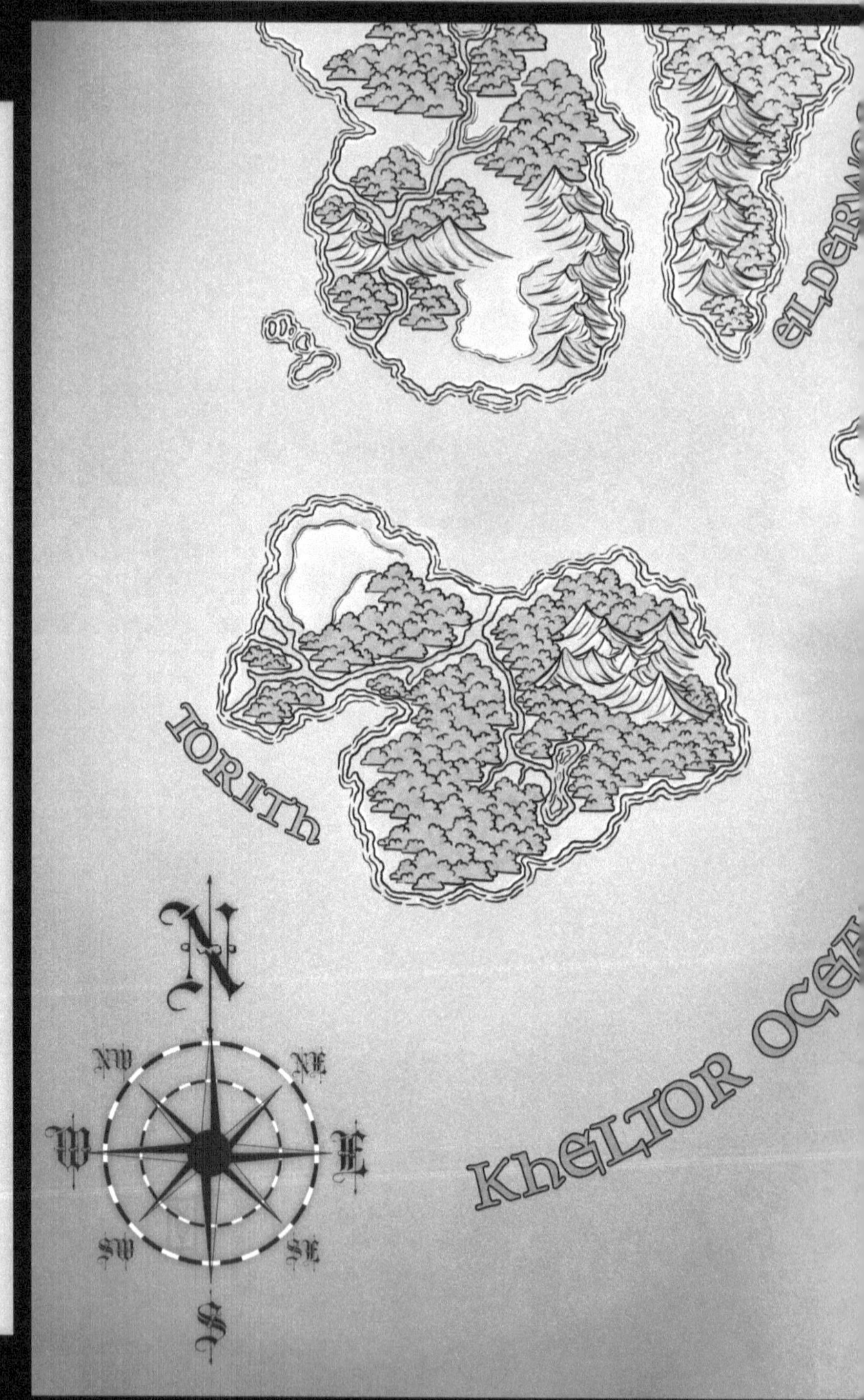

ELDERWO
TORITH
KHELTOR OCEA
N
NW
NE
W
E
SW
SE
S

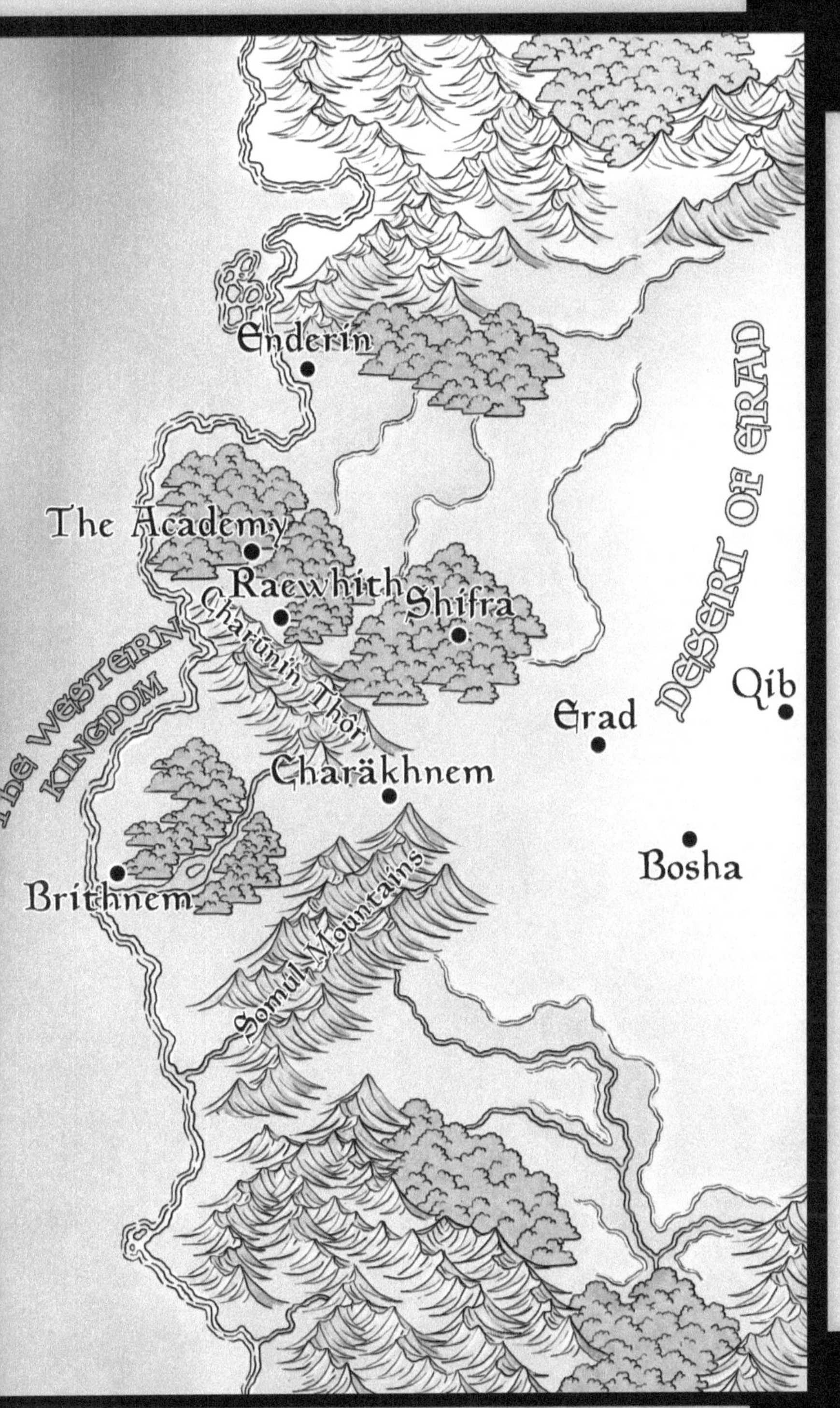

Enderin
The Academy
Raewhith
Shifra
Charunin Thor
Charäkhnem
Brithnem
Somul Mountains
The Western Kingdom
Desert of Grad
Erad
Qib
Bosha

GRAY
FORES
GRAND
market square
PORT
amiran
academy
MON PÁRINATH
ROY
wa
SHORE
LITTLE
MARKET

BRITHNEM
N
W
E
S
MAZE
FARMERS GUARD
ABRECAN GATE
SCROLLWAY
STONEWAY
ARENA
TESTING GROUNDS
OTHELIN RIVER
GRAY FOREST

1

BELIK

Master Belik had three reasons to burn the palace.

It would demoralize the people of Brithnem, bring its soldiers to him, and split their attention as they tried to salvage treasures and lives from the castle. If he hit the right pressure points, surrender would come quickly.

Belik limped down the wide, shadowed hallway of Mon Pári-nath, flanked by high-ranking Tanyu, and weakened from his encounter with that traitor Bard. Though his breath came labored, power ran like iron through his veins after watching the boy bend backward through the sheer force of Belik's mind. It should have been gruesome, but all he'd felt was grim fascination. Rightness.

Finding the royal bedchambers when he'd arrived had been easy. The buzz that constantly vibrated at the corners of his mind spoke of traversing these halls a thousand times. He didn't remember consciously following Chetana in years, but as soon as he set foot in the palace, he knew the layout like a memory.

The First and Third Keepers had been in their rooms, in bed with their wives. Each had a coterie of four soldiers guarding the door. One problem with royals was that they lacked imagination. All the guards were exactly where he expected them to be. When the black-clad Tanyuin warriors had arrived, striking out of the dark like vipers with their knifing teeth, the soldiers had no time to scream, much less draw their weapons. They dropped like sacks.

Belik ordered the Keepers to be killed painlessly. Mercy had gripped him at random. It didn't matter if they bled or not, if they suffered or not. The only thing that mattered was that Cúron's and Atael's deaths be undeniable and deliberate.

After the chaos, he would escort the soldiers off the palace grounds. The Tanyu would station themselves inside the beating heart of power, with the sea behind them, giving themselves access to limitless resources.

Most of the work of conquering a kingdom wasn't physical, but mental. Once the people believed the Tanyu had won, then they had. Resistance would wane, and everyone would become more and more convinced that this was how it ought to be.

All it takes is belief.

Tanyuin Masters had repeated those words over and over again. Belik set his mouth hard as he took another uneven step, cursing his bad leg in frustration.

Belik had believed in Firian. The moment he first saw the boy, he knew this was the one who could make the Tanyu great, could make *him* great.

Belik's earlier protégé, Anewa, had gone far but ultimately failed, getting irreparably Lost in the Unreal, despite Belik's efforts to save him. Belik needed someone even stronger. And for a long time he didn't think anyone could live up to his expectation.

Firian was the exception. His intensity had been obvious from the moment he arrived at the Tanyuin Academy. He would do whatever it took to become a Master. Too many Learners started by doing what was asked of them and assuming they would rise through the ranks. Idiots. A Master was not only a master of the Tanyuin arts, but of his own fate.

Firian had practiced often enough and hard enough to earn even Belik's grudging respect. Firian might have more scars than Belik did on his own body. Scars proved his effort—that he pushed himself to the edge of what was possible. More than once, Belik had been forced to grab Firian out of the Unreal before he believed in his own death.

He took a sharp breath through his nose at the memory. The air was filled with an underlying must. It had seen blood. He huffed it back out again, eyeing the shadowed corners. This hall wouldn't be quiet for long. Even now, footsteps and shouts filtered through the hazy air. Took them long enough. He halted in the center of the elaborate corridor. Master Nedi, the leader of physical training after Jovan died a few months ago, towered on his left. Shiro, a young Tanyu about nineteen, Firian's age, stood at his right.

There had obviously been questions about Firian's whereabouts. Most thought that they were acting on Firian's orders.

In the few seconds of peace they'd had since they entered the palace, Belik told several of them that Firian's true plan had surfaced—using them to eliminate the other Keepers so he could rule with Kiria alone.

Close enough to the truth.

In a different way, Firian had betrayed the Tanyu by suddenly acting the coward. Belik included some vague nonsense about Firian's exhaustion after using his killing ability, so the others wouldn't be as afraid to attack him if he showed his face. When he showed his face.

Belik's chest felt hard as stone with disappointment. How could Firian fall prey to the same vice Belik had years before? The injustice of it scratched at his heart. He'd been so careful to make Firian loyal only to the Academy. He'd raised him as he would have raised his own son, if he'd gotten the chance. And *still!* He gritted his teeth.

That girl had gotten her claws into him so deeply there was nothing Belik could do. Waiting outside the capital city of Brithnem, ready with an army, Firian had simply called off the attack. Called it off. Because some girl told him to. It didn't matter that she was the Second Keeper. That should have made her opinion matter *less*.

It was almost impossible to think that Firian could be so spineless. Especially when justice was this close.

A group of armored Kingdom soldiers appeared around the corner. Only fifteen. Over half of them had light blue cloth across their shoulders marking them as palace guards. One of them caught Belik's attention. He wore many insignias the others didn't and was the first to direct the others toward the Tanyu.

Belik needed to speak to Kingdom generals. He could start here.

The approaching soldiers rushed forward, swords drawn. The Tanyu didn't move. A corner of Belik's lip curled upward. These soldiers had such fierce expressions as they came on. Despite their fervor, they would attack in a spearhead formation, probably all using their right hands to wield identical swords.

At a twitch of his head, two more Masters materialized from behind him to stand by his sides. He communicated with their minds in the Unreal, out of earshot of the charging soldiers. "Everyone but the leader."

The fight was brief. The Tanyu, both in black, whirled through the crowd of soldiers like ghosts. A couple missed opportunities—Belik's eyes narrowed—but the warriors exploited vulnerabilities in the armor and the soldiers soon dropped. The leader, who appeared to be a general, at least, stood with his arms wrenched behind his back, face to face with Belik.

Shiro ripped off the man's helmet and threw it away with a clank. The leader was middle-aged and sandy-haired, with high cheekbones and almond-shaped eyes. To the soldier's credit, he didn't openly quail before the Tanyu, but a white rim shone around his irises.

Belik resettled his glasses on his nose. The air was getting smokier. "I would like to speak to the other generals."

The man's mouth closed in mute defiance.

Belik sniffed. There was no time for this. "Tell them I'll meet them just outside the barracks in an hour. I have an offer for them."

Confusion replaced the insolence in the man's face, which was an improvement, at least as Belik's plan was concerned.

"Something good," Belik clarified, as though speaking to a child. "Of course, they can refuse it." He regarded the man meaningfully. Refusal meant death—surely he could understand that. He'd just watched all these men die.

The man eyed the weapons around him warily, as though he could fight them off with mere awareness. But more than everywhere else, his eyes landed on Belik's face, meeting his gaze.

"The Keepers are dead," Belik explained, "and I don't want this to be bloodier than it has to be."

"Lies!" the general spat, the word ricocheting out of his mouth.

Belik backhanded him casually. "You'll see their heads in the arena square before sunset tomorrow."

The man's pale lip twitched convulsively, though whether from sorrow or horror, it was difficult to tell. Faint crackling sounded in the distance as Belik let the moment stretch, grow heavy with significance.

"It's done," Belik resumed. "The Tanyu have control of the

city. You can take my offer and be part of restoring peace, or you can doom your soldiers to painful deaths. You know our reputation, what we can do. There's no Keeper to stand behind. One hour." He growled the final words one by one.

The Tanyuin Master released the general and gave him back his sword. The gesture seemed to baffle the man, but he slowly sheathed his weapon and left.

When the general was out of sight, the Master trailed him down the hall and out the door, silent as smoke, which was filling the space.

"Outside," Belik told the others. He had an hour before he could deal with the other generals. The Masters around him could stop anything but a fight with truly overwhelming numbers. And it took more than a few ordinary soldiers to take down a Tanyu. If he moved quickly, they wouldn't have time to plan an attack coordinated enough to take him down, and now the military leaders had the draw of his offer. Imminently generous, and most of them would see that. What were riches for except to direct power?

Shiro opened the exterior door as Belik passed through. Even the glass in the door was decorated. Were these Keepers trying to compensate for their lack of military imagination by keeping everything pretty?

Apart from a couple indiscreet Torithians and border patrollers from Tánuil hauling loot from the burning palace across the gardens, it was a quiet night. Even now, with two of the three thrones standing empty.

He needed to empty all three. They'd find the girl soon enough. He'd make sure of it. His mind shuffled backward a few paces, a few minutes.

Bard, that deserter, had bought her enough time to get away. In the rush of the initial attack, no one could sense where she'd gone. Firian knew, but he'd already made his preference clear. He'd choose her safety over the Academy.

Honestly, Belik didn't regret the time it took to kill the boy. Another Tanyu could have done it quickly, but Bard seemed like he would make a good first victim, since there had to be victims. A little smaller than male Tanyu tended to be, and too weak for violence, he was unlikely to fight back. And he had betrayed the Academy. Run off to spill their secrets to Kiria, the girl who had her barbs in Firian. No one betrayed the Academy to that extent and lived.

Belik had felt young and powerful again as he showed off his new ability for the first time. It was simultaneously horrible and thrilling to open his eyes and find Bard's spine bent backward and blood leaking from his ears. Shiro was the only one near him at the time, but he had been suitably impressed. Impressed wasn't the word. As Bard's body collapsed, Shiro was terrified, awestruck.

Hopefully Belik would never have to use that power against another Tanyu again, past or present. That part rankled. That, and the fact that little Bard had been a friend of Firian.

The perfume of flowers softened the air around him as he moved quickly across the flagstone patio of the garden. This false peace wouldn't last. Time was against him. Right now, he needed to get inside the one place he swore he'd never go: the Amiran Academy.

2

FIRIAN

Firian heaved out a shaky breath and readjusted the body he carried across his shoulders. Bard's limp form was surprisingly heavy and unstable, even though Firian grabbed his wrists tightly. His arm wrapped around the crook of Bard's knees, even though that meant limited mobility for that hand. If a guard came to kill them both, he would have to drop his friend and fight.

No, the guard wouldn't come to kill Bard. Only Belik wanted him dead, and he thought he had finished the job. Only the faint warm breath against Firian's left cheek suggested Belik was wrong. Bard was alive, but barely.

Something warm and wet slid down Firian's temple and dripped off his jaw. Blood. Bard's blood.

Firian bit back a groan as he picked up his pace. He needed a doctor. Now. The only one he could remember was the doctor who had come for Salaar, the Amir Firian had killed in his sleep several months ago. He barely recalled what the man looked like, much less his name.

With palace guards after him, and Belik no longer an ally,

Firian was on his own. He fought back panic. Getting out of this enormous tomb seemed like it had to be the first step.

Which doors would Belik and the other Tanyu have used? Judging from the silence, they would still be unguarded for a few moments. Firian conjured a map in his mind, ticking off the options. Belik wanted to kill, to conquer. One choice stood out. It was what Firian would have done.

If Firian had had a bad leg, that is.

There were high windows no one bothered to guard that could be easy entrance points, but Belik couldn't reach them. Firian had shown Kiria last year. Her two friends had been there, too—the Third Keeper and his brother.

His brother, Jori.

Firian blinked hard, willing himself to come out of the Unreal. He hated to admit it, but shock sometimes thrust him into the Unreal without his knowledge. If he didn't realize his mistake about reality, he could be Lost forever in that imaginary space.

He'd realized quickly this time, at least. Jori Calthwaite sprinted toward him in a radically unlikely way. His billowy white shirt and open embroidered vest flowed around him in his speed. His gray boots rose to uneven heights on his legs. When he saw Firian, he skidded to a halt and drew himself up like a fighter in a children's story. Like he'd never really fought anyone before. His face was chalk white.

"Where's Kiria?" he demanded, too loudly. "Is she alive?"

Firian couldn't break out of the illusion, so he spat back, "Yes! Where's a doctor?"

Jori's chin trembled with his next words. "You didn't kill her?"

Firian adjusted his hold on Bard's wrists, jogging him further up on his shoulders. "No. A doctor!" At this point it didn't matter if what he saw was real. Bard was dying.

Jori squinted at Bard, as though seeing him for the first time. "Is that Bard?"

Firian cursed. "Yes. I need a doctor *now!*"

Jori waved him forward, breaking into a run. "Here, here," he said.

Firian followed Jori's kicking heels, eyes darting to all the details he and Kiria had changed. The purple of the carpets, leaves of the *sachion* trees, frames of the portraits, panes in the windows—everything was right. He wasn't in the Unreal. This was really happening.

Jori ducked into a small storage room. He jumped high-kneed over bags of dried food and piles of silk blankets like someone who had done this hundreds of times. Bundling sheets in his arms, he threw them out of the way, revealing a small square door underneath, set low into the wall. It came up to Jori's thigh.

Firian calculated whether he could crawl through with Bard in his arms. It was challenging, but he could make it work if this was the only way. "This leads to the doctor?" he demanded.

"We have to get out," Jori said, his voice desperate as he started to force open the door.

Bending forward so Bard would stay in place from his own weight, Firian grabbed Jori's throat and forced him to his feet. "Is this the quickest way?"

Terrified tears streamed down Jori's face. "Please..."

"Is it?" Firian gave him a shake. Bard's legs began to slump off his shoulders. He let go of Jori to catch Bard behind the knees again.

Jori fell to the floor, gesturing helplessly to the tiny opening. "There's a doctor through here."

"Then go." Firian kicked him, galvanizing him into action again. He had no time for panic, no time to think. Bard's body was still warm against the back of his head, but he couldn't be sure he felt breathing anymore when his own was so erratic.

As Jori lunged headfirst into the opening, Firian eased Bard to the ground, considering all the ways to haul him through this space that must be only for emergencies. He took Bard by the armpits and dragged him to the opening, getting himself inside first, and then Bard after him. It was an awkward arrangement. Bard was lying partly on top of him with his back against Firian's chest, but Firian found he could push his way along with his legs while still holding onto Bard.

There were no lights in the tunnel and very little air. The claustrophobic smell of mold and dampness permeated his nostrils. "How far does this go?" he hissed.

Jori's voice sounded far ahead of him. "Just this way."

That didn't answer his question, so Firian just focused on going as fast as he could, pushing off with his feet as he dragged Bard's limp body. Again and again and again. A faint heartbeat pulsed beneath Bard's arms. He was still holding on. The earthen floor of the tunnel scraped Firian's back as he forced himself backward, heedless of anything in his path. Part of his shirt ripped loudly, shredded by the pebbles.

Finally, light fell over them. Firian's head cast a black shadow over Bard, so he couldn't see his friend's face, couldn't see if more blood leaked from his eyes like tears. With renewed energy, Firian kicked against the walls and tumbled out onto wet grass. The light had come from the moon. They were outside the palace walls, though where exactly, Firian couldn't tell. Surf crashed in the distance and the shadowy shapes of buildings rose over the grassy basin where they'd emerged.

Jori was already sprinting away. Firian cursed repeatedly under his breath as he bent down to pick up Bard. Jori had to be running for the doctor. If he was running to get away from the

Tanyuin invasion, he was a gory coward who deserved worse than what Bard was enduring.

Firian's breath seized. Bard's light brown face had gone gray. He still had a pulse, but he was fading fast. Even a doctor might not be able to save him. "Come on," he muttered as he pulled him up again. The flowing breeze cooled his back and confirmed his suspicion that much of the shirt had been torn away. He was probably bleeding, but it didn't matter.

He eased Bard's unconscious body to the ground. No warm air feathered against the back of his hand when he held it against Bard's mouth. Too much time passed between thick heartbeats before a sign of life appeared.

From the top of the knoll, Jori and a man ran toward them. "Here's a doctor. It's a doctor," Jori said when he reached them.

The doctor was tall and thin, middle-aged, with a hanging lip and a wary eye, like some homeless travelers Firian had seen. Despite looking as though Jori had woken him from a deep sleep, the man looked at Bard with precision and concern, and Firian had no other choice. This doctor had to help, or there was no hope to save his friend. Maybe hope had already left.

The doctor knelt next to him, checking his vitals.

Firian stood above them, unable to walk away. But a second task assaulted his mind, now that this one was done. He couldn't do anything more to help Bard. His life or death was out of his hands now. He'd done what he could. Even with those reasonable words, he lingered. Was there nothing—*nothing*—more he could do?

Bard's eyes were glued shut with blood. The backs of his hands were filthy from rubbing against the walls of the tunnel. Firian watched his chest to see it rise and fall, just once. Then he could leave. It felt like a long time before he saw it.

He swallowed. "Give him the best treatment," he told the

doctor. "He lives." He said it like an ultimatum. When he glanced up from Bard, Jori had already gone.

Spinning around, he saw the palace rising behind him. They'd gone just past the wall enclosing the palace grounds. In there was Belik.

Without looking back, he dove into the dark passageway, running like an animal on all fours. Belik had defied him, tried to kill Bard, taken control of his men, gone after Kiria... The crimes went on in an endless list. All the lies and manipulation he had endured came back like bitterness on his tongue. How had he not seen this coming? "Gore," he muttered and pushed himself to speed up.

He burst through the other side of the tunnel, colliding with a basket of candles in his speed. They rolled across the floor as he leapt over them to get to the hallway.

As he emerged from the storeroom, he grabbed a long strip of cloth, tying it around his palm as he ran. Where was Belik? He tightened the end of the knot with his teeth.

Belik wanted the Tanyu to have control of Brithnem. He hadn't given the Keepers a peaceable option, so he would take what he wanted. That meant that he would follow the method he taught Firian: disable the leaders and have the public swear you in on whatever they deemed holy. In this case, the Sacred Scroll. Firian hadn't brought his copy from the Academy since Brithnem was known to have duplicates. If those tactics didn't work, he'd threaten their lives and the lives of those they cared about.

Belik had already gone after the Keepers. Firian cast his thoughts toward Kiria again. He still felt the distinct buzz of her presence on the edge of his thoughts. She was in distress, but not dead. For now, anyway, she was safe. Hopefully she'd found someplace to hide until he could put this right.

He looked down at the carpet rushing beneath him and took

a slow breath. *This is the best way to help her. She might not take my help now anyway.* The thought did little to dissuade him from going to find her, but it did enough. He would find out more about Kiria later.

What about Cúron and Atael? There was no time. Checking on them would mean wasting time looking for Belik. Belik was the one who needed to be stopped. He had betrayed Firian in the worst way possible. Even the thought brought the taste of blood to Firian's mouth.

He had to be at the Amiran Academy. It was the only place guaranteed to have copies of the Sacred Scroll. Few of the Amir would consent to crown Belik the leader, or Keeper, or whatever he demanded. But he had to be there.

The closest exit brought him past Kiria's bedroom again. Hopefully no guards would slow him down.

Even as he thought it, he heard footsteps behind him. It didn't matter whose they were, Kingdom or Tanyu. Firian stopped dead and whipped out his knife. Eight Kingdom guards in silver and blue ran toward him, swords in hand. Behind them was a strange orange glow. The fire on the outer edge couldn't be raging so fiercely that its light reached that far.

The truth dawned. The palace itself was on fire.

But that wasn't why the guards were running. The fight in their eyes showed they were coming for him.

He spread his legs in a fighting stance. Eight against one. Normally, those weren't great odds, but the fire in his veins made him feel superhuman. He had to find Belik. These people were just roadblocks. There wasn't time to explain that he wasn't the enemy. They wouldn't believe him anyway.

He sliced a warning in the air with his knife as he scanned the space. If he used his killing ability to wipe them out at once, he'd weaken himself too much to go after Belik. He wouldn't risk it.

Statue, window, plant, chandelier.

Creativity and simplicity. The words of Master Asoka, the woman who'd taught strategy at the Academy, came back to him. *Those make the best plans.*

The first two guards reached him.

With his wrapped hand, he grabbed the first soldier's sword by the blade and swirled it around into the man's knee, where the armor was vulnerable. *One down.* His other hand dug the dagger under the second soldier's arm.

Crouching by the injured bodies, Firian made the next soldier hesitate, unwilling to swing a weapon so near his writhing comrades. Mistake.

Firian slid the sword and dagger forward, parallel on the carpet. The hesitant soldier looked down. It was the entry Firian needed to vault over the men on the ground and plant a hard kick in the man's chest, sending him tumbling into the man next to him.

Both blades were in Firian's hands again. With another precise kick, he left the two men nursing broken bones. *Four down.*

A thrown knife incapacitated a fifth.

He parried a thrust from the next soldier. Most Kingdom guards heavily favored their right sides. Firian's observation over the last year had detected five primary moves that all seemed to master. Such a limited repertoire.

Keeping his eye on the two others, Firian fought the largest guard, probably the most experienced as well. Each parried thrust flung his opponent's sword in the direction of one of his comrades. Such action hamstrung both enemies at once.

Use everything at hand. You are part of the environment.

But he couldn't let the fluidity and rush of battle distract him from his mission. He didn't have time to waste here.

He switched the sword to his left hand and disarmed the

man with his right, protected by the cloth. A slice across the front of the helmet left his opponent crumpled on the ground.

Releasing his energy in a yell, he yanked down one of the large potted trees between them, leaving Firian with the exit. They stumbled out of its way, momentarily distracted. Firian raced in the other direction, watching the view from the windows.

He'd seen the Amiran Academy on the palace grounds before. It wasn't hard to find. He didn't wait for a door that might be guarded. The tied cloth guarded his hand against glass shards as he leapt through the nearest window frame.

Belik would have other people with him. If the Master had gone alone, palace guards would kill him for treason. If he went with a group of armed Tanyu, they could fight off the guards or hold Amir hostage, or however he thought best to get their attention and their pledge of loyalty.

The dome of the Amiran building rose beside the manicured gardens behind the castle. Columns surrounded its covered portico and round lanterns hung around the entire circumference. He knew those lights. His father, a glassmaker, had sent Firian to learn the family trade. All those white lanterns came from Raewhith, his hometown, but they were patterned on the colored lanterns of Shifra that Kiria loved so much.

His heart thundered as he charged toward the building. It was foolhardy to run in a straight line and in plain sight, but he didn't care. He could take down any Tanyu one on one if he had to, and it was a matter of extreme urgency. He couldn't slow his blood enough to hide in the shadows. Kiria, Bard, now Belik—it was too much. His body was alight with urgency. He barely felt his feet fall on the flagstones.

As he vaulted a green bush, he spotted the first Tanyu. It was just the sliver of an arm behind a column—there, and then out of sight. Almost a trick of the eye in the darkness. Without those globed lights, he might not have noticed it. Nothing else stirred.

He flew toward the column, catching the ankle of the traitor and then gripping them by the neck. He spun around to see Xan, a Tanyuin girl a couple years older than he was, stone-faced, hair braided back. She had fought with him under Tiev when the Tanyu had launched a fear campaign against the Kingdom. Before Firian became the Tanyuin Head and called off that war, which Belik had started up again. He tasted coppery blood in his mouth.

"Where is he?" he snarled in Xan's face. She looked confused rather than afraid, though her pulse raced in the web of his hand.

She could have brought her arms up to snatch his hand away, but didn't. Unable to speak, her eyes flicked from his face to a spot to his left. Adrenaline shot through his body. His hand flexed under her jaw as he turned around enough to see over his left shoulder. No Belik.

Until today, he had never had bad blood with Xan. For a heartbeat, he wondered what to do. Then he boxed her on the side of the head, knocking her out. He caught her as she fell so she wouldn't hit her skull on the stone floor. Belik was the only one who should die for his crimes.

He swiveled to the door directly behind him and yanked it open. A narrow, winding staircase led out of sight. There was no way to see if anyone lay in wait above.

Belik had taken control of the Tanyuin forces against Firian's will, so he had to know Firian would retaliate. Belik had pitted them against one another. Only one of them would make it out of the capital today. The thought made him catch his breath in a rush of emotions he couldn't name.

"Firian."

He whirled at the sound of his name. He knew that voice. It sounded as measured as ever.

"I'm glad you joined us." Down the walkway stood Belik, flanked by Tanyu. Shiro and Nedi were at the forefront. Blood speckled both their faces and their hands were stained dull red. Light from the burning palace lit Belik's face, highlighting the bruise purpling his jaw. Firian's heart pounded against his chest, the sound rushing in his ears. Before he knew what he was doing, he hurled himself at the Master.

Something hit his shins and he vaulted face-first to the ground. His arms were immediately pinned behind him and bound. White spots burst in his vision, but he tucked his knees under himself, getting ready to spring. He tried to explode upward, but the weight of many bodies held him down.

He reached toward the Second Level. These people were blocking his way to Belik... that traitor... that murderer...

"Firian." That hateful voice again. "They're just doing what I ask. If you kill us all, you'll kill good Tanyu and maybe yourself if you're not goddamn careful."

A shard of deliberation sliced through Firian's rage, and it said that Belik was right. Choking on fury, Firian opened his eyes. He was on his knees, his wrists attached to his ankles. Air felt trapped inside his ribcage. Stars still followed his vision as he narrowed a glare at Belik.

"There," said Belik. "I figured you'd be angry, but I finished our mission. I removed the Keepers and the city belongs to us. So don't be an idiot, and join us."

Rage clouded Firian's sight. He spat in response. Behind his back, he writhed his hands. Shredded bits of his shirt blew against them, but he wouldn't be able to slip the bonds unless he broke his thumbs. It wasn't time for that yet. He might still need his thumbs.

"This is what we've been working for all this time." Belik

inhaled through clenched teeth. "We know what you did, but there's still time to... atone." He fixed Firian with a look, impressing on him his crime of letting Kiria persuade him not to attack Brithnem. What Belik didn't understand—among many other things—was that the decision had been Firian's alone. It pained him, even now, but any other choice would have broken her heart, made him the monster he didn't want to be.

Firian would never apologize.

A muscle in Belik's jaw twitched and his nostrils flared. "Firian, I'm giving you a chance. Take it."

If the choice was between death and joining this man, the choice was easy. But Firian was fairly sure there was a third option. He didn't like it, but it lay in wait down in the Second Level, where everyone's brains and hearts and lungs pulsed with life. Firian suspended himself above that abyss, ready to plunge in if Belik made a move.

When Firian didn't answer, Belik's eyes narrowed. He nodded once to the Tanyu next to him, Master Nedi.

Nedi, huge and imposing, walked forward with purpose. Firian realized what he was going to do a second before it happened. Pain exploded in his temple and everything went black.

3

____

BELIK

BELIK DREW his mouth into a tight line as he watched the limp body of Firian being carried away, bound. All that strength, all that potential, tied up in another girl. He saw his own mind in those bonds. Chetana held a string he could never shear away, no matter how much he wanted to, no matter how much he hated it. Hate was easier than fear, more powerful, so he had chosen that a long time ago. He would kill her if he ever got the chance. The one who had seduced him, betrayed him...

Belik's lip curled. They were so close—literally moments away—from making their dream a reality and Firian had to screw it up out of a misplaced sense of... what? Honor? Lust? Whatever it was, Belik wouldn't beg. His road had been much longer than Firian's, though he had grown fond of the boy. Maybe Firian would realize his stupidity.

"What the gory hell was that?" Master Ardal demanded from behind him. "He's the Tanyuin Head. He'll kill you. He'll kill *us*."

Belik tore his eyes from Firian, whose hair flopped over his face, mouth lolling open as he disappeared past the light of the everlasting round lanterns.

"I didn't see you stepping in," he responded coolly. Master

Ardal had never impressed him. He taught World Events at the Academy, but he was rusty in action.

"I know not to put a target on my back."

"As you're doing now?" Belik raised one eyebrow meaningfully.

Despite a flash of apprehension, so quick it might never have been there at all, Ardal didn't back down. He'd argued with Belik before, although most Masters knew better than to try. "What did he do? If this is a coup, it's messy. Master Kess has many people on his side."

Messy? Maybe. Belik shrugged his massive shoulders, setting his expression into a glare.

Shiro stepped in to answer. Belik had told enough Tanyu to accomplish the initial mission. Word just needed to spread. "He only ordered the Keepers killed so he could rule with Kiria. That's why he disappeared. He helped her escape." The younger Tanyu's eyes flashed with hatred. He felt Firian's betrayal more than most, since Firian had accidentally killed his friend Rian when Kingdom soldiers raided the Academy.

"He wants to distance himself from the strike now," Belik added. "It's all right, Ardal. He lied to all of us. Turns out he had a *katah* with her." He felt his own anger rise with the word. This part was truth, and it made him seethe. "Firian was going to leave us all to rot. No justice for what the Kingdom did. You knew the victims of the attack on the Academy. I did too! So I'll get revenge with or without him." There was no one who could refute his story, but he'd have to remember the details so he could repeat them. His lie might as well be truth. "How else could she have known we were coming? Coward," he spat. "She left them all to die."

"She wants to be with Master Kess?" someone else asked. They were like children, all lapping up gossip. Firian had had plenty of girls. Why were they surprised about one more? Kiria was a child, no more than eighteen. Of course she'd want to be part of the grand play Firian promised with his power and his name.

Belik tried to prepare for the unpredictable, but was often disappointed when people acted exactly as he expected. No one was original anymore. Firian could have been. He could have gone somewhere...

"She won't show us mercy after this, if Firian gets his way." Belik grunted. "Hopefully he'll come around."

"He could have killed us all just now," Ardal insisted again.

"He could do that before." *Before the killing ability made it easier.* "I'll put it right." *And hopefully Firian will start thinking with his head and not his dick.*

Belik was tired of talking. There was work to be done. Right now, the generals in the barracks were no doubt arguing among themselves about the best course of action. That, or following attack protocol. Belik had stationed many Tanyu there to settle things before he arrived.

Belik turned to Shiro. White light from the round lanterns warred with the waning firelight, dominating opposite sides of the Defender's face. The sky had turned gray with the morning, but none of that light bled in. Belik was already sick of this soft place with all its religion and reminders of her.

"Advisors," he grunted. Shiro and another Tanyu ran to gather them.

He loped after them slowly, rounding the corner away from where they'd taken Firian. The weakness in his leg had gotten worse since he used his new ability on Bard. Someone appeared around the corner. His stomach jolted with nerves.

Just a Tanyu. He cursed himself. Death didn't frighten him—his plan would work, he was reasonably sure—but his body reacted with anxiety now that he was so close to his son. Seething anger layered under his skin, at himself, at her... He hadn't seen his son since he was a baby, and since he was three-quarters Khelê, he didn't have to bear any resemblance to either of his parents.

Shiro and his companion returned with three Amir in tow. They stood with regal dignity, as though standing before Belik were beneath them. Belik fought the urge to spit on one of the gory prisses' boots. They all wore the same grayish blue robes, but the one on the left was the oldest, with dark, thinning hair slicked back. In the center was a younger one who looked like a stereotypical Kingdom man, deep-set eyes, fair skin and dark hair. On the right was another man who might be the same age as the one in the center. It was difficult to tell. He was clearly Khelê, having very large eyes and a small mouth. His irises might have been tinged with purple.

Belik scrutinized the ones on the center and the right. The man on the left was too old. Surrounded by the buzz of the other Tanyu, it was difficult to tell if any of these men had the Talent. Any son of his had to have it. "The Keepers are dead," he said. It would be true of all three soon enough, and the more people he told, the more plausible it sounded.

All three let out cries of horror.

Belik studied them impassively before continuing. "I need one of you to announce this to the people, and to inform them that the Tanyu will take ownership of the city at the next new moon."

"What proof do we have?" the oldest demanded hesitantly.

Belik stifled a smirk. "We'll show you later. Which of you will give the announcement?" Fractionally, he paused. "What are your names?" In the silence that followed, his heart started jogging in his chest. This was it. If he was right—and he was rarely wrong—this would be the moment he would meet his son.

"I am Parohim," said the eldest, "and this is Daelon and Reynard."

Daelon. Belik locked eyes with the one in the center, taking in the high-necked collar, the scholar's hands, the lined eyes, the youthful mouth, the straight nose. Daelon's skin wasn't dark like his mother's or pockmarked like his. A hint of defiance was the only sign Belik could detect of his parents' deadly personalities. His breath caught in his throat as Daelon looked him in the eye. His eyes had the tired look of someone who read too much but hadn't yet gotten glasses. He would need them in time. He was Belik's son, after all. A royal advisor. An Amir.

No scars at all.

He swallowed down the trapped air. Chetana had ruined their son. Daelon was a man of words, not action. He couldn't defend his home against the Tanyu. He couldn't even help his princess, or Keeper, as she was now. His only son, and she had twisted him with her own priorities, told him that the Tanyu were bloodthirsty and cruel, while the Amir were soft and merciful. His face grew warm with blood. His son. His only son.

He shifted his weight, his badly broken leg throbbing as though the fight with her had been yesterday. Daelon was the prize he had lost. By then, he'd already lost Chetana.

"Which of you will give the announcement?" he asked again, willing for Daelon to speak.

All three remained stonily silent.

About to call on Daelon, he stopped himself. He had to make an example of anyone who refused. "You," he said to Reynard.

"I will not," the Amir replied calmly. "I will not sanction a cruel leader while my Keepers might still live. God would not have it so."

Belik ground his molars. He should have expected this pigheadedness. "You will, or we'll kill you."

Constriction in his neck tendons revealed the Amir was nervous. "I can't betray my Keeper, my kingdom, or my God."

Before Belik could respond, Daelon spoke. "*God supports the just man's cause and dawns upon him light in darkness.*" In his eyes burned a fire, admittedly small, that made Belik almost proud. It had to be about the Sacred Scroll, though. Everything did with these people.

Belik turned back to Reynard. "You won't do it?"

The Amir's huge eyes widened almost comically. "No."

Chewing his cheek, Belik gave one nod to the Tanyu behind Reynard, who went down in seconds, his neck cracking loudly through the night air.

Daelon and Parohim recoiled in horror, shuffling away from the body and uttering guttural sounds of dismay. But they didn't fight back. Did they have any nerve, any mettle at all? Who could watch one of their own go down and not attack the one who did it?

His gaze brushed past his son again, standing tall but too docile beside Reynard's body. Had Chetana ever told him who his father was? About to call on Parohim, he stopped. His curiosity burned him from the inside out.

"You," he said.

Daelon stiffened.

Belik's heart hammered. To be announced by his own son would taste more like victory than any other part of this so far. Someone had to recognize the greatness of the Tanyu. If not Firian, then his biological son.

"My name is Master Belik, a Tanyu of the Academy," he said, staring into his son's eyes.

Something in Daelon's expression went slack with recognition and dread, but he didn't say anything.

"I need you to announce that the Keepers are dead, and that

the Tanyu have taken the city. It will be made official at the next new moon."

The recognition in Daelon's eyes gave way to pain. His mouth strained as though pulled by misery. Belik could see his shallow breathing. All the little adjustments resulted in a horrified grief.

Was he this sad about the Keepers? Belik considered for a moment if he could allow that as a legitimate reason to be so upset.

"No," Daelon managed. His brow lowered and he glared up at his father with a clear message: *How could you? My own father!* So he didn't want to admit the relationship. Fine.

Belik felt pressure building in his blood. His gaze ticked to the Tanyu standing behind his son. He didn't nod.

"The Tanyu have taken the city," Belik repeated. "You can support what's inevitable—" *Or you can die.* But the words stuck in his throat.

"I will not sanction you," Daelon said again, more clearly this time.

"Do you have another quote for me?" Belik barely hid the derision in his voice.

He might have imagined it, but it looked like Daelon leaned forward. "*God uproots the tyrant.*"

The Tanyu behind him started forward. Holding up a hand, Belik was barely quick enough to stop from breaking his neck as he had broken Reynard's. Belik's mouth had gone dry. Anger swam in his thoughts, but he couldn't have his own son killed. It shouldn't have mattered so much, not when there was so much at stake, but he'd found an unexpected weakness in himself. Later, he would redress the issue, but for now, he couldn't do it.

Flicking a look at Shiro, he said, "Daelon will send food down to Firian. Show him where he is."

It was a dangerous job, but it accomplished Belik's purposes:

throwing Firian an obvious lifeline, and keeping his son alive. If Firian threatened Daelon or injured him in his reckless anger, at least Belik wouldn't have to watch.

Two weaknesses.

Fatigue lapped against him. After a few more hours, Belik could rest and start the hard work of prying them off his mind.

4

KIRIA

Kiria tore herself away from the thin, dirty window where she had been watching the palace burn, a billowing black plume just on the other side of the walled grounds. If she ran out of here, she could be there in minutes. But what could she do? How could she save the dead, or take her kingdom back?

Tears burned like smoke in her eyes. She sniffed them back and steadied herself on shelves laden with emergency provisions.

The tunnel through which they'd all escaped fed into this storage cellar. A larger room with more finery was visible through an open doorway. That was it, the entire safe house— just some basic supplies in this room and the second room large enough for several people to lie down. A temporary reprieve.

Her serving girls, Candrae and Vayci, took her arms gently and steered her toward the bigger part of the compound.

The main room had no windows at all. Stifling. This room had been decorated to be more comfortable, but it still felt sparse and unnatural, despite the purple and blue flags of Brithnem draped from the ceiling. A few formal but utilitarian pieces of furniture had been arranged, grouped into a sitting area, working space, dining area, and a bunk, all in a space no bigger than her royal bedroom.

With the four reserve guards in there already, the space felt cramped, a mockery of her title as the Western Kingdom's Keeper. Hopefully not the only one still alive.

Candrae, quietly crying, settled Kiria into a chair. Her long blonde curls fell disheveled in her smudged face. The upholstery of the seat suggested luxury that Kiria wanted no part of right now. The city was under attack. Horrible things were happening. She couldn't let herself think about all the possibilities. The likely possibilities. The memory of Chetana's horrified expression after coming out of Cúron's bedchamber made Kiria's throat close until she couldn't breathe.

She couldn't breathe.

Gasping, she stood and waved to Vayci, who already stood by her other arm. Her eyes stung as panic crawled up through her chest.

"Just breathe," Vayci said. "In through your nose... that's it... and out through your mouth."

Kiria repeated her shuddering attempts until she could drag air into her lungs again, feeling deflated as an empty set of clothes. Who else had escaped? Was her mother okay? Was Atty? Jori?

"Is Chetana back yet?" she whispered. Her former Amiran advisor had disappeared through the cramped emergency tunnel as soon as she'd deposited Kiria in the safe house. She didn't say why she was going back.

"Not yet, My Keeper," one of the guards replied before Candrae had the chance. He was young, with a large tattoo on his face. She didn't recognize him. Maybe a newly inducted recruit.

Kiria shook as she took another breath. Chetana would risk her life for more than one person in the palace: her son Daelon or Kiria's mother Merian held the top of the list. It was possible that she would go back for Atty too. As the Third Keeper, he was technically the most important person there, since Kiria was in this compound and Cúron was...

She sank back in the chair as her strength left her. Leaning forward to look back to the other room where they'd emerged from the tunnel, she hoped to see Chetana's short reddish-brown curls coming through the opening. But there was nothing.

A loud noise jolted her out of her seat. Legs trembling, she shot glances at the serving girls. Their wide eyes confirmed she hadn't imagined the sound.

The guards leapt to attention.

Again, someone pounded against the safe house. Her heart leapt into her mouth. Chetana would return through the tunnel, wouldn't she? Who else knew she was here?

A sudden alarming idea hit her. Firian would know. Their connection often allowed him to know what she was doing. Was he coming for her? Why? Hadn't he done enough? Watery rage engulfed her. Or was it violent sadness? Firian had no right to come after her, not after she'd willingly given herself up to him to save her people. Maybe he'd changed his mind, not only about ruling the Kingdom, but also about owning her.

Earlier that night, he had given her an ultimatum. *Was that tonight?* It felt like weeks ago. He said he wouldn't attack the city if she gave herself up to him. He promised. Eventually the solution was painfully clear. Brithnem was worth more than her life and reputation. Without telling anyone, she had gone to the abandoned farmhouse where he told her to meet. He had kissed her, and then... he had let her go.

If she'd thought this outcome was even a possibility, she never would have left. She wouldn't have jeopardized her city and the people she loved. The thought flushed her dark with anger and regret.

The events of the night had been so breakneck that she hadn't had time to think about the meaning of that encounter, except to see that Firian had broken his promise. He had attacked her beloved Brithnem, breaking her last shred of trust. The memory of loving him tasted bitter in her mouth. Rancid. Piece by piece, he'd ruined something that could have been so good. She should have known it could end this way. She knew him better than most, and she'd seen the creature that tugged him toward greater violence. He'd given into that monster within. Maybe he was coming for her now.

Her stomach clenched painfully, emotions roiling like an ocean in tempest. Even she could never have predicted how far he would go in his quest for dominance. In a far corner of her mind, she doubted he *could* go so far, that he'd ordered this attack at all. But that was just more evidence of her weakness. She should be far beyond those delusions now.

The pounding had stopped, but a small scraping like a rodent's nails took its place. No one moved toward the door except the guards, standing with weapons raised.

As they all watched in horror, it burst open and someone fell inside. Kiria gasped. Vayci stumbled backward a couple steps and Candrae covered her mouth with both hands.

Dust billowed in after the figure, obscuring him for a moment. A pick, like a hairpin, dropped to the ground.

"Jori! Oh my god!" Kiria flung herself toward him, wrapping his neck hard in her embrace.

"Kiria!" He held her tight, shaking, planting rough kisses on her cheek. One of the guards hurried to shut the door behind them.

Sobs rushed out of her. She let them go on Jori's shoulder as she clung to him. Tears poured faster than she could wipe them away. One of the metal buttons on Jori's vest pressed against her collarbone.

Jori's back hitched. He was crying too. How had it come to this? Were they the only ones left? Time froze as they cried into each other's clothes and hair.

Sucking in uneven breaths, Kiria let him go. "You got out," she said. "Did you see anything? Do you know what's happening?"

Jori looked like a man haunted. Even at his worst moments, she'd never seen such desolation on his face.

Her gut twisted. Her instincts were wrong. They had to be wrong.

He swallowed convulsively, as if trying to force the words out of his throat. They stuck for a while, and he couldn't speak.

"What happened?" she made herself ask.

He fluttered his fingers, the only gesture that looked recognizable, as he summoned up his words. Kiria's chest felt tighter and tighter the longer he paused. The pressure built through her entire body.

A noise behind her made everyone jump. In the next room, Chetana stood tall and dark. Almost grateful for the interruption, Kiria dashed toward her. Her feet skittered to a stop when she saw Chetana's face. The Amir looked like a harbinger of death.

Penned in by bad news, Kiria steeled herself as best she could. She had to know more. It was her duty, and those were her friends. "Did you learn... anything?"

Chetana's expression filled with pain and horror, but in her eyes was a fierceness that made even Kiria quail before it.

"They got Atty!" The words ripped from Jori like an arrow.

Kiria's knees went weak as she turned back to face him.

"I saw. And Haved..." Jori was shaking violently.

Candrae scrubbed the tears from her face and helped him

sit. His arms and legs convulsed at random as though he were freezing.

Kiria came closer. Jori pressed his palms to his eyes, shuddering again, and then reached for her hand. Her presence seemed to calm him, though she felt anything but calm. She squeezed his fingers.

Breathing heavily, he continued. "I was... going out. And I saw Tanyu. Just..." His eyes became perfect circles. He snapped with his free hand. "They were fighting Atty's guards. So I ran back—all those tunnels—you know I know all the ways."

She nodded.

"I was going to warn him." He gritted his teeth as more tears came. Kiria felt them in herself too. Jori's voice broke as he said it again. "I was going to warn him." Inhaling sharply, he crushed her hand in his grip, not realizing he was hurting her. The rings she wore dug into her skin. "When I got there, I... They were... They were dead on the bed." He closed his eyes, his breaths coming faster now.

In a daze, she motioned for Vayci to bring him water. Kiria could barely understand his story. She felt like she'd been stabbed, that life was draining out of her, but she couldn't cry. Something worse than sobs sat heavy in her chest. *It can't be true. They can't be dead. Atty's not dead. He's my friend.*

Candrae beat Vayci to the task and pressed a cup into Jori's trembling hand. At the touch, he opened his eyes again, meeting Candrae's gaze. He didn't smile, but there was gratefulness in his look. The water splashed as he brought it to his lips. He lowered his cup to his lap, his attention on Kiria again. "I tried to find you, to make sure... I ran, but you escaped. I'm glad he was right. I knew it, or I would have come after you."

"What? Who was right?"

"Bard..." He stopped, winded again. He tried to take another drink.

Was Bard still alive? Kiria waited impatiently. In the whirl-wind of her thoughts, she hadn't thought enough about him. She sensed Chetana stiffen near her.

"He needed a doctor," Jori continued, shaking his head. "It was that Tanyu. He said you were all right."

She scrunched her brow, confused. "Bard said I was all right?"

"No, Firian."

Shocked, Kiria let go of Jori's hand, her attention instinctively drawn toward the door. "You saw Firian? With Bard? Is he here?"

"Here?" Confusion and grief distorted his features.

A tiny breath of relief escaped her. "They were together?"

He nodded, gulping the last of the water like a shot of liquor.

"What was he doing?" Her head spun. She had too many questions. Shooting a look at the door, she added, "Bolt it. If it can be bolted any more."

"Taking Bard to the doctor. He didn't look all right."

Did that mean that Firian wasn't behind the attack after all, or just that he didn't expect Bard to get caught in the crossfire? "Was he... ordering the attack?"

Jori waved his head back and forth, almost in a stupor. "I don't know."

"Did he talk to any other Tanyu, or...?"

"Just saw him with Bard."

Helping Bard wasn't definitive proof that Firian wasn't behind the attack, but even the hope of it gave a little water to her parched soul. Maybe she didn't have to add another betrayal to the list of evils done tonight. *And he didn't harm Jori, a member of a Keeper family.* Her tiny hope grew brighter.

There were more urgent questions than wondering about Firian's moral limits. "Do you know about anybody else?"

"No." Another tear squeezed from his eye as he handed the cup back to Candrae.

Sickness overcame her. She turned away, afraid she might throw up. Atty was dead. Haved was dead. Jori was alive. Firian was alive. Bard may or may not be alive...

She swiveled to Chetana with the same question.

Chetana's glowering sadness proclaimed her news before she told him. "Cúron," she said grimly, as though beginning a list, "and Varinna."

Jori cried out.

Kiria fought to remain composed. "Kader?" Kader was their ten-year-old son, heir to the first throne.

"I didn't see him. Without a body, it's likely that the Kepron was able to escape, but I don't know with certainty. I'm sorry, My Keeper."

Her title sounded odd in this safe house. She wished Chetana would call her Kiria. The familiarity would be comforting, especially considering the way Chetana was still looking at her. They all needed as much comfort as they could get. But more than that, they needed justice.

Kiria flexed her hands, nails digging into her palms. "We have to make a plan."

One of the guards, a large blond man, stepped forward. "We must take you farther away from the palace," he said in a low, clipped voice. "Your safety is the most important to the Kingdom."

That was true. With Cúron and Atty gone, she was the only monarch left. But the passivity of the suggestion made her skin crawl. Despite grief filling her like a lethal disease, she had to do something. She couldn't let her city burn. "Okay," she said. "Where?"

"We have a place prepared," answered the only female guard among the four.

The memory of Carradoc swarmed over her. A Tanyu in the fortress hidden in plain sight. Would all Tanyu side with the invaders, even if they were in different cities or countries? It was a stupid question. Of course they would.

So where could they go that was safe? Safe from Tanyu, safe from Firian? If he was hellbent on finding her, he would do it. They could only buy time.

Weakness overcame her. She sank into the seat next to Jori. His nearness was comforting even though he was holding his head in his hands. When had she last slept? She didn't feel tired, only weak, but she knew she hadn't slept for days. Or maybe one day?

Dimly, she noticed a change in the light streaming into the storage area by the tunnel's mouth. She stood up hazily, and went to see.

Chetana followed her. She hadn't told Kiria her news yet. Kiria didn't want to hear it, because part of her already knew that the tragic news hadn't stopped coming.

The Amir set a dark hand comfortingly on Kiria's shoulder as they both peered up at the smudgy window.

"It's Mother, isn't it?"

Chetana's fingers tensed. Answer enough.

Emptiness had replaced Kiria's earlier desperation, like the undertow of a wave that would surge again into mad whitecaps with time. Her poor, lovely mother.

"Daelon?"

"I don't know."

The grayish-yellow morning fought with the violence of the firelight through the high, narrow window. Despite everything, the sun was rising.

"We'll take it back from them, My Keeper." Chetana's profile was red-eyed and resolute.

Kiria's thoughts fluttered unevenly. *Them.* The Tanyu. Firian, who, despite helping Bard and not murdering Jori, still led the army. The boy she'd once loved who had become utterly unrecognizable. How could he do this? How could she have not seen what he was?

Her insides weren't large enough to fit all the grief. But they could fit the same tenacity she saw in Chetana's eyes. That burning resolve to make things right. To take back the Kingdom and save the friends that remained.

5

———

FIRIAN

FIRIAN WOKE WITH A JERK. His head throbbed. The air felt acrid against his nose and throat but he wasn't bound anymore—a small mercy, but it was mercy. Why hadn't Belik just killed him?

He jumped to his feet. His vision narrowed with the quick movement, tilting the ground beneath him. He caught himself and focused.

The events of the night rushed back, almost collapsing him under their weight. The offer to trade the Kingdom for Kiria, letting her go, the attempted murder of Bard, Belik's betrayal, realizing she didn't love him... How had it come to this?

He was in a cell, the air smoky and dark. Judging from the haze, he must be in or near the palace. Floor to ceiling bars blocked him from the rest of the small space. On the other side of the bars was nothing but a blank antechamber, a space for standing. His was the only cell. The quality of shadows at the end of the rectangular room suggested a bend leading to steps or a longer hallway. Yes, there was the jut of the lowest stair. He was alone.

Firian thrust his arm through the bars, feeling for the lock. On one side of the crisscrossed bars was a box with a large keyhole. The burns he'd received on his arms as he ran through the fields of the outer edge a few hours before protested against the rough treatment. They weren't deep, but still stung with any pressure. Firian hadn't noticed the pain until now.

He shoved his finger into the keyhole and felt around. No latch gave; no hint of its internal mechanism brushed against him. He scanned the walls for hooks, shelves, ropes—anything that could help him, but there was nothing.

If his environment couldn't help, his next recourse was to communicate through the Unreal. He could feel for someone he might be able to trust. Bard was incapacitated, but Firian had still been popular among many of the other Tanyu, even those he didn't often talk to. He lunged below.

The force of the shock flung him stumbling against the wall. In his desperation, he hadn't immediately felt the Sentry placed over his mind. This was worse than anything they'd done to him so far. He yelled and punched the stone wall. The blow broke the skin on his knuckles but kept his bones intact. A dark smudge smeared the wall and the bite of pain felt good.

He sucked in a breath. Did he believe Bard and Kiria were alive because he hadn't felt their panic, hadn't felt the pain of their leaving? Was a Sentry strong enough to hide a truth that devastating?

He forced himself to stay calm, but the effort left him trembling. He hadn't felt so helpless since he was a child hearing his father's drunken footsteps coming toward his room.

No one had placed a Sentry on Firian since... Belik. It was his fault last time too. Firian's bloody hands curled into fists. Belik had ordered a Sentry after discovering that Firian kept spying on Kiria even after she gave no new information.

That had been months ago. He was stronger now. He could go to the Second Level. He could kill from there. He had practiced skills no other Tanyu could achieve. Even Belik hadn't managed to kill Bard. Not yet.

He had to get through. Standing tall with legs spread, he brought air deep, deep into his lungs. Setting his jaw, he closed his eyes, calling on his considerable focus. With all the violence he could summon, he dove down again.

For a few seconds he knew nothing but pain, bursting from his head to his extremities. Sheer willpower kept him there a second longer. He burned from the inside out, pain ripping from a thousand exit wounds. Another second. Maybe he would die. *All it takes is belief.*

With a gasp, he released his hold. Opening his eyes, he landed heavily on his hipbone as he collapsed. Another gasp brought up vomit. He wiped his mouth with the back of his hand, reeling from the smell. His headache had spread to the base of his neck, throbbing along his skull. He refused to die. Not when he had to kill Belik.

Pale light, then quiet footsteps cut through his pain. He froze and then forced himself to stand. Through the metal grating he saw a figure wearing the high-necked robe of an Amir, holding a torch and something else in its hands. As his vision cleared, he recognized the man.

It was Kiria's—what? Friend? Advisor? Daelon was his name. Firian felt a handhold, a crack in Belik's plan. He knew something about this Amir. "Daelon?"

The man's expression remained bereft and wary but he approached Firian without slowing or angling away. He laid a cup of water and hunk of bread on the ground just outside the bars. Belik didn't intend to kill Firian now if he had someone bring him food. Perhaps this was a peace offering.

"What's going on out there?" Firian tried to keep his voice kind, but the question came out as a demand.

Daelon ground his teeth. "Your people are taking over everything," he said. "They've profaned the holy place."

"What did they do?"

"You don't deserve to know."

Firian glared but kept his composure. "I won't be in here long," he managed. "If you tell me, I can stop them." Seeing the indecision in Daelon's eyes, he added, "I'm obviously not on their side."

"They've killed the Keepers," Daelon said thickly, going greenish pale.

Firian's gut dipped. The blackness of the shadows reached out for him, constricted his throat. *No.* "Is there proof?"

"I haven't seen it." The desolation didn't leave his eyes.

"Kiria's still alive." The words came out before Firian could bite them back. Maybe he needed to hear them himself, like a fresh breeze through this forsaken, fetid place. The Amir needed to hear them too. If Belik had shown no proof, then Kiria wasn't dead. She couldn't be. Firian refused to believe it.

Daelon's mouth fell open. He blinked with raised eyebrows. A tear slid down his cheek. When he closed his mouth again, he muttered something under his breath. A prayer, maybe. Then suspicion entered his gaze again. "Are you sure?" he asked, each word clear.

"Yes." Kiria was alive. Bard was alive too. A Sentry couldn't hide something so monumental from him. That belief kept the last bit of ground from crumbling beneath his feet.

Daelon wrung his hands before dragging one over his face.

A moment of panic took Firian. If Belik actually thought that Kiria had been killed, then he had just told someone a fact that could send new assassins after her. One more look at Daelon dispelled his fear. This man, at least, wouldn't tell Belik. He was loyal to Kiria. Besides, Firian doubted Belik would allow an Amir into his presence when it wasn't necessary to his plan.

"Don't tell anyone," he said, just in case. His tone bore a threat he didn't verbalize.

In his place, Kiria wouldn't threaten Daelon, but anything that could give her additional minutes to escape had to be tried. What would Kiria do, if she were locked here? She wouldn't accept the fate of Brithnem. Just hours before, she showed what she was willing to do to save it. The memory tasted like shame.

Daelon's pupils contracted, flame flickering across them from the torchlight, but then he gave a sad smile, as though death wouldn't be so bad after all he'd witnessed. Then he nodded. "I don't have a key," he admitted.

It wasn't an offer of help, exactly, but it was close.

Quietly, the man turned to go, leaving the torch burning in a bracket and providing helpful light. Soft footfalls faded to nothing in the distance.

Iron rust from the bars had left bloody-looking red marks on Firian's arms, which he hadn't been able to see before. He grabbed the two items and pulled them inside his cell. They could be poisoned. The drink Belik had sent him after Firian had called off the raid had some kind of agent in it that knocked him out. This could be the same. He'd get water after he was out of this prison. He crushed the bread. Just hard crust and doughy insides. Nothing else.

All he'd needed to do was alert some of the Tanyu that this *wasn't* his plan the moment he realized Belik acted in his name. They would have pulled back, even disposed of Belik for him. Now he couldn't contact anyone. Panic had made him stupid.

Black despair threatened to close around him with the finality of death. He was trapped. Belik was taking control of Kiria's city. The only people he cared about were as good as dead, and they hated him. He had failed. He had failed. Just as his father had predicted. The words he'd heard as a child played in a hectic, overlapping loop.

Why'd we even keep this scut? Worthless, gory, stupid kid...

He felt hollowed out. The echoes bounced inside him until he couldn't take the noise. He screamed. He even startled himself with the shredding sound. The worst things he could think of, all the curses and all the pain he kept inside his head, burst out in barely coherent shouts. Wrapping his fists around the bars of his cage, he rattled hard until the veins stood up on his arms and blood from his knuckles dripped down to the floor.

Deflating, he grimaced. His heel hit the bread crust on the floor as he backed up.

He would not give into despair. He would not. Belik would not win.

6

———

KIRIA

THERE WAS no time to mourn. The five people in the safe house had pulled the upholstered seats into a rough circle. One guard stood by them. Three others had stood by the door after Kiria voiced her fear that Firian might try to find her. Candrae and Vayci sat back as though abashed to sit in such company, but Kiria and Chetana sat forward. Jori lounged, listless. Half the time he seemed not to be listening or following their train of thought.

"So no one knows whether Kader made it out of the palace?" Kiria looked at the guard nearest to her, the blond one who held seniority over the others, but got no answers. That had to be their first priority, to make sure the three Lines were safe. "How can we find out?"

"I'm sure the Tanyu will announce which leaders they eliminated," Chetana said bitterly.

"We can't wait that long, if there's a way to find out sooner," Kiria replied. Besides, the idea of waiting for such a horrible report turned her stomach. "We should try to find him now. The Tanyu will be looking for him if we aren't."

"And us," said the soldier with the face tattoo.

The big blond guard, old enough to be the younger one's father, shut him up with a look.

What they needed was more information. God knew Kiria didn't want any more bad news, but if the heir to the First Line was alive, then they needed to make sure he stayed that way. If they knew what the Tanyu did, they could make better decisions. With her sanity hanging by the thinnest thread, she needed all the help she could get.

Firian would know all about the attack. Kiria wrung her hands, running her thumbnail along the length of her fingers. She didn't want to see him, not when he was probably the engineer of all this horror, despite being seen with Bard. What if he made more demands? What if he found her even as they were talking?

"I don't think I should contact Firian directly. It could just draw him here. We need a plan first." Her muscles tensed at the thought. She didn't need to explain further. The rumor of her relationship with Firian had run through all the palace personnel.

"I don't think he's in charge," Jori struck in.

"He's the Tanyuin Head," Kiria said drily, surprised that Chetana hadn't replied first, considering the Amir's hatred of him. Instead, Chetana's expression implied that she agreed with Jori. Kiria raised a brow at her.

"Yeah, but I saw him carrying Bard out of the palace," Jori said. "Why would he do that?"

"He was *carrying* Bard?" It would be hard to direct an attack and save someone at the same time—someone the Tanyu harmed in the first place.

"And he didn't harm you. Did he?" Chetana asked.

Jori shook his head, shifting uncomfortably in his chair.

Kiria's mind whirled. It felt like betraying the memories of those she lost to consider that Firian might have kept his word after all. What did it matter now anyway? "But he must have ordered the attack. Who else could have started something like that?"

"I know who it was," Chetana said. She had that faraway look she often got, as though she were about to prophesy. Even the serving girls stared at her, hanging on her next slow word. "Belik." The sounds of the name rolled in her mouth as though she'd already tried every variation, tasted and spat each syllable.

Master Belik was Chetana's *katah*, Daelon's father? The one who had incapacitated Bard outside her room?

Kiria knew that name.

Firian trusted him. Belik had been his teacher when he first arrived at the Academy. He had taught Firian about the Unreal. Did that mean he knew more about it than Firian did?

"Master Belik?" she echoed. "He and Firian are close. Are you sure they aren't working together?" The idea made her shudder. Anyone who could frighten Chetana was truly dangerous.

"I don't know. They could be, but Belik killed our family." She meant multiple things by those words. "He is... treacherous. He is capable of turning on the Tanyuin Head, of taking power for himself. I am surprised he didn't do it sooner."

"Maybe he couldn't."

"Oh, he could have."

The others watched their faces in rapt attention, bouncing from the Keeper to the Amir and back. The room felt airless, as though everyone held their breath for fear of missing a crucial word.

Jori swiped a hand over his face. "How do you know him?" he asked Chetana, who ignored the question.

"Something's gone wrong with his plan," she said stiffly, with almost a twinge of fear in her voice.

Jori looked at Kiria next, who didn't supply an answer either.

If Chetana didn't want everyone to know about her *katah* with the enemy, she would respect that desire. She knew it all too well.

"Do you know what his plan is? His next move?" Kiria asked instead.

"I think he has a few objectives," Chetana replied curtly. "The most obvious is taking control of the city. That's what we need to focus on."

"So, there's a new Tanyuin Head?" asked the tattooed guard. This time, the blond one didn't shush him.

"For our purposes," Chetana said, "we'll act as though there are two."

Reluctantly, Kiria cast her a look. Chetana seemed to divine its meaning at once before Kiria even asked the question. "Could you find out more about his plan?"

Chetana's dark eyes hardened. "I can't gather information from Belik. He'll know where we are immediately. It would just draw him here."

So there it was. The truth. Anyone in the room who knew about *katahs* would understand now. Jori straightened a little out of his slouch.

Belik had been the one outside Kiria's room during the brunt of the attack, the one Bard had confronted to give Kiria a chance to escape, the one who had made Chetana so afraid. Firian, on the other hand, had saved Bard, left Jori alone... Certainty solidified within her.

She dropped her voice and her eyes. "So Firian didn't order the attack." Something stirred in her, writhing and alive. The emotion was strong but unnamable.

Firian was still at large, his allegiances unknown, she reminded herself. Based on their last intense but confusing meeting, he could go either way. And still had the means to find her if he wanted to. *When.*

Jori shrugged a shoulder.

The female guard wasn't so nonchalant. "If he didn't order the attack, does that mean he's on our side? If this Belik has turned on him, wouldn't he want some kind of revenge, if not justice?"

Kiria heard the real question: *Could he be our ally?* She'd hung onto that possibility so many times and the rope hadn't held her in the end. If she could avoid another disastrous alliance, she would. Yes, Firian was powerful, but with so much at stake, she couldn't take the chance. "It's too soon to tell," she evaded.

Chetana mirrored Kiria's meaningful look from before.

"Once we get farther away from here, then we can discuss the possibility," she added, to end any more prying. Calling on Firian, now, would break the fragile hold she had on rational thought, the ability to plan and mobilize those under her command. As it was, horror and sorrow and rage and exhaustion pressed in around her like stifling blankets, kept at bay only by the jabs of her forward motion, her planning.

Chetana's dark eyes fell to the floor as though she were searching for something. Her full lips wrinkled with a sneer that touched the bottom of her septum ring.

"We could leave the city." The voice sounded small and far away. Kiria smiled. Vayci never gave her opinion, but if there were ever a time, this was it.

Chetana looked kindly at her. Vayci looked down to avoid her gaze. "If the people find out the Keeper has left, they could lose hope. That cannot be our first resort."

"But it's not a bad idea," Kiria added, though she agreed with Chetana.

"Belik will try to set Tanyu at all the exit points of the city," Chetana continued. Her expression was bitter and knowing. "Until we know the danger, we should not run toward it. Our duty is to Brithnem, in Brithnem." She looked at Kiria for confirmation.

She nodded back.

"We have to stay here?" Jori stretched backward on the seat, craning his neck to see the room upside-down. Clearly, the idea didn't appeal to him.

"Yes," Chetana snapped, "at least we've chosen a more secure location."

"Yeah, this one's not the most secure," he admitted, scratching his ear.

Kiria cast a nervous glance at the outer door. It had been relocked, but it still felt like flimsy protection.

"Are there any other ways out of here?" she asked Jori. She didn't see any, but that didn't mean they weren't there.

Jori gestured toward the tunnel. "No. Just those two."

"Will you be able to hide me when we move?" Kiria asked the guards. The only other time she'd been in hiding was with Firian, and she'd been far away from potential enemies most of the time.

"Both of you," Chetana corrected.

Kiria knit her brows. The insistent words were slow to register.

"Both of you need to be protected. The Kepron is the heir."

Kiria felt faint, each realization disorienting. Even after Atty had been crowned, she hadn't given the idea much thought. That Jori could become a Keeper of Brithnem was beyond imagining. Yet here they were. Atty was dead. His dream of having a family to succeed him had died also. The only clear option for the Third Line was Jori. Kiria was the Second Line. *Where's Kader?* she wondered again. *Has he been killed too?*

Jori rocked forward, running a hand through his hair. He shook his head a few times as though shaking his words loose. "No," he said simply.

Chetana was businesslike. "It is not your—"

"No!" Jori leapt aggressively to his feet.

Kiria sat back, away from him. The longer she watched his strained face and flashing gray eyes, the more she softened with understanding. In his place, if Atty were her brother, she would probably act the same way. Her heart contracted with shared pain. "We don't need to worry about that yet," she said. "You need to stay safe one way or the other." She laid a hand on his arm. "I need you."

He jerked away. Slumping back in the chair, he inhaled a few shaky breaths.

Candrae was on her feet, ready to serve. The girls weren't used to sitting by while others needed anything. Jori needed more than a cup of water this time, and Kiria wasn't sure that anyone could get it for him. "A pillow," she said, just to give Candrae something to do.

One of the guards—a round-faced man with pink skin and dark hair—stepped forward respectfully. "My Keeper, I could go and investigate Kader Calthwaite's location."

Kiria drew her hand into a fist, considering. They had few guards as it was, but Kader's safety had to be a priority. That way, at least, there would still be one person alive from each of the three Lines. She cleared her throat. "Go. Once he's safe, we'll have a clearer path to regain power." *If he's safe.*

She looked sidelong at Jori. His hair tumbled over one eye, and he didn't meet her gaze.

7

BELIK

BELIK GRIMACED. All these stairs were killing his legs. Why did all Watchmen need to be in the highest place in the city? They had a sputtering level of Talent, but that Talent could be used anywhere. Still, people liked their mystical beliefs about the job. They liked to believe that all the news coming from these high cells was perfectly accurate, removed from the biases of the world.

As though they've never met a person before.

"Do you want to pause?" Shiro asked just behind him.

Belik started to snarl at him but thought better of it. "Maybe to answer that stupid question. No."

Behind Shiro's head of dark hair were two more Tanyu. Only one was visible in this blindly winding staircase. In front of him walked one more. Four should do it. Maybe he'd add a couple more.

The problem was that no one could be spared from their duties. There weren't enough capable people as it was for all the tasks that needed to happen simultaneously for a smooth takeover. Manning the city wall alone took too many people. Several others stationed themselves around the barracks to keep the army true to their word to back the new reigning champions. Some had resisted, of course. Skirmishes. What rankled was that the Tanyu hadn't closed the net, plugged all the holes to prevent renegades from escaping. Dozens of soldiers had. Belik's forces could deal with them when they showed their faces again. The rest of the military's doubt was in Belik's favor, and they were held in tentative check by the few generals to whom he had promised generous riches.

During the raid, a few Tanyu had stood out as his most loyal supporters. They were the ones who cut the Keepers' throats, who didn't cry and moan about where Firian was. Weapons in his hands.

He struggled up a few more steps. He was being a fool—pain subsided in the Unreal. In an instant, he was there. Thoughts of Chetana floated like damned ghosts in the corner of his eye. It was all he could do not to whirl around and fight her, but he knew she wasn't really there. If she had been, there would be no mistaking it. Instead, he swirled colors against the black like flavors in a pot of soup. He floated in the midst of them, touching the silky texture of the colors floating by. This is where he went if he wanted to completely forget where he was. It was as good as sleeping.

Almost. Belik hadn't slept since this raid began. After this crucial task, he could rest for a short while before continuing. Delegate to Master Nedi and Shiro until he could join them again.

His foot reached the top landing. He came to himself again. The room at the top of the palace was large and circular, ornate and white. Around the windows there was yellow discoloration. A man sat cross-legged on a lush deep purple rug. The Watchman looked placidly at them as they entered, his old face scored with deep wrinkles.

"Are you the Watchman?" Belik asked, though he already knew the answer.

"Yes." The voice was husky from disuse. The single word came out clearly, but a little like a sigh.

One of Belik's eyes squinted behind his glasses. "What is your name?"

"My name is not important. You are the Tanyu who have ravaged my city," he said, making no move to attack or defend himself. The Watchman's breath sounded loud in the quiet. How much had he already told neighboring cities?

"I would like to know it," Belik said.

"My name is Velmay Rancin." The man's tone was the same as before, even and breathy.

That was enough. Belik jerked his chin in the direction of the old man. He averted his eyes at the moment Shiro snapped his neck. The man's death was necessary, one of a short list along with the Keepers, and the soldiers who resisted. The Watchman controlled information.

Belik scratched his ear, trying to replace the sound of the crack with something else, then looked carefully at the man's face. Slowly, he came closer. The impending trip back down the staircase occupied as much of his thoughts as the man slumped in front of him.

The man's skin was smooth like tooled leather. His eyes had been gray. That much he'd noticed as soon as they'd walked in. He sat with the quiet poise of a man who had never had anywhere else to go. Typical Kingdom bone structure. He'd just gotten a haircut. As Belik circled, he saw the perfect edge to his hairline. The man wore chipping paint on his nails. That surprised him, though he couldn't have said why. He stretched his jaw, ready to begin.

With the ease of a bird in the air, he entered the Unreal. Instantly, he had sharply-cut hair, badly painted nails, and soft leather skin, scored with age. He knew the Tanyu with him were doing the same.

After taking a moment to modulate his voice, he reached toward the Watchman in Redshore. "Lady Kiria, the Second Keeper, has run away with Firian Kess, the former Tanyuin Head, compromising the safety of Brithnem in this time of crisis..."

8

———

KIRIA

EVEN WITH THE GUARDS' help, the journey from the safe house to the tannery was a frightful one. The sun was up, shining traitorous light on their passage. All the neighborhood buildings served to shelter them, but also became a terrifying maze of blind corners.

The young guard with the tattoo on his face gave Kiria the swath of blue fabric that draped across his shoulders. She wound it across her own and over her head. She'd dispensed with her Beauty before the attack began, which deepened her disguise.

Jori had no God-given power to change his looks and, until now, never would have wanted to. Even in his listlessness, though, he moved with a secrecy even the guards couldn't rival. He'd always known about every nook and exit, every hiding place around the palace. Sneaking into places he shouldn't was his forte.

Chetana also seemed to melt into the air any time Kiria wasn't looking. For all her height and imperiousness, she could be stealthy too.

As the sounds of waking people, opening shops, alarmed

voices, and marching feet surrounded them, Kiria's heartbeat tripped and her feet felt as though they'd been attached the wrong way. Phantom pains from her long-ago arrow wounds surfaced and ached.

They only saw one figure in black.

Not Firian. Still, Kiria stopped moving at the sight. It was a man with a light beard, standing in front of one of the main warehouses in Grand Market Square. A small crowd surrounded him, as though to ask for news. The agitated postures of those in front of the Tanyu told her they knew some of what had happened in the night. Something like a wail rose from among the voices. Hands gripped other hands.

Jori shoved her from behind, forcing her beyond the gap between buildings that allowed her to see. The strip of light passed over her face and left her in shadow again. Had the man seen her? What was he telling her people?

An irrational part of her wanted to march up to the man, dramatically reveal her identity, and confront him for all the evils he'd taken part in. She wanted to be a hero, not this skulking fugitive.

But there was nothing more foolish she could do than that, she reminded herself, the intrusive image of dead guards rising to her mind. They had to take this carefully.

Words, light as dust on the breeze, floated across her as they snuck forward, keeping to alleys and backways. Many reflected shock and mourning in their sound; others, serious discussions about what to do. But only one conversation, close enough to their destination that she could hear more, stuck to her after they entered the tannery.

"My cousin says the heads are in Arena Square."

A gasp. "All of them?"

"Not the Second Keeper."

A noise of pain. An obscured reply, and then, "Do you think she's with them?"

"I thought she might pull something like this." Machinery drowned out the next words but caught up at the end of the sentence: "...sympathizer."

"Are we safe? Will she keep us safe?"

"Looks like Tanyu are the ones in charge, not her. Just keep your head down."

THE TANNERY WAS SITUATED close to one of the smaller gates to the north, far from both the palace and the Abrecan Gate. Its position, unattached to the palace, made it more secure than the safe house, but Kiria didn't feel safer. The interior was unsettlingly alien and also small to house her, Jori, Chetana, Vayci, Candrae, and the guards who assisted them. One of the guards —the only woman, with freckles and narrow eyes—said the tannery belonged to her uncle and that it was easy to defend, at least temporarily.

The floors and walls around them were stone. Raised rock platforms rose to Kiria's hips, covering about a third of the floor space. As soon as they arrived, Jori jumped on one to get some breathing room, but he stumbled backward into a pit cut in the rock. Three identical square pits had been carved into the platforms, like huge basins. Judging from the foul-smelling swill left behind in the bottom, they'd been used for one of the more unsavory steps in the tanning process. She didn't want to know exactly what.

Large wooden paddles leaned against one wall along with an assortment of metal instruments Kiria was glad weren't in the hands of the enemy. The guards concentrated themselves at the entrance, blocking enemies' way in but also blocking their way out. The round-faced guard left to check for news of Kader as soon as they'd arrived. How long would they have to stay here?

The morning-bright room smelled tangy with animal musk. Outside, she could hear people in Grand Market Square working, haggling, hauling—all far away but echoing through the stillness of the room. The tension she'd heard in their voices on the journey here persisted, as did their words, which echoed, echoed, echoed in her mind, pinging uselessly but forcefully against her thoughts. She had no room for more pain, but it lurked at the door, ready to pounce whenever she found reprieve. *I thought she might pull something like this. Will she keep us safe?* How could anyone think she'd have a hand in this? Did her people know her so little? How many others felt the same way?

She suddenly wanted her mother there to tell her it would be all right. The longing for her grew into physical hurt.

Jori sat on the lip of a cold brick oven built into the wall, one knee propped up. He looked almost insolent, halfway between depressed and carefree.

The smell, the small space... It all felt oppressive. The ceiling made the room too low, too cramped. Anxious energy kept Kiria from relaxing.

When a knock came at the door, she started but was almost glad for the interruption. No guard moved to welcome the intruder. A loud voice came from the other side. "Amir Parohim has informed the people that the Keepers are dead! Tanyu have taken over the city! Come to the palace Mon Párinath at the next new moon to witness the crowning of the new ruler!" The end of the rehearsed announcement faded as the stranger moved onto another building with the news.

Tense silence fell. Kiria's chest constricted. The voice repeated the news farther down the street. With every repetition, the betrayal became more and more real.

"You look all right to me," Jori said.

Kiria caught his eye, but she was too stressed to smile. Instead, she turned to Chetana. "Why would Parohim make that announcement?" Cúron's advisor had always hated Tanyu, which made him happy to support the First Keeper's anti-Tanyuin agenda.

"They threatened him," she declared.

"But you wouldn't give into their demands if you were threatened," Kiria said, refusing to accept such a simple explanation.

"Not if they threatened *me*," she replied.

Whom they could threaten that would make Parohim overturn so much he had striven to build? The Amir didn't have any family. He had chosen to dedicate his life entirely to the spiritual wellbeing of the Kingdom. And, although his personality grated at times, he had done a good job of it.

Her breath caught. "Kader." Cúron's son. It had to be. Nothing else would make him spread these lies, this propaganda. "Do you think they have him?"

Chetana lowered her eyes in confirmation. Thick black lashes shadowed her cheeks.

A hissing sound at the door meant that the round-faced guard had returned. His companions let him slip inside. The man stood at attention, his helmet gleaming in the morning light. "My Keeper, the Tanyu have taken control of the Abrecan, as well as the Elidyr and Drein. They seem to be moving in both directions away from the main gate in an effort to control the outer wall."

Kiria pictured the city, arranged roughly in rings leading out from the seaside palace all the way to the city wall. Five primary gates and a few other minor doors provided exits. Chetana was right. Master Belik was cutting off their ways of escape one by one.

"They haven't reached Ana'h Gate yet?"

The man shook his head, but his expression was doubtful.

Her mouth went dry. "We'll be trapped."

Chetana looked grave. Jori shifted uncomfortably in the oven opening.

"We were not planning to leave the city, My Keeper. This changes nothing," Chetana replied.

Still, a new kind of claustrophobia sent her thoughts spinning. If they were going to take back the palace and regain control of Brithnem, they had to formulate a plan now. The new moon, had he said? That was in two days. That left no time for coming and going from the city. Her guards could drum up the surviving military still loyal to her...

Her head hurt. When she had studied military strategy with Daelon, she hadn't imagined it would feel like this—less like a game of Indisfate and more like jumping off a cliff and hoping for water instead of rocks.

"What about Kader?" she asked the guard. He hadn't led with information about the Kepron, so she didn't expect anything hopeful.

"Nothing definitive," the soldier replied, "but it looks like he may have escaped through his emergency tunnel as you did. No telling whether he could get out of the city." His face darkened.

Unlikely. Kader was so young. Was he afraid, waiting for someone to help him? "We have to find him."

"A few of us are attempting to find him."

The Tanyu would be on the same scent. The soldier's stormy expression halted her bleak train of thought. "A few of you?" she asked. "Where's the rest of the military? What else did you find out?"

He wet his lips. "Master Belik has promised land and wealth to the commanders in the barracks. He killed two who didn't take his offer and tried to revolt. The rumor is that you're all dead, all the Keepers. There was nothing left for them to fight for." Maybe he was close to those rebel generals. His words definitely sounded like excuses for people he cared about.

Or they think I'm a traitor, she thought bitterly. "Then we have to let them know I'm alive," she exclaimed. "And Kader too, probably. That we're both on the Kingdom's side."

Jori raised one hand, a small, reluctant gesture to add his name to the list. Kiria nodded in acknowledgment. She hadn't gotten used to thinking of him as the Third Line representative. Neither had Jori.

"That will let Belik know," the tattooed guard piped up.

"He already knows," Chetana replied drily.

"Some managed to get out during the fighting, looking for you," the guard told Kiria. "Not everyone has gone over to the Tanyu."

That anyone would defect, and so quickly, made her gut feel heavy. They probably felt that they had no choice after hearing the Keepers were slaughtered. Doubt plagued her, though. Before the attack, her leadership was heavily questioned. And after it too, apparently.

Now that she was the only living Keeper, would she have enough clout to reestablish the thrones? She had risked more than anyone realized for Brithnem already. She'd been prepared to sacrifice everything, and would do it again if it would guarantee safety for her country, and especially for her friends. Even if it meant working with Firian. She cast a glance at Jori, whose lip curled in disbelief.

They were desperate, and time was against them. They had to try to contact the Tanyu who might be on their side.

If the people in this tannery didn't get the upper hand somehow, Tanyu would hunt them all down and kill them, and, based on the depraved style of the attack, they wouldn't deal justly with her people either. She thought of Lord Ruler Thraddock. Firian had set up his head in the square, just as

Belik had made a spectacle of the Keepers. The thought made her ill.

No, it was too soon to contact Firian. He was power and skill, but not strategy. For all his brute force and Talent, he hadn't studied large-scale warfare as she had.

Casting her eyes around the unfamiliar space, she wished Bard were here. Bardhon Tanery. She wondered if his name had any connection to a real tannery like this one. Bard could beat Firian at the game too. He wasn't a fighter, but he had the same goals as they did: beat the Tanyu and take back the Kingdom with minimal loss of life.

She cringed at the memory of his back as he faced death on her account. "Jori." He lolled his head in her direction. "Do you know where Bard is?"

"There's a doctor." He flicked his fingers in a vague direction.

"Could you find him again?"

"Kiria," he said, screwing up one side of his face in a grimace, "I don't know..."

She set her mouth in a firm line. "Can we try?"

"What's the point?"

Chetana nodded once toward Jori. "You remember what the Kepron said. He's probably not alive."

Kiria rounded on her former advisor. "Could you check?" Chetana had the Talent. Maybe she could feel Bard's thoughts. Kiria wasn't sure she was advanced enough to do that yet, without knowing right where he was.

Chetana let out a breath and closed her eyes. The last expression was admonishing before her lids shut.

Kiria waited a few breathless seconds as Chetana's lids fluttered. When she looked back at Kiria again, the answer written there made Kiria wilt. "I don't sense him anywhere. I think he is dead."

Tears pricked at Kiria's eyes.

Seeing her distress, Chetana added, "He died nobly. He redeemed himself from those Tanyu at the end and helped to keep you safe." She set a hand on Kiria's shoulder. The words barely comforted her.

"Yeah, we don't need him to come up with a plan anyway," Jori said, but his tone was far from cheerful. When Kiria turned her attention to him, he was staring at the wall above the pits, glassy-eyed.

Everyone here deferred to her to make the decision. Of course, it was only right. She was the Keeper, the only one left. She squared her shoulders. "Belik is supposed to be crowned on the new moon," she began, looking at Chetana. The thought mortified her, but running through ideas like this hardened her resolve and strengthened her hope.

"And the whole city will come out to see him." Kiria mused for a moment. "Do you think we could overcome the Tanyu at the gates during the coronation?" As soon as she said it, she realized that, although the people of Brithnem would come to watch a coronation, there was no guarantee that other Tanyu would come too. In fact, securing the perimeter would be one of their first concerns. She waved a hand. "Never mind. You say that Firian isn't in charge. It's only Belik?"

"It seems so."

Kiria looked at the guard who had gleaned information, who offered no more surety.

"Firian wasn't exactly subtle," Jori struck in.

Seems wasn't good enough, if they could afford better information. The uncertainty was maddening. She had to check. Chetana had said that contacting Belik would alert him to their location. Firian could find them without Kiria's cooperation. As it stood, he was the one with the power—to find them, to battle Belik, to turn the tide of the coup—and she needed to take that power back.

"I'll see," she said thickly, and closed her eyes. She hated the thought of feeling Firian's presence again, calling for it, but she would just check quickly if he was alive, at least. And if he really wasn't behind the attack, if Belik had acted of his own accord, and Firian had only come to the palace to save Bard, then there was a cobweb's chance that he might want to help them depose Belik. That would mean he meant what he said when he let her go in that farmhouse, his skin flushed with desire and mind obviously roiling against itself. It would mean that he finally denied his baser impulses. A fierce longing seized her for that to be the truth. She'd wanted there to be hope for him for so long, had defended him when no one else would, defended him until there was no excuse for him anymore...

She angled her mind toward the palace, though she could sense Firian from anywhere. At least, that's how it had been before.

Now there was nothing. Nothing at all. The darkness of the Unreal wasn't just empty of his immediate presence, but it was as though it had no knowledge of him. The familiar sense of his mind, always so close, was absent. It was like going home only to find a stranger who claimed to have lived there for years, with the furnishings to prove it. It was confusing and *wrong*.

"Firian! Firian!" she called. "I know you're there."

He didn't answer or materialize as he always did, dark-clad shoulders and knowing look. Blue eyes under heavy brows.

"Firian!"

No whisper rose to acknowledge her cries. Just a blank, endless emptiness tinged with pain, as though small but painful shocks webbed over her skin.

Firian was dead? It was the only explanation. He wouldn't leave her alone like this. Killed, then, either by Kingdom soldiers or Tanyu. Kingdom soldiers had never been able to match him. Even if they had, the news would have spread quickly. Her guard would have learned about it, along with the news of the commanders. The likelier scenario was that Belik, another Tanyu, had killed him.

Firian had kept his word.

This wasn't how she thought Firian's death would feel. His last agony must have been covered up by her own. The hope that she and Bard had held for him was gone, all that potential squandered.

Fury, hard and rough as charcoal, filled her gut. Belik killed Firian the moment he chose to do the right thing.

She opened her burning eyes and shook her head. "Yes, just Belik," she confirmed. Her voice was a croak. "We have to stop him before the coronation."

"Sounds easy," said Jori. "We'll just sneak in and stab him in the back. It's not like the Tanyu control every entrance." He brought his legs off the ledge to the ground. Leaning his forearms on his knees, he eyed Kiria.

She barely registered his words, tilting to the side as weakness overcame her. Jori couldn't expect her to have every answer. He wasn't the only one who experienced a traumatic night.

Releasing a breath like someone fighting not to drown, she turned to Chetana and the guards. "How do you think we—?"

"You need to rest, My Keeper," Chetana said, hovering her palm above Kiria's hair as though she would touch it, but then dropping her hand.

When Kiria blinked, her vision went blurry. She needed to tell them, but the words wouldn't come. Weariness settled in her limbs but the spastic movements of her mind kept her from lying down. Her thoughts sputtered like a dying fly—at rest one second and flailing the next.

"Yes," said the blond guard, "for now we'll see how many soldiers we can muster to your cause. We'll let everyone know you're alive. We can plan after you rest, My Keeper."

Kiria's insides formed a knot. "I think Firian's dead," she said, swallowing.

Chetana cut a serious look in her direction, more concerned about Kiria's wellbeing than the news that Firian had died. There was a hint of fearful determination too, since Belik was now unequivocally in charge and there was no hope of Firian as a temporary ally.

Jori raised tired eyebrows as he dragged three pelts into the enormous cold oven. "You all right, my girl?" he murmured, laying them out without his signature flair. Something told her he couldn't handle the weight of anyone else's grief right now, so she didn't answer.

No one else responded to her announcement, instead regarding her with grim looks. To them, Firian's death was a key bit of news, something to consider when moving forward. It was something different to her, a private world of confusion and anger and sadness for what might have been.

Kiria felt heaviness and grief transform her motions into the movements of a mannikin, hard and stiff and automatic. Exhaustion pressed on her aching head. As she helped Chetana work one of the wooden paddles off the wall, unconsciousness sounded like welcome relief. Perhaps sensing her fatigue, her serving girls came up on either side and took it from her. It was surprisingly heavy, so she was glad of the help.

In a short while, they had used the paddles to cover the raised stone pits, creating more spaces to sleep. Kiria still chose to sleep in a corner of the floor so she could feel the press of walls against her back and know that there was no mysterious animal substance underneath her. Besides, it was darker here, more sheltered from the sunlight filtering in.

The rolled pelt crackled as she laid her head on it. From her corner, she could see Jori, already asleep on his perch. If none of this had happened, they would have been preparing for Dedication Day today, instead of figuring out how to stay alive while Tanyu hunted them. Amir would choose selections from the Sacred Scroll and musicians would compose new pieces. Jori and Atty would eat extra helpings in anticipation of the fast.

A hot tear ran down her temple into the stiff fur. *"Do not fear, for redemption will come to you. While you are surrounded and the shadow of your destruction overcasts your skies, salvation will come."* How was that possible now?

9

———

KIRIA

THE *SACHION* TREES in the wide palace hallways had been stripped to skeletal sticks. Pictures hung askew. Broken glass littered the ground near the walls. Beams of light crisscrossed madly through the windows, casting green and blue light. The end of the corridor looked as blackened as the depths of a well.

Kiria picked her way barefoot through the debris, observing each piece of wreckage as if it held the clue to a mystery. Confusion, more than fear, filled her at the sight. The blackness of the hall, though, unsettled her more than anything else. Monsters could be lurking there and she wouldn't know until they sprang out, like creatures of deep water.

The shadows beyond converged into a figure made of smoke. She squinted at it, but it just regarded her as a wild animal would. Although the shape had no eyes, she could tell it was there for her.

She stopped walking. The niggling feeling that she should do something about this quiet intruder worried at her mind, but she couldn't remember exactly what she was supposed to do.

The curls of smoke floating off the figure made her aware of an acrid smell in the air. It felt sharp in her lungs. As the air became thicker, she focused her attention on breathing. Dragging in a breath became more like exercise than reflex. It was interesting, like an experiment. How far would this go?

When she looked up again, the shadow was almost close enough to touch. The darkness drifting from its shoulders ribboned into her lungs. She pulled it in as she saw some men do to their pipes in neighborhoods near the wall.

Smoke surrounded her, obscuring her vision. Was she the shadow? Had she been looking in a mirror? Tendrils of smoke wreathed around her arms. Her hair floated up like a ghost. She'd stopped breathing, but it felt natural. She was suspended in darkness that trailed its fingers over her skin.

White light, sudden and violent, blinded her and she fell back, skidding over pebbly glass. The back of her head hit the rug before it bounced up so she could see what had happened. She eased herself up on her elbows, breathing heavily. Clarity returned to her vision.

Chetana floated near the roof like a goddess of war. Her orange dress waved around her ankles. Glaring down at the shadow creature, she held her hands in front of her as though they were weapons.

Another ball of white light exploded from Chetana's hands. Kiria squeezed her eyes shut, unable to stand the brightness. When she opened her eyes, a red dot followed every time she blinked.

The distortion made it harder to see when the hallway stretched, becoming enormous. Or maybe she shrank. Either way, the ceiling rose out of sight, though only the shadow had grown to match the building. It loomed huge above her. Kiria cowered, no bigger than its foot. Smoke from its body snaked toward her.

With a loud, grating ring, a three-pointed blade appeared in the hand of the shadow creature. One point of the crossguardstyle edges could pierce straight through Kiria's tiny body. Her hands and forehead went clammy.

Chetana's determined expression didn't change. Nothing so far had surprised her. With a start, Kiria realized she had grown too, or maybe they both had. The creature still looked huge, but Chetana matched it. Its blade swung forward.

Kiria clasped her hands over her mouth to stifle a scream. Horrified, she couldn't look away.

Chetana's image flickered like fire and the blade fell harmlessly through her, lodging deep in the hardwood floor below.

Kiria jumped to her feet, finally understanding. This was a dream.

When she moved, Chetana flicked a glance toward her. For a second, the Amir looked glad. She flashed three fingers down at her sides.

Two fingers.

One.

Kiria woke up gasping. The pelt she'd used for a pillow lay unrolled against the wall. Panting, she sat up, placing a sweat-slicked hand on her chest as she struggled to calm down. The smell of dust and fur and dung filled her nostrils.

Chetana appeared, crouching at her side. Their eyes met in understanding.

"Thank you," Kiria whispered, holding onto the vain hope that she hadn't woken anyone up.

Two guards, the young one and the blond leader, instantly stood above her. "Is everything all right?"

Chetana looked up at them. "The Tanyu attacked the Keeper in her sleep. I'll watch over her."

The guards didn't move from their position close to Kiria. They loomed over her, hemming her in. The tattooed one shifted as though he wanted to help but didn't know how.

"Thank you," Kiria told Chetana again. "I didn't know you

could do that." The image of the Amir floating so menacingly, so self-controlled, still filled her mind.

Chetana pressed her lips, offering no explanation. "I'll watch so you can sleep a little longer. It'll protect your mind from any intruders."

Now that she had caught her breath, Kiria sat up more fully. It was bright in the tannery, perhaps midday. Her heart still beat hard with the aftershock of the nightmare. "I need to know how to do that."

"It takes a long time to learn, My Keeper."

"You'll teach me later," Kiria said, not minding her protests. Chetana had the Talent; so did Kiria. Maybe she couldn't shoot light from her hands, but she could fight in the Unreal somehow. She could learn helpful tactics. Besides ordering the army, she had nothing to do here but wait and pray. And learn to fight.

Chetana must have sensed Kiria's resolve, because she didn't protest again. "As you wish, My Keeper. Get some sleep."

10

BELIK

After making his announcement as the Watchman, Belik somehow made it back downstairs, pain shooting up his bad leg with each step. After getting no sleep the night before, he needed to rest, to make his mind sharp again.

A few hours later, he emerged from one of the smaller, fresher bedrooms, which he'd kept heavily guarded, and exhaled. He'd sent Shiro and Nedi with jobs so the takeover didn't flounder in his temporary absence. The weighty exhaustion brought on by lack of sleep and killing Bard had lifted, and Belik felt ready to begin again.

Daylight came through the windows, along with talking and footsteps and screams. Everyone busy.

Belik nodded at Master Nedi, who'd returned from his duties at the barrack and now stood closest of the four he'd tasked with guarding his room. "The cell," he grunted.

He couldn't get Firian out of his mind. Something like guilt jabbed the back of Belik's sternum. Somewhere, he had failed Firian, who had believed him with reckless confidence. Firian was many things, but temperate wasn't one of them.

Belik knew he should feel bad for egging Firian on, but he

couldn't force any feelings of remorse. Years and years ago, he and Sias had been friends, but that was before. Before his leg was ruined, before the *katah*, before he was demoted to a teacher. Firian *was* a better Head, while it lasted. Taking over the city and ultimately the Kingdom was going to be their crowning achievement, the glory of the Tanyu on full display.

While he caught a few hours of sleep, the blaze in the palace had been put out. Belik had ordered that fire only be set in the Main and a few other strategic locations. Most of the smaller areas of the palace, like the Watchtower, weren't badly affected. The issue was spectacle.

The five of them trod through the bright gardens where there was less smoke in the air to a partially hidden hatch in the ground near the barracks. Master Nedi heaved the trapdoor up with one huge hand, revealing a darkened staircase leading below. Belik indicated that they should all stay above while he went down alone.

The air grew smokier in the humid space. Firian's energy coiled like a snake waiting below. He waited for his eyes to adjust before he stumped down the final two steps.

At the bottom of the steps, he turned to see the cell. Iron grating covered the space at the end of the cave-like narrow room, a body's length of space behind it. The door looked secure, reaching seamlessly from floor to ceiling. A rancid smell turned Belik's stomach.

Firian crouched behind the door, glaring hatred. The fire in his eyes would have extinguished Daelon's quiet resistance.

His gaze moved to the crumbs at Firian's booted feet. "You didn't eat the food I gave you."

Firian didn't answer, except to stand, muscles tensed, ready for a fight. Belik didn't intend to give him one. It was odd. Firian's energy and drive should have been broken, at least temporarily, by Bard's death.

Belik's failsafe hadn't worked. Gerand's insistence that a *katah* would serve as useful insurance was nothing but wasted work. Well, maybe not as much work as he had anticipated. Firian had always been attached to his little friend, though Belik couldn't understand why. Bard's classes had only solidified their connection into something potentially deadly.

Young Firian, who claimed he didn't have those kinds of attachments, had two *katahs*. Belik hadn't planned his connection with Kiria. With Firian's reputation, he'd assumed that Firian would seduce the beautiful princess and leave without the mark of a *katah*. Bard he'd planned. Firian was like a son to him but Belik was also a Strategy Master—he always had to know people's weaknesses. And Bard was Firian's weakness. Unless...

Belik walked closer to the bars. The Sentry protected him from a Second Level attack. Behind the bars, Firian could do nothing but yield or rot in this cell. "It's working," he said, much as he would have back at the Academy. "The Amir have announced that the Tanyu have taken over the city." He was going to add that the Keepers were dead too, but if Firian's *katah* was anything like his had been with Chetana, the constant rumble of her presence, even with the Sentry, wouldn't let him believe the lie.

Firian's heavy eyebrows lowered over his flashing eyes. His hands became fists at his side. If Firian weren't acting like a child, he would understand.

Belik continued, lowering his voice. "These people are used to having multiple rulers. I could figure something out for you if you stop being so gory stubborn."

Every minute that passed made Firian's redemption less likely. If he didn't get on the right side, Belik would have to have him killed. He'd be too great a threat to their plan, even if he later pretended to agree. Belik chewed on something caught between his teeth. All this time, all this work... He liked Firian. Why couldn't he see reason?

Finally, Firian spoke, his voice low and menacing. "You went against my orders." His jaw flexed as though he wanted to add more, but choked back the words instead.

"We had a small window, Firian," he explained, trying to be patient, but he bit off the words with increasing bitterness. "Attacks can only be this painless if you act quickly. You weren't in a state to make demands, so I acted, knowing you'd come around."

"I told you to turn around and leave the city alone!"

"We were at the gates!" Belik came so close to the bars that he had to angle his head up slightly to glare into Firian's eyes. "We couldn't—"

"You murdered innocent people." Firian's chest was heaving.

"So have you."

A crackling silence, thick as oil, fell between them. As Belik felt the force of it, numbness shot through his hands. Certainty began to settle in his mind. He tried shrugging it off. He'd examine it another time.

"Revolutions take sacrifice, Firian," he said, more gently. The ice in Firian's glare hadn't melted. Gore, he had a strong will. Belik found himself wishing he'd given Firian more time to cool off before attempting to turn him around.

"I saw what you did to Bard."

Firian could only mean one thing. Belik twitched one shoulder in a shrug. "I figured it out."

Firian was trembling. Belik would get nowhere with this boy. That sense of certainty hadn't left him. It kept settling slowly, like a feather he kept blowing upward to keep it from touching him. There had to be a way to redeem Firian, to make him see that the Tanyu deserved to rule Brithnem, to put the Amir in their place, to right all the injustices they'd endured over the years. Firian *had* believed those things until Kiria convinced him otherwise.

Belik exhaled in frustration. In all ways, Firian was more his son than Daelon had ever been. A disappointment now, and a danger, but he'd handled him up to this point. He wouldn't give up on Firian now. Not yet.

He turned to go.

"I'll kill you."

Firian's words made him turn back. The tone and expression left no room for doubt. Rage radiated off him like heat.

In anyone else, the threat would have been laughable. Belik held the power here. Maybe Firian knew that Belik wouldn't kill him now—couldn't, because of their bond, all the hours and days and weeks and years spent together. Did Firian know him so well, or was he really so reckless with his own life?

Why did he have to make this so difficult?

"I don't think so." Belik climbed the steps to the fresh air without looking back.

11

KIRIA

Kiria woke well before the dawn as she usually did, though this time she had wasted almost an entire day. Rubbing her eyes, she sat up and wrapped her arms around her knees. As she looked blearily around, pre-dawn quiet lay heavy over everything. The freshness of the morning turned the faint body odor into something not quite as offensive as it had been in the heat of the day. Two guards stood at attention by the door. Candrae and Vayci lay snuggled together against the raised pits. She hadn't woken them. Jori slept too, sprawled messily in the oven opening, one arm hanging out and a look of concentration on his face.

Beside her, Chetana sat cross-legged. A slight hunch of her shoulders as she opened her eyes revealed how tired she was. Amir always maintained stick-straight posture.

"Thank you," Kiria mouthed, realizing that she should give Chetana the opportunity to nap before diving straight into her fighting lesson.

The quiet in the room suddenly became even more profound, as though her ears had stopped working. Chetana had taken away the Sentry.

Kiria gave her a pointed look, indicating the other sleeping forms around the tannery. She had permission to sleep.

Chetana's expression showed little relief, just steadfastness. But after a moment, she laid two fingers on her temples and began to rub them wearily. Kiria leaned forward and breathed, "We'll do it after you get some rest."

Chetana nodded and lay down, her breaths deep and measured almost from the moment she touched the floor.

Getting up this early was awkward now. She didn't have space to herself, she couldn't leave, and Firian would never meet her again... It was unwise to practice in the Unreal alone after Chetana had done so much to protect her mind as she slept. Her advisor should at least be able to sleep one time without worrying about her.

Her advisor.

Her insides twisted. Chetana wasn't her advisor anymore, not since the vote to get rid of Firian as the Tanyuin Head. Her son Daelon was. He didn't have the Talent, so none of them could be sure he was still alive. Were the Amir all hostages? Had they burned in the fire? The options were almost too terrible to contemplate. Yet Chetana still maintained her composure. Kiria doubted she could do that if not only the Keepers, but also her only son, were dead.

This morning there was little to do but mourn. The round-faced guard, whose name was Merrick, had started to alert the commanders and soldiers still loyal to her to get ready for a meeting, but some needed time to escape the palace grounds, if they were able to manage it. In the meantime, they all had a deep breath before sprinting again.

Everyone else woke up slowly: her girls first, who tried to be helpful as best they could, then the extra guards, who replaced the ones who had stayed up all night, then Chetana again, and finally Jori. Kiria had been awake for a long time before they all received water and a bite for breakfast.

"Okay," she said as she stuffed the last piece of biscuit into her mouth.

Chetana didn't need more prompting. "My Keeper," she said, as though these words had been simmering in her for some time, "it's been a long time since I learned how to fight."

"You did a good job last night."

"But I might not be the best teacher. I gave up that life long ago to pursue the ways of God." It looked like she wanted to say something else, but stopped. When Kiria didn't respond, Chetana sighed. "It's best if we sit," she said, crossing her legs and spreading her skirt over them.

Kiria did the same.

"What are we doing?" Jori asked, jumping down from his perch with a kind of cheerless enthusiasm.

Chetana cast him a sharp look. "*We* are practicing something dangerous and difficult that you cannot partake in."

"But those are my specialties."

"It's the Unreal," Kiria explained, freshly glad for these lessons. Jori's dreams were in more danger than her own since he had fewer tools to use to defend himself. *Thank goodness they didn't attack him last night!*

Jori rubbed his hands together and sank cross-legged next to them. "Oh ho! Then I'm going to watch."

"You'll just see two people closing their eyes."

"Fascinating," he replied, staring at them as though they'd already begun.

Chetana set her jaw and resolutely turned to Kiria. "You will have to tell me how much you already know."

After a glance at Jori, Kiria felt almost self-conscious. She hadn't worked on this Ability with anyone but Tanyu. It felt weird to do it in front of anyone else. "Let me show you," Kiria said, closing her eyes.

She created the palace hallway, as she'd done a hundred times. No, she realized with a painful twist, this was the palace hallway as it had been. This version of it didn't exist anymore. She set everything in place, checking the details. Would Chetana notice something she had left out?

The Amir appeared, exactly as she'd looked in the smelly tannery a moment ago. Even so, she couldn't help looking regal. After gazing around the room, she shifted her attention to Kiria. "This is quite well done," she said.

Pride bloomed in Kiria's chest.

"Now, what do you know of fighting?"

She shuffled through the things she'd heard and seen.

Bard's ball of blue light. *Focus on it like it's a real thing. Act like it's a real thing.* Firian's cryptic hints. *Every window is a door. Everyone has weak points, so exploit those. The eyes, the throat, the groin.*

"Not very much," she admitted. Fighting here wasn't like studying war tactics with Daelon.

Chetana rubbed her lips. Apparently, she wasn't surprised Firian hadn't taught her to fight. She was silent for a while, considering. "The key is to make the other person *believe* they're hurt," she said finally.

"How?"

"You have to believe it. You have to create it. There can be no doubt."

It sounded easier than it was. Her disastrous first attempt to recreate Bard's ball of water proved that. Her heart sank. "These are Tanyu..."

"They believe," she said, raising her eyebrows. "If you surprise them, you can win even against a Tanyu."

Kiria longed to ask how Chetana knew all this, but she didn't want to derail the lesson. "How?" she asked again.

"They always believe they have the upper hand. They believe their training is their luck, that they are gods in this space." She paused. "You show them they are not."

"Give me an example."

"Of course, My Keeper." The royal title created distance between them again. Kiria eased back. "You are sleeping. You see a Tanyu come. Do not be passive. Change the background to something you know better than they do. It will take some of the strain from your mind."

Kiria nodded. The hallway they stood in was already one of the places Kiria knew best, so she didn't switch it to something else.

"Can you change your appearance in the Unreal? Have you used your Beauty?"

"Not there, but I think I could."

Perhaps the shimmering moonlight glinted against Chetana's dark eyes, but it looked as if she were astonished by that answer. It was natural, Kiria supposed, for people to assume she'd used her Beauty around Firian when they'd been together. There was a lot that others didn't know about them.

"Maybe that's how you could surprise them," Chetana said.

"What do you mean?"

"You had a *katah* for several months. Could you look like Master Kess?"

Kiria cringed. She hadn't had time to process her feelings about Firian's ultimatum and his too-recent death. To look like him felt too vulnerable, an admission of how much she had studied him. Maybe even a violation of whatever was left of his memory. "I've never tried," she hedged.

But Chetana had latched onto the idea. "You won't be able to outfight them in a couple of days. You must resort to those tactics that will give you the best chance of winning. You said you wanted me to teach you. This would be a good first step."

Kiria had pictured doing what Chetana had done—levitating, shooting weapons from her hands, but not this. But she didn't have the luxury to protest.

She concentrated on her memory of Firian. He was a head taller than she was, blue eyes, dark hair, lean but muscular... She put each thing in place, including the black Tanyuin outfit and the little white scars. Even this slight height difference gave her something like vertigo. She compulsively pushed the hair out of her eyes and almost startled at the sight of the large, calloused hands. She flexed them open and closed once, assaulted by an odd mix of emotions.

When she looked back at Chetana, who stood at eye level now, she seemed impressed.

"Won't they be able to tell, though?" Kiria asked in Firian's voice. It wasn't always Firian's appearance that alerted her to his presence; it was something distinctive about his mind, something else that she could feel before she could see. Surely Tanyu were better at distinguishing people than she was.

"Eventually," Chetana conceded. "But all you need is time."

"What if I need to hurt them?"

"You just need to stop them."

Kiria had a strange feeling of déjà vu, like she'd had this conversation before. "Okay," she said. Stopping an attacker long enough to wake up unharmed was the first step. It sounded weak compared to what she knew others could do, but at least it was something. She thought of Bard's game with the glowing ball. "So, if I turn into Firian, then what?"

An idea came into Chetana's eyes. "Surprise them. Do something simple, like this." She stepped back, giving Kiria a look that warned her to get ready, which was difficult since she didn't know what to get ready for.

Hot, white light exploded from Chetana's core, drowning the space in blindness. The glare faded as soon as it had come, but Kiria couldn't see anything but vague dark shapes.

"You changed," Chetana said from somewhere in the murk.

Kiria sensed rather than saw that she was right. In the shock, she had returned to the plain appearance she usually had in the Unreal.

"Try it again." A new, commanding tone took over.

Kiria obeyed, piecing together the Firian illusion again. It was easier the second time. She also had to replace items in the hallway that had puffed away like smoke in her surprise.

"Ready?" Chetana asked.

Kiria nodded, feeling stronger this time. Maybe she was just channeling Firian. She did feel that she could do more this way, but that was foolish. In the Unreal, anyone could do anything.

Light consumed her again.

In the ensuing darkness, Kiria rubbed her hands together, feeling for the raised scars. She'd kept the disguise intact.

"Very good," came Chetana's voice.

"How do you do that?"

"It's fairly simple, but effective, as you see. And it harms no one."

At this point, with everything that had happened, Kiria didn't think that was an advantage.

Her arm twitched. It twitched again. Immediately, she looked for the difference she had planted in the background to remind herself that this wasn't reality. Her muscles seized with nerves. The last time she'd felt odd sensations like that, she had blurred the line, even forgotten the line, between what was real and Unreal. This time, though, she was in no danger of forgetting where she was.

Without telling Chetana what she was doing, Kiria opened

her eyes. The brightness of the tannery actually matched how far her eyes had adjusted from the last assault of light.

"There you are. I thought you had fallen asleep." Jori was poking her in the arm.

She swatted him away, annoyed. "Jori! I told you it doesn't look like anything."

Sitting cross-legged across from her, Chetana opened her eyes as gracefully as a swimmer. She didn't even acknowledge Jori. "Is that enough for today, My Keeper?"

"No." Kiria shot Jori a look. "Let's keep going."

Jori's fragile jollity broke. With a sullen look, he slumped back to the oven.

12

FIRIAN

THE ENCOUNTER with Belik left Firian breathless with anger. *As though anything could be the same!* But Belik had insisted on talking to him as he always had, the careful, ruthless advisor. Firian didn't think that Belik's keeping him alive was much of a mercy, but his old Master clearly thought it was.

Firian hadn't lied or exaggerated when he said he would kill him. He would find a way to do it, if Belik didn't give up trying to convince him and killed him first.

Time stretched on. The stink in the dungeon from emptying his stomach earlier only intensified. Without a window, there was no foolproof way to tell how much time had passed. Since that first meal of bread and water, no one had brought him food. He'd gone without before, but the lack of freedom and information grated on him.

Most of all, he missed the Unreal.

He couldn't even check to see that Kiria was still safe, that Bard had managed to save her after all. All of Belik's Tanyu were probably searching for her. How long could she survive? He closed his eyes, fighting against despair. He couldn't check on

Bard either, though he grew more hopeless by the minute. Even with the aid of a doctor, Bard was probably beyond recovery.

There were other reasons Belik cut off his access to the Unreal. Without it, he couldn't deny his lies or recruit others to his side against Belik. Skipping over the First Level to the next was impossible, so he couldn't use his killing ability either.

Stripped of his mental weapons, he resorted to the physical. He ran through muscle strengthening positions until he made himself sick with exertion. Push-ups, sit-ups, everything he could think of to keep himself in perfect shape as he waited like an animal to be unleashed.

His black shirt had been ripped up to his mid-back in the tunnel. Edges of the torn pieces felt stiff with blood from his reopened cuts. Disgusted, he threw the shirt to the side.

Again and again and again, his gaze darted to the base of the steps, illuminated by Daelon's guttering torch as well as thinly filtered sunlight. He couldn't stop staring, hoping someone would appear. Anyone but Belik. He needed news, allies, supplies, *something*. Wouldn't anyone come to him? Many Tanyu would stand by him if they knew he was alive. And Daelon had said something about a key.

Hours later, he stood fitting one of his boot clasps into the keyhole, fishing for a latch. The Tanyu had taken his boot knife, of course. Pinching with his fingertips, he swiped the piece of metal from side to side, trying to scrape all the walls of the lock, but the clasp was too shallow to find purchase. Cursing, he snaked his seared arm back through the bars. The crook of his elbow was red and raw from hooking it around the iron grating.

Crouching, he reattached the fastener to his boot. He refused to give up, but he was running out of options.

A door squeaked. He jerked his head up and stood. Someone was coming down the stairs in a pool of light. It was day, then.

The footsteps were lighter and more even than Belik's. Amir

Daelon appeared, holding a platter of food. He paused at the foot of the stairs, squinting like a blind man before moving forward. The flame had gone out hours ago. If Daelon struggled to see, others would too. Firian tucked away the small advantage in case he needed it later.

Daelon's face looked gaunt as he approached the bars and set down the food. A misshapen piece of meat, though it wasn't clear what kind. Firian's mouth watered, but he didn't grab for it. The last time Daelon was here, Firian had ordered him not to reveal that Kiria still lived. Something about the Amir's expression said that he kept the secret. No sign of a key, though.

"Have they found her?" he asked, hating that he had to rely on this Amir for information.

"They haven't told me," Daelon replied. He sounded as though he hadn't slept in days. "I think they would inform us all if they did."

Firian agreed. Belik would want to make it clear that the people of Brithnem had no other ruler to pin their hopes on. Belik's war was psychological as much as it was physical. Kiria was a neat end to tie up.

The news should have made him feel heartened, but the gnawing unease didn't go away. They hadn't found her yet, but it was only a matter of time until someone did.

Daelon's hands hung limp at his side. Those hands could do something to turn the war, but the Amir hadn't practiced beating his body into submission, learning to be a weapon. What use was the Scroll now? Brithnem needed a hero, someone to fight against these injustices and win. Yet Firian stood behind bars in this tiny cell and Daelon walked free.

Energy burned beneath the surface of Firian's skin as the longing to be released came over him in a rush. With Daelon, he had a little leverage, at least. A temporary ally. Another chance.

"I could check on her," Firian offered, angling for friendship.

Daelon frowned.

"In the Unreal. Like your mother has."

Skepticism twisted Daelon's expression, but he waited for Firian to continue.

"I can find out where she is. I just need you to help me."

Daelon's gaze softened, still distrustful. "You took the Keeper hostage, you killed our soldiers, you led your troops here... There is little reason for me to believe you."

Firian didn't try to deny the Amir's accusations. Laid out like that, his crimes sounded horrible. Was that how Kiria saw him too? As a dangerous war criminal?

"I'm in here," he said, spreading his arms. "We're not on the same side, or they would free me." He licked his dry lips. "I want revenge."

"Revenge is not the same as justice."

Amir had a comeback for everything. In this case, revenge was justice. "You obviously need help, and I can help you. I understand how they work, what they'll do next. I can communicate with Kiria. I can kill Belik. You need my help." His pulse was racing. Daelon had to see he was right. What other chance did they have?

Still, Daelon fiddled with his sleeve for a while before he answered. When he looked back into Firian's eyes, his face was hard. "You could kill my Keeper, so I can't take the risk. You act as though Brithnem doesn't have anyone willing to defend it. We will prevail in this conflict, and we'll do it with those who are loyal to us. Maybe you can one day prove that your words aren't lies, but it's not today."

Firian vibrated with anger as he watched Daelon turn and shuffle back up the steps. Darkness settled over him again.

If Daelon weren't so blind and stubborn, he could help him find the Sentry, at least.

Mental claustrophobia closed in. Firian had nowhere to go.

Drawing in a deep breath, he ran a hand through his greasy hair. Getting Daelon's help was the obvious solution. Maybe it was too obvious. Remembering the years of strategy and mental warfare he had taken, he ran through scenarios in his mind.

Possibilities are currency. Always think of more. The words were Belik's, but they were right.

He sat cross-legged and pulled the plate of food through the bars. The hunk of meat wouldn't fit through the square, so he had to yank it hard by the bone to make it squeeze through. Reddish rust coated the meat from being scraped over the grating. He sniffed the offering. It didn't smell rotten or poisoned. In fact, the roasted meat smell made his mouth water. He forced himself to eat slowly, savoring the juices. Long ago, he'd found that he could survive on less food as long as he focused on what he had.

The meal had to be a weak gambit from Master Belik. Good meat wasn't cheap, yet Firian, a prisoner, got a large share. It gave him energy and bought him a little more time before Belik snipped his life like a loose thread. Two good things in a world where everything had gone horribly, unthinkably, wrong.

Despite chewing slowly, even sucking on the fat and gristle, the food was gone too quickly. Just a bone left in his hand. A memory prickled the back of his skull. Something about a prison cell and a meat bone...

His eyes went wide when he remembered. Three good things. Bard played Indisfate with one wooden figure that didn't match the set: Corso, the great Tanyuin warrior. Long ago, before the Keepers, he had been imprisoned—*in this city!*—but he made a miraculous escape. In all its variations, it was Firian's favorite story when he was young.

He stared at the meat bone in his hand. It was knobby on both ends. Gripping one side, he cracked it against the ground once, twice. On the third strike, the bone broke, leaving a jagged edge, needle sharp. A smile spread over his face.

Kicking the smaller piece skittering to the side, Firian stood and wrapped his arm around the bars again. He fit the pointed end of the bone into the lock, careful not to press so hard that it snapped off. Feeling around, the point scraped nothing but the flat walls of an empty box. Readjusting his body, he tried a different angle, one that eased the raw space inside his elbow.

Then, there! There! The point caught on a small protrusion in the keyhole. He held his breath, pressing himself harder against the bars. With tiny movements, he traced the bone fragment around the latch. One side had a groove deeper than the others. That had to be it. Hooking the point into the groove, he pried the bone sideways. The thin point would break off any second. The groove was so deep in the lock that it might be a long time before he found anything else to do the job. *Stay on. Stay on. Work!*

A heavy groan of metal and the door eased forward.

13

FIRIAN

FIRIAN'S HEART SKIPPED. The door was open. He was free.

Fire licked through his veins as he ran to the bottom of the steps. He had to regain control of the Tanyuin forces, take them from Belik, but first he needed to find the Sentry holding his mind hostage. Then he would know if Kiria and Bard were alive.

Even freed from his cell, he felt the claustrophobic, low-hanging buzz of the Sentry in the corners of his consciousness, its white noise replacing the music of possibilities.

Still clutching the bone fragment, he crouched at the foot of the stairs and listened. A tiny sliver of bright light rimmed one side of the trapdoor at the top.

Where would Belik keep a Sentry? He swallowed down a lump of humiliation at his ignorance. He'd trusted Belik with the details and had been too distracted by Kiria to learn them all himself.

The white-hot image of her Beauty appearing in the farmhouse struck him like a physical blow. He hadn't allowed himself to dwell on her, but now the memory of her filled him with longing. She had only come to protect her people from invasion.

She didn't want him. Would all this have been different if she'd loved him?

He wished he could hate her. That was an emotion he knew well, but instead he was filled with a chaos of thoughts. Could he blame her for not loving him?

From this distance of time, her stricken expression and trembling fear spoke more of courage than anything. He could have taken her for himself, and she knew it. Yet she'd come anyway. Bard's voice, insistent and clear, had told him to let her go.

But it was all for nothing. Belik attacked the city anyway. Firian balled his fists.

Beyond the trapdoor, people were talking. He should have asked Daelon where his dungeon was. Kiria, to his knowledge, had never been down here, so he had no sense of where it might be on the palace grounds. It felt hot and humid, but so did all areas of the castle just before autumn came. If he was close to the Kheltor, then the door muffled the sound of waves too much to prove it.

He could burst out and hide, unless they'd set a guard above the entrance. Voices suggested that he was close to a populated area. Well, an area populated by Tanyuin forces, at least. Now, Shiro, Xan, and Makai spoke to each other in clipped voices. They would notice if the trapdoor swung open.

"...loitering when there is so much to do!" This, from Master Makai's deep voice.

"I've been stationed by Master Belik," Shiro replied.

"He's not the one with the orders. That's Master Kess."

"He's turned," said Xan. "Not with the Tanyu anymore."

"Not with the Tanyu," Makai scoffed, his disdain for her comment clear even though the conversation was muffled.

"No, he helped the Keeper Kiria escape," Shiro supplied.

Below, Firian blinked. Did people believe all this?

"He hasn't been here," Shiro continued, as though that proved his point. That snake.

Something about the silence made Firian guess that Master Makai was the only one who didn't realize that he was practically standing on Firian's prison. If only he could reach out with his mind.

Other sounds, running, a brief fight, more conversation, now overlapping, made it maddeningly difficult to hear any more.

His isolation was an asset. As he craned to look up through the darkness, he knew no one was coming. If he waited until nightfall, he'd have a better chance of slipping out unseen.

Despite practicing patience all his life, the wait sounded interminable. His muscles grew taut and his breaths shallowed at the thought. *I can do it. I'm the Tanyuin Head.* He looked up in defiance at the glowing exit. This time he whispered it aloud. "I am the Tanyuin Head."

Even if they set a guard above him, *he* was their rightful leader. They should see that. Someone should challenge Shiro's gory lie and find him.

Belik could only have taken over because the other Tanyu were used to taking Firian's orders from Belik's mouth. Apparently, during the attack he'd undermined Firian's reputation enough that they were willing to accept Belik as their new Head, but that would be short-lived.

What had he said? Firian's blood heated to think of it. Had he told them all about Firian's *katah* with Kiria, how he had let her go with a promise not to conquer the city?

Did that decision make him weak? Maybe it did. At the time, though, he knew—he *knew!*—that his decision was the only one that wouldn't make him a monster. He had done it for Kiria, for Bard, for that part of himself that rebelled against being the villain.

His thoughts swirled as he waited for the light to change and fade. He shucked his black shirt back on, despite the rips in the back. Easier to hide that way once it got dark. The stifling presence of the Sentry made it hard to take a full breath.

Finally, the voices sank to silence and only the palest glow, perhaps night lanterns from a nearby building, seeped around the side of the trapdoor. He quieted his breathing, straining to listen. Nothing. Adjusting his grip on the sharpened bone, he clutched it in his fist, the scars on his hands barely visible in the darkness. Taking a steadying breath, he felt adrenaline course through his veins. He might not get another chance.

3... 2... 1...

He burst through the door, catching it before it flipped against the ground, and set it back in place. All silent. Though it was night, the darkness of his cell made everything look bright in comparison. Amiran Academy in the distance to the left, farther away the ocean, palace behind, a low building closer on the right, grove of trees ahead. Kingdom soldiers moved around the low building. A barracks. Then why weren't they fighting against Belik? Had they accepted his rule? What threat or promise had Belik made them? Firian scowled at the passive soldiers and sprinted lightly over the grass to the trees.

The buzz of the Sentry was coming from the palace.

Across the lawn toward the palace gardens, small movements probably meant Tanyu were patrolling it. If he had organized this attack, he would have made sure that the palace grounds were locked down despite the partially unusable palace. Wisps of ghostly smoke still floated on the air, eking from paneless windows blown out by the fire.

This was his test. He turned the pointed bone in his palm. He only needed to disable the Sentry. It would be easier to kill his way through, but the thought made him sick. Who would he be killing? Shiro was with Belik. Though not a friend, Firian didn't want to kill them.

He followed the trees toward the castle until their shelter disappeared. The ornately carved walls showed many entrances —doors, windows, cellars—but which would be unguarded?

By virtue of being a Tanyu, any soldiers that remained loyal to Kiria would want him dead. By virtue of being Firian, Belik wanted him neutralized.

With each step he considered who would side with him and who would side with Belik once it became clear that everyone had to choose a side. The groups played like drumbeats in his mind.

Tanyu would be split. Friends of Rian—the Tanyu Firian had accidentally killed when the Kingdom invaded the Academy— would probably side with Belik, as well as those who were more ambitious, unwilling to give up the current plan of conquest. Some would come back to Firian out of loyalty or fear.

Torithians and border patrollers would side with Belik because he'd give them free reign for their bloodlust and greed.

If Firian could go back to the Academy, the Sentries would help him. He freed them, after all. In that moment, he realized just how helpful—and how gory frustrating—they could be.

Belik had suggested that Master Gerand look after the Academy in their absence. Did that mean she was on his side? Firian wouldn't be surprised. Gerand had never thought much of him, but she was a capable commander, which is why he'd agreed to leave her in charge. She was also the sister of Kiria's advisor—what was her name?

The answer hit him with force. Chetana. Belik's *katah*. Firian had never put that together. Belik hated Chetana but worked closely with Gerand, a *katah* Master. Was Gerand trying to free him from the mental bond with Chetana? Firian didn't think that was possible.

In any case, regaining rulership of the Tanyu might not be as easy as going back to the Academy.

Firian crouched and sat back on his heels. What would he do in Belik's place? As much as he hated to admit it, he and Belik thought very much alike. The main doors would all be watched, since the Kingdom always guarded those, taking care of the most obvious routes first. He cast his eyes up. The roof was too risky to climb. Which meant no one guarded it.

With the bone, Firian drew three lines in the dirt at his feet, one straight with two adjacent wings, like an unfinished octagon. Inside the shape, he drew a small circle—the Amiran Academy. He enclosed the drawing in two parallel lines representing the city and the sea. If he did climb the palace walls, he needed an angle where he would less likely be seen.

All the flourishes in the stone work made for good camouflage, if he could just find a divot or alcove that stretched all the way up. He looked up from his drawing to the palace itself peeking through the trees. Shouldn't there be a drainage system or something?

But of course it wasn't so easy. Glancing back at his drawing, he obliterated it with his hand. He had to go and hope he could find a spot like the one he envisioned. It was that simple and that difficult.

Nothing facing the road to the city. The Keepers would want the most visible part of the palace pristine. Same with the ocean-facing side. The edges, then. Those were his best chance.

He stilled his breathing to observe the space in front of him. No immediate threats.

Quick as a shadow, he ran.

The palace wall offered one-directional protection, so he sprinted to it, arms pumping. At the wall he turned like a mouse, sticking close to the stones. His muscles tensed at every door, but their modestness meant that they were servants' entrances. No visible guards.

Just a few more seconds...

A door opened toward him. Without thinking, Firian slammed into it, crushing whoever was emerging outside. A scream and a foreign curse. Torithian.

Firian gripped the door with his free hand, yanking it back. He was right. A Torithian he barely recognized slumped against the wall, clutching a broken arm. Blood poured down his forearm, dripping into the pile of fabric at his feet. No, not just fabric. Tapestries of the royal families. How had those survived the fire?

The dark room was meant for some kind of food preparation. Wheels of curing cheese sat on the floor and on shelves. Beside the pirate's left shoulder was a pile of cheesecloth. The man's eyes bulged to white as Firian stuffed the bone in his own teeth to free his hand, grabbed one of the cloths, and rapidly gagged him as he kicked and cried out in pain. The gag pulled the man's face tight. Considering more restraints, Firian determined that the looter was in no condition to run. One of the legs looked broken too.

Knocking him out, Firian left him and moved on, shutting the door quietly.

No one else appeared as he raced to the narrowest part of the palace. Heart hammering, he turned and tipped his face upward. Mon Párinath was taller than the Tanyuin Academy, maybe even twice as tall. A flap of movement revealed the edge of one long flag. There was no recess for drainage here, as he'd hoped. But there was a section that had reliefs on either side that would at least shelter half his body. It would have to do.

Throwing away the bone shard, which would fall out of his clothes, injure him, or get crushed if he held it in his teeth, he started the climb. His adrenaline was starting to wear off and even the practice in the cell hadn't made his muscles optimal, as they'd been before the Kingdom attack. Before Belik had killed all those people...

He pushed the thought away and kept reaching for the next handhold. He needed speed even more than secrecy. His biceps burned and his fingers strained to hold onto the stone. Falling wasn't an option. It didn't matter how much it hurt, or if his shoulders dislocated. Pain was temporary. He couldn't fail.

If he didn't get inside the palace, he might never taste the Unreal again. If he didn't disable the barrier, he couldn't have all his powers to stop Belik for his treachery both against him and the Kingdom. Against Kiria. Against Bard. People he wouldn't see unless he survived this climb.

Another burst of energy brought him near the top. The resonant flapping of the flag sounded loud now.

He wrapped his arm around the topmost stone and dragged himself over. Rolling onto the roof, he leapt to his feet.

No unsheathed weapon. No cry of alarm.

His vision of the palace roof when he had fought Bard hadn't been far off from the truth. He must subconsciously have seen Kiria here. The roof was covered in patterns of walkways and miniature green lawns, like its own garden. On enormous poles the long blue flags of Brithnem swung in the breeze. It was almost peaceful.

Scanning the parapet, he found a door. Resisting the urge to rush toward it, he focused again on the pain just out of reach. Where was that Sentry?

His vision went blurry as he pressed into the web of pain blocking him from the Unreal. As his physical senses dulled to fire, the Sentry's location became clearer.

He broke off his focus, gasping from the effort. His mind felt shredded. But he knew where to go.

14

FIRIAN

APART from the burned stairs and the acrid smell of smoke and two more Torithians carting off treasures, Firian reached the Sentry without much incident. He was being kept in a tiny room on the ground floor by himself to focus. Firian entered swiftly and closed himself inside. The space was so small that the two pressed against each other. In his trance, the Sentry didn't try to move away. The smell of parsley wafted up between them.

Firian's head felt squeezed tight. This place was black as blindness, not only to the eyes, but to the mind, and he hated it.

"Let me go," Firian demanded.

No answer.

"Can you hear me?"

A change in the cadence of the man's breath told Firian he did, but the barrier remained immovably intact.

Firian reached for the man's throat and held it. "Let me go." This scenario felt uncomfortably like when he and Bard had raided the Sentries' prison and freed them all. Firian had later tracked some of them down to appease the previous Tanyuin Head. Little good that did.

Giving the Sentry's neck a shake, Firian squeezed harder.

The message should have been clear. Did the Sentry think he had no hope of freedom, of doing anything but this mind-numbing, dehumanizing job?

"I'm going to kill Master Belik," Firian whispered. "And then you'll be free."

The man swallowed under Firian's palm.

"Let me go." Firian said it more slowly this time, as though he were easing open the cell door latch.

"You won't give me freedom. You're Tanyu," the man rasped, barely audible.

"So were you."

The Sentry broke off the barrier. The dam broke, letting in the flood of the Unreal. Firian fought back a gasp of relief, releasing the man's throat. So there was really hope he could do this. He hadn't realized any doubt before, but it must have been there, because now it was gone.

"If you don't free me, then kill me," said the man in the darkness. He was deadly serious.

"What's your name?" Firian asked, feeling the dark weight of his words.

"Lev Aramin."

"It's done."

The Sentry fished for Firian's hand, solidifying their pact.

Eager to go, Firian said, "I'll get you out of the palace, but you never saw me."

"If they find me..."

"I can't do any more than that. I need to end this, and I can't have you around." Normally, he would have told the Sentry to stay to buy more time, but Firian's absence was sure to be missed soon. There was no guarantee Firian would come back to this part of the castle to free Lev unless he did it now.

Before opening the door, Firian felt in the Unreal for Kiria. Was she alive?

A knot balled in his chest in the grasping second before he sensed her presence.

Then, there it was! Relief flooded him. It was faint and wreathed in too-familiar sadness. She had a Sentry too, but not a very good one. Had Belik set up both of them? Firian could break through this Sentry if necessary, so there was no need to track down whoever was blocking Kiria's mind. At least she was alive. She was alive—not panicking, not hurting, not dying. Despite the odds against her, alive.

And Bard? His chances were slimmer.

Almost fearfully, he cast his mind toward Bard next. Right away, he found him. Alive too!

But the brush against the Unreal made Firian pause and go further. The setting solidified around him. Yellow grasses, worn dirt paths, high-pitched roofs with intricate wooden carvings... This was Enderin. Dust motes floated above the surface of the ground, glowing in the sunlight. White clouds spaced themselves evenly across the bright blue sky. Firian knitted his brows. Something about the light or colors was wrong.

Bard was here somewhere. "Bard!" Firian called, ignoring the fake people who turned to look at the disruption. One woman with a kerchief shook her head at his brashness.

From behind a grassy hill that bent the road, Bard appeared. He wore a rough-spun gray shirt with worn brown leather accents. His black eyes grew wide with surprise and delight as he broke into a run. "Fir! What are you doing here?" he cried, colliding with Firian in a hug.

Firian stiffened. Had Bard forgotten their last encounter in the Unreal, the one that felt like a door slammed shut?

Bard let go and spun around. "Have you been here before? Why did you come to Enderin?" His lilting accent sounded even more pronounced here. Then his expression darkened. "You're not planning to take it over, yeah? We don't need the Academy. Look!" he said. "It's too big. You're here for something else."

A chill crawled down Firian's spine. Some details here were too perfect. A loose thread jutted from the neck of Bard's shirt, gnats swarmed around Firian's face, a broken piece of pottery— maybe a plate—lay halfway buried in the dirt beside the road.

Bard was Lost in the Unreal.

"Bard," he said, keeping his voice steady, "where are you?" Belik had asked Firian the same question not too long ago. Since the Master was the only person he knew who had practice in Retrieval, he took the same tactic.

Briefly confused, Bard pointed behind him. "I'm staying at home right now, if that's what you mean." His face lit up. "You're welcome to come! You should come. Meet everybody!"

"No, where are you really?"

Fear tinged Bard's expression like a film. "What are you talking about? I'm here."

That was all the confirmation Firian needed. Staying in the Unreal, he returned to reality enough to function in both. He left the Sentry's closet, Lev behind him, keeping his eyes open for soldiers. Freeing the Sentry meant shattering the illusion that Firian was still under control. But it was what Kiria would have done, and it took mere seconds to coax the man to follow him.

If Bard was Lost in the Unreal, that meant he would lie comatose in real life. By Firian's calculation, which was flimsy at best, the doctor had taken Bard a full day ago. Maybe two. Even when Firian dropped him off, Bard had been unconscious. How long would the doctor try to keep him alive if he wasn't regaining consciousness?

Firian's head spun as he tried to remember where to find the storage area with the tunnel that had led him to the doctor the first time.

In the Unreal, Bard still regarded him suspiciously.

"You're not here," Firian said carefully. Based on what he knew of Belik's work, it was delicate—more than a matter of turning the sky green to prove a point. If he made some grand gesture, Bard would assume he was dreaming, retreat deeper into his delusion, and be even harder to convince the next time. Bard had to come to his own conclusion, realize for himself that he was Lost.

"Fir, I have no idea—"

"Think! Where are you?"

Now annoyed, Bard nodded rapidly as he answered. "Why do you keep asking? I'm right here. I'm in Enderin." He looked like he was casting around for another sort of answer that would satisfy him. "My family's back there. The ocean is that way." He pointed.

"How did you get here?"

"What are you talking about? I took a horse from the Academy."

He was running out of questions. "Where's the horse?"

"Do you want it back, or...?"

"No, I just want to see which one it is."

Bard scratched the back of his head, sending his hair spiking in new directions. "Okay. Stable's this way." He walked past Firian on the path.

Firian gazed a moment longer at the perfect recreation of Enderin, so similar to what he'd seen when he docked there after the victory on Torith.

A scrabble of rocks made Firian whip around to see Bard on his hands and knees in a glowing cloud of dust. Firian's heart clenched. People didn't trip in the Unreal.

"You're okay," he said tersely, reaching down to help him up.

Breathing hard, Bard stared at the ground, as though he were too weak to reach up until he caught his breath. When he clasped Firian's forearm so he could haul him to his feet, Firian's gut flipped with the memory of Bard lying all but dead in front of Kiria's bedroom. *I'm sorry. I'm sorry.*

Firian swallowed hard. "What happened?" Hopefully he sounded unconcerned.

Bard dusted himself off before walking ahead at a slower pace. "I just rolled my ankle or something. I'm fine, mate."

But Firian couldn't shake off the terror that his friend was dying.

BARD SEEMED to forget about Firian's concern after they'd been walking for a while. Firian was glad, but not sure how long Bard could keep limping along this dirt path to the stables.

As quickly as he could with the Sentry following, Firian snuck down the hallways of the palace back to the storage area where Jori had shown him the tunnel leading to the doctor. Tanyu, Torithians, and Kingdom soldiers appeared now and then, but Firian expertly evaded their notice. A few he had to incapacitate, leaving more evidence of his escape, but with Bard's life running out like grains through a sieve, Firian couldn't afford slower stealth. He suspected that most didn't want to be in this section of the palace, still smoky and more badly burned than others.

The space was just as he had left it. White tapered candles littered the floor, now partially melted from the heat of the earlier fire. He hadn't bothered to return the cover last time, so the tunnel entrance sat exposed. Firian gestured to Lev Aramin, and then to the hole. The Sentry wasn't fast, but he was silent, a shadow of a person. This was where he could make his own way. Now Firian had to run, and he did, dashing through first, but not before he caught a hint of gratefulness on Aramin's face.

"Rissa thinks she's as tall as me now," Bard went on. "But I don't think so. We'll have to measure. She is tall for a girl…"

"Mm hm."

Firian kept the Unreal in view as he hurtled through the tunnel, running on all fours. The damp earthen wall pressed down on his spine whenever he bounced too high.

"I'm definitely taller than Elsi. And Aline's just a kid." Bard winced, a pain unconnected to his inane conversation.

"Mm hm." He had to keep him talking. "What about Jac?"

That sent Bard on another life update for a while. He half-listened as Bard explained how a local carpenter had asked Jac to help him restore homes that had been damaged in the Torithian raids, but Jac had refused, choosing instead to extend his stay with the Endrian army.

Surely the end of the tunnel was getting close.

"…staying in his room until he gets back from the war. Mum says we'll have to share when he gets back. Yeah, he won't like that very much, I don't think." Bard laughed and coughed.

The tunnel exit! Firian could see it in front of him, glowing softly in the moonlight. He vaulted toward it and burst through into the grassy hollow. Springing to his feet, he circled once, sucking in a breath of fresh air. No Tanyu, no Torithians, no Kingdom soldiers.

The doctor had come from over the lip of that hill, away from the direction of the palace.

"You okay?"

Firian's attention snapped back to Bard on the dusty road. "Yeah. Yeah, I'm fine."

Bard squinted at him, obviously doubting his flippant answer. "The horse is over here. You know, if something's wrong…"

"I'm fine." He was sprinting over the night-darkened grass. A line of buildings edged the field at the top of the hollow. Which one was the doctor? He wished he could ask Bard, but his friend wouldn't even understand the question.

Cautiously, Firian slowed. He would have to check them one by one. The delay set his teeth on edge.

Firian crouched against the building on the end of the row, hoping to sense Bard's presence. No. The next building. They almost looked like houses. No. Impatience clawed at his throat. No. No. No.

"Thass not... my horse..."

Firian's heart froze. The voice had come from the real world. He knew that murmur. Bard was talking in his sleep. A well of memories sprang up to choke him but he pressed it back down. The sound had come from the next building. He scanned for entrances. Of course, he could just use the door. Doctors always kept their doors open.

Would there be guards inside? He considered how he looked. Even those who hadn't seen him as the Tanyuin Head would know he belonged to the Academy, the enemy. The back of his shirt was shredded from crawling through the hole the first time. He quickly rubbed the red rust off his forearms. It gave him a murderous look. Some of the color remained stubbornly embedded in his skin. *Oh well.* He usually had a murderous look.

The doctor had seemed willing to help Bard without knowing who he was. Maybe he didn't take sides.

Firian smiled grimly at his own thought. Everyone took sides.

He pushed the door open. It gave easily.

The room smelled like powders and chemicals. Heat from the torches made sweat break out on Firian's skin. He felt painfully visible. Dark hallways led to more small rooms beyond. Physician's assistants moved between them, reacting smoothly to the moans of soldiers.

The hang-lipped doctor appeared. He quickly took in Firian's bedraggled appearance, betraying some surprise. "Hello, how can I—?"

"I'm here to see the patient."

"He's not well."

So the doctor did remember him. He followed Firian into the smaller rooms, protesting faintly. "You're... one of them. I'm afraid you can't—"

Firian silenced him with a look. The man closed his mouth, but his watery eyes brightened with defiance on behalf of his patients. Firian liked the doctor more for it.

He turned back to the short row of doors, nose crinkling at the smell, significantly worse than in the brightly lit entry. Four rooms, each neatly appointed with a bed and various medical tools. Every room, Firian realized, bore some hint of Brithnem colors: light blue and deep purple. Maybe the man was an official doctor of some kind.

In the darkness of one room, a figure lay on its back, covered with a sheet up to its neck. It had black hair.

Firian rushed in. Bard didn't respond or wake. Strands of hair stuck haphazardly to the sweat on his forehead. At least blood no longer crusted his eyes. The doctor must have washed it off.

Looking down at his friend, a moment of helplessness washed over him. He couldn't just snap at him to get up. He couldn't shake him until he woke, grumpy and sleepy. He had to convince him of the painful truth first, that he wasn't at home with his family, but on the verge of death because of a brutal attack. Despite the heat, a chill coated Firian's body like rain. It could take a long time, and he had a demand for vengeance that couldn't wait much longer.

"Gore," he breathed, rubbing one eye with his palm.

"He hasn't regained consciousness since he was brought in," a voice behind him said gently. "It's unlikely that he will."

Firian turned his head only enough to look at the doctor from the corner of his eye. "I said he lives. So he lives."

"So you did."

He turned his attention again to the brightness of Enderin. Bard was staring at him. "What is it?" Bard demanded.

Firian considered, breathing in the faint smell of horse manure. This illusion really was a masterful piece of work.

But there was no time. "You're Lost in the Unreal."

Bard's lips twisted in annoyance. "That's just mean."

"No, you are."

In the doctor's room, Bard slurred a few incomprehensible words.

"Seriously, Fir, stop it." He looked irritated rather than afraid.

Firian drew his bottom lip between his teeth, looking for a way to get the truth into his friend's skull. He had to be subtler or he would make him retreat further into his own mind. Inspiration struck.

"Look over there." He pointed to a barn-like structure ahead of them. It had a hitching post in front. The lintel and post were both carved in the Endrian style. "Okay, I'm going to count down. When I say 'one,' a white horse will walk out the door by itself."

"Is this some sort of game? You want a wager?"

"Sure," he conceded. Anything to make Bard pay attention. "I bet you ten coins."

Bard's eyes rounded. "I don't have ten coins. I just have..." He fished around in his pockets, looking a little embarrassed. "Four tokens."

Firian waved his protest away, staring at the barn door. "Shh!

Look!" He waited until Bard was staring too. "Three... two... one."

A magnificent white stallion trotted out of the building, dancing with Firian's own agitation.

Bard rounded on him, his heel scraping the dirt as he pivoted. "How did you know? I can't pay you, you know. I never agreed to the—"

"Bard! You're Lost in the Unreal. That's how I knew that horse was there. I made that horse!"

"You're not God." Bard didn't meet his eyes now, almost as though he were talking to himself.

Seriously? This isn't enough? Firian huffed a breath through his nose. When he spoke, he softened his tone. "I'm not trying to trick you. You got attacked. So..."

"Attacked?" Bard asked distantly. He was getting further away, sheltering more firmly in the depths of his own mind.

"Do you remember anything?"

"About what?"

Firian had no idea where to begin. Did he remember the Kingdom attack on the Academy when Firian had killed all those people? Did he remember abandoning Firian, calling him a monster before going to Brithnem? Did he remember seeing Kiria's Beauty, which she didn't hide from him? Did he remember stepping out in front of Belik to give her time to escape?

Instead, he said, "Do you trust me?"

The question seemed to jog a memory in Bard, who looked like he suddenly doubted his answer. Uncertainty crept into his eyes.

"Trust me now. I'm trying to save you. Just follow me." He closed his eyes dramatically, encouraging Bard to imitate him. "Go up, not down."

"There's a down?"

"In real life, you're lying in bed in a dark room. I'm standing there. That's what you should see."

Firian heard Bard's breathing quicken with fear. "Really?"

"I'll explain it all later. Just follow me."

Firian opened his eyes and exhaled. Strong herbs permeated the space. Bard lay lifeless before him. *Up, come on!*

Nothing.

Movement, not of trees or clouds or lanterns, stirred outside the window. Black forms headed toward the medical building, unmistakably Tanyu. Firian's chest seized. What reason could they have to come here unless they had found him or were coming to kill Bard?

He licked his fingers and put out the lantern by the door. Darkness would give them momentary cover.

The Tanyu outside disappeared, heading apparently toward the road that opened to the building's main entrance.

Firian rooted himself beside the bed, though every fiber told him to jump through the window and escape. Another moment more. Firian himself had been Lost in the Unreal. It could take a moment to orient himself. *Come on, Bard. Damn it!*

Seconds ticked by like the footsteps of approaching Tanyu.

Behind his lids, in the faint light of a dying moon, Bard's eyes moved.

15
———

KIRIA

"Let me out."

Kiria rolled over to see Jori facing the guards by the door in a brutally petulant mood. It looked dark outside.

Her eyes felt as scratchy as the pelt beneath her head. She must have just fallen asleep. The long, tense day trapped in the tannery, waiting for word from the military to begin concocting a plan in earnest, had sapped her strength. A strange buzz assaulted her senses, unconnected to her exhaustion. Chetana looked down at her and she remembered the Sentry.

"My Kepron, we can't let you leave."

Jori touched the blond guard, who blocked his path, more to make his point than to move him out of the way. He lowered his head. "I'm about to lose my mind. The least you can do is give me a couple hours of freedom." There was something fragile in his voice. He was begging.

"I'm sorry, My Kepron." The guard made to lay a hand on Jori's shoulder.

Jori twisted violently away. "You are going to let me out." He sounded close to tears now.

The closest guard opened his mouth.

"Then bring me something to drink." Jori held up a hand, ticking off items as he had done with Kiria since she was young. He jutted up his thumb for number one. "I've been through hell the past couple days... we all have." It seemed as though he wanted to add more to his list but couldn't bring himself to voice it. His fingers crumpled in on themselves. He got close to the guard's face instead. "So let me out or bring me that drink. I'm going mad in here."

"Jori," Kiria called from her makeshift bed.

Glowering, he turned to her. His waistcoat was soiled by hours spent in the oven opening. His red-rimmed eyes almost scared her.

"It's late," she said.

He cursed and kicked over a roll of leather like a child before turning back to the guards on full alert by the only door. After regarding them a moment, he held up a finger. "You know I can figure out a way." He raised his eyebrows, some of the old Jori coming back.

Two of the guards exchanged glances. Apparently, they did know.

"My Kepron, I—"

Loud knocking reverberated through the tiny room. Kiria started, sitting full upright.

"See, fate has spoken!" Jori cried, as though he were already drunk.

Urgent voices from outside the door demanded to come in, identifying themselves as Kingdom soldiers. The guards opened the door cautiously, then gratefully, as they saw two of their own outside. They bustled quickly into the already crowded space. Jori was forced to back up to make way for them.

Kiria trundled to her feet, anxious for information.

The two newcomers searched the room for her. When they

found her, they bowed respectfully. "We have news of the Kepron."

Kader. "What is it? Is he alive?"

"He is alive. He escaped the initial attack and is on his way north."

Kiria let out a breath. A motley semblance of the Keepers still lived. Ten-year-old Kader represented the First Line, she the Second, and Jori the Third.

"Who's with him?"

"His guards."

Kiria's thoughts faltered. If these soldiers had been able to find out all this, surely the Tanyu also had means of figuring it out. Kader was very likely being followed, and what could a child do against a Tanyuin warrior?

She set her jaw. "We have to make the Tanyu think he's dead, and we have to make sure everyone knows that *I'm* alive. That may give them hope, and prevent more soldiers from giving in to Belik's leadership. The new moon is tomorrow. Tell the commanders still loyal to us to meet in the paper warehouse today at sunset." Earlier that day, they'd worked out the next location, this time large enough to house a sizable meeting and close enough that they wouldn't have to travel more than a few buildings over. Sunset would give enough time to relocate and rally. "We'll need a better place to meet. And get me something to write with."

Her notebook with all its ideas about bettering the Kingdom still lay in her bedroom, probably nothing more than smoldering ashes. A list, or a visualization of a raid on the palace, would help center her swirling thoughts.

"As you wish, My Keeper."

"And?" Jori prompted.

The guard hesitated for a moment, glancing at Kiria before responding. "And a drink for you."

16

FIRIAN

Bard's eyes were still closed as he lay back on a sweat-soaked pillow. The skin had a grayish pallor under his black hair. Firian frowned. What if Bard couldn't walk?

Well, they didn't have a choice. Tanyu were coming for them. He couldn't tell how many, and he didn't want to fight all of them by himself. Bard could too easily get caught in the crossfire, killed during a negligent breath. They had seconds to escape from the medical building, if they managed to escape at all.

He shook Bard's arm. There was something unnatural about the stiffness of the limb. Firian forced himself to keep his grip, bending down close. "Bard!" he hissed, pushing him. "Get up!"

"Aahgnn!" Bard exclaimed so loudly that Firian flinched.

At least that was a good sign.

His eyes darting to the door to check for movement, Firian pushed Bard so hard that he had to catch him from falling off the bed. Finally, the black eyes squinted open, focused on Firian, blinked. Bard had always been slow to wake up, but his evident concentration as he fought to keep his eyes open wasn't typical.

Firian swallowed on a dry mouth. Every second wasted

meant they were both in more danger. By himself, he could take on a few Tanyu, but protecting Bard and preventing him from sinking irrevocably back into the Unreal complicated things.

"Get up," Firian demanded, a little more loudly than before.

Bard looked at him with the absence of sickness or distraction. "Where...?" he murmured, unable to form more of a question.

What if he couldn't carry Bard fast enough or far enough to save both of them? Could he still stop Belik, make sure Kiria was safe? The list of painfully urgent duties sent impatience like static webbing over his arms, his chest, his neck, his head. He could hardly bear it.

Bard winced and forced himself into a sitting position. He leaned back heavily on his right arm.

Firian's heart jumped. There was a chance. A chance that Bard could walk out of here.

"We have to go," he whispered.

Bard's expression didn't change.

Anxiety wormed back into Firian's body. Then Bard swung his legs over the side of the bed and stood. Unbalanced and still squinting, he wavered and fell.

Firian threw an arm behind his back to catch him. He didn't remember Bard's being so heavy. Gripping him around the ribs, he wrestled him fully upright. Instead of holding on, Bard's left arm hung heavily at his side. There was something dead about its movements.

Dazed, Bard stared straight ahead. He wasn't all right. But he wasn't dead either. He nodded, a small movement but enough to jolt Firian back into the urgency of the moment.

Their best chance was going through the window. Firian hauled in a deep breath. He'd have to get Bard through, make him stand again, and only then could they run as fast as Bard was able to go.

But he had no choice. *They* had no choice. Firian wouldn't leave him here. Neither Bard nor Kiria would die today, not while they had the true Tanyuin Head making sure of it.

A FEW HOURS LATER, Firian held Bard up, half carrying him through a wooden gate set in a low stone wall. Across a green lawn that stretched toward the beach lay a large manor house, though it looked too big for a residence.

Firian had crept painstakingly northward through the city, perhaps unconsciously following Kiria's mind, though he didn't actively search for her, focusing instead on getting Bard out of the city. Many of the shop doors were shut, making it fractionally easier for him and Bard to sneak through unseen. Knots of people ran through the streets, though, despite the hour, feeding the impression that violence lurked right below the skin of the city. Endless footsteps of soldiers and civilians reacting to the upheaval at the palace sent Firian hiding when all his training told him to go out and fight. But Bard couldn't fight, and his safety couldn't be risked. They spent too many long minutes crouched in alleyways or lying out of sight on cart beds or behind trash heaps, with Firian's hand over Bard's mouth to stop his sleep-talking noises. He wasn't asleep, of course, but he wasn't quite conscious either. It was like trying to run with a sleepy child.

Skirting Grand Market Square, which seethed with unrest, they finally made it here, outside the walls of Brithnem.

A tiny gate in the massive city wall had been patrolled by only one Tanyu, Bohai Lira, an Eradi Defender who used to live on Firian's hall. Hall Masters had tested them together when Firian was a Learner. Bohai couldn't hear well out of his right ear, and had grown to favor everything on the left. It was a simple matter of timing to undo the lock and creep through to the other side.

Here, the Gray Forest abutted these mansions, each like a tiny palace of its own. The leaves, some beginning to turn unseasonably yellow at the edges, hid the buildings from view. A fine place for Bard to lie low for a while.

Not a sound came through the many windows, but that didn't mean someone wasn't sleeping inside. The sun was rising on a cloudy, wet day. Everything looked gray, from the trees, to the grass, to Firian's own hand.

Moving like a blind man, Bard shifted a foot in front of him, and then another. He smelled like chemicals and herbs that made Firian's head woozy.

Firian stopped walking. Their escape had already seemed endless. Scanning the enclosed lawn, he spotted a copse of trees far enough away from the house to avoid notice. He sucked in another steadying breath and moved. *Just keep moving.* It was all he could do.

All the pieces—so many pieces!—out of his control.

He couldn't think about it. The possibilities blinded him. At least he hadn't gotten Lost in the Unreal again.

Had he?

He looked down at Bard's messy black hair that swept over Firian's cheek as he held him upright. *Turn red,* he ordered, and stared, waiting. The hair didn't change. Still black. A manipulation that simple would have been possible even if he were Lost. He puffed out a shallow breath of relief.

They reached the group of trees at last. He lowered Bard to the ground. Deep shadows slashed across his face, the dawn sun doing little to alleviate the darkness.

"You can sleep here," Firian said quietly.

Bard's eyelids fluttered, and then he cringed as though he

hurt all over. Even that slight movement made the undergrowth crackle underneath him.

Firian's forehead furrowed with concern. "I can't get you anything else right now, but you're out of the city." The doctor had been just outside the palace grounds, not nearly far enough from the heart of the conflict.

Bard looked like he wanted to say something, maybe many things. Firian hesitated. Did Bard remember the moment he saved him from the palace?

Bard's eyes widened until he looked haunted. "Fir," he whispered. "I can't move."

Relief at hearing his voice gave way to deep-seated worry. Firian's stomach tightened. "You can move," he said. "You just—"

"My arm." Bard's gaze shifted down to his left hand lying in the dirt.

"Sure you can move." Firian squatted beside him.

After a moment, the fingers still hadn't budged. Firian didn't want to look up at Bard, who he knew was probably looking at him with panic. He couldn't take it. Not today.

"You can move," he repeated, this time rubbing Bard's forearm back and forth in his hands as though he were trying to start a fire. Bard's skin felt cool and damp. Probably the weather. When he let go, Bard's hand dropped uselessly back to the ground.

Helplessness threatened to choke him. This *had* to work. Something had to go right. He gestured for Bard to try again. Bard's chest rose and fell in quick gasps.

A finger twitched.

Firian jumped to his feet, pointing. "There!" he said more loudly than he meant to. "Keep doing that. You'll be fine." He glanced at the brightening sky and shook out the arm that had held most of Bard's weight during their walk. The Unreal beckoned, calling with poignant urgency. He had to take care of Belik. Now.

"What?" Weakness made Bard much less talkative than usual. But at least he was talking.

"If I'm not back in half an hour, get inside that house. There'll be food." He pointed to a hatch at the side of the manor. "I'm going to make this right. I'm going to kill Belik."

17

BELIK

EVERYTHING STILL SMELLED like mold and smoke. Belik only stayed in the gutted palace because the Amiran Academy made him feel trapped with its tiny monkish cells and domed upper room devoid of escape routes. From here, he could command his forces, prepare for the coronation, and quash the feeble resistance presented by the minority of Kingdom soldiers and civilians.

Leaning back against the headboard, Belik shifted against the sumptuous blankets of one of the royal bedrooms untouched by the brunt of the fire. The Main was conspicuous with too many opportunities for entry. Though he had slept in a smaller room before, this place served as his headquarters for now. Surrounded by other Tanyu, without closing his eyes, he dipped into the Unreal.

Master Gerand waited for him in the darkness. She looked no less severe than in real life. Her ashy brown hair met in a tight bun at the back of her head, pulling the light skin away from her eyes. Though only his own age, her thin lips faded in unattractive lines into the rest of her face. She wore Academy black without the long coat. The only hints that she was Chetana's sister were her height and her indomitable attitude.

Part of him loathed this woman, but she was a strong ally, and he'd be a fool not to admit it. She'd been on his side since the beginning, or at least since Belik's break with Chetana so many years ago.

"We got news that you had taken the city," she said. "Is that true?"

"It is." He had ordered all tunnels, closets, and rabbit holes searched until there was no cellar or safe house left. The Tanyu would finish their thorough search within a day. Security at the wall and harbor was strengthened until even Belik could hardly see a feasible way through. All the silly martyred civilians proved the strength of their position. "It will be finalized tomorrow."

"Did you get them all—the Keepers?" Gerand asked. "You don't want anyone for the people to rally behind."

The straightforwardness that had initially drawn him to Gerand's sister Chetana grated on him now. The same thought had been eating away at his mind. *Kiria and Kader gone in the wind... Gore!* But he knew he could get them. Tanyu combed the city for them, starting with the medics and associates and moving systematically toward the wall.

A young boy and a teenage girl? How hard could it be? He'd eliminated all other threats. Well, Atael's dissipated brother hadn't shown up.

He fought to keep his face impassive. There were too many loose ends. The last thing he needed was Gerand nagging him about it. "Yes," he lied, and then amended, remembering the rampant rumors in the city about Kiria's survival. He couldn't keep those voices silent much longer. "By tomorrow all three bodies will be displayed."

"Well, that's something. Chetana?"

He clenched his jaw at the name. "Not yet. She ran."

Gerand narrowed her eyes. She suspected something. "She ran?"

They both knew Chetana didn't run. "We couldn't find her," he amended. "She's not our first priority."

"No." The syllable lifted at the end, unfinished. Belik knew Gerand felt almost as betrayed by Chetana as he did, and their bad blood went further back. Their goal was respect and power for the Tanyu, but the tantalizing idea of revenge tugged on both of them.

"We've secured the palace grounds," he said. "All we need until the coronation ceremony."

She continued to give him a skeptical look, but neither of them liked to mince words. The *katah* Master waited for more information. Then it struck him. According to Firian, the princess had the Talent. Gerand could declare *katah*, or send someone else to do it.

Firian already had one with Kiria, but he wouldn't kill her. His gut hollowed at the thought of his protégé. Firian was supposed to be part of this victory. Knowing Firian's implacable drive, it wasn't likely that he could make him come around. But it was worth one more try. Firian wouldn't completely turn his back on the Tanyu, but if he continued to fester in that cell with murderous thoughts, that's exactly what it would amount to. No, Belik wouldn't give up yet.

He eyed Gerand, considering. If he asked for a *katah*, he'd have to admit that he'd lied about taking care of all the Keepers. All they needed was a little more time to find her. If she became a problem, he'd turn to Gerand.

"You'll let me know," she said.

"Yes."

A sudden, rushing pressure squeezed at his chest, at his head. It threatened to crush him, to eviscerate him from the inside. His vision blackened. Without another word to Gerand, he sank painfully down to the Second Level.

Firian.

How the hell had he broken the Sentry?

In the Second Level, Belik could press back against the attack. It felt as though fingers let go of his windpipe. Now that he could breathe again, with nothing but a dull headache left behind, he created a background. The Main. Firian stood before him, legs spread, head tilted down with a murderous glare.

Belik curled his lip. "Are you here to kill me?"

But the answer was in the attack.

"Yes."

This time Belik felt as though his skin were stretching from the inside. It felt *wrong*. Like he would burst, entrails through skin. He calmed and pushed back.

Concern glinted in Firian's face and was gone. His posture now looked more forced than powerful. Belik had been practicing too.

"I don't want to kill you," Belik said. How close was Firian that his ability was working? During practice, Belik always needed to be within sight of the rabbits. If Firian weren't primed to assault him, he could warn his Tanyuin guards. No time now.

Firian flexed his jaw. He'd always been hasty, always grabbed for everything when he wasn't ready. "I don't care."

Belik searched his face. Not having a Sentry probably meant Firian was out of the cell. Sick pride welled up in Belik's gut. Where was the boy, then? "You have a right to be angry," he said in a measured voice, "and so do I. But you can't kill me."

"Watch," Firian snarled, lunging forward, growing larger, filling the space. His towering form gripped a sword. He swung.

"Wait, Fir!" Belik said in a lilting voice, in a body that matched Bard's. He threw up his hands in front of his face.

Firian halted, blinked just once.

It was enough of an opening. Still in Bard's body, Belik plunged a knife into Firian's shoulder. The blade cracked through sinews. Blood spattered his face as he tilted the room to make Firian fall from the shock.

Firian clutched his wound, biting out curses. The blades melted into nothing, but the pain was real.

"You're good, Firian, but I've been at this a long time, and I've shed my weaknesses." Now Belik was the one towering over Firian. "In real life I'm surrounded by Tanyu. Even you couldn't take them all by yourself. And here, I can match you."

Firian looked positively feral. Though Belik knew he was right, his heart stuttered, and he cursed it.

"You know I can get to you," Firian said through gritted teeth.

"But I know you won't. You're my only family, Firian. I've always taken care of you."

Firian spat blood and saliva on Belik's boot.

"I could have let you die a dozen times," Belik continued, his blood turning hot, "but there's something—something!—I saw in you. If it weren't true, you'd be dead now."

Glaring, Firian stood up again. Wetness seeped into a larger circle on his shirt.

Why wouldn't Firian see reason? Why wouldn't he join him? Belik was not a forgiving man, but Firian had an olive branch in his face and was throwing it away. "Think it through!" he snapped. "You kill me, and then what? You aren't an idiot, but your gory stubbornness is going to get you killed. Don't be blind! If you kill me, you'll have two options—take my place or countermand the order. If you replace me, you'll have the responsibility for all those deaths on your head." *And that damn girl will never forgive you.*

Firian had killed a lot of people, but he wasn't used to it yet.

He would feel the weight of the Keepers. Belik had dulled his conscience for the cause a long time ago.

"I'd be a better ruler than you," Firian snapped.

"You *are* me, Firian! Don't pretend you'd do anything differently. If you didn't rule like me—if you let the princess back on the throne with you—you'd destroy what Tanyu have fought for." He scoffed. "She won't forgive you. Stop living in a fantasy." Belik drew himself up. "Say you kill me. If you pretend like none of this ever happened, go back to the Academy, you'd give up all we've gained here. The Kingdom will put such a target on our backs that none of us will get out alive. You'll be a traitor either way."

Hesitation finally shone in Firian's eyes. His chest rose and fell more quickly. He'd hit a nerve.

"Or," Belik said, speaking more gently now, "you can come back. I'm your only ally. We've always had the same vision for the Academy."

A new expression, something vaguely defiant, crossed Firian's face. Belik cocked his head. *Not his only ally?* Was he thinking of Kiria, or...? "Bard's alive, is he?"

It made sense now. Firian's strength, his ability to escape the cell. He didn't look weakened at all. Rage pulsed through Belik at his own incompetence, but he swallowed it down. Firian didn't need to answer. The answer was written over every line of his body. *Gore!*

"I'm the only ally who can help you," Belik revised. "I'll let you take the lead. I'll take the fall for the Keepers. This is happening one way or another." He rubbed his glasses between fingers of his shirt. The action always calmed him. Replacing them on his nose, he looked straight at Firian, all in black, coiled as a spring. Belik's mind raced through all the tricks he knew. Even injured, if Firian chose to attack, another fight would be even. "You're either with the Tanyu or against them. You have to make a decision."

Belik had too many issues to deal with already. He couldn't have Firian Kess of all people running around, mucking up his plans. He felt the foolish urge to pray that he would see reason. Not Firian's strong suit.

Across the patterned floor of the Main, Firian never broke eye contact. But he was wavering.

It's not a difficult choice! Even in the throes of his *katah* with Chetana, Belik had never turned his back on the Academy. Not once.

He had to make the choice even easier, apparently. "If you don't join me, then run. Go home." This would only stall for time, but if Firian headed back toward the Academy, it would be easy to waylay him, to use forces still at the Academy to stop him instead of his forces here, which were already stretched thin until reinforcements arrived. As his mind whirled, he liked the plan more and more. "When I could tell you were still dallying with that girl on our way here, I switched out the Tanyu in charge of Raewhith."

That got a reaction. Just a blink and a skipped breath, but enough to see he'd gotten Firian's attention. Belik's over-caution had paid off.

"She likes me more than you and will do what I say. At my word, she'll look for your arrival and report to me. I've been in contact with her every other day. If she doesn't hear from me... well, I would hate for anything to happen to your sister. It takes two weeks to get over the mountains, doesn't it? But you could do it in ten days."

He met Firian's gaze. *Come with me.* For once, the strength of his will might not be enough to bring Firian back to his side. Belik wouldn't stoop to ask again.

Firian's eyes flashed. "I'm going after Kiria." The words came out clearly, decisively. In an instant, he disappeared.

Belik stood alone in the Unreal Main, filled with nothing but the vapor of rage and disappointment. To run was to choose.

Firian could have wiped his sins clean, but instead he turned his back on the Tanyu. He chose to be a traitor.

18
___

FIRIAN

Firian sucked in a breath, clutching the shoulder Belik had pierced in the Unreal. He yanked down the neck of his shirt to see how bad the injury was. The movement made him grimace in pain. The cut was bleeding freely down one side of his chest. *Gore...* This wasn't good. He glanced down at Bard, who sprawled on the grassy ground, mouth open. His skin looked ashy, even in the rain starting to fall from streaky clouds.

Firian crouched beside him and put a hand on Bard's chest. Very slightly, it rose and fell. Firian's lungs ached with relief.

He stilled his trembling hands. Belik had looked at him curiously when he asked about Bard. He had expected Firian to be weakened from Bard's death. That was when Firian knew that Kiria wasn't safe either. Despite the news that she had died, Belik had to know she was alive. Otherwise, the question wouldn't have been about Bard—an inconsequential player in Belik's eyes—but about Kiria. So he'd made the only decision he could. He'd bought her time.

But how much time? Tanyu would be out looking for him in force, thinking he was headed toward Kiria's location, but Firian had to go north to save Brett too. He pressed the heel of his hand to his forehead. There was too much. He had to get to his sister, had to save her, had to save them all.

Again and again, Belik's words played in a dizzying, relentless loop.

Bard's alive, is he?

I'm your only ally.

You have to make a decision.

And then what?

He could have killed Belik, ended it all there. His nose flared with the force of his breathing. Was it cowardice? Firian had never run from a fight before. Others could accuse him of starting fights but never running from them. Now this was the second time he had failed to kill Belik when he had the chance. What was wrong with him? Why couldn't he finish the gory traitor?

Thunder rumbled in the distance. The trees didn't offer good protection from the rain, and the dark clouds presaged storm. He had to get them under shelter.

He scanned the length of lawn leading back to the manor. It looked abandoned, but all large houses did. He smacked Bard on the arm without looking at him.

"Get up," he said, gripping Bard's bad arm.

Bard's body twisted, forehead furrowed. Whether it was from sleep or confusion, Firian couldn't tell.

"We're going in there. This will be it, the last time." *The last time you need to walk.* He forced the thoughts away again. They led nowhere he wanted to go.

Wavering and disoriented, Bard struggled to his hands and knees, and Firian pulled him the rest of the way to his feet.

With a nod, they limped unevenly together from the semi-shelter of the trees toward the manor. It didn't take long to find a trapdoor at the side of the house with stairs leading down to a cellar. Firian's chest constricted as they descended the steps.

This felt too familiar. Living in darkness, picking the lock, help-less against the Sentry...

"Fir."

Bard's soft voice made Firian realize he had stopped on the stairs. He forced himself to go down the rest of the way into the deep brown darkness. Wood rot and cool, moist earth made the space smell inviting compared to the hole where Firian had been kept. There was also the bready tang of ale. He swallowed. He hadn't eaten anything since the hunk of meat in his cell. It felt like ages ago.

Though rain splattered through the open door onto the stairs, Firian didn't close the door until he could light a lantern bolted into the wall. He'd had enough of darkness for now. Later, he'd overcome his inhibitions, but now he wanted some-thing to go right. No more darkness.

The soft lantern light glowed over warm wooden barrels. Some had spigots. Piles of other miscellany sat in corners. Leaning towers of crockery, half-hearted stacks of rough-cut fire-wood, trunks with lids propped open by the amount of fabric inside.

He opened one of the trunks and threw a few blankets on the floor behind him. He ripped one into strips and bound his aching shoulder, remembering the times Kiria had passed her sash across his body to bind the cut on his back. He should run, send the Tanyu off Kiria's scent, but fatigue had caught up to him, and he was well hidden. As he reinforced the exit door so he would be alerted if anyone tried to get inside, his muscles moved sluggishly. In this rainless space, closed off from the rest of the world, exhaustion hit him hard. His breaths became labored and his mind dizzy from lack of blood and sleep. He couldn't run tonight. After a short, reviving sleep, he would decide what do to.

Almost before Firian rolled up two pillows, Bard had fallen

asleep again. Firian lowered himself onto the blanket near him, scooted forward so his face was under a barrel spigot, and took huge mouthfuls of ale. He savored its heady coolness on his tongue.

Casting his eyes to the corner, he spied a cup among the dishes. Tomorrow he would make Bard drink too.

Wiggling back onto the makeshift bed, he curled on his side. A deep ache filled him like water in a drowning man's lungs. He took deep, steadying breaths as he looked at Bard asleep in the lantern light, and thought of Kiria in danger in her own city but willing to give her life to protect it. He should have been angry, but he was too tired. His eyes grew hot as he fell headlong into sleep.

19

—————

KIRIA

Kiria watched the sun set through a slim slit in the cloud cover. Only a moment, but she caught it. Rays of light shot through the falling rain, shining bright against each drop chasing down the windowpane. The beauty of it made her heart clench. And then it was gone, black as midnight. She swallowed. The light spoke of what they had all lost, and all they still had left to lose.

She stood in near darkness, in a storage warehouse in Grand Market Square, larger than the tannery, with her top remaining military leaders. Chetana had come too, but no other Amir had been able to leave the palace grounds. Her group had moved as soon as word came that Tanyu had already searched the nearby building.

It had been a hectic and terrifying afternoon of trusting her guards to keep her safe. In a fight, Tanyu had the upper hand, so, to avoid one, the guards hid her and the others, sometimes separating them for long minutes. The tannery had fallen under ordinary notice, because the sweeps of the city took in even the lowliest outbuilding. Some of her people fought back against the sudden invasion, but the scuffles didn't last long, from what she could see. Near misses and huddling in alleyways and garbage heaps, her guards' instruction and her insistence that the Tanyu would be thorough, perhaps could track her down by her mind alone...

A breathless hush stultified the room. No chairs had been set out. A wooden stool sat squat in the midst of them in case someone needed to lay out a document. In this murk, it would be hard to decipher text. The walls, made of wooden planking and dotted with lantern brackets, were suggestions in the shadows, along with systems of pulleys in the ceiling. All the inky corners made her uneasy. A Tanyu in black would have all the shelter he needed to surprise them.

All eyes were on her. She wore the fresh clothes they'd found in the safe house, and she'd put on her Beauty for this official meeting. Still, her nerves felt frazzled and her fingertips numb. Without other Keepers and their Amiran advisors, the meeting seemed incomplete, as though they couldn't begin until experts arrived. But as she scanned the mismatched group, the earnest faces hungry for hope, determination welled inside her.

"Thank you all for coming," she said, clearly but quietly. "Master Belik says he plans to be crowned tomorrow at the new moon. As soon as he is, it'll be more difficult to get to him. The Amir, the military, and the people will swear to serve him. Many will believe that he's sanctioned by God." She thought briefly about how most people thought that about her too, and yet there were dissidents, even against her reign. There was a sour kind of hope in that now. "We have to strike before he's crowned, before everyone is forced to swear loyalty to him."

"We will not, while you live," said Lanthe, a Khelê military commander who, despite Belik's offer of wealth, had ordered her troops to fight back once they discovered the palace was under attack. Tanyu had killed almost all of the soldiers under her command before she changed tack and went to find any Keeper who remained alive.

Others, like Royce, the large blond guard with a square jaw who had helped Kiria since the safe house, joined in with agreement.

A wry smile rose on Kiria's lips. "Thank you. I don't doubt your loyalty. During the coronation, his security will no doubt be increased, but it will all be centered around him. We need to strike where he doesn't expect us if we're to have any hope of success." There was little hope to begin with, but a surprise attack could accomplish what they needed. The loyalty of a few talented soldiers might end this crisis. Doubt gnawed at her, as sickly as a disease, but they had to do something even if hope was slim.

She ran through the ideas she'd formulated in the hours leading up to the meeting. Everything Daelon and Firian had taught her, every game of Indisfate, everything she had learned about the Tanyu fed into her plan.

"On the night of the coronation, we'll send in an assassin, someone who can kill Master Belik from afar. Our best archer. As a precaution, soldiers in plain clothes will go posing as the audience. There's a cache of emergency weapons in the Main. The soldiers can use those if it comes to it."

The weak light from nearby buildings drew a slash across the blond guard's face as he shifted his weight. He held his helmet under his arm. "Excuse me, My Keeper, but what guarantee do we have that the Tanyu have not already confiscated those weapons?"

"We have no guarantees." The unbidden image of Firian floated before her mind, followed by the litany of those she had lost. The too-recent horror threatened to choke her.

She threw back her shoulders and looked at Jori to ground herself. He held one elbow in his other hand, abnormally uncomfortable. Before, he had never relished political or military meetings. Now, he had nowhere else to go and had to face the invasion head on. He returned her gaze with almost a pleading look.

She shifted her attention to Chetana. She needed allies, but, with each inspection of the room, she felt a little bolstered and still very alone. These people would do her bidding, even unto death, but who was there to tell her it would be all right? Who would hold her hand and give her strength? Take some of the terrible weight of responsibility that never should have fallen on her back alone?

"Then some of us should bring weapons to the coronation," the tattooed guard resumed. Kiria still hadn't caught his name. She'd have to ask later.

"You'll be searched," growled Royce. Always like an older dog with a young pup, those two.

"Yes," Kiria admitted. "Probably, but we'll arrive early, act natural. Our soldiers can take up the entire audience, leaving other citizens who come to watch unable to get in and having to watch from afar, if that's possible. If we take up all the space closest to Master Belik, any other audience members can be clear of the fighting."

"That sounds risky." As time had gone on, the tattooed guard spoke up more often, despite frequent looks of consternation from Royce.

"It is..." she agreed, waiting for his name.

"Viktor." He stepped a little closer so she could see him better. Viktor was the youngest among the guards. One half of his face was covered in a Khelê tattoo, this one an oversized *laird* flower, the symbol of peace.

"Viktor. But so is any plan that has our troops intentionally going into a Tanyu-occupied area."

"But what about the Tanyu on the grounds?" Lanthe asked. "We don't know how many there are."

"That's true," Kiria admitted. "Is there... Do you think that more of our own soldiers will join the Tanyu in resisting us?" The suggestion sent shivers spidering down her body. Could the dissent against her reign run that deep? If the conversation she had overheard meant anything, it did in some circles. This attack, at least, would demonstrate that she had done nothing to encourage this overthrow, the death of her friends... Again, bone-deep loneliness rose up to drown her as surely as the blank eternity of the Unreal.

Lanthe swallowed, the muscles in her bone-white neck tightening. "I think it's more likely that they won't engage."

"And wait to see who wins so they know who to support?" Chetana asked, disgusted. "Has anyone consulted the Amir about where their loyalty should lie?"

An awkward pause followed. Were the Amir even alive to consult? The air felt chilly around them. Rumors suggested they were alive. That had to be enough for now.

Kiria cleared her voice. "So the priority will be to kill only Master Belik."

"What about the Tanyuin Head?"

A lump of unexpected emotion rose to her throat. "Firian Kess is dead. Killed in the fighting. Master Belik has taken his place."

"But..." One of the commanders, a man with a lined face, looked skeptical, and even touched the stool in the center of the circle with his fingertips. "What about the Academy raid?" He spoke as though Firian were unkillable.

But no one was unkillable.

Kiria shook the hair out of her face. "He was dangerous, but someone managed to kill him." She wouldn't go into detail about his last day. "He's not a... a factor anymore." Thinking about his death made her deeply angry—at him, at the situation, and especially at Master Belik.

She wanted to scream, to be safe, to be alone, but she

returned to the plan. Her words came out more labored, like a cart that had gotten something stuck in the wheel and had to work it free. "At the beginning of the ceremony, on Petra's signal, you'll form a unit and move in formation toward Master Belik."

"Do we know where he'll be located?" asked Lanthe.

"No, he could be in the Main. He could be on the lawn or on a balcony. We'll no doubt learn right before the ceremony begins, so we won't have time to adjust our plans. We'll have to be prepared for a variety of scenarios. My guess is that he'll do it in the Main. Regardless of the location, form up tightly enough that no one can get inside. The Tanyu's only options will be to attack from the side or from above."

Lanthe cast a quick glance to the general beside her. *Above?* her eyes seemed to say.

"Some of you will bring shields and weapons concealed in your cloaks, things that wouldn't immediately spark suspicion."

Viktor frowned, stretching the *laird* flower almost comically. Others shared his confusion.

"Like cooking tools, or farmer's supplies," Kiria supplied.

Jori's face twitched, though it was difficult to tell if it was from amusement, pride, or skepticism. The result was a dark, sardonic smirk.

"I know what it sounds like. But at least that way our soldiers won't be entirely weaponless in case of the worst." She banished the image of the guards lying dead outside her door. "We'll hope the weapons cache is untouched," she continued. "Use shield for above and weapons for the side. Even Tanyu can't break through that." *I think...* She did her best to be confident.

Bard's story about Firian's ability to kill people without touching them sliced through her thoughts. Could others do that too? She'd never heard of such a thing with anyone else. "Once you've killed Master Belik and gained a position of strategic advantage, announce your allegiance to me and the Keeper Lines."

The plan sounded simple enough. Too simple, in fact, but maybe that was the strength of it. The coronation was their best chance, with Master Belik on full display and the Tanyu coming out of the shadows to support him.

"Won't they be suspicious?" asked the skeptical commander. "We won't come across as a civilian crowd. There will be no children, no elderly."

Kiria chewed her lip. "We can't risk civilian lives in this."

"Of course not."

"Looks like it'll be cold tomorrow," Viktor piped up. "That'll give our troops an excuse to wear cloaks big enough to hide their features."

Kiria smiled at his support. "Thank you. I think this could work. We need to strike quickly, before they feel balanced, and before the people of Brithnem give up on us." *On me.*

20

____

FIRIAN

FIRIAN SUPPRESSED a groan as he woke. His whole body felt sore. The lantern had gone out during the night, leaving the cellar in darkness. A freshness in the air and light seeping down the steps said that it was already morning. How long had he slept?

He rolled to his knees and lit a lantern hanging from the wall for better light to inspect Bard lying beside him. Bard lay on his back with his mouth wide open. The angle of the rolled-up pillow tilted his head to the side. Some color had returned to his face. When he woke, would he be lucid? Would he be able to move his arm? Would he remember anything from the past few days?

Something pressed on the hollow of Firian's throat when he considered that Bard might not remember their reconciliation. Maybe he would wake up and call Firian a monster again, blame him for all this carnage, afraid and angry when he realized the two of them were alone.

The comfort of the musty cellar closed in around him. The feeling of safety had been a lie. Only exhaustion had convinced him otherwise. Whoever owned the house could come in at any moment and catch them sleeping. Thunderstorms usually didn't put Firian to sleep; they kept him awake. But he'd obviously slept for hours without waking once. That meant he had only nine days to get to Brett before Belik would make good on his threat. He had to leave as soon as he knew Bard and Kiria were safe.

Settling back on his heels, Firian eased into the Unreal. It felt true, almost cleansing. He'd spent almost no time there the past few days, and his mind was in need of space.

He hadn't seen Kiria, either in the Unreal or the Real, since the night he'd let her go back to the palace. His jaw tightened uncomfortably at the memory.

He deserved her opinion of him, since he just let her go on the run without helping her. But what more could he have done?

It was different now, as though more than just a few days had passed. Had his ruse worked to keep her safe? Now that the initial adrenaline had tempered down to uneasy embers, he cursed the feebleness of his plan. It was stupid. But hopefully it bought Kiria a few hours.

He had to check on her. It didn't matter if she woke and cursed him. At least he'd know she still breathed, still fought. All that life couldn't be snuffed as easily as someone lesser. Only his intimate knowledge of death allowed him even to consider the possibility, and it chilled him like sickness.

He reached toward her, mindlessly creating a wooded road around himself, morning sun casting shadows like black pillars across the path.

Through the trees, she appeared, fully dressed, fully aware of him.

Astonishment and relief made his breath halt. She was all right! She was here! His eyelids fluttered as though he'd forgotten to blink, and his hand ran through his hair to smooth it down. He knew the gestures were inane even as he did them, but his body felt foreign with surprise. When he'd let her go, he'd felt the pang of loss, assuming he wouldn't see her again. Yet here they were again, and she had never been awake before he was. The thought teased a trace of joy from him. Then he noticed her expression.

She stared at him as if he were a ghost, a fierce line drawn between her brows. One arm moved across her torso with an unconscious air of protection. Her eyes were fire, shock lighting their amber depths. "Firian?" she breathed, hardly audible. "I thought you…"

His words wouldn't come. She looked at him with intensity that stole his breath. The furious question in her gaze made him pause. Was she that surprised to see him here? Did she think he had died in the fighting?

As he looked at her, memories assaulted him—memories of her, distraught and angry as he kissed her. Memories of her glee when she beat him at Indisfate, or the way they held each other so desperately after he beat the Torithians, or her presence when she saw Brett and his mother for the first time in so many years, or when she pushed him away after his success at Archer's Point.

And now.

Now the recent past was hot between them, true and painful like a room ablaze. Like the palace.

"You're all right," he said, relief evident in his voice.

Lines fanned from her eyes, denying his statement. After all that had happened, none of them were really all right.

Because Tanyu had taken over Brithnem. His Tanyu. They'd killed the other Keepers.

"Did you do this?" Her voice was a hush; her body trembled down to her closed fists. The next time was a ragged shout, wet with emotion. "Did you do this?"

"No!"

Fearless, she charged him, snarling, eyes red. He didn't step back as she struck him hard in the chest. She glared inches from his face. "Where were you?"

Firian's face flushed hot with frustration and guilt. He should have been there to help her, but how could she think he had caused such horror, killed people she cared about? "Master Belik—I told him to leave and he refused. He took control of the Tanyu and... you saw what he did." There was no time for a full explanation.

"Are you with him now?"

"No," he cried, losing patience. "I'm not with him. I told you." The hurt and disbelief in her eyes were hard to look at, but he held her gaze. Low in his gut, urgency lurked. Words that needed to be spoken. But the most urgent was her safety. "Are you someplace safe?"

Her silence was frosty. She stepped away. "If you're trying to get our plans—"

"No," he repeated.

She wasn't safe inside the city walls. Belik would find her, and he would kill her. Judging from her demeanor now, she was still relatively secure, probably surrounded by guards. Otherwise she wouldn't be here talking to him. There was still time.

His breaths came sharp and quick. "You have to get out of the city."

Air puffed from her lips in a sneer, her eyes full of pain. "My people need me. I won't run at your suggestion."

"But you—"

"Remember that question you asked me?"

There had been many questions, but yes, he knew the one she meant. *Am I a monster?*

She let the silence draw out in the air between them. Answer enough. Every second dug into his gut.

"Okay," he finally said, his lip curling. He could deal with that later. Right now, Belik was stalking Kiria. This wasn't a game. Even Firian's pride had to halt for a moment. "Kiria, I'm serious. You have to get out. Belik knows you're alive."

She retained her new composure. "I'm not surprised," she said. "We've been telling the people."

"Kiria."

"They have to have hope!" A wild tinge of red came back into her eyes. Her chest rose and fell, heavy with emotion. Her voice quieted. "I need hope."

A confession.

An accusation.

So do I. "I didn't want this to happen," he said gently.

"That's why you brought your troops here," she said, dead-pan. Her eyebrows rose.

He opened his mouth, closed it again.

"Unless that was only to blackmail me into being with you."

A muscle ticked in his jaw. Everyone he cared about was slipping away from him across a chasm he couldn't breach. He couldn't take much more. "Just... get out. He will kill you." He was surprised by his own breathlessness.

Her nostrils flared, sad but defiant. "He's the one who should be afraid. And you, if you come here."

She doesn't understand. He wanted to drag her out of the city himself, take her somewhere safe, turn back time... His fingers twitched but he held himself back. Taking her anywhere in the Unreal wouldn't accomplish his purpose.

"I..."

But she didn't want his help. He'd have to find some other way to coax her out of harm's way.

Out of options, the truest statement came out, bald and obvious. "I don't want you to die."

She gave him a curious look at that, her red eyes searching. Accusation and vulnerability at once. There was a breath of hesitation as her face cycled through myriad emotions. Maybe she would start crying. The look was hauntingly similar to the one she'd given him before running out of the farmhouse.

"I don't either," she finally said, the words quiet and almost confused. But then her expression cleared like the sky. "And we won't."

Before he could speak again, she disappeared.

We? She didn't mean the two of them. They would never be *we* again to her. She meant others. Who else had escaped? Maybe Jori had caught up with her. He was still alive when Firian had left him. The thought gave him a modicum of comfort. Kiria wasn't alone. At least, not completely.

After taking a moment to recover from the conversation, he came back to reality. He dug the palms of his hands into his eyes. His jaw was getting sore from grinding his teeth. She *had* to get out. How did she not see the danger she was in? Cúron and Atael had been killed by Tanyu. She had to see the risk. And yet, she didn't go. Even as he felt sick with worry, he was proud of her. Stubborn bastard that he was, he wouldn't have left either.

"F'r?"

He turned. Bard was sitting up.

Lightheadedness swept through Firian. Bard was sitting up on his own. Did he hate him too?

In hindsight, he realized that he should have told Kiria that Bard was with him. Maybe that would have proven his sincerity.

"What happened to your shirt?" Bard made a sound that might have been a laugh, but it sent him into a coughing fit. He leaned forward, bending almost in half with the force of his wheezing.

Firian rose to his feet and shoved a mug under a spigot. Dark brown ale sloshed and foamed into it. When the mug was half-full, he set the cup in Bard's hands. Only the right one curled around the handle. His stubborn left arm hung limp at his side.

Still, seeing his friend conscious was a relief, and a welcome respite from the pain of seeing Kiria.

His mouth quirked up when Bard began to drink. He was okay. He was okay.

After a long moment, Bard lowered the mug again. He winced with his last swallow. "Where are we?"

"Some big house."

Bard's eyebrows drew downward. "I don't..." His half-finished sentence sounded husky, his voice creaky with disuse.

"Master Belik attacked you. But you're all right."

His face twitched a few times, as though he were trying out different movements. "I thought that was... a dream or something." As he said it, memories seemed to return. He stretched out his stiff thumb with his other hand. "Where's Kiria?"

"Inside the city somewhere."

"Are we not?"

Firian shook his head. "Just outside." After a pause, he added, "She needs to get out. Belik is looking for her too. It won't take him very long to find her."

Bard set down the mug, looking around as though seeing the room for the first time. He squinted, smacked his lips. Firian tensed, waiting for Bard's recognition that this was all wrong. The information seemed to take a long time to sink in. Bard's eyes grew large again. "My hand."

"I know," Firian said quickly. "You can move it. It's just hard." Crawling forward, Firian rubbed Bard's left arm. It had gone clammy again. "Here. Try."

The thumb twitched, more a tiny muscle spasm than a controlled movement.

"See? You're fine."

Bard set his mouth in a line that silently disagreed. He stared at his hand for a while, his fingers making miniscule movements. A trickle of sweat beaded down his temple. When Bard's dark eyes met Firian's again, they were sharper than before. "What happened?"

The question held new weight. Behind it, Firian heard all the warnings from their time as roommates. *Don't do that or they'll kick you out.*

What was Firian's role in all of this? That was what Bard really wanted to know.

Honestly, Firian wasn't sure how to answer. He'd been so intent on stopping Belik that he hadn't asked himself how much of this was his own fault. Bard's gaze made him ask himself the question. He hated the uncertainty of the answer. He was the Tanyuin Head. Some of this destruction had to be his fault. He'd been spineless, foolish, weak. His nose flared at the thought of the last word. He worked so hard—*so hard*—not to be weak. His whole life was dedicated to it. Yet here he was. In a basement with one other renegade Tanyu while Belik stole his authority and threatened Kiria.

"I don't know," Firian said quietly.

Bard seemed to read the sincerity in his voice, and nodded. The two sat in silence a long time.

Firian's stomach felt hollow and his blistered feet ached. He hadn't noticed before. He also didn't remember taking his boots off, but he must have done so in the night. He flexed his toes.

Bard took another slow swig of ale. When he lowered the mug, his gaze flickered between Firian and his own useless hand.

Firian wasn't good with words. Nothing he had said to Bard, Kiria, or Belik had made anything better. With those three, he couldn't hide behind prepared lines and a sense of mysterious power. Of everyone in this world, those were the people who knew him best. He had no clue what to say to Bard, but something had to be said. The interior pressure made his empty stomach roil.

"Why were you here in Brithnem?" he finally asked in an undertone.

Bard blinked. "I had to stop you. But I... I didn't want you killed."

So you went to Kiria. Firian nodded, feeling oddly numb. The anger that he normally held so close didn't come to him now. It felt right to speak the truth. No more lies or posturing.

"I didn't want you to leave," Firian confessed. This cellar full of ale and junk had transformed into a space where there were no consequences for truth.

The only other time he'd felt this way was when he had talked to Brett in the room they'd shared when he was very young, maybe six. He hadn't thought about those times in years. After a particularly bad day, he or Brett could call a night meeting if they couldn't sleep. They'd wake up together and sit cross-legged on the floor and talk until they felt better. After the initial misery had worn off, they usually tried to make each other laugh. Silent fits of giggling meant that the night meeting was over and they could go back to sleep.

"Yeah, I figured," Bard said, echoing the words he'd said that day just before he abandoned the Academy.

Another bout of silence fell over them. A breeze tickled through the shredded back of Firian's shirt. Were these really the same clothes he was wearing when he met Kiria, and then carried Bard to safety? Maybe Bard was right to laugh.

"I saw you try to save her. That was stupid, you know." Firian smirked at him, proud.

Bard smiled back and coughed. "I know. Didn't get very far." His face fell again. His finger ran along the side of the tankard, and then he looked up as though realizing something. "You saw that?"

Firian shrugged. The word tugging at him now had so long smacked of weakness. Tanyu didn't get involved in an unintentional *katah*. He already had one with Kiria, but the evidence was overwhelming—he had two.

"Huh," Bard said, coming to his own conclusion, inevitably the same one. It was that uncanny ability he had to read Firian's mind, to know him almost better than he knew himself. "So you're going after Belik now." The statement held a question beneath it. *Where does that put me?*

"Yeah," Firian answered, standing and opening the chest full of fabrics. The new knife wound twinged under the bandage. He would just have to attack Belik from a different angle as he headed back to Raewhith and figured out allies that Kiria could trust to help her. "I have to. I mean, I ordered the Tanyu to stand down."

Bard's mouth quirked.

"Belik ordered the attack anyway. He killed... You were there." He looked away and exchanged his ravaged Tanyuin shirt for a new one from the chest.

"Would you have done it?" Bard angled his head with an evaluating gaze.

"Not all that," Firian said lamely.

"You would have burned the fields, yeah?" Bard murmured into his mug as he took another sip. There was a new fearlessness in Bard that took Firian by surprise. His boldness had grown back at the Academy, but it seemed to have solidified into a permanent aspect of his personality. He was still Bard—still cautious, still attentive—but now his strength of conviction was rising to the surface. He wasn't afraid of consequences anymore, not as he had been.

"Yeah," Firian admitted. "Maybe."

"But there was something with Kiria, I think."

Bold indeed. "Yes," he said carefully. He didn't want to think about it. What he thought was a mercy had made her distraught. So he'd changed course, gone against his impulses, and released her. The right thing, the good thing, Bard would say, and yet Firian felt like shit whenever the memory surfaced.

The night meeting had hit a wall.

"If I was in the palace..." Bard began. A sudden gasp sent him into a violent fit of coughing. He had to set down his mostly empty mug of ale to keep it from sloshing in his hand. The dead arm looked pointedly immobile when the rest of him was moving.

Firian waited until the fit passed. "I got you out," he explained, answering the unspoken question. A sharp smile twisted his lips. "That's how my shirt got all..." He gave a dismissive gesture.

Bard's black eyes sparkled, even though he still looked confused. "There was a doctor, though. I think."

"It's... There's more, but I did get you out of the palace."

Bard flexed his bad hand slowly. It had loosened somewhat, but it still looked like he was squeezing some tough, invisible object. "We need to figure out who's still on your side."

"I can't stay long, though. Belik said he'd... hurt my sister Brett. Remember her? I've got to leave." Belik's control bound him as surely as ropes. He cast a glance at the cellar trapdoor. Even this conversation was costing him valuable time.

"Once you gather support, then what are you going to do?" Bard asked. "You're not just going to kill Belik and that's it, yeah?" The implication hung in the air. *You could have done that already.*

"I don't know," Firian muttered.

"You do know," he said, not lifting his eyes from his own struggling fingers. "Kiria should be in charge." His gaze flicked up and then down again, not sheepishly, but pointedly. Her name sounded strange coming out of his mouth. He didn't even add "Lady" or "Keeper."

Firian froze. Admitting it would make it real. The same idea had crept into his thoughts, more and more frequently, coloring the choices he made, but he never looked at it straight on. It stayed in the periphery. He wasn't sure he was ready to turn his head and agree.

Did it really come down to this—him *or* Kiria? The question almost made him huff in impatience. Of course it was either him or Kiria. It would never be the two of them together.

But Kiria didn't trust him, didn't want his help, not after all he had done. He'd opened the door for Belik to kill the other leaders—not deliberately, but Kiria didn't see it that way.

He stayed silent. When he focused again on Bard, they gave each other a painful, knowing look. Firian's chest constricted. *I'd improve our defenses and alliances... and do my best to make peace... People will protect something they love...* He pictured the rioting and slander she had endured because of her alliance with him. The way she had defended him when no one else in Brithnem took his side. The way she played like a sorceress to his better nature, taking what was hardened with fear and anger, and enticing him toward choosing good.

If you don't love me, why did you come?

Because I love them.

Bard was right. Something inside him struggled against it like a wild animal, but Bard was right.

He had to get Kiria, just Kiria, back on the throne.

21

FIRIAN

FIRIAN NODDED, dropping hard on his tailbone beside the chest of fabrics to steady himself. Words wouldn't come. That nod, that agreement, meant losing some of his identity—giving up a dream of power instead of feeding it.

Creases formed at the corners of Bard's mouth. Was that pride in his eyes?

Firian cleared his throat. "You can't travel very far, can you? Not very fast?" The words sounded empty and obvious, but it was something safe to say.

"Probably not." He shrugged apologetically.

"Then... maybe we'll figure out where Kiria is—I can find her—and you can communicate with the Tanyu for her." Kiria had mastered certain elements of the Unreal, but, as far as he knew, she had only met with him and couldn't communicate well with anyone else there. She would need a more experienced Tanyu at her side. She already trusted Bard—far more than she trusted him, at least—so maybe she would accept his help.

"Yeah," Bard replied. "Yeah, that's good." He stretched his fingers back with his other hand.

Firian would head to Raewhith and then the Academy, pick up anyone left there and in the surrounding cities, and head back down to the capital. On the way, he would communicate with the Tanyu and figure out whose side they were on. Without Bard, he could move much more quickly. With the urgency he felt, he could bring an entire force down to the Brithnem in just over three weeks. Hopefully before it was too late. Between new troops and Tanyu still loyal to Firian, they might have victory.

He would, he realized, have to tell his allies that they were fighting for Kiria. How many would abandon him?

"Fir, you're serious?" Bard wasn't just talking about having him work with Kiria. He meant conceding the throne.

In the corner of Firian's consciousness, a buzz sounded, another mind that wasn't Bard's. He sat up straighter, motioning for Bard to stay quiet. Bard's look of surprise soon gave way to understanding. He sensed it too.

There was definitely a Tanyu outside—maybe one who believed Firian's ruse that he was going after Kiria.

Firian hauled his boots back on, gritting his teeth against the searing pain. With another warning look at his friend, he opened and closed his hand, indicating that Bard should do the same. Bard needed to flex that hand if he ever hoped to use it normally again.

The pocket at the side of his boot was empty. No knife. He scanned the room, chose another tankard, and broke it. Bard cringed at the noise, but now Firian had a weapon. It was just a jagged handle, but it could do damage if necessary.

Something stilled in Firian before he jumped to his feet. This person was a Tanyu. One of his. He closed his palm more tightly over the curved handle, hoping he didn't have to use it. Better this than his killing ability, though.

Carefully, Firian snuck out of the cellar to meet their pursuer. The air was fresher outside, with the cool bite of after-storm. The lawn grass looked greener, as though a layer of dust had washed away.

Firian's boots tread silently over the thick grass as he angled toward the other mind. Back toward the ocean, toward the front of the house. That was where he felt it most strongly. His stare skipped over the mansion's windows, the trees—anywhere a hidden person could be watching him.

The Tanyu wouldn't have gone inside the house if they could help it. Still, Firian avoided the view of the window in case the owners were home.

Down the embankment toward the sea? Firian ran swiftly toward the door in the low wall that opened onto steps leading down to the beach.

The little door slammed back against him.

As he'd expected.

He backed up and shouldered into it again, sending the unknown assailant tumbling backward before leaping again to their feet with a hissed *"yabesh!"*—a Charäkhni curse. Firian slipped through the opening to see who it was.

Tesni, the girl who had lived on the opposite hall. She had tan skin and dark reddish hair pulled back in a sleek braid. Her cheeks were flushed with exertion, as though she had run far before encountering Firian. Dirt smudged her black Tanyuin outfit. She didn't wear the long coat—better for tracking.

He held out an appeasing hand, the one without the jagged piece of pottery. "Tesni," he whispered.

She regarded him warily, a knife in her hand. Her gaze expertly scanned him from head to foot, snagging on the broken handle in his grip. But she didn't advance, didn't attack. Maybe she was thinking about the way he could kill her without a word or a movement.

"Master Kess," she replied.

"You were sent to follow me."

She didn't deny it. "Just to follow."

Did Tesni think that Kiria was here? Was it worth trying to keep up the charade a little longer for Kiria's sake? He decided not to mention it, to let Tesni draw her own conclusions. "Tesni..." He was hardly sure what to say. "I didn't give the order to kill the Keepers."

She betrayed little surprise. "No?"

"No. Master Belik acted on his own. I never betrayed the Tanyu. You know I wouldn't." Saying the words felt like drawing poison out of a wound. Grueling, painful, but cleansing. A relief.

She scrutinized him. "Then come back," she said finally. There was a question in her eyes, a genuine request.

Her look made a small flame of hope leap in his chest. "Not yet. The Tanyu are split. Belik has enough support that he'd go after me. And I have things to do."

"What do you need from me?"

Firian let out a breath, almost a sigh, and relaxed his stance. Tesni lowered her knife. "I need you to see who's still loyal to me. I am still the Tanyuin Head, but Belik's lies..."

Tesni nodded once, a soldier in his army. "You'll kill him for insurrection."

Firian paused. Yes, he did want to do that. But if so, why not simply order it now? Belik's words echoed in his mind—*what then?* He needed time to think. Killing Belik to offer Kiria the Kingdom would mean exposing the Academy to punishment or extermination.

"Eventually," he replied. When Tesni's eyes narrowed, he added, "Leave him to me."

She lowered her head at that, apparently understanding, though Firian wasn't sure he understood himself.

Firian's new revelations—and probably the fact that he'd only had ale to drink in the last many hours—made him dizzy. If it had to be either him or Kiria on the throne, then she deserved to rule Brithnem more than he did. The truth itched, like a fine shirt against skin that wasn't used to finery.

He'd spoken no more than a few words to the Defender, but they were in accord that they had to stop Belik. She would be a valuable ally inside the walls while he rushed back to Raewhith to protect Brett and gather reinforcements, in case a few loyal Tanyu near Belik weren't enough. They had to be. A well-timed strike could end Master Belik. Kiria just had to be poised to take advantage of the opening.

That was where Bard came in.

Tesni had gone back to the palace, drawing Tanyuin eyes elsewhere while Firian reached out to other potential allies.

Soon, he'd take Bard to find Kiria, but the idea of treading carefully around Tanyuin minds while sneaking Bard back inside the walls sounded too precarious.

One thing at a time: allies, Kiria, Brett.

A plan was already forming when he ducked back into the cellar to find Bard leaning against one of the ale casks, half-asleep. His friend had gotten better, more aware, since Firian had brought him here, but the heavy way he slumped against the wooden barrel showed he wasn't fully recovered. Bard's hand, still claw-shaped, lay in his lap. The mug sat by his other side.

Only when Firian got closer did he stir. A few rapid blinks later as though his eyes needed to refocus, Bard asked, "Who was it?"

"Tesni."

Bard's eyes grew bright with the obvious question. *For or against?*

"She wants to help me."

Settling cross-legged across from Bard, Firian drew in a few breaths. It had been too long since he'd had the luxury of entering the Unreal like this, seated, fully focused. Mostly focused, at least.

Less than two weeks to get to Brett, but if all went to plan, Belik would be taken care of by then. No war. Just one quick battle.

Firian closed his eyes.

Master Makai first. The deep-voiced Tanyuin Master who'd led him to the Academy the first time seemed like a good place to start. Firian knew he'd been asking about him, at least, and they'd never had issues with each other.

Firian recreated the gray stone room of the Head's office in the Academy, and called to Makai. The man appeared almost instantly, the consummate professional, dressed in the customary long black jacket, which swayed around his booted feet.

"Master Kess," he greeted. The last syllable rose slightly, betraying his surprise.

Firian stood behind the desk he knew so well. Fragments of flags from Raewhith, Imlin, and Archer's Point festooned the front. Though urgency sang in his blood, he felt at home too. On his brow sat the metal circlet of the Tanyuin Head. Where was the real thing now?

"Master Belik defied my orders not to attack the capital," he began. "He committed treason against the Tanyu and against the Western Kingdom. I need to know whose side you're on."

Lines of concern scored Makai's dark brow. "Treason?"

"I chose you because you can see how horrible his actions are. I will stop Belik with or without you. Are you with me?"

Fractional hesitation.

Blood began to rise to Firian's face.

"If you'll take back the crown, I'm with you."

Neither Makai nor Tesni knew that it wouldn't be himself on the throne, but Kiria. Firian kept his secret for now. All he needed was enough allies to win a battle against Master Belik. He could deal with the fallout later.

Firian released a breath. "I thought so," he said approvingly. "Tell no one. Meet me in the Unreal in seven days, at sunrise. I'll gather others, and we'll end this."

Not everyone was as anxious to join Firian's cause without asking more questions. Firian didn't tell doubters about the meeting. He couldn't afford a greater risk of weak links.

In the next two hours, he found twenty Tanyu who overtly sided with him. Under normal circumstances, that would be more than enough. But Belik had beaten Firian head-to-head plenty of times, both in the Real and Unreal. The memories tasted bitter.

All that would change in seven days, when Tanyu loyal to Firian would attack Belik together in the Unreal. Seven days sounded like a long time to wait, but he couldn't guarantee Brett's safety any sooner. In seven days, he would be about two days from Raewhith, closer if he were lucky. The Tanyu waiting for Belik's response wouldn't get it, and Firian needed to be able to reach his sister before that person decided to take action against her. Seven days was risky, but it could work. In one week, Belik would be dead.

22

BELIK

Amir Parohim cut a nervous glance to Belik. The two of them stood together on the raised dais, dressed in finery, looking out over the remnants of the Main. The watered-down smell of smoke scratched against Belik's lungs, but at least a cool breeze whispered through the broken panes of glass. Metal lines arched through the empty spaces like winter trees. Charred remnants of Brithnem flags still hung high above by the ceiling.

The fire hadn't brought down the enormous statues of the founders either, but smoke had discolored them.

Sickly orange and dark gray settled into the grooves of the Scroll passage etched along the ceiling, enhancing the words. Belik pursed his mouth to look at them.

Ash—the burned remains of three thrones—had coated the floor until Belik ordered some of the remaining palace servants to clean it up. Most of the servants had survived the coup, and with Amir performing some of the least savory duties, there had been plenty of help for menial tasks. The room had to look splendid. Those Brithnem people liked pomp. This was just the sort of thing they'd lap up like dogs.

Belik was never going to be crowned at the new moon. Of

course, it was important that all the citizens and the Amir thought so.

Tomorrow, Dedication Day, was a much better choice, more symbolically significant in the minds of the people, and a day when most of the city fasted, and would be less likely to fight back.

Today, the new moon would teach the people to fear. It was a temporary but necessary measure, to make sure the rebel faction of the military was killed or cowed.

A chair, salvaged from the wreckage, sat on the dais. Only one, not two. Belik looked at it almost mournfully.

Fury built in his chest. A *katah*, again. Firian really was like him. Except he was younger and stupider. Headstrong, with even more on the line. Tanyu were on the cusp of ruling the entire Western Kingdom, and Firian would rather be on the run.

Belik's mouth felt sandy. He fought the urge to spit.

Shiro jogged toward him, stopped, and stood smartly. "Shall I let them in, Master Belik?"

"Yes."

"As you would have it."

The huge double doors opened immediately and hundreds of citizens filed in. Belik scanned the ranks hungrily. No children. No elderly. Many wearing oversized cloaks. He almost laughed—would have, if it hadn't been so insulting. With Kiria and possibly Kader still alive, he expected some clique of the army to retaliate against his rule, but this was childish.

Warriors manned the entrances, searching all the visitors before they could enter, but they'd clearly allowed the people to bring personal items with them, even incongruous ones. Tanyu should know better than anyone that harvest flails or coin purses or even baskets could be used as weapons. Perhaps they thought these people too weak to use them well. It was unwise to discount an enemy, no matter how predictable.

A flicker of movement caught his attention. Turning, he saw more spectators outside the broken windows. *A little better,* he admitted. It would be more challenging to contain them all out there as it would be in here.

The flaming lanterns and booted feet shuffling across marble floors made the only sounds. Too late, he considered music. Eh, he'd already bowed enough to their delicate sensibilities. Silence was where a Tanyu lived.

Parohim seemed disturbed by it, though. His slicked-back hair was practically quivering with tension.

Belik leveled him a glance. The Amir would go through with this. He'd watched as Reynard, advisor to Atael Calthwaite, died instantly at Belik's command. Visible fear had stuck to Parohim like sap ever since, binding him to Belik's will until it dulled, which could take years if Belik kept giving him reasons for terror.

Parohim blinked long and steadyingly in reply. He could have been praying. Always God, always the Scroll, with these people. As long as the Amir planned to crown him, Belik didn't care how Parohim felt.

One more scan of the room assured him that the princess hadn't come herself, just sent her cronies to deal with him. A twinge of disappointment tugged at him but it dissipated quickly. Of course she didn't come herself. She'd have been a fool if she had. Kiria was naïve, but based on the way she was able to manipulate Firian so thoroughly, she wasn't a fool.

Once everyone had filed in, the people quieted, looking up at the dais with anticipation. Belik watched a line of sweat form at Amir Parohim's temple. Searing silence cut through the room like a dare.

Belik had Tanyu stationed along the walls, in front of the dais, around the building, in the hallways—all with strict orders to kill any Brithnem soldier they saw who didn't wear a sign of

Tanyuin loyalty: a simple scrap of black cloth pinned at the neck of the uniform. Hesitation had flared in some of the warriors' eyes. Tanyu could be brutal, but this was a higher level of brutality than usual. These younger Defenders were largely untested in anything except rigorous drills, so Belik had made it known that disloyalty would come with harsh consequences.

Firian flashed through his mind again, staring at him with murder in his eyes from behind those rusted iron bars. It would have been cleaner to kill him, make him an example and start fresh. But he couldn't. Even now, he knew he wouldn't do it himself. Taking over the Academy and then the Kingdom hadn't initially been Belik's plan, but Firian was so perfectly placed to do just that that the temptation had been too much to resist. And why should they resist it? A more perfect opportunity would take another twenty years to materialize, and he'd done his share of waiting.

Belik nodded at the Amir beside him, prompting him to speak.

"Welcome," Parohim said, with a volume that sounded hollow in the large space. He wrung his hands.

Shifting from the audience. Hands reaching under cloaks.

"This is a... momentous day for Brithnem. Thank you all for coming." His eyes flickered up to the smoke-damaged words along the ceiling. He blinked hard as though he had to get rid of dust, and his throat bobbed. *"Forever shall you worship God. In whatever you do—"*

Outside, something hissed and thwacked against the building. Parohim halted his recitation to look. An arrow clattered down the chaos of metal lines in the window frame before falling out of sight. Heat climbed up Belik's neck, not due to the fur stole he wore for the occasion. That was too close. Accidents like that couldn't happen.

Two Tanyu vaulted through the openings in the window to

drop on the other side before Belik halted any more from going. They couldn't all leave when there were enemies in here too. "Enough!" he snarled. The quiet inside the room allowed the word to carry.

Parohim looked at Master Belik as though to ask if he should continue.

A moment later, the crowd outside surged apart with gasps and screams of surprise. A huge black-jacketed figure led a man, half lifting, half guiding him toward the window that the arrow had hit. The Tanyu held the would-be assassin's arms behind his back. The archer's right bicep bled freely through his dark green shirt, and the paleness of his face made the stubble on his chin look like something that was drawn on. His expression, however, was resolute. The man, mid-forties maybe, had the look of someone who had seen war. It was a Tanyuin expression.

"The Second Keeper lives!" he shouted.

Tanyu could have simply killed the archer when they found him.

Pandemonium erupted. Shouting, men and women flung themselves at the bases of the four huge statues. The grating of swords being unsheathed rang through the Main.

The bases are hollow.

Why hadn't they checked more thoroughly for weapons caches? The carved-out bases of the statues were right under their noses. Belik clenched a fist as several Tanyu sprang forward to quash the predicted rebellion. The area behind the sculptures quickly became choked but the weapons still passed from the hands of killed soldiers to the living.

Parohim ducked and then straightened, clearly unsure of what to do. Belik hadn't warned him about what was coming. "You can go," he told him. The man ran to the opposite side of the room. There was no exterior door there, just an entrance into an office—

a dead end—or statues and blown-out windows. The cowardly Amir would still be necessary for the real crowning ceremony tomorrow. It was best that he not get caught in the carnage.

In the commotion, no one else even saw the death of the archer.

The Kingdom soldiers fell back from the statues—*how did we miss a weapons cache like that?*—and threw back their cloaks, slicing out shields and holding them out in an overlapping pattern around and above them. The shielded mass of Kingdom soldiers pushed forward.

Then Belik lowered himself into the Unreal to speak into the Tanyu's minds. "Now."

At the word, shadows materialized into black-clothed Tanyu. They moved without the huffing and screaming of the Brithnem soldiers. Inner poise. Reigned-in rage.

Small knives darted from corners as the front of the mass of bodies reached the front of the dais. Two Brithnem soldiers slumped to the ground, leaving a momentary break in their shield wall. One of the shadowy Tanyu jumped into the opening, moving artfully and felling six more soldiers inside before falling back, injured. The opening was wider now. How long would they pretend that their shields were an impenetrable defense?

Looking down, he saw a Tanyu Defender standing in front of the dais run through by a sword, overwhelmed by the force coming forward. So far, the only one down. Blood leaked out on the stairs, dripping and smearing with the fighting.

His heart thudded in his chest, his new power just out of reach. Was it worth it to try again? Unless Kiria herself were here, it would be useless. Killing someone as Firian had been able to do was draining. And Belik wasn't good at it.

Bard was alive, after all.

A sword clanged against the top stair as someone fell forward with the force of his swing. Belik took a step back.

The shields over the heads of the Kingdom soldiers rippled like bronze and silver waves. It would be difficult to fight one-handed and keep that awkward position for long. The soldiers had considered unusual possibilities—an attack from above—but didn't consider what addressing them would cost. Maybe they were learning after all. Belik nodded at one of the smaller Tanyu, a young girl whose name he didn't know. Her eyes glinted back at him. She had the same idea.

With a leap, she landed on top of the undulating platform of shields. She stabbed downward just as she skipped to another shield a safe distance away. Stab, jump, stab, jump. By the time she'd killed a dozen of them, the shields angled down again, removing the flat surface she'd used to her advantage. The young Tanyu nimbly leapt back to the ground.

Without protection from above, the cloaked soldiers were twice as vulnerable to attack. Belik saw one more Tanyu go down, but the soldiers died in droves. They fought forward, always looking to their front. They parried and thrust as all good soldiers were taught to do, every move predictable, like a child in a sporting match.

He toed the blood leaking down the sword-made crack in the marble and waited for the din to die down. It didn't take much longer, and he was safe, surrounded as he was by a ring of warriors around the dais.

Shifting his attention, he spied a similar scenario playing out on the grounds outside. Without the enclosed space, it would be harder to herd the rebels all in. But he trusted his Tanyu to do what he said. Most of the time.

The metallic smell of blood washed through the room. The back of his throat rose in response.

If he was going to keep this power, and if the Tanyu were

going to follow him despite not enjoying his every order, he had to make sure that they knew what would happen if they rebelled.

Firian had rebelled. Everyone knew it. He'd rebelled against his own, against all the Tanyu, leaving them leaderless.

Tesni had returned without information about Kiria's location. A ruse. Belik should have expected it. Firian's connection to the princess was the only excuse he had left to keep him alive. Based on this attempt on Belik's life, it seemed likely that Kiria was still inside the city, gathering support, raising hopes for the Keepers to rise again. Belik could find her without Firian. Every person she met was a leak, a weak spot in her hiding place. He already had Tanyu hounding her at night, filling her with nightmares. But the girl had some kind of Sentry now, so she'd parried their recent attempts.

Chetana must be the one standing guard over Kiria's mind. He hadn't sensed Chetana's death, and who else could it be? No one else in the Keeper's camp, besides the girl herself, had the Talent. His blood chilled at the thought.

With a jerk, he ducked, all instinct. Only afterward did he register the arrow he'd seen flying toward him. Another assassin? He glared from the weapon embedded at an angle in the window frame to the place where the attack had originated. This time, it came from the opposite direction, outside, removed from the fighting. The fight against the soldiers had died down enough that a couple Tanyu, including the girl who had leapt on the platform of shields, could be spared to race off in the direction where the arrow had come. His blood boiled.

Better, he thought bitterly.

Another arrow whizzed at him, aimed lower. This time he hurled himself sideways. The blood on the toe of his shoe painted the story of his movements. That he had backed away. That he had cowered.

No, not cowered—lived.

When no more arrows came, Belik tore his gaze from the view of the empty grounds where the second archer was hiding. The arrow had caught one of the Kingdom soldiers in the leg. Tanyu had all but won the skirmish in the Main, with only a few holdouts.

A slim black figure, one who had run at the first sign of another attacker, leapt into the room. Running up to the dais, she stood smartly before Belik, a soldier to a general. "We got him, Master Belik," she said with a surprisingly girlish voice. "Would you like us to show you the body?"

"No," he said, waving her away. "Finish this."

His skin still sang from the near miss, but after a few moments, he steadied his breath and watched as the Tanyu utterly routed the rest of the Kingdom fighters.

Kiria's fighters.

The initial sweep of the city hadn't turned up the princess. At first, Belik was furious, but the more he considered it, the more he thought it would be better to wait than to send more people after her now. Secure the palace and later the city. Find out who was working with her, if there were any leaks in the newly submissive barracks. Use her defiance against her. Then they could crush any uprising more decisively, without anyone to view her and her cohorts as martyrs.

The hushed thudding of fleeing boots whispered outside. Belik nodded at a Master standing outside the broken window. Let them go. A couple survivors could tell the tale, run to other traitors and reveal their positions.

A ghostly quiet settled over the Main. Belik found three Tanyuin bodies. The rest were Kingdom. Spreading blood obscured the inlaid mosaic symbols of the Three Lines.

The girl approached him again. Other Tanyu fought to keep

the horror out of their eyes, but not her. *Interesting.* "Where would you like us to move the bodies?" she asked.

"Set up a few outside the palace, by the street. Burn the rest."

"As you would have it, Master Belik." Her tone was clipped and efficient. Dark, silky hair fell in sheets to her chin. He recognized her dimly but they had never interacted in any meaningful way, despite her wearing a black Master ring. She couldn't be over twenty-five. A new Master, then, one of the last created under Sais Jairon's rule.

So far, Belik had Shiro and Nedi to carry out his orders. Another would be welcome.

"What's your name?"

"Enktuya Baloraat."

Eradi, if he had to guess. She had the eyes for it.

"Find me when you're finished. I have more work for you."

Power didn't materialize on its own. It was held by decisive action and a loyal coterie of followers. *Always have a backup plan. Even when you've just executed a company of soldiers.*

23

KIRIA

It was late but Kiria couldn't sit. She paced, her serving girls following her with their eyes. She could tell the two of them were tired, but no one would be able to sleep until they heard how the assault against Belik had gone.

Had the plan been too simple? Had it worked?

She rubbed feeling back into her hands. She wanted to do everything and nothing. What she really wanted was news, but none had come.

Except that Firian was alive.

Seeing him alive shot sparks through her veins. She hated him and loved him. It was enough to drive her mad. She needed to focus on the attempt to unseat Belik, but her thoughts repeatedly wrenched her toward Firian and the desperation in his face when he told her to get out of the city. It was in his best interest to get her out of the way whether or not he still pretended to care for her. He did seem sincere in one thing, though—he wasn't in league with Belik. In that, they were allies.

She had told the others right away, but that news had quieted in the wake of this infernal hush. This wait for news that didn't come. Firian had become nothing but a complication they could deal with if the attempt on Belik's life failed. Well, more than a complication, but something no one was ready to face fully just yet. Yes, he could find her here, but, judging from his former behavior, he wouldn't threaten them, and she could even play along, pretend to work together, until it became impossible to continue.

Guards watched her, Jori watched her, Chetana watched her. It grated on her thin nerves.

Kiria had gone over the plans again and again, self-soothingly, until the others were no doubt sick of hearing about them, about the contingencies, about what they would do if the soldiers succeeded, about what they would do if the soldiers failed...

Finally, she'd fallen silent, resorting instead to remembering the moves Chetana had shown her for defending her dreams against Tanyuin attack. She hadn't been able to master many of them, but she could levitate, disappear briefly, look like Firian.

Did the lack of news mean that there was no one alive to deliver it? Her head ached with nerves. Waves of thoughts flowed and subsided.

A knock.

She nearly flew to the door. With a hand against one of her shoulders, the blond guard named Royce stopped her from opening it herself. She couldn't show her face until it was clear who stood on the other side.

Her heart galloped as Royce cracked open the door. The words from the other side were maddeningly obscured, though she strained every nerve to listen. The door closed again. The guard turned a grim face to her. He shook his head.

She let out a breath, anguish pooling inside her.

"They failed?" Jori asked, incredulous. He turned to Kiria. "Belik is still alive? Didn't we send *two* archers to assassinate him? And all those soldiers?"

"Yes," she answered. She had known it would be a gamble, but she prayed it would be one that paid off. The company of soldiers would all have the same goal—to kill Belik. The risk was huge, but with that many, couldn't they accomplish that task?

No. They'd failed, the force of the Tanyu too strong. Chetana's expression mirrored the way Kiria felt—disappointed but unsurprised.

Immediately after the counsel when they'd met to decide how to kill Belik, Chetana had started to reach out to some of their nearest allies, but, without a clear directive, the effort petered out, depending on this news.

This failure.

"Because of the attack, Master Belik is still uncrowned," Royce added.

"Who was at the door?" Kiria asked.

"One of ours from the meeting."

The hair on the back of Kiria's neck prickled. Lowering her brows, she asked, "How many survived?"

"The final count is unknown, but it sounds like only a few. Civilians also got caught in the fighting. Tanyu slaughtered them."

Gut swooping, she traded looks with Chetana. "We should get out of here," she said, sparking Candrae and Vayci into motion. "If only a few soldiers survived, then they're definitely being followed. They're looking for me." She shot a glance at Jori. "And you."

Jori scowled but didn't argue.

"What's a place they wouldn't know about?" she asked him.

"What do you mean?"

"One of your places."

"Ah." He pivoted back and forth on the balls of his feet, the only evidence that he was pleased by the question. "For all of us?"

She raised her eyebrows in response. *Obviously.*

He cast his eyes to the ceiling. "There's a place not too far."

"Great, where is it?" she cut in, hoping he would speak more quickly.

"It would take us out of the city, though."

Kiria froze. Out of the city. She couldn't leave now, when her people needed her. "Where?" she asked again, cautiously this time.

He looked at her seriously now. His voice lowered. "Do you want to leave the city, darling?"

The guard with the tattoo on his face spoke up. "My Keeper, there is another safehouse, the one meant for the First Keeper and his wife. We could go there."

Kiria's heart sank, not just at the all-too-recent memory of Cúron, but at the impracticality of the plan. "No," she said, "that's too far away. And the Tanyu have surely found it by now. The other safehouse too," she added, cutting off any mention of Atty. Jori felt raw as it was. "Do you have any other ideas?" The question was directed at the guards, at Jori, at anybody who could help them.

Jori inspected his fingernails. "There's a tunnel beneath a house one street over. It goes under the wall."

Two of her guards exchanged furious glances. But this was no time to bemoan old security risks—it was time to avoid new ones.

She heaved a breath. *Another gory tunnel.* "You think it would be safe?"

Jori nodded, slowly at first, and then with more conviction. They would still be close enough to the city to influence it, to encourage the people. The important thing now was not to get caught by any Tanyu who had followed the messenger. There could be someone lying in wait at that moment. They had no time to lose.

"We'll take Jori's way," she said, turning to the guards.

Candrae and Vayci had already packed most of their belongings. There weren't many to begin with. Most of them had burned in the palace.

All eyes shifted to Chetana, the most experienced user of the Talent. Calmly, she closed her eyes. Maybe it was that Firian didn't always close his eyes when he did it, but there was something more mystical about Chetana's power.

After a few moments, she opened her eyes and nodded once. She sensed no Tanyu in the immediate area. They were clear to go.

A hand touched her shoulder. Jori was putting a cloak on her. "Don't forget our disguises."

"My face is a disguise." She hadn't worn her Beauty since the meeting with the generals. How many of them had gone to Belik's coronation themselves? How many of them would she never see again?

He hooked her chin with one finger. "You look like a Keeper to me," he said, his voice oddly quiet.

She closed her mouth. Unexpected emotion prickled at the edges of her eyes. Jori could be sour when he felt caged or down, but that look meant that he trusted her. That he would follow her. She nodded at him and cleared her throat.

He released her chin and took a packet of provisions from Candrae, who hadn't handed it to him.

Kiria gathered the folds of the cloak around her. "Show the guards where to go."

"Will do, love."

"Who owns this place?" the tattooed guard, whose name was Viktor, asked Jori, frowning.

He only waved his hand in answer.

It was a legitimate question, Kiria thought. The tunnel that ran under the wall had emptied them out into a space that looked like an enormous, low-ceilinged, underground house or bunker, with plenty of open spaces where many people could gather at once. They stood in one of the largest now. Everywhere she looked was an opening somewhere else. Cursory investigation had unearthed a makeshift kitchen and bedrooms laid with abandoned, moth-eaten blankets and enormous pillows. Haphazard decorations—expensive-looking colored lanterns and snagged tapestries—suggested that this was a place frequented by some of the wealthier families. Nothing had been cared for, only used for wild festivities. A great assortment of bottles and clothes and masks and dishes had been crammed unceremoniously into corners.

"Ah!" she cried, going toward one pile and holding up a lyra. Her instrument had no doubt burned. She squeezed the neck of the instrument and avoided looking at the others as she felt sorrow threaten to overwhelm her.

"I've come here a time or two," Jori said. "Always the best parties when no one knows."

"The partygoers know," Chetana replied acidly.

"But not the Tanyu."

"For now."

Kiria turned to see Jori spread his arms wide. "I found a place. Here. It's big enough for all of us." He pointed to the serving girls. "You could have your own room, darlings. Doesn't that sound good? There's probably even food around here somewhere." He bustled to a doorway.

"It does sound good," Kiria admitted. "Thank you for finding this place." Words hung thick in the air. They could stay nowhere for long. All their moves so far had been too short-sighted. Because of that, the Kingdom had lost good soldiers, some of whom she knew personally.

She cast a glance at Chetana, who seemed to understand exactly what she was thinking.

"We'll be safe here tonight, and tomorrow..." *Tomorrow.* Tomorrow was Dedication Day, a day of fasting and prayer and remembrance. How had she forgotten? Looking around again, she realized they all would be spending the holy day here, in this cavernous party den.

Sounds of items tossed carelessly across the floor crashed through the wide room. Royce set his jaw with obvious irritation. "Jori!" Kiria called.

He emerged, one brow raised.

"Tomorrow is Dedication Day."

His shoulders slumped. "Everyone's still fasting?"

"Well, we certainly need the prayer."

"Isn't there a story," he began, twirling one finger through the air, "about an army who lost because they were weak after fasting? Hm? Don't want to be caught off guard. I doubt Kader is celebrating."

The mention of Cúron's son sent a twist to her belly. They'd received no updates after learning that he had escaped north, a maddeningly vague report.

"We're observing Dedication Day," she said firmly. "We need a day to think, to regroup. And pray. We can use the time to contact our allies as well, see if anyone knows where he is." She held up the lyra in her hand and waggled it with levity she didn't feel. "I could play."

After choking back his first response, he said, "That wouldn't be so bad. Thank you, love." Apparently giving up his search in that area of the underground house, he approached her and took her free hand in both of his. "If that's what you want, it'll be lovely. Just..." He looked around. "Unorthodox." He shuddered, then brightened and spoke in an undertone. "I remember one party here last summer. Unbearably hot. But someone brought firecrackers—"

"Inside?"

A wry smile stretched his features. "Oh, you're no fun."

Here was a hint of the old Jori, the one she liked and leaned on. She gave Jori a sideways hug that lingered.

Chetana began speaking to the guards, and Candrae and Vayci tidied up to prepare the space for a Keeper. *Almost two Keepers*, Kiria thought again, holding Jori closer. He mirrored her movement.

Her plan had failed. Words came back to her as from a forgotten dream. *There are possibilities all around us. Every window is a door.* She would get up and try again.

"The Kepron is right." Chetana's voice—and, even more, her words—startled Kiria upright.

"What?"

Her advisor stood between two guards. All looked grim. "Belik will try to use the holy day to his advantage. I guess that he'll crown himself tomorrow when Brithnem has less strength and strategy to fight back."

Kiria swallowed. It made perfect sense. Even if Belik did crown himself—she shuddered to think with whose crown—it didn't change the ultimate plan to take back the Kingdom. There were the trappings of power, its symbols, and then there was the real thing. Belik crowned would present new problems, but nothing she couldn't face. She had to believe that.

"I'm afraid that..." Chetana closed her mouth.

"What?"

"My Keeper." Chetana's tone was deadly serious, one full of horrible confidences she needed to share.

Taking her cue, Kiria broke away from Jori and headed into a different room with Chetana, trying to brace for more bad news. How much more could she take? "What's wrong?"

"My Keeper," she began again, "I have made a decision."

Kiria froze stiff with dread.

"I must go back to the palace." She dropped her eyes. "I've given you what I was able, but I cannot continue. I will send a new messenger for you. I'll figure out a way for you to have all you need. But I have been away from my son for too long." Her face was etched with pain. "Daelon is still alive, and I fear Belik plans to use him to get to me. I thought my duty was with you, as it is, but blood cries louder." Anguish drew a fierce line between her brows as she gazed down at Kiria, not asking for permission but understanding.

Kiria's eyes had gone misty. She struggled not to feel selfish for forgetting the depth of Chetana's struggle. Kiria missed Daelon too, but she had the entire Western Kingdom to think of. They all had given what they had to give. "When will you leave?" she asked simply.

"I will sleep to gather my strength, and then I must go back."

Kiria bit her lip, mind whirling. Chetana had helped her defend herself in the Unreal, and she was the primary person who could communicate with Tanyu and Watchmen alike. Was Kiria strong enough in the Unreal to do the same? It would be better if someone other than the Keeper could convey messages. It would potentially keep their location more secure.

If Kiria commanded it, Chetana would stay. Probably. But she couldn't command it. If Daelon had more hope of surviving this storm if Chetana left to be near him, then Kiria had to let her go. They'd all lost loved ones. Kiria would sacrifice a slice of her own safety if it meant that she didn't have to lose one more. The trade wasn't even worth considering. The gain was infinitely greater than the risk.

"Very well," she agreed, an image of her own mother rising

in her mind. Merian would have made the same choice Chetana was making now. "I just have one request."

"God willing, I will grant it."

"I would like one more lesson."

Chetana's eyelids fluttered with relief. "As you wish."

⁂

WHEN A KNOCK SOUNDED at the door, Unreal knives evaporated from Kiria's hands.

It wasn't a loud knock, but no one should have been knocking on the door leading outside. She opened her eyes, emerging into the Real. She sat cross-legged across from Chetana, to whom she gave a questioning look. Though she said nothing, Chetana's dark eyes went stern. Her advisor had much to worry about, but the look still sent Kiria's pulse racing. Kiria flexed her now empty hands and turned her attention toward the opposite end of the room.

A short staircase led up to the ground level. Royce and Viktor had turned cautiously toward the sound.

Kiria stood, feeling less vulnerable if she could run. It wasn't Belik, of course, or else Chetana would have sensed it. Was it a different Tanyu?

Royce cracked open the door at the top of the stairs. Then he stepped backward down the steps, alert but not afraid. Kiria let out a breath.

"It's Master Tanery, My Keeper."

Kiria laughed, here then gone, the noise bursting out of her before she recognized it. Joy and disbelief surged so strongly through her veins that she couldn't keep it in.

Bard appeared, ducking his head so he could see into their underground space.

Jori leapt up from the corner with surprising speed and took

Bard's head in his hands. Bard tried to shake him off but Jori held on and turned Bard's face toward Kiria. "Ah! Kiria, my love, you told me he was dead! Look! Look! Why did you say that?"

Chetana had been the one to confirm it, but the Amir looked as bewildered as Kiria felt.

Jori didn't wait for an answer. He looked into Bard's eyes, finally releasing his face and instead resting his hands on Bard's shoulders. "Are you all right, darling? You look a bit wobbly."

It was true. To escape Jori, who was blocking his path, Bard stepped off the last two stairs sideways. Instead of having a Tanyu's sure poise, Bard had to steady himself. A smile crinkled the corners of his mouth, but he heaved a breath as though even that tiny exertion had cost him something.

"Get him a chair," Kiria ordered.

One materialized almost immediately. Bard looked grateful to sit down.

"What happened?" she asked, standing before him. The air was cooler by the door, even though it had been shut again. She didn't realize how much she longed for fresh air.

"My Keeper..." Royce spoke her title as a low warning. His meaning was obvious. Bard was a Tanyu. Was he not in on the coup?

Kiria shot the man a glare. Bard had risked his life to save hers. She wouldn't doubt his loyalty now.

"I thought you needed me," Bard said.

Jori flashed a grin, quick and sad.

"Bard..." Kiria felt tears well up in her eyes. She swallowed. "I saw you face Master Belik for me. How did you get here?"

"Firian found me."

Jori cursed joyfully. Kiria shushed him.

Although she was glad Bard was alive, she wasn't ready to hear a glowing report about Firian. She knew more about what had happened the night of the attack, and she doubted Firian had told Bard about it.

Bard was silent for a few seconds more, as though he wanted to say something else, but couldn't for some reason. His breath smelled like ale. Jori must have noticed too because his eyes sparkled as though laughing at the mad coincidence.

"He took me to a doctor and then got me out again before Belik's people could find us." He side-eyed the guards standing above him with a mix of apprehension and determination.

Beside Kiria, Chetana narrowed her eyes. "Were you with him just now?"

Bard closed his mouth.

Her heartbeat rushed. *Yes, then.*

The soldiers braced to run out, but Kiria gestured for them to stand down. Firian would already be long gone, and running out would only betray their location.

"You need a Tanyu, I think," he forged on. "For messages, and to know what's going on."

"They can find us through him," Chetana told Kiria quietly.

"They can find you through Kiria too," Bard responded.

Chetana raised an appraising eyebrow.

Kiria scrutinized him, looking for injuries, but found none to explain the weakness. He held his fingers oddly in his lap, as though he were gripping something that wasn't there, but his hand didn't look broken.

"I want to help you," he insisted. His black eyes bored into hers.

After a pause, Kiria said, "This is good." She turned to Chetana. "You can go back and Bard can stay with me."

Chetana's gaze darted across the floor, as if searching for an objection. Finally, she inclined her head. "As you wish, My Keeper." Relief laced her words. "But..." She sighed. "He's probably correct that you're being tracked at this moment. You need to get farther away from here."

"I think so too, yeah," Bard said. "They can find us here."

Jori looked aggrieved at the insult to his hiding place. "Then why haven't they done it already?"

Bard fiddled with his hands. Something wasn't right about the way his left arm moved. He lifted his forearm and hand all in one piece, as though it were made of wood. "I don't know. I can guess."

"Then guess," Kiria said.

He lifted his eyes to hers. "My guess is that Belik will want to use you, or call you, or want you on his side or something."

The suggestion made her stomach writhe. "On his side?"

He nodded, a little less rigorously than before, but it was such a familiar gesture that Kiria smiled. "Yeah. I'm not sure. But you're the Keeper, and he hasn't found you yet. I'm sure he's figured out you're alive."

Royce stirred. "Everyone knows My Keeper is alive. We told the populace, to keep their hope alive that this disruption will soon be over."

Disruption. He made the attack—the *murders*—sound like a bout of bad weather.

The guard's words merely seemed to deepen Bard's conviction. "Then he won't want that. Yeah, he'll want you for something... special."

Jori glanced at Kiria, almost fearful. She straightened her spine. "I want to be here to give my people hope," she said, her chest tight as she said it. The words seemed like the right ones, so she forced them out, but if duty hadn't tethered her to the city, she would have followed Bard's advice without question.

Jori set a hand on her arm. "You also want to live."

"Has Belik only taken over the palace grounds?" Bard asked.

"The whole city," Viktor answered.

"Is he crowned?"

A shadow passed through the room at the mention of the lost battle. Bard's brow twitched as he sensed the atmosphere shift too. "Yes?"

"No," Kiria answered heavily. "We think he'll do it tomorrow."

"That'll be it. Probably. He'll want to... get you before the coronation. Maybe for the ceremony."

Chetana's full lips had flattened to a line. It almost looked as though she had changed her mind about returning to the palace.

"You too," Bard said to Jori.

"Me?" Jori splayed his hands over his chest in a gesture of innocence. "What have I done?"

"You're the heir to the throne. Right? Kepron?"

As he always did when the topic came up, Jori turned touchy.

Without warning, Bard slumped over, his head heavy as a child's. Kiria and Jori caught him from falling off his chair.

"Water!" she cried, and Candrae went to fetch it.

Bard's dark eyelashes fluttered open and he gasped in a breath.

"You're not dying on me?" Jori asked, his tone artificially light. Lines Kiria had never seen on Jori's face until the past few days deepened.

"No, mate," Bard said, though his voice was barely more than a whisper. Maybe it was his word choice, but something seemed to remind him of where he was. A Tanyu among hidden royalty. He braced his hands against the seat of the chair and sat up as Candrae rushed forward with the cup.

"I think we've asked enough questions for now," Kiria said. "You need to rest."

"You've got to get farther away," Bard insisted, his voice a little stronger now. "Trust me."

Something dark passed through her mind. "Did Firian tell you that?"

"He's right, though."

"Would he follow me if I left?"

She and Bard were suddenly the only people in the room. Pretense was reserved for opponents, not allies.

"Not if you go east."

An odd reply. "Do you know what's going on between Firian and Belik?"

"Yes."

"You'll tell me as soon as you've rested." Kiria looked up at Chetana. Assuming Bard had the inside information he claimed, he could communicate as effectively as her advisor could. Now was as good a time as any for Chetana to return to Daelon. Bard could even check on Chetana to verify that Daelon was still alive. Kiria took a deep breath. "You can go," she told her.

This time, Chetana did not protest. She leveled a look that spoke more than words could. Warnings, instructions, and love passed between them. "I would have abandoned all else for you."

Kiria nodded, her eyes beginning to sting.

"Remember what I taught you, My Keeper."

"So many things," Kiria replied, squeezing her hand.

And without another word, Chetana was gone.

24

FIRIAN

EIGHT DAYS.

Firian had eight days to get back to Raewhith; otherwise, Belik would order Brett hurt or killed. He could make the trip over the Charúnin Thôr that quickly at the peak of his strength, but he was weak from the knife thrust to the shoulder and little sleep.

One of the manor houses at the far end of the beach row had especially magnificent stables that were now one mare short. He rode furiously to the foothills, the pounding hooves beating his thoughts into an empty trance.

Bard was with Kiria. That would help her navigate the dangers of the Tanyu, at least. They both lived, for now. In a few days, the small group of loyal Tanyu would join together and attack Belik in the Unreal. And, as soon as he could, he'd return in force just in case to make Belik relinquish control. That was as far as his practical thoughts took him. Daydreams—of Kiria choosing him, of killing Belik before he hurt Bard—played through his mind like breezes through the air. Here one second, then gone, only to return minutes later.

Low in the saddle, Firian urged the sweating horse to go

faster along the uninterrupted stretch of beach. The Gray Forest rose to his right, darkness turning the leaves a murky orange. It was faster riding this way than through the trees, at least until he reached Redshore, the seaport, which wouldn't be for another hour. He needed all the time he could recover.

It was already nearing autumn, which meant that, although it was balmy here, snow could fall over the mountains at any time, slowing his progress. The idea shortened his breath. Belik wasn't one to give grace. He'd probably only allowed him to get to his sister as a concession to the ways they'd served each other over the years. There would be no more mercy.

The horse's hooves splashed in the surf and the beast skittered to the side. Drops of sea water spattered Firian's legs. Firian was no expert rider, though he had ridden plenty of times before. His anxiety must have gotten to the mare. He lowered his voice, murmuring soothing words, and calmed his body, guiding the horse back on course. He'd switch mounts at Redshore. Once he reached the mountains, with their treacherous rocks and climbs, he'd go on foot, but for now, this was the fastest way.

Bard's familiar presence arrived like the scent of cinnamon.

"Everything all right?" Firian asked, momentarily taking his attention off his ride to find him in the Unreal.

"We're okay," Bard affirmed. He had created a low, windowless space made of sandstone. Looked like it could be the place where he and Kiria were hiding.

"Have you left yet?"

"No. We're leaving after Dedication Day."

Firian huffed. He'd forgotten about the holiday. A few people at the Academy celebrated it every year, but they were the minority.

"Fir, it's about the Kepron." No one else inhabited the large room, and it made Bard look small, though he stood up straight.

"Jori?"

"Kader."

The young one. "Did they get him?"

"We don't think so. Not yet. Do you think you… do you think you could convince Master Belik he's dead so they don't go out looking for him?"

This didn't sound like Kiria's idea. She was furious with him. But she would want the boy to be safe. With Kader, they'd have all three Lines accounted for. "Do you know where he is?" Maps flashed through his mind. He didn't have time for a stop. He barely had time to slow, as long as he could force his body to keep going.

Bard shook his head, sending black hair askew. "Heading north, is all they know."

Firian sighed. "Bard, I can't—"

"You don't have to stop. Can't you talk to Tesni or something? Figure out some proof that Master Belik would believe?"

In the sandstone room, Firian tapped his leg with his thumb, considering.

"It would matter a lot to her," Bard persisted.

If Belik discovered the deception, any plan could compromise Firian or the people he was starting to amass on his side. But Bard was right. Kader's safety was a priority for Kiria, a key step in pursuit of her goals. The boy didn't matter much to him —he'd never seen the Kepron before—but she could be worrying about him even now. Maybe he was one of those she'd given herself up for the other night. One of those she loved.

Something fierce tugged at his heart. "Okay, and if I catch a rumor of where he is, I'll let you know. I'll make sure Belik thinks he's dead. Don't tell Kiria it was me or she might not believe it. Just tell her the Tanyu aren't going after him anymore. That he's safe."

Bard gave a curt nod, his expression somehow impish and

concerned at once when he looked up. "And tell me about your sister too, yeah?"

"Yeah."

Firian wished he'd come up with the idea to help Kader. Now that his mind spun with ideas about how to accomplish the task, it was definitely possible to do while he rode on his way to Brett. It was almost a blessing to be able to focus on something other than his own failures. Before long, though, a simple solution presented itself.

Firian talked to Tesni, to a couple others still in Brithnem who sided with him, and they divided tasks. Firian would contact Watchmen to the north, directing them not to make the Kepron's escape public if they saw him. Another Tanyu would find a personal token in the Kepron's room and another would cut off the small finger of one of the casualties of battle. Both would be sent to Belik.

Firian didn't fear that Belik was watching him. The Master was so busy mucking up everybody's lives that he wouldn't spare more than a thought or two on Firian now that he was headed to Raewhith. At best, Belik would think that Kiria was up this way too, that Firian was going to join her, as he said.

No, to make sure his plan was executed, Firian was watching Belik instead.

25

KIRIA

KIRIA DIDN'T SLEEP that night. She kept running her hand over the neck of the lyra until she was afraid she would destroy the strings with the constant friction. She had no appetite, so fasting wasn't a burden.

It would be a strange Dedication Day without Chetana. She had always been a key figure in the holiday since Kiria was a child. She and Jori and Atty would complain about having no food to eat, and then they'd all go to the upper room of the Amiran Academy and listen to the new composition. During the music and recitations, she, at least, would regret her earlier griping. The holiness of the moment would envelop her as it always did and she would thank God for all they'd been given. The day before usually gave her some trepidation because of the seriousness of it all, but she ended up loving it every time.

Last year, both her parents were still alive. They'd held hands in the upper room. Kiria hadn't yet revealed her Beauty, and she'd looked at their display of love with anticipation for her own future.

She scrunched her eyes tight and clutched the lyra close to

her chest like a talisman. How much had changed in one year! It didn't seem possible. She had been a different person then.

Blinking back hot tears, she stood. If she was going to command her group to pause for a day of remembrance, they ought to make it a day not only to remember the trials of the founders but the trials they'd just endured themselves. They could honor the dead. She had to face it sometime or another. Shuddering a little, she turned the pages of her mind to the horrible list of those they'd lost.

Cúron.

His wife, Varinna.

Her guards.

The soldiers of yesterday.

Haved.

She stopped, choking on her memory. After a few sniffling seconds, she turned the last pages, the ones she didn't know if she could face.

Her mother.

Atty.

They deserved to be remembered. They all did. Jori wouldn't be ready, but there was never a good time to comprehend loss. Dedication Day was the best chance they would have for a while.

Candrae and Vayci slept fitfully on the other side of the space Kiria had chosen for herself. They didn't take up Jori's offer of a separate room. Kiria was surprised she hadn't woken them. It was no wonder they were exhausted after the past few days.

Vayci rolled over. When she saw Kiria already awake, she trundled to her feet, blinking sleep out of her eyes. As though the two were connected, Candrae woke up too.

"Girls," Kiria said gently, "today we'll make arrangements for a funeral service for the lost, just before the evening song. You can help me."

"Of course, My Keeper," they replied nearly in unison. Then Vayci leaned her dark head forward. "May we get you anything this morning?"

"No. It's Dedication Day." Kiria realized she still had the lyra in front of her as though it were some sort of shield. Now that Chetana was gone, Kiria would not only provide the music but maybe even the Scroll recitations. The thought brought a grim pleasure. Daelon would be proud of her.

The day passed in a blur of tears and prayers. Bard looked a little lost through it all. He'd never celebrated the holiday before, but he happily filled in wherever he was needed. In the afternoon, they prepared a service honoring the lost.

The ceremony was over too quickly. Everyone shed tears, several spoke about people they had known, prayers were lifted, but it all ended in a flash. Through most of it, Jori held her hand so tightly he bruised her fingers. To his credit, he seemed to realize how important it was for them all to face the tragedy they'd endured. Maybe it was good that the ceremony was so short. None of them could face the truth for long. Kiria squeezed his hand back. He sniffed loudly in response. Neither of them was a graceful crier. Even Bard, who hadn't known any of the causalities well, had tears running down his face as each part ended.

Afterward, Kiria needed to clear her head. The weight of her grief clogged her lungs, making everything sluggish. If she was also going to play the music for Dedication Day, she had to get some air.

Calling over two guards as she tightened the black mourning cloth around her wrist, she said, "I'm going outside. Just for a moment."

They seemed to understand because they didn't protest, but

silently followed her up the stairs to the woods outside. Her skin instantly cooled in the twilit air. Trees rose around her and she could feel the ocean nearby, though she couldn't see it. She drank in the freshness, just breathing. Fireflies flitted under the green trees nearby, blinking in and out of sight like magic dust. The sight brought new tears to her eyes. Something about the beauty made her wish she could share it with those they had lost. Atty would have loved to show this to Haved.

As though on cue, someone emerged behind her. Probably another guard to call her back, remind her that being out in the open was unwise, especially tonight. She swallowed her tears and turned.

"I was hoping to be alone. Plan foiled, I see," said Jori, sauntering up beside her with his hands in his pockets. He didn't smile, but his words aimed at his signature levity.

"Don't act like you didn't hear me." She watched the fireflies silently for a few moments longer. "You'll never be alone, Jori."

He made a strangled sound, as though he were trying to swallow but couldn't quite manage it. He turned it into a barked laugh. "You always know the words to say."

"*I* do?" She faced him. "I've always thought that of you."

He gazed listlessly into the distance. "Today, you have the words, my dear. I don't... have much of anything."

She waited until he turned to her. "We've all lost too much," she said quietly, not wanting to spoil the forest's peacefulness. "But none of us are alone. We have to remember that."

He raised one skeptical eyebrow. "We're a small group now."

"Stop protesting. I've got you. We have each other. We can't forget what we still have."

A small smile crept its way across his features. "You could be a Keeper, with all these speeches." He gave her a quick kiss on the cheek. "Thank you, love."

They stood together in the quiet a few moments more before

heading back downstairs. It was easy to forget that the outside world held so much danger for the two of them. She would think twice before going above again.

Most of the people, listless and thoughtful from sorrow and lack of food, hadn't left the common room, with its piles of random items in the corners. After being outside, the space felt hot and stuffy. A sheen of sweat clung to her skin.

Earlier that day, she had written a new piece of music for Dedication Day. With only one day to prepare, she thought it sounded rusty and a little cliché, but hoped that the others wouldn't think so. Viktor, with the Khelê tattoo, had volunteered to recite from the Sacred Scroll, and that took a bit of the pressure from her to provide yet another ceremony for everyone.

She took the lyra from the corner where she'd left it and started playing without any announcement. The few hushed sounds ceased. The interplay of minor and major keys matched her feelings. The lingering notes had a swampy, ringing quality as she drew the bow over the strings. Overlaying everything was sadness, but she couldn't forget there was still hope, and that she was the face of it. The movement of the bow soothed her, focusing her thoughts into melody.

At a key change, a spike of apprehension tore through her, unrelated to the music. She lengthened the note she was playing to buy herself time to focus on the feeling. Because it wasn't connected to anything directly at the moment, which probably meant that Firian was experiencing it instead. She didn't know what to make of him surviving the attack. Part of her had nearly collapsed with relief, but another part had burned with so much anger that it had been difficult to speak. Why should she be relieved, when he'd all but engineered the pain they were experiencing?

She closed her eyes, leaning into the melody, which she had practiced enough times that day to do automatically, and let herself sink into the Unreal. She didn't want to meet him, but if he had information she needed, then she couldn't let her feelings get in the way of helping her people.

No, not apprehension. She'd misread the feeling. It was anger, just as sharp and searing. He hadn't invited her to join him in his mind, so for a while she couldn't see anything. Where was he? Although she knew he could see her at odd times, she couldn't do the same with her level of ability.

"What's happening?" she whispered in the dark, risking detection.

Firian was instantly by her side. "Belik."

The darkness transformed into the partially burned-out hull of the palace façade. One of the balconies still remained stable. On it stood Belik and Amir Parohim, lit clearly by a row of lights constructed on the terrace. Belik wore a fur stole over his black Tanyuin uniform. The entire scene was hazy, as though she were watching a memory or a dream. Firian wasn't creating this himself, then. Belik appeared most clearly, so maybe he was watching Belik and she was able to see this only through their *katah*. Nothing seemed impossible with Firian.

Parohim was saying something, but she could barely hear it. Why was the advisor helping Belik? She and Chetana had never figured out why he would turn. Kiria had never liked him much, with his slicked-back hair and oily voice, but he had always been loyal to the Keepers.

Parohim raised his hands to the sky, clearly in a prayer. Where was Daelon? Was he all right? The dark oranges and blues of the sky moments ago had given way to velvety black. Belik stood silent and regal above a nervous, mixed crowd who had come out to see. It was no wonder that they looked anxious after what happened at the past coronation.

It was as they feared. Belik was being crowned today.

Her empty stomach churned. *God help us.* Was this really

happening? She glanced at Firian. He wasn't looking at her, but was staring at Belik with far-seeing eyes, his hands clenched into fists.

She turned back. This was actually happening. Somehow, Firian was seeing it in reality. There was no time to ponder how.

The coronation wasn't as beautiful as the original ceremony, with its symbolism and vows. This was stripped down to the skeleton: a prayer and a crown.

Her skin prickled as she spied something metal in Parohim's hand. She squinted to see whose crown Belik had decided to use. They'd all been left in the palace during the chaos of the attack. Breath caught in her chest as she recognized the gold diadem Cúron had worn as Keeper, but it had grown, become more elaborate. Bronze and silver teeth made the crown menacing.

Bronze, gold, and silver.

She ground her teeth. The bronze belonged to Atty, the good ruler he had slaughtered. Gold, to Cúron. And the silver—that was a statement. He was coming after her power. He would crush whatever was left.

Parohim lifted the gorgeous crown high and placed it squarely on Belik's head. Something in Kiria cracked. This moment had seemed like a terrible part of a story, something looming but destined not to happen because the hero would ride in and stop it. But no one stepped forward.

Kiria turned her eyes again to the crowd. Black-clad Tanyu stood amongst them, glaring watchfully. Angry heat bit the corners of her eyes.

"As the God-blessed Keeper of the Western Kingdom," Parohim shouted, "Master Belik now requires every citizen to swear allegiance to him." The Amir glanced nervously at Belik as he spoke. There was an unspoken warning in the words.

Belik shifted his weight as though it pained him to stand.

"You will take a knee," he said. His rough voice wasn't loud, but deep and carrying. "You will swear on the Scroll."

How many loyal soldiers were left? Kiria searched the crowd. Many had died the day before in the failed attempt on Belik's life. Were there others trapped inside the city walls? There must be.

Slowly, a few began to sink to their knees.

Did they really think that God meant for such a thing to happen, for such a ruthless man to lead them?

One man resisted, standing stubbornly, but three Tanyu approached him. They didn't have any weapons she could see, but the meaning was clear. The soldier's options were loyalty or death. One of the Tanyu put a hand on the man's shoulder. After looking at the Tanyu defiantly, he obeyed. More followed, until all the men and women, soldiers and civilians alike, knelt on the ground.

Kiria wanted to stand forward, to yell. *I'm still alive! Don't follow him. There's still hope!* She watched helplessly as Parohim led them all in a recitation of loyalty, the Amir first, the people repeating.

"Tanyu will make the Kingdom great," Belik continued after the vows were complete. "Rather than forcing our will upon you, we'll give you a choice. All the cities that belong the Western Kingdom will receive both riches and independence, provided they swear continued allegiance, if they choose to turn from their former queen."

A movement to her right made Kiria glance at Firian. He was mouthing the word *Keeper*.

"She ran away instead of helping you, but she can make it right. If she agrees with my order to give you wealth and independence in exchange for loyalty, she can come forward and we can make a bargain together."

"Don't go," Firian said sharply.

"Obviously not," Kiria spat back.

"If you help the fugitive queen, you don't deserve my offer."

Kiria felt cold inside. Belik was trying to turn her own kingdom against her. Would anybody listen?

"All this... unpleasantness can be avoided if Kiria comes to me and agrees to give you what you deserve. If not, you'll know what kind of leader she is. I suspect she will choose to rebel against you all, since she ran away with the last Head of the Tanyuin Academy. No matter what she does, I will restore order and justice here in the Western Kingdom, even if I have to do it myself." His gaze cut sharply to Parohim, who took it as his cue to pray an end to the ceremony.

Kiria was shaking. She had no intention of bowing to Belik's wishes, no desire to negotiate with someone who had killed her friends and family and stolen her kingdom. Her face felt hot with the force of her fury. She let out a few breaths as she watched the ceremony and the crowd slowly snuff out like a candle until only curls of fragrant smoke were left.

Belik's words played again and again in her mind. How many of her people would listen and feel that she was withholding something good from them? Would any of them hunt her? The thought made her dizzy, as though the ground shifted.

Firian spread out a hand toward her—maybe she actually had wavered on her feet; she hadn't eaten anything that day, after all—but he let it fall back at his side. His dark eyebrows were drawn down, his jaw cut in a hard line.

Watching him made her feel reckless. "You don't support him?" She'd asked the question before, but the answer was so essential that she had to ask again.

His expression didn't shift as he stared out at the empty place where the crowd had been. "No."

"Is this real?" Firian could create all of this if he wanted to, even the haziness of it, but why would he add details that would incriminate both of them?

"Yes."

"Then what are you going to do?"

He turned to her. His blue eyes burned with a fierce emotion she couldn't place. "What I have to."

"That's not an answer." Then, remembering Bard, she added, "Did you help Bard here last night?"

He hesitated before nodding, a small echo of Bard's repetitive nods. "You need him more than I do now."

This all felt odd. It was as if he was changing so quickly that she couldn't keep her eyes on him long enough to tell what he was doing. She knew Firian—she had thought she knew him. But that was all before he offered to trade her for Brithnem's safety. Now she didn't know who this boy was.

She narrowed her eyes but just said, "Yes, I do." *Are you on my side?* For some reason, she couldn't get the words out. The other questions had come out easily, all demands. This one question didn't feel like the others. It tasted like vulnerability and she didn't like it. "Is he going to tell you what we do?"

He tipped his mouth thoughtfully. "Not everything."

These non-answers drove her crazy. "I don't want him to tell you everything."

"That's fine. You could check up on me instead, you know, if you're worried." He spread his mouth in something that could have been a smile but wasn't.

"I trust him more than I trust you, so he'll stay with us."

His expression got smaller but turned into something closer to a real smile. "Okay."

Will you kill Belik? It was the other question she couldn't stomach. If Firian hadn't done it yet, something was stopping him. Whether it was inability, or the two were secretly working together, or something else, she didn't know.

A phantom pain pricked at her arm. She looked down but saw no stinging bug or anything else that could have bitten her. It must have been from the Real.

Up and up through the haze she went until she opened her eyes in the underground room lit by torches and faces, so many faces, looking down at her from above. She squinted against the firelight and took a big gulp of air. An arm wrapped around her back and helped her to sit up. She realized she was still clutching the neck of the lyra. It had fallen beneath her when she collapsed, its edges digging into the back of her upper arm. Pulling it free and setting it on her lap felt like moving through water. Voices were talking over each other.

Candrae and Vayci were there, of course, but they weren't among the talkers. Kiria looked at them and they ran off to fetch water and something else that would probably help far more than these people's questions. She stifled a grunt as she sat fully upright. "Belik..." she said. "He crowned himself the new Keeper."

26

KIRIA

"You're sure about that?"

Jori's question was sincere, but it still gave Kiria a headache. "Yes, I'm sure."

"How do you know? Was Firian there?"

She, Jori, and Bard sat cross-legged on the ground together after Kiria had been too shaky to stand. Her guards stood behind them protectively, as though danger were going to burst through the door at any moment. Maybe it was.

"That's how I could see. But he wasn't helping him."

The round-faced guard scoffed. "Well, he's not helping us."

"He's against Master Belik," Bard confirmed. "We talked about it."

The reminder did nothing to improve the guard's mood, apparently, since he eyed Bard with greater suspicion after that.

"It doesn't matter what Firian's doing right now," said Kiria. "What matters is what Belik has done. He's wearing the crown, and he made all the audience swear their allegiance. Even Amir Parohim was afraid to go against him." The mention of the advisor brought Daelon to mind. Hopefully they would hear from Chetana soon that he had survived the attack.

Jori pouted and shifted his weight, sighing. "Then what are we going to do?"

"The Tanyu are able to find me because of the Talent. I think we need to get away from here until we can regroup and attack from a place of strength." Kader's guards had the right idea after all. The idea of running from Brithnem brought her physical pain, but it could be for the best.

Bard stopped drawing in the dirt with his finger, evidently surprised by her shift in mindset.

"My Keeper," Viktor interjected, "isn't there still a way to communicate with our troops on the inside? I know many of them will still be loyal to you."

Many of them. She didn't like the implication. *Many others won't be.* But it made sense. Belik had made them swear on the Scroll that they would be loyal to him. He threatened them and their families. "We need more firepower," she replied, shoving away the thought of Firian's ability to kill, the one that had obliterated the Kingdom forces they'd sent to the Academy several weeks before. He hadn't offered, and she wouldn't ask. "So we'll go to our other cities, rally the armies there. With troops on the outside, we'll have a better chance than relying only on those trapped inside Brithnem."

"Do you think they'll all come?" Bard had asked that morning when she suggested the urgent need for more allies.

"They'd better," she replied. "Can you communicate with the Watchman?"

He shrugged one shoulder. "Sure. What do you want me to say?"

She paused. The Tanyu had certainly gotten to the Watchman in Brithnem by now. She wouldn't risk their lives on the possibility of his disloyalty or death. "How about Watchmen in other cities?"

"Yeah."

"Then contact the ones in Rantoul, King's Heights, Redshore, and Arrow that we need their urgent assistance."

He nodded, slowly at first as he considered the names like a sum, then faster as he grew more confident. "Sure. I can do that right now, yeah. Is there a place I should tell them to meet?"

She looked down. "Nowhere yet. Just tell them to muster their armies. I need an idea of how many there are first."

"Shouldn't we bring them here, darling? It's the inevitable next step," Jori had interjected, overhearing their conversation. "We can hunker down, wait for reinforcements. Sounds like a plan to me. Better than gallivanting across the countryside."

"Not yet. It's not quite that simple. And we won't be gallivanting," she said. "We have to get out of reach of the Tanyu first, to preserve the Keeper Lines." She poked Jori's knee. "Yes, you too. And then we can come up with a plan of action. We know that the Tanyu are braced for an attack." Even as she spoke, she felt braced too, tension knotting the muscles in her shoulders.

Bard's jaw worked with the mention of Tanyu. Some of these invaders were his friends. The less bloodshed on either side, the better. But she would do what it took to bring justice back to the Kingdom, even if it meant danger or death.

"Where's Cúron when you need him?" Jori muttered. Kiria frowned at him, but he gave her a sad, impish smile.

Dedication Day was effectively over after Kiria's announcement about Belik. The services were over, the lyra put away. Royce, who had fallen into the position of head guard, talked urgently to the freckle-faced woman, Lilith. Hopefully they would have some good input later.

"So where are we going, then, if we aren't staying in this choice location?" Jori gestured to the underground room he'd been so proud of.

"Rantoul is the closest, if we go directly east. That's probably our best chance right now." It had seemed secure during her return stop on the coronation tour.

"The one with the racing track?" Jori asked. Their guide for that part of the city tour had been a cute, curvy girl Jori hadn't stopped flirting with until she handed them off to an older man with a short beard styled as his father Aylmor's had once been.

"How do we know that the Tanyu haven't anticipated that move?" asked Viktor.

"We can't know," she snapped, then felt bad for her tone. She rubbed her forehead. "But it's something, and we have Bard to look out for us."

Bard raised his chin slightly in acknowledgment, perhaps feeling the pressure of the position he held as the only Tanyu among them.

"We'll have a warning, at least," she clarified.

Jori popped up his eyebrows at Bard. "You can handle that, right?" he asked. "If my girl says you can."

He could. Bard had gone up against Belik himself when he'd come to murder Kiria. He'd stood his ground in the face of almost certain death.

Dimples appeared in Bard's shy smile. "Yeah, that's true," he agreed. "I can do that."

BARD'S USEFULNESS to her cause still didn't mean she needed to forgive him for keeping her awake now. They were all shipping out before first light, first to Rantoul to gather support from her own cities, and then onto Charäkhnem to join with their forces. The idea was to overwhelm any counterattack Belik could cook up. Between the Kingdom towns and the massive force King Ganesha could bring from Char Visil, it should be enough.

Kiria had elected to sleep in the great main room along with everyone else so the guards could take shifts looking out for everybody at once. After the evening they'd had, the unspoken consensus was that they wanted the company too. She nuzzled her head against the pillow. It had been found in one of the smaller rooms and smelled like pipe smoke.

"So you just... kept the shields under your cloaks?" Bard asked in an undertone. In a room as quiet as that one, any noise carried.

Royce sat across from him, temporarily off duty. With his helmet off, he looked almost more formidable. The tendons in his thick neck suggested he could crush Bard to smithereens. "That's what they did," he confirmed.

"And they didn't search you?"

"I don't know. Probably. They thought we were ordinary citizens." He heaved his large breastplate across his crossed knees and started polishing it.

Bard shook his head. "I... I could have told you how that plan would go."

Royce blinked at his audacity, the rag pausing in his hand. "Then tell me, what could we have done to reverse any of this?" It was a challenge more than it was a question.

"Well, the first attack was a surprise, so I don't know—"

"So was our move."

"Not in the same way."

In the pause that followed, Kiria started to drift off into warm sleep, sailing on that silence.

"Hey, any word from Adelisa? She's your daughter, isn't she?"

Kiria cracked opened her lids to see Jori settling himself beside Bard and Royce, breaking some of the tension between them.

"I haven't heard from her," Royce replied grimly. "We won't get a full count until we're inside."

Bard squinched up his face, trying to remember. "Is she the one—?"

"Runner," Jori supplied.

Kiria suddenly remembered where she'd heard the name. Adelisa, a young servant in the palace, was part of a squad who fixed broken things—broken pans, mortar, furniture—and she was one of the fastest in the beach races Jori loved. He'd bet on her more than once.

"What do you mean?" Royce asked, moving onto the next piece of armor.

"Have you never been to the races?" Viktor whispered from where he stood on duty above Kiria. She was getting to know all the guards well. Viktor was the youngest among them, only eighteen, like she was.

"Stay at your post, soldier," Royce growled before turning back to Jori. "What races?"

"At the beach," he said easily. "Nothing untoward."

Bard's mouth quirked in a smile.

"I beat Adelisa once," Viktor added.

Jori raised both eyebrows high. "Then it wasn't during one of the races."

"It was! Last spring—"

"Enough," said Royce, holding his shining helmet in one meaty fist.

After a moment, Bard asked, "She's your only daughter, yeah? I'm sorry you haven't heard from her."

"I have seven children."

"Busy man," Jori muttered.

"I'm one of six!" Bard quietly exclaimed, delighted.

The slope of Royce's shoulders softened. "Are you? Where are you from?"

"Enderin."

Jori leaned toward the soldier, imitating Bard's accent. "Listen to him. I thought that much was obvious."

"There's more than just Enderin up north," Royce replied. "I went there twice during the Torithian War."

"Did you?" Bard was leaning forward now too, his black eyes shining with news of his home country.

Jori frowned. "Am I the only one who hasn't been there? What is there to see?"

"Everything!" Bard's prompt response made Jori smile in surprise. "I'll go back when this is over, eventually, I think. I need to visit my family. My brother got married and I have... I have a niece or nephew, only we've never met. You understand, sir."

Royce looked pensive a moment before responding. "I do."

Jori squared himself at Bard. "So all there is to see is your family? That's not a long list of sightseeing options, unless they're spread out, hard to find, like mythical creatures." He looked far away at the wall past Bard's shoulder. "Oh, there's one! I think I spot a Tanery."

Bard smothered a laugh, but Royce rolled his eyes. "I wasn't there for sightseeing."

"Granted," said Jori. "But your eyes were open. There's nothing?"

"There's the ocean," Bard supplied.

"We've got that."

"But it's different."

"Bright pink?"

"Uh... wilder. We've got cliffs and *sachion* trees outside the main city. You should see the buildings. Your houses are just gray. Not... to be... not to offend anyone. But ours match the families. I think I saw some Endrian work in the palace. Woodworking?"

"Go on."

"Have you ever tried *orfinskal*?"

Jori plucked a handkerchief from his breast pocket and offered it to him. Bard shoved his hand away.

"*Orfinskal*?" Bard persisted. "It's like porridge, but with oranges and honey and nuts?"

"I had your cinnamon toast one time."

"That was you?"

"Of course it was. Pretty good. I ordered it from the kitchens next day." Jori turned his attention back to Royce. "Enderin can't be all bad. There's *alfinskat*."

"*Orfinskal*," Bard corrected.

"*Orfinskal*."

Royce set the helmet aside. "Yeah, I tried it. I could never get used to the way they keep the leaves in their tea, but we ate the Endrian food when we had to."

Bard's mouth flattened. Apparently, he didn't like his local cuisine insulted.

"We leave before dawn," Royce said, more gently now. Kiria heard fatherly care in it. "You two should get some rest."

"I never rest," Jori said grandly. "I only pause."

Bard quirked an eyebrow. "It's all right. You can sleep," he said, as though guessing that some fear lay behind Jori's declaration. "How are we traveling? Horses? I... I'll need to sleep sometime, but if I can ride with someone tomorrow... you know, sleep in the saddle for a while, I'll watch you tonight."

Jori's eyes widened in pleased surprise. "Oh ho! You want to watch me sleep? But we haven't so much as held hands."

Bard's cheeks darkened. "No. No, I mean, the Tanyu will come after you. You're their biggest target, after... My Keeper." His eyes shot to the guard. Maybe he felt he had to use her formal title in front of him. "They'll come in your dreams, maybe tonight, yeah?"

Jori grew serious, his gaze sliding to where Kiria pretended to sleep. "What about her? Kiria needs this more than I do."

"She has the Talent, at least."

"Check with her." Without waiting for someone else to do it, Jori crawled over to where she slept.

"My Kepron," Viktor began hurriedly, "don't—"

Jori gently shook her shoulder.

Kiria sighed and looked up at him. "Do you really think I could sleep through all that?" she whispered.

He smiled roguishly. "Then you heard, love. What do you think?"

She sat up slowly to look him in the eye. "Chetana taught me what to do. Or she started to before she left yesterday. I can take care of myself."

"Don't lie, darling."

"Never."

Jori cocked his head, unconvinced. "You're dreaming peacefully away and a Tanyu comes to kill you—you'd know what to do?"

"I have a plan, yes."

"So I should let this one watch me in my sleep?"

"Definitely." Her face warmed. Why hadn't she thought of suggesting it herself? At least someone had. "He can ward them off, or at least wake you up in time to avoid getting hurt."

"You're going to stay up all night?" Viktor asked Bard, dropping the pretense of whispering. More than one person groaned. For a guard that was supposed to be silent, he had a lot to say.

Bard gave one of his rapid-fire, repetitive nods.

Viktor reached in a pouch by his side, retrieved something small, and threw it at Bard. "Helps me stay awake."

In Bard's palm lay something that looked like a seed pod.

"You chew it," Viktor explained.

"Well, that's that," Kiria said, shoving Jori playfully away. "Now please, please, be quiet and go to sleep."

27

BELIK

Sandalwood. It was always sandalwood first. Belik snuffed, as though he could rid himself of the smell that meant Chetana was near. During this whole gory campaign, he'd felt her presence, but had successfully ignored it so far. A lifetime of practice had given him excellent skill at that. But he hadn't been crowned more than a couple hours before he started to feel it again in force.

She wasn't in the Amiran Academy—he'd had it searched— or else he would have killed her right there. If Amir weren't valuable assets, he would have burned the infernal place down with all of them inside, in honor of her memory. Except for Daelon, maybe. As it was, they made good servants.

As pacifists, the Amir didn't frighten him with rebellion, but as scholars, they could be capable of spying, so he ordered them locked in their Academy at night.

He pushed aside such gloomy thoughts, readjusting in the uncomfortable chair. The air still smelled smoky here, but this was the Keepers' quarters farthest from the worst of the damage. Third Keeper's quarters. He had all the bodies taken out days ago and placed in the arena plaza, but the room still had the uncomfortable feeling of recent failure. His most reliable allies —Shiro, Nedi, and the girl named Enktuya, who'd taken charge at the first coronation—stood around him. He'd just sent away the Tanyu taking care of the thin troops commanding the wall. If Chetana's presence got stronger, he'd send out a search for her, but at the moment he could hardly spare the warriors as he took total control of the city and crushed the mushrooming attempts against the Tanyu's rule. Now was the time to lock down the city tightly and to kill those who opposed him. Quick and simple, but requiring all hands. Finding Chetana was not the kind of job he'd trust the Kingdom troops to do. She'd once been part of Original Plan, the radical group that had sent her to assassinate him, once upon a time. No, if it became necessary, he'd find her himself.

"A Defender," said Shiro after checking the door.

Belik waved his hand impatiently. A ruler's work was never done. The crown, melded of all three royal diadems, sat on a cushioned pillow beside him, ready to be wielded like a weapon when necessary. One day the Tanyu would have the palace, have the wall, have the city, have the Western Kingdom, but he wasn't quite there. In the meantime, it was always meaningless interruptions.

"Master Belik," said a Tanyuin Defender, approaching him with head bowed. The stocky, light-skinned boy held out a carved wooden box. The markings didn't distinguish it as coming from any particular culture—no Endrian *sachion* trees or Charäkhni golden eagles.

"What's this?"

"It arrived… from Master Kess."

Belik's eyebrows darted downward. *Firian?* He was supposed to be on his way over the mountains by now. He snatched the box and opened it. Inside, next to a curl of paper, lay a small human finger severed at the second knuckle. He cast a shrewd glance at the messenger, but the boy looked back steady and guileless. The Defender hadn't manufactured this grisly present.

Belik pinched the slip of paper and read it. *Kepron Kader is killed and no longer a threat to you. Give Brett more time. Three days.* The handwriting looked masculine, but there was no way to test its authenticity.

"Where did you get this?" Belik demanded.

"Master Turgin, on the wall."

"Your name?"

"Lazlo Gram."

He'd have to question Master Turgin about where he received this package.

"It's a finger," Belik explained, gauging Lazlo's reaction.

The boy's features remained immovable. A good Tanyu, with no sign of guilt or innocence.

The bloody stump could belong to Kader. As he began to accept the possibility, his body felt alight. If the Kepron were dead, that was one less loose end to track down. Who else could it belong to, unless Firian had infiltrated the Tanyu here in Brithnem? There was no way to check if it came from one of the previously dead bodies, since all but the royals and would-be assassins, put on display, had been burned.

Kiria, then, was the only royal left. And the Calthwaite prince. Belik could deal with both of those in dream attacks. No Tanyu would even have to leave their post. It was elegant. Suspiciously easy.

He snapped the box lid closed. Oak. Still better than sandalwood.

28

———

BARD

BARD POPPED one of Viktor's seeds into his mouth. They tasted bitter, like fenugreek, a spice his cousin used to use in all her food. It was never his favorite. He'd always liked sweets better.

Slow breathing surrounded him, lulling heaviness into his limbs. But he could sleep in the morning. Now he had to defend Jori. Of course, being awake at night and asleep in the day like a barn cat reinforced that he was an outsider. He was already Tanyu—too soft for the Academy, too Tanyuin for his family. At least here his differences could help someone.

Jori slept recklessly. A small smile dimpled Bard's cheek as he looked at him. The Kepron's mouth was wide open, wavy hair falling back from his forehead. Never careful. If he was going to survive Belik, he'd have to learn some caution.

He'd suffered so much. Bard forced down the last seed, smile fading, trying not to think what he would do if one of his own brothers were killed, and slipped into Jori's dream.

Nothing was distinct, as though everything were happening underwater. The forest Jori wandered through looked born from the sea too. It wasn't made of trees like any forest Bard had seen, but sea kelp or upside-down jellyfish, the tentacles and transparent veils waving in an unfelt breeze. Red birds with slim bodies and long wings flew among the pale green appendages, squawking to each other.

The environment was incredible, as imaginative as anything a Tanyu would come up with. It set Bard's mind ablaze and brought an open-mouthed smile to his lips. So beautiful and strange.

Jori looked up for a while. Faces appeared between branches —fleeting glimpses gone in a blink. These seemed to confuse him, but the dream still felt tenuously peaceful.

Bard stayed out of sight. He could have set a Sentry instead of watching the weird, unruly beauty of this dream. Every murky corner was decorated with thoughts the way every Endrian house was decorated in carvings and strings of shells. Setting a Sentry would have been simpler. But the idea scared him.

The memory of those people, once Tanyu like himself, forced to become Sentries until their Talent and identity faded into nothing but pain. His heart squeezed. Back in Tánuil, Wells had told him a little, but Bard never pressed him. The image of pale, dirt-smeared people with hollow eyes was enough to haunt Bard for the rest of his life. He'd rather watch and defend every crazy dream Jori had than set a Sentry night after night.

One translucent branch bent down toward Jori as though curious. Its sinuous arm wrapped around him tight.

Was another Tanyu here? Was this an attack? Bard felt for another presence but found none. An ordinary nightmare.

As Jori struggled, Bard's breath grew shallow. Shouldn't he help him anyway, since he could?

Before he could decide, the ground tilted and spun, folding in on itself, the branch taking Jori with it. As though someone had turned a page, a new scene appeared. Jori was still bound by the plant creature, but now the space was now smaller and emptier. It was a rectangular box, splashed with different colors. The walls closed in slowly, or maybe it was the colors themselves, but everything was contracting around them, getting smaller and smaller.

Another figure appeared nearby but Jori didn't seem to notice it hadn't been there all along. Bard looked closer.

Kiria. She looked already dead, purple-pale and wrapped in layers of clammy tentacles.

Jori called to the birds in the forest, the red ones that had swum in the air above him, but his voice was muffled. He tried to scream, his mouth open wider than it was in real life as he slept, but the sound grew quiet, instantly stifled.

Bard's stomach tightened. He knew that feeling. No voice. Shouting when no one could hear.

Then, the touch of another mind. Subtle. This Tanyu was probably older and more experienced. The buzz became more distinct, but Bard saw no one.

He raced to the surface of the dream and burst out into the Real again. Jori hadn't moved or changed his expression. Only Bard knew what was happening inside his head. He shook the Kepron's shoulder, but he didn't stir. When Bard shook harder, Jori only smacked his lips and rolled over.

Urgency pressed against Bard's chest. If Jori wasn't waking, then Bard would have to help him from inside the dream. Hopefully he hadn't lost too much time. Dream time was different than waking time.

In a flash, he was back. The dark walls were still lowering, getting closer to the prone forms of Jori and Kiria, trapped in their bonds. Bard's nose wrinkled. If the walls touched Jori, he'd wake in seconds.

This probably wasn't part of the Tanyuin warrior's attack, then.

Never wake them up. That was what his Masters had

instructed Bard before they sent him to terrorize the people of Brithnem during the fear campaign. Ah, he'd hated that. Hated it. Done all he could to avoid hurting anybody.

Even though closing the room wasn't the Tanyu's primary tactic, Bard hated to see Jori trapped like that, about to be crushed. He eased into Jori's consciousness, made himself known as he gently directed the dream to change, for the ceiling and walls to expand.

Jori followed him with his gray eyes, curious, no longer panicking. A small spike of relief ran through Bard. But something was still wrong. The feeling of the other presence hadn't left. This was too easy.

The dungeon-like room shifted sideways as the forest had done, pitching like a wave into a variation of the scene. Kiria's body disappeared. The long ceiling became a wall hung with tapestries. A small blonde girl was kissing him. Jori's eyebrows rose in surprise and then delight.

Bard inhaled sharply. *Nothing like the captain, yeah?* He'd never forget what his *katah* with the Torithian captain Tibor Wat had made him witness. Images stuck to his mind like tar. Poor, used girls, naked bodies with bruises, sour kisses, and nights that brought pleasure only to the captain. He wished he could scrub his mind clean.

Jori wrapped his arms sweetly around the girl's waist, broke the kiss, and said something indistinct, a playful smirk on his face.

No, nothing like him. But it still felt invasive to spy. Bard squirmed.

The shift that followed was slight. Jori stopped talking. He stopped moving, and so did the girl. His eyes slid out of focus.

Bard snapped to attention. She was the Tanyu. Had she shifted the dream to this to distract him, lull him to airless sleep? Bard couldn't will away the girl—somebody must have chosen to look that way since she didn't seem familiar at all—but he could do something.

He sent an enormous red bird barreling at the couple, flying low enough to brush both their heads. Jori's eyes focused for a moment. Good.

But the Tanyu saw him too. "Leave us alone," she laughed in a girly voice.

Bard's skin crawled. "He's... needed at a meeting."

"Ha! Just two more minutes." The steely eyes belied her innocent words. Jori still held her loosely.

Make them passively accept what's happening, the Masters taught. He needed the opposite.

"What do you think?" Bard asked Jori.

"I think?" Jori replied, looking as though he'd forgotten something.

The girl planted another kiss.

Bard glowered. Jori wasn't catching on. Though it was risky, Bard rapidly took in the details of the little nook and added realism to it, solidifying it. It was a relief, actually. The dream had been so murky, Bard felt he had trouble breathing. Now the stone walls had depth, and the tapestries had clear design and texture. The air smelled a little like cinnamon. Why not?

Just like practice. But he hadn't practiced fighting in the Unreal for a while. Didn't think he'd have to again. He took a deep breath and released a piercing gust of wind from his palms. The tapestries whooshed upward and the Jori was slammed back into the wall with a grunt. The force made him release the blonde girl—the Tanyu, whoever it was—who whirled on Bard.

He brought the red bird back, its long gleaming beak clacking. The dusty smell of feathers joined the scent in the air. It picked up the blonde girl by the back of the collar.

Instantly, a spear flew at Bard. He shrank to avoid it. It didn't even look like the girl threw it, but the weapon definitely came from her mind. *Believable but unexpected.* That was a hard line to walk, but she apparently had practice.

Bard was no Firian, but he had practice too.

The huge bird dropped the girl. Instead of hitting the ground, she sank into it as though it were a pit of tar. The ground roiled and bubbled, pitch black and sticky. It covered the girl's arms and left angry red burn marks. Bard chewed his tongue but didn't let up. She was going to kill Jori, heir to the throne and one of his few remaining friends. Someone who didn't dismiss him or mock him or fear him. Someone who actually seemed to like him.

The image grew grotesque, but finally, mercifully, she disappeared. Hopefully her real burns weren't too bad. He needed to really frighten her so she didn't come back.

When he looked to the side, Jori had disappeared too. Bard came back to the Real, the mild scent of cinnamon replaced with faint body odor. Jori was stirring. Uninjured. Awake.

Bard smiled reassuringly when Jori opened his eyes. He had the same expression he'd worn in the dream, confusion, like he'd forgotten something important. He ran a hand through his hair and turned over to see where he was. His attention returned to Bard, who didn't feel as sleepy as before. Either the fight or the seeds had done the trick.

"That wasn't..." Jori trailed off, instead lifting one eyebrow in a question.

Bard nodded. "It's okay," he whispered. "You can go back to sleep."

Jori's mouth turned downward in perplexed amazement. "That was amazing. I'll try to get in more trouble."

"Please, don't do that."

The mischievous glint in Jori's eye offered no promises.

29

———

FIRIAN

WHEN THE BOX arrived for Master Belik, Firian immediately shifted his attention back to the Real.

As soon as he did, exhaustion cried out in his bones. He'd been riding as hard as the new horse could stand for a long time. Between his trips to the Unreal and the endless ride, he'd almost lost track of time. The sensation was like dizziness. Squinting at the horse's mane bobbing before him, he fought to find his footing, to remember how much time was left to save Brett. The ground swam. Even when he looked up, the mountainous landscape moved like water. He ground his teeth with frustration. Time to stop.

He pulled up on the reins and the sweating horse obeyed immediately. They were well clear of Redshore, traveling along fairly well-trodden roads. Despite wearing the brown shirt he'd taken from the chest in the ale cellar instead of his customary black, he knew he could be recognized. Still, it was faster this way, and speed mattered most now.

He heaved in a breath of sea-scented night air and dismounted. Beside him, the mare tossed her head in wide-eyed agitation. What would Kiria have named this horse? The question caught him as a more serious one would have. He faced the beast and looked into its deep brown, glossy eyes, rimmed with lashes. Keeping a hold of the reins steadied him. Gore, he was tired.

Move or sleep.

He gazed down the lantern-lit road running parallel to the sea. Was Kader safe somewhere north, or was he another corpse that Belik would soon find... or make? Belik was no fool. He'd suspect a trick, and if he caught Firian spying on his mind, that would only deepen his suspicion. Still, better to check to make sure that the ruse had actually worked, and that the young Kepron was safe from further pursuit.

He led the mare off the road into the trees, where he could sleep without prying eyes. The poor beast was covered with sweat. Pursing his lips, he stroked the mare's long nose. He should have changed horses more than once, he realized as he eased off her saddle and bridle. Well, at least they were resting now, and there was good vegetation for her to eat here.

As he lay down, his last thought was that her name should be Laird. Kiria would like that.

FIRIAN HAD ALWAYS REGARDED sleep as wasted time, but when he woke a few hours later, he had to admit that he felt much better. Now he could ride and trek afresh. Brett's life depended on it. Though he hadn't seen his sister since the shocking encounter in Raewhith, he knew she was on his side. When the world abandoned him, his sister never would.

Laird, the mare, wasn't happy to continue. She threatened to nip at him as he put her tack back on. He patted the side of her head once, reassuringly, before leaping in the saddle again. His muscles ached, which was good. He could regret the break less if he knew he had pushed himself far enough to hurt.

Now, maybe, he could sneak a look into Master Belik's mind. Was Kader safe? Could he tell Bard he'd succeeded?

Casting his mind back to the palace felt strangely off-kilter. That was the place his mind had gone to be with Kiria, but now it was Belik's domain. The knowledge burned. At least he could do this to help her, to show her that he didn't condone Belik's violent overthrow. Soon—but he reined in his mind. Thinking too far ahead was disastrous. The simple fact was this. Firian would kill Belik for what he had done. He would make things right. Beyond that, his ideas shied like a horse at an unexpected barrier. He couldn't ask himself why, not when there was so much at stake already.

A direct confrontation. It was a gamble, but it was best. If Firian had really killed the Kepron, he would own up to it directly.

Firian cleared his mind. *Meeting up with Kiria in the north, saving Brett, picking off heirs to the throne to buy time...* He inhabited the (mostly) false reality he wanted Belik to believe. Now, where to meet? Statues and tiles and stained-glass plates and soaring ceilings came together in a replica of the Main. He smirked in grim satisfaction at the sight.

Belik was not long to appear on the dais beside him.

The wound in Firian's shoulder shot pain across his chest.

The Master didn't wear a crown, but he might as well have. He scratched the side of his head casually and took in Firian, up and down. Though his posture was relaxed, his eyes shone bright with wariness. Apparently, he determined that nothing was different about Firian except his attitude.

Firian's muscles tensed, even in the Unreal, but he held his black rage in check. When they'd met before, his hatred nearly drowned him. Now, he was diplomatic—at least, as diplomatic as he ever got.

"I want time for my sister," he said. Could he kill Belik now? Maybe, but he needed Belik to call off his allies from harming Brett. And who knew if Kiria was in a position to retake the throne? Bard had said they'd leave after Dedication Day, and that was yesterday.

Belik grunted, waiting for more.

He'd have to sell it, then. *Okay.* "I..." He swallowed. "I found the Kepron. Kader. The young one." He allowed a flash of the hate he felt to surface in his gaze. "I made it fast. I had to kill his escort too, but he's gone."

"Where?" In the Real, Belik would have sat on the throne beside them, but here, his leg didn't hurt. They were on equal ground.

"I killed him in a tavern between Brithnem and Redshore. Where they were hiding before moving on."

"Which inn?"

"What?"

Belik repeated the words.

This was a game, a calculation. Firian fished for a name. Hadn't he passed an inn...?

"I don't know the names of all these gory places," he said.

Belik's law clenched. "And the body?"

"You got your gift," Firian snarled. The idea of killing a child... Disgusting.

Belik leveled his gaze, and the gravel in his voice deepened. "The body."

Firian's chest constricted with fury. "I gave you part of it. Do you want the rest?"

"Where is it?"

"Burned by now for all I know! I didn't stay. I doubt anyone would recognize him. He was wearing average clothes and the only royal token I found on him is the one I sent you. Now, do I have my three days?"

Belik scrutinized him longer. Firian didn't flinch. A deed as horrific as he'd claimed to have done would earn him, at a minimum, that extra time.

"Three days," Firian repeated, jaw clenching. He truly could use the time. With only seven days left, he could run out of time if snow had reached the mountains. It wasn't unheard of this time of year.

"The First Line is dead?"

At the words, a rabbit's breath of pause shook Firian. Had Kader been a shield for Kiria? She was all that was left of the Second Line, as far as he knew. Now that the threat of a living heir to the First Line had been dealt with, would Master Belik spare more Tanyu to hunt her down? The thought made him sick. Still, "yes" was the word he heard himself say.

Belik's barrel chest expanded in a heavy breath.

"Three days," Firian said again.

"Two," Belik replied, mouth quirking as though they engaged in some sort of game.

A hand might as well have gripped Firian's throat, for the rage he felt. He had to leave. Now. His curt nod might have come off as a twitch, but he didn't care.

He came to, sucking in the cold morning air. The leaves, ripening to orange as he went north, and clean chill brought him to calm as he rushed along the road.

He could do more than this. He'd saved the Kepron, but Belik had to be stopped. Soon, his own allies inside the palace would take care of that.

30

———

KIRIA

THAT MORNING, Bard lay slumped over the saddle horn of Royce's chestnut mount, bobbing with the movement of the horse. He'd stayed up all night defending Jori's dreams. Exhausting work, even at the best of times.

Kiria looked back at Brithnem, her city, right before it went out of view. Was it her imagination or was the air still hazy above the palace? The black sky was lightening to gray, cooling the tips of the far waves. City Beautiful.

Where was Chetana in that tangle of stone buildings? Was she safe? If her *katah* with Belik was anything like hers with Firian, Belik would know she was near. When Bard wasn't so drained, Kiria would ask him to check on the Amir, make sure she was safe. Maybe they would learn whether Daelon was alive.

Their group wasn't taking the main roads, so it would be slow going. The pace grated against her nerves. It was a straight shot east to Rantoul, then Charäkhnem, much more direct than her coronation tour had been.

"Kiria."

She turned to Jori, who looked more serious than usual. It

was probably the earliness of the hour. Despite his claim the night before, he loved to sleep in.

"Bard told me he set a watch over Kader's dreams as well. Thought you'd want to know."

"He watched two people himself?"

Their words fell like leaves in the burgeoning autumn. Pre-dawn chill swept over their faces, and birds sang in the quiet.

"He said there was someone else to watch Kader."

She lowered her brow. "Another Tanyu? He should have told me."

"It was the middle of the night, darling. We had specific instructions not to wake you, if you remember."

"But another Tanyu!"

"I know, love, but maybe we don't have a choice."

"There's always a choice." The words echoed in her thoughts, dripping like an indoor pool. She shook off the feeling. "Who is it?" *It had better not be Firian.*

"He says he was a 'Sentry' back home. Abused by the Tanyu so he has no love of them. Blocks the dreams or something. Says his name is Wells."

"No love of the Tanyu?" Kiria replied. "He is one of them."

"So's our boy."

She chewed her lip. Bard was the exception. Theoretically, there could be more like him. She cast a glance in his direction. His mouth was open, eyes closed, crazy hair fluffed in the wind. Royce, holding the reins, towered above him.

"I'll speak to him later," she said finally. The two heirs were her responsibility. Hers alone. Atty and Cúron weren't here to support her. She stiffened her spine. "You shouldn't go making decisions like that without me."

He narrowed his eyes. "You can't have it both ways, love. You insist I'm important—"

"You are."

"—and yet I can't act like it. Which is fine."

But it didn't look fine. His expression turned sullen.

Kiria adjusted her grip on the reins. "You just... Jori, you know yourself. Have you ever been responsible?"

"I heard there was a time when I was eight."

"Lies." She smiled. "You are important. You are... the Third Line. But you didn't know where Qib was!" Her coronation tour had only been a few months ago, and the name had slipped his mind during the party when they both met Princess Haved for the first time.

He placed one hand on his chest in horror. "Oh, Qib! Well then, I can never rule."

Kiria rolled her eyes. "You know what I mean."

"Do I have to be more intelligent? I've heard I'm very dashing."

"Not the same thing."

"And fabulously brilliant."

She sighed. "You have to know where Qib is, and who our allies are, and how to enforce laws."

Halfway through her sentence, Jori's attention drifted elsewhere. He pointed ahead of them. "Is that a blue wren?"

"Am I boring you?"

"Oh no. Taxation and legislation have been my constant source of pleasure for years." He eyed her, deadpan.

"That's what I mean. You have to get more serious about this stuff."

"Many have tried. Many have failed."

"Jori!"

He released a breath and held her gaze now. "Don't squash my sense of fun. Not now." There was a hint of pleading in his tone.

For how long? Jori couldn't avoid responsibility forever, not with so much at stake. "Just think about it."

His attention lingered on her only for a beat before he gasped and fell back to maneuver around her. "Look who's awake!"

"Not awake," Bard slurred, closing his eyes again.

Jori clucked his tongue, casting Kiria a quick conspiratorial look. "We were just talking about that person you sent to help the Little One." That was their unofficial code name for Kader while they traveled. It wouldn't do to have strangers overhear that another heir was alive.

"Wells," Bard murmured, doubling over on himself in an apparent effort to get more comfortable.

"My Kepron," Royce said above them, snapping the reins, "let him sleep."

Jori held up a finger. "Very quickly, very quickly." His voice was soft, but he spurred on his own horse to keep pace.

Kiria followed, hedging Royce's horse in on the other side. "Does he know... if Kader is still free? If he's been caught?"

In an admission of waking, Bard raked a hand through his hair and scratched his head hard. Heavy shadows ringed his eyes. A pang of guilt sparked through her at forcing him awake. "He hasn't," he answered. "They won't get him."

Relief flooded her body. Then his effortless tone struck her. Was it just that he was still shaking off sleep, or did he know something more?

"Biscuit?" One appeared in Jori's hand. He broke it in half and offered some to Bard, who waved it away, but then thought the better of it and took it gratefully.

"So good," he said through the second mouthful.

"Only the best. It's old, but I always keep some in my—"

"How do you know the Little One won't get caught?" Kiria interjected.

"Firian," came Bard's swift reply. When he looked back at

her, however, something like indecision wavered in his gaze a moment, as though he'd said too much.

"What about Firian?" She asked the question carefully, unsure what to expect.

Bard swallowed the last bite of biscuit. "He made Belik look the other way." A one-shouldered shrug. "Convinced him Kader was dead. He's not! He's not."

"How?"

"Do you really want to know how?" Jori asked, peering through the gap between Bard and the horse's neck. Then, to Bard, "You can tell me later—I'd love to know details."

"It's... It'll work," Bard said. "No one will look for him, at least not for a long time. He said not to tell you it was him." Something like defiance crossed his features.

Firian helped her? Helped *Kader*, who could do nothing to advance his cause?

She held her breath. "Does he know where the Little One is?"

Bard shook his head and swayed in the saddle. Royce caught his stiff left arm before he fell.

"Sorry," Bard said, righting himself.

Jori patted Bard's knee. Royce glared at the hand so close to his own leg.

"It's fine," Kiria said. The landscape around her blurred, secondary to her thoughts. "Get some rest. Now we can all sleep easier, with that information."

Bard gave a wide smile that split his whole face. "Yeah."

Kiria trotted ahead of the guard, leaving Bard in peace. Hopefully Jori would follow her lead. Bard had more than earned the rest. It crossed her mind that she had forgotten to ask about Chetana. She'd ask him about her once he woke in a few hours.

Because of mysterious actions by Firian, Kader was safe

somewhere. The Three Lines intact. She felt lightheaded. Glad. Confused. *How* had he done it?

And with the Sentry over Kader's mind, she didn't need to worry about a nightmare attack on any of them. She smiled, and it felt strange. All this time spent in terror and horror and grief. Finally, now, some good news.

Some very good news.

31

KIRIA

Rantoul lay on the far end of Á Quihilmar, the Gray Forest. The large town spanned the river. The mayor's residence rose like a miniature fortress on one bank. Beside it, threaded among trees, were shops and theatres and money changing stations. Well-dressed citizens bustled along the streets, stopping by the various businesses and entertainment options. Ordinary citizens lived across the river on the larger half of town, where the structures were noticeably more dilapidated. Warehouses, factories, smithies, and small farms took up that side. Two bridges spanned the Apothelin River, connecting the disparate sides.

As they approached from a distance, Kiria was struck by the beauty yet odd segregation of the town. On her coronation tour, nobles had ferried her from one sight to another, but they never crossed the river. From where they were, only the mayor's tall residence, and a sliver of the activity happening on either bank was visible until they came closer. Then the town walls shut out much of the activity within. A large portcullis closed the gap that allowed the river to run through the town's center.

Near it, outside the walls, children played along the riverbank on the poorer side. One small boy, shirtless despite the early snap of autumn, perked up to see Kiria's little group approaching the more affluent side. She waved at him. Without wearing her Beauty, there was little danger of being recognized. The boy waved back before screaming joyfully and rushing at the cold water with the other children.

After a few hours on the road, Bard had reluctantly woken up and let the Watchman of Rantoul know they were arriving. Their entrance that afternoon held little fanfare, unlike her last visit. This time, she was disguised with her plain face. With violence so close by, the guards at the walls had insisted on seeing their agreed-upon verification: the top of the royal tattoo, whose point ended at the nape of her neck.

Now they all sat around the mayor's large wooden dining table. Every guard but Viktor, who was carrying everyone's bags to their quarters, had joined them in the room, opting for additional caution. Bard was nursing a cup of tea, Jori a cup of wine.

The décor here had a seafaring flavor, though they were several days from the Kheltor. On a side table sat a large model of a naval ship. A row of cylindrical metal lanterns had been hung above the long table. This room had windows too, unlike the grand dining room in the palace. One was ajar, letting in cool air. Every other place she'd been to since the safe house had felt like a closed box, a prison. This felt open.

The mayor of Rantoul, a young man in his twenties with thick, closely cropped brown hair and a round emerald earring in one ear, sat with them. He stretched his long legs out, his chair angled sideways to the table. He was obviously trying to look relaxed, but he held his body tense and his shrewd gaze kept returning to her as though she were a puzzle to be solved.

"Mayor Emeric," she began, "thank you for taking us in during this time of need." The words felt false, rehearsed, although she meant them. Tonight, she could sleep in a real bed. For that alone, she was grateful.

"It was no trouble, My Keeper," he replied evenly, adjusting his posture and pulling up his chair. "In fact, it was a delight. It's good to be able to do something positive. I'm horrified by the events."

"Yes," she said, her limbs suddenly heavy, "but the Three Lines live on and the traitors must meet justice."

Jori dropped his eyes.

She picked up her tea and blew on it. "That's why we came to you. I need your army to assist us in taking back the capital. We must act quickly. We're calling on other cities as well, all around the Western Kingdom."

"I'm honored you stopped here first." He inclined his head, but kept his eyes on her.

Relief and suspicion battled for supremacy inside her. There was something scrutinizing about his piercing gaze, something that went beyond respect and loyalty. She needed these Kingdom cities on her side. The memory of Belik's promise to give wealth and freedom to anyone who refused to help her sat sour inside her.

"And who are my guests?" Emeric gestured to the others. An emerald ring flashed in the light.

"This is the Kepron Jorrim Calthwaite, and this is our friend, Bardhon Tanery."

His eyes lit up at Jori's name. "A pleasure. I thought I recognized your face."

"Yes, well, it's a memorable face," Jori replied.

"But *your* name," Emeric continued, turning to Bard, "I regret to say, I haven't had the pleasure of hearing before." Friendly dimples appeared in his cheeks, but his eyes sharpened.

The tea in Kiria's stomach made itself known. Should she tell the whole truth, that Bard was a Tanyu? As Keeper, she could do as she liked, but having a Tanyu by her side might undermine her credibility. Belik was already trying his best to do that without her confirming negative rumors.

"He was a Tanyu but he's on our side now," Jori piped up. "Bard's communicating to the Watchmen for us. Best of the lot."

Emeric cut a glance at Kiria. She saw his mind working.

"He's from Enderin," she supplied. Maybe the fact Bard's family was an ally would repair some of the damage Jori might have done by outing him as a Tanyu.

Bard nodded, absently twisting the black Tanyuin ring around his finger with his thumb.

Emeric noticed the action. "I see," he said, leaning back again. "I must say I'm surprised to see you traveling with a Tanyu after all that's happened. What, if I may ask, happened to the Tanyuin Head?"

Kiria set down her tea. A blunt question required a blunt answer. "Master Belik supplanted him when he attacked the capital," she explained.

"Did he die in the fighting?"

"No."

Their eyes locked, a challenge in the look. Why would Emeric challenge her? Did he not believe her? Again, Belik's speech rose to her mind.

She put her shoulders back. "He's not our concern right now."

"I think"—here, he tapped a finger against his lip—"that I have some right to know if I'm going to help you. Don't you think?"

It didn't escape her that he said *if* not *when*.

"He's heading over the mountains right now," Bard supplied. The last red rays of the evening sun fell in a slash across his cheeks and nose.

"I didn't help Master Kess organize any sort of attack, if that's what you're insinuating," Kiria said, when Emeric's attention flashed back to her. She swallowed. "My family were casualties in the fighting."

"Your private affairs are hardly my business, My Keeper. My apologies." He pressed a hand to his chest and briefly bowed his head.

Private affairs. "Accepted," she said flatly.

He waved a female servant forward. "Drienne, check on the dessert and tell us how long until it's ready." She swept from the room to follow his orders. It was early for supper, but Kiria had requested a meal immediately after all their traveling. "I'm simply looking out for the welfare of Rantoul. You must understand."

"Of course," she said.

"So, I have to ask. How do you come to travel with a Tanyu at all? Did he renege on his kind? I've never heard of a cowardly Tanyu. Wicked ones, we've seen ample proof. Again, I mean no disrespect."

Jori perked up, his eyes darting between Emeric and Bard as though he just realized what was happening. "Excuse me, you might not mean it, but you're managing it just fine. It sounds like you're insulting my friend here."

"I meant no—"

Bard tipped his mouth and waved his good hand to dismiss the slight, but Jori squeezed Bard's shoulder and shook him lightly. Bard rapidly set down his tea to keep it from spilling.

"Bard was with us during all the... unpleasantness. And before that night," Jori said. "He left the Tanyuin Academy before any of this happened. He saved my girl—your Keeper. He's more heroic than any of us, and takes less credit. You excepted, my dear, as always," he added to Kiria. "And with a little help, his hair could be better than yours." He leaned forward, scrutinizing the handsome mayor. "Probably. But that's not the point. If you're going to slight my friend, then you could find yourself paying higher taxes for a year."

Itching powders in bed, a duel, a public dunking in the river, Kiria might have expected from Jori to persuade him, but taxes? She wouldn't follow through with his threat, since the common people didn't need to pay for their leader's lack of tact. But maybe Jori was listening to her after all.

Emeric looked at her for confirmation. Was Jori someone to be taken seriously?

She smiled mirthlessly. Though she tried for her mother's easy grace, it didn't come as easily to her. Still, diplomacy seemed to be breaking down. Somehow, she needed to repair it, put Emeric's fears at ease. "We're not working with the Tanyu," she explained, "but we are working with Bard. He isn't like the rest."

Bard readjusted his shoulders as though his shirt were on crooked. His cheeks had gone dark, but his eyes shone with delight at the compliments.

The mayor's jaw jutted as though he were a reprimanded child. "My apologies."

Jori raised his eyebrows and took another drink.

"In fact," Kiria said to Bard, "if you could contact Charäkhnem and let me know how many troops they plan to send. Take a guard with you."

"Sure. I'll go right now." He bounded up from his seat so eagerly that a servant flinched as she gathered the mayor's glass.

Once he was gone, Kiria said, "He could do it at the table, but I wouldn't want you to be uncomfortable."

Jori looked at her approvingly over the rim of his cup, as though she'd just won a point.

"I assure you I wouldn't be uncomfortable…"

"It's the convulsing," Jori added. "That gets some people."

The mayor frowned, looking sorely ganged up on.

"Now that you know he's no threat," she said, thinking they might have taken their comments a little too far, "you know that you have nothing to fear from us. I want the Tanyu out of the capital even more than you do."

"No doubt." Emeric laced his fingers together. Taking a breath, he looked up again. "I should have known better than to question your judgment. I hope you will forgive me. With all the uncertainty surrounding the attack, and the conflicting reports about you, My Keeper, we have been warier than usual."

"I understand that," she conceded, although it was unsettling to hear more about conflicting reports about her. Would the mayor think like those citizens she'd overheard in Brithnem? Did he think she was a weak leader, sacrificing those she loved to succumb to her passions? No leader was universally loved, but that memory stung like a new wound every time she thought of it. "What are the conflicting reports, exactly? In Brithnem, I wasn't in a position to hear much news beyond what my guards brought me."

Emeric blinked a couple times before answering. Not a good sign.

"Sometimes they paint an unflattering picture," he admitted, running one hand through his short hair. "Now I see they were mistaken about your character."

"But what do the reports say?"

When the mayor hesitated, Jori said, "It's an easy question. Do they say she's as tall as two people standing on each other's shoulders? That she's a muskrat, a murderer? What?" He flung his hands in the air.

"They conflict," Emeric said delicately. Looking at a servant behind him, he said, "Bring out the dessert now."

Could he stall any more obviously? She stopped herself from crossing her arms in annoyance as the servant left the room. She hadn't come through the trauma of watching her world burn to be strung along by this man. The time for prevarication was long gone.

Emeric angled his chair again before continuing. "I had heard something about how you were... involved with the Tanyuin Head, and that you let them into the palace. I was shocked, of course, and knew you would never have done such a thing."

Jori glowered at the mayor. He all but said, *Damn right.* Kiria didn't deign to respond, but still felt heat creep into her face. Hopefully he wouldn't see her blush.

"I also heard that you refused to give aid to Kingdom cities who helped you," he said.

She quirked an eyebrow. Belik's coronation speech had traveled quickly.

"I knew right then that I was listening to lies."

"What aid?" she asked carefully. "We've always treated our allies fairly." The Keepers had always helped the other cities of the Kingdom—fostering trade for their economy, sending troops when they were in trouble, assistance after disasters—all with the assumption that the Keepers could rely on them to fight on their behalf. But Emeric sounded like he meant something else, something more.

"There's substantial danger in helping you," he said. "The entire force of the Tanyu is against you. It will cost great loss of life. The leader of the Tanyu said he would pay for our armies to stay out of the conflict, but I knew you would give more for us to help you."

"Pay?" Jori repeated. "We don't normally do that, do we, love?"

"We do. We give fair compensation," she said icily, finally understanding the young mayor's game. "We promise nothing extra for helping us. We depend on loyalty to the Keepers."

In her periphery, she saw Royce tighten his hands on his

sheathed sword. Emeric saw it too, but he persisted. "A promise would be a show of good faith. Your reputation—pardon me—is tarnished at the moment. Not rightly, I know!" He opened his hands in a gesture of peace. "Giving from the palace stores could help restore some of that trust in your leadership. My suggestion comes from a place of loyalty, believe me." He laid one hand on his heart.

"Unwavering dedication to the throne would start to end those rumors too," she replied, her heart clenching.

"It's... difficult."

"Which part?" Jori asked. "Loyalty, justice, honor? I'm curious."

Emeric shot him a look. "None of those things." Then he added, "Kepron Calthwaite. You must see things from my position. Many people are believing these vicious rumors. I could mobilize them with the right... monetary incentive... but without it I'm afraid my hands are tied."

"Cúron and Varinna Calthwaite, Atael and Haved Calthwaite, Merian Arioc," Kiria recited. The names felt like ash on her tongue. To bring them up in the presence of this mercenary member of the Western Kingdom felt almost sacrilegious. But words came rushing out, her blood ringing. "The Tanyu have gutted the capital and we require your assistance. We have been good leaders to your town in the past. I believe we even assisted in the floods last year? I can't promise you riches if you come because I don't have access to my own stores, and even if I did, I wouldn't empty our coffers so you could feel more comfortable about doing the right thing."

Jori leaned forward as he listened to her, wide eyed, as though this were a sporting match.

She had too few allies to be rash, but part of her wanted to rise up—as Firian undoubtedly would do—and order Emeric to be arrested.

She was so tired.

Bard came back at the same time as the servants who held dishes of lemon-flavored ice. He looked like she felt, gray around the edges. Pressing his lips together tightly, he eyed Kiria, a request to speak with her.

Something was wrong. She sat up straighter. She would have been glad for the excuse to leave, except the reason looked like it could be nothing good.

"I'll hear this news. Save the dessert for another time," she said, standing. "Mayor Emeric."

Jori swiped a dish as he followed her and Bard out of the dining room. "He's awfully handsome," he exclaimed around a large mouthful of lemon ice. "Too bad he's a conniving bastard." His eyes grew large and he looked down at his dish. "Mmm! There's mint or something in this. We should ask our..." At the sight of Bard's stricken face, his words vanished on the air.

"What's wrong?" Kiria asked. Seeing a cadre of Emeric's guards posted nearby, she added, "Here, let's get to our rooms." Their floor of the tower wasn't particularly large, and they found their guestrooms quickly.

Gathered in her simple, nicely appointed bedroom, Kiria and Jori turned wordlessly to Bard.

"They aren't coming," he said.

Kiria's body went cold. "What do you mean they're not coming?"

Bard scrubbed the back of his head with his knuckles. "The Watchman said that the alliance is dissolved."

"But... Haved!" she protested. "They must want to avenge her death."

Jori made an uncomfortable noise in his throat.

"They... they said Belik's returning her to them, so they want out of the conflict," Bard said. "Those were his words."

This is impossible. "They just want her body, and they'll be satisfied?" The thought filled her with nausea. She hadn't pegged King Ganesha as a coward. Her hands balled into fists.

"No." Bard shook his head. "She's alive."

Jori went bone-white, almost blue.

Alive? Kiria clasped her hands in front of herself to keep them from shaking. She couldn't believe it yet, just in case. But the news sent lightness to her bones. "Didn't you... see her?" Kiria asked Jori gently. If Haved was alive, that changed everything with Charäkhnem and gave them one less friend to mourn.

Jori moved uncomfortably, as though itching to get out of his own skin—his neck, his shoulder, his arm. "Yeah."

"Are you sure she was...?"

"It looked like it." His voice sounded dry and hollow.

Kiria wanted to ask details, but Jori was on the verge of breaking already. She couldn't push him further. Instead, she turned to Bard. "Did Charäkhnem have proof? Could Master Belik be lying?"

"Yeah, they seem pretty sure."

"Is there a way you can check?"

Bard's attention darted around the room, searching possibilities. "Maybe."

"Try. Tonight. And tell us in the morning."

Whether or not Belik was lying, she could no longer count on Charäkhnem's support. Could she count on anyone's? Her mind flashed to Chetana. The last time Bard checked on her, she had said something about sending help if she could. But what kind of help could be enough if her own allies—her own kingdom!—refused?

"I've also got to..." Bard pointed at Jori, who was still too flabbergasted to speak, a rare look on him.

"Right." She sighed. "We'll find out soon. You take care of Jori."

Jori's dish of lemon ice was forgotten in his clenched fingers. "I thought…"

"It's okay," Bard assured him, tentatively patting him on the arm. "You know, maybe she's all right. That'd be good, yeah?"

Jori took a gasping breath as though he'd realized he was holding it.

"It's all right," Bard repeated, holding his arm now and leading him toward the door. "Which one's your room?" Bard's reassuring lilt faded as the boys left.

Alone, but for her serving girls, she took a fortifying moment to consider the day. After she contacted the Watchman, she'd return to her conversation with Emeric. It wasn't late, and she didn't have time to waste with his games.

32

BARD

Jori wrenched his arm out of Bard's grasp. As soon as he did, he patted Bard's hand absently, murmuring, "I'm sorry, darling. I'm not... I won't be able to sleep."

The past few days, only getting snatches of sleep, made Bard want to crawl into bed immediately, but he nodded. His news had shaken everyone. "At least Haved's alive, yeah?" They stood in front of Jori's bedroom in the mayor's residence but they made no move to enter.

Jori gazed sidelong at Bard, a vulnerable expression in his stormy gray eyes. "You didn't hear anything about...?"

Bard's throat tightened. *Atty.* "No. I'm... I'm sorry."

Jori tossed his wavy hair as though shaking off the thought. "I knew that. I knew that," he said quickly, breathlessly.

"It's okay," Bard said, bringing his voice low. It really was. If Bard lost one of his siblings, even though they hadn't talked more than a couple times the past few years, he'd be devastated. The very idea made his chest tighten. "It's normal." With the words came a spark of defiance. It had to be normal to grieve a huge loss, even though the Academy might deny it. Well, he'd defied the Academy in many ways. The knowledge gave him grim pride.

Muscles flexed in Jori's jaw as he looked away, dashed away a tear with a brusque hand, and straightened. He looked up and down the hallway but no one stood there but the two of them and Lilith guarding Kiria's door. Who was he looking for?

"We'll just get a quick drink, then. You're coming, of course." Jori said it casually, but Bard hadn't been chosen as a companion for a long time. Hadn't realized how starved he was for company until that moment. He felt alight. This was wicked—asked by the Kepron of the Western Kingdom. Jori's title jumped to mind as though they hadn't become friends already. Jori was kind to everyone, so the invitation shouldn't have struck him so forcefully, but it did. Why did so many powerful people want to spend time with *him*?

"Yeah. Yeah, let's go!" Bard cried.

Jori's mouth stretched into a dimpled smile as he pretended to clean off his cuffs. One side bulged a little where the sleeve hid the black mourning cloth he and the others had worn since Dedication Day. "We'll find out where they keep the good drinks in this place," he said, heading off down the hall.

Shouldn't they take a guard? But they were already out of sight of Lilith. Maybe there would be more of them in the next section of the tower. Even Emeric's guards would be useful as backup if anyone were to attack Jori. Not that Bard expected that, exactly. Still, it was better to be prepared, since Jori was being targeted, and he had no combat experience. Did he?

"We'll be fine."

Bard's attention snapped back to Jori, whose eyes laughed at him.

"You look worried."

"Can you fight? I mean, have you learned to use a weapon?"

Jori's smirked. "That's how I spend all my free time. That's why I have six knives currently strapped to my person. Care to guess where?" He paused and spread his arms wide.

Bard grimaced and laughed at the same time.

"We'll be fine," he repeated. Then he leaned close to Bard's ear. "Best case scenario, I get a little drunk and you have some impressive fights in my dreams. Worst case, I die."

His bluntness made Bard startle. "Yes, that is the worst case."

"Only a little," said Jori, resuming his walk toward the staircase. "I mean, it's generous to call that the worst case, isn't it?"

"No," he replied firmly, trying to catch Jori's eye, but he wasn't taking the bait. Did Jori mean that?

"Aw, you'd miss me. Say nice things about me when I'm gone."

"Don't joke."

They trotted together down the long staircase. At the bottom, Jori veered left, past two guards at the base of the steps. "I have a nose for these things. Ah!" He pulled up short, staring at a servant Bard recognized from the dining room.

Short and prim, with Endrian-dark eyes, she was just coming out of a side room, carrying a tray with little silver bowls on it. Sensing Jori's attention on her, she stopped uncertainly.

Jori approached her with his signature ease. Just moments ago he'd been in shock. No one could tell to look at him. It was amazing to have that kind of control, that command over himself. It wasn't the Tanyuin kind of control, the kind Bard always struggled with. It was the kind of thing that made a person popular, magnetic.

"Oh, is that the dessert from earlier?" he asked, grabbing one of the bowls off her tray. Disappointed, he set it down again. "Empty," he explained to Bard before turning back to the girl. "Darling, I was wondering if you could fetch us some of your best wine." When she hesitated for a beat, he added, "Jorrim

Calthwaite," pointing to himself, "Bardhon Tanery," pointing to Bard.

Her face lit up with recognition. "Yes, of course. Shall I send it to your room? Would you like any food as well? Eggs with capers?"

"No, no, dear. Wine sounds lovely. What was your name? I know I heard it and I'm shocked at myself for forgetting."

"Drienne." She tucked a strand of brown hair behind her ear, clearly flustered at Jori's attention. The Kepron seemed to have that effect on most people. Candrae, Kiria's serving girl, couldn't look at him without blushing, anyway.

"That was it. Rolls off the tongue." Jori winked at her and turned back toward the stairs. "Easy as that," he said, speaking to Bard again as they headed up.

"How do you do it?"

"Ask for drinks? Well, you need the right vocabulary. Send. Wine. Sometimes ale. Sparkling's best."

Bard chuckled despite himself. "No, I mean, put everyone at ease."

"I hardly do that."

"You did just now."

"I suppose I could have yelled at her," Jori answered with mock thoughtfulness. "But she seems like a nice girl."

Bard made a frustrated noise. "You know what I mean."

"You, at least"—Jori stopped to point dramatically at Bard's chest—"aren't relaxed by my presence. Or, what did you say? 'Put at ease.' I keep you up all night, fighting on my behalf. Sorry that lot fell to you. Can't imagine." He raised his brows apologetically.

"I don't mind." Bard waved his hands, revising. "I mean, it's fine. I can do it, and I'm glad. I want to keep you safe." Finally, his Tanyuin skills used for something more than spying and killing. After he left the Academy, he missed the Unreal when he didn't have it, but, for a while, who could he have talked to?

Firian's expression as Bard closed the door to his office for the last time still haunted him. He'd seen that face before, but never directed at him. It cropped up in nightmares even now. Crazy that he and Firian were still friends after everything. He should give him an update about this stop, ask how his side of things was going. He'd find a moment before Jori went to sleep.

Despite the exhaustion and the stress, it was great to stretch out his mind again in the Unreal and feel powerful enough to help.

Jori smiled lopsidedly at him. "Could you fight? With all the knives I have on me?"

For some reason, the question made him squirm a little. It felt sincere, despite the fact that Bard's hand had stopped twitching when he tried to move it. It was stuck for good. Without it, how much of his limited physical training would still hold up?

"In the Real?" he asked. "Sure, yeah. I'm not..." He almost named Firian and stopped himself. Jori had good reason to dislike him. No point in extending that dislike to Bard too.

"Ah, I'd like to see that."

They reached the bedroom again to find Viktor so pale his tattoo looked like it was pasted on top of his skin. The guard exhaled with relief at the sight of them.

"My Kepron, why weren't you here?" he asked tightly.

"I had protection," Jori assured him, laying a hand on Bard's shoulder. Warmth filled him at the compliment. It was a compliment, right? Must be, after the nice things he said about him to Emeric earlier. The memory brought his hand up to his hair. Was it really that good?

"Always tell us where you're going," Viktor said, grumpy now. "I was about to tell the Keeper you were missing."

Jori flashed him a grin. "We're back, see? Don't worry Kiria about us." He pushed past Viktor to get into the room. "Unless you hear screams or something," he added as an afterthought.

After assessing the room, Jori bounded onto the chair in the corner and crouched there like a bird. His gaze took in the bed, the pictures on the walls, the chest of drawers. It looked a lot like Kiria's room next door.

Just watching Jori made Bard realize how tired he was. A yawn forced his mouth wide. He covered up the gesture by scratching the back of his head as though it didn't matter.

"If you want to sleep tonight—" Jori began.

"No." Bard stretched and shook out his shoulders. He gave a sniff to end the argument before it began. A second afterward, he realized that was a tactic he'd picked up from his mother.

"You know, with a Tanyu watching my every move—don't mistake me; I'm flattered—it's a lot harder to go where I want, sneak out a window, get away from all this." Jori gestured wistfully toward the window, raising himself enough to sit on the back of the chair with his gray boots on the seat. Bard didn't point out that they were at least three stories up.

"Sounds kind of fun," Bard admitted. "Where would you go?"

"I don't know. That's the fun part. Who knows what's going on out there?" After a moment, he said, "Not that I blame you. Escaping from a Tanyu, now that would be something..." A dreamy look stole over his face, the expression children got before stealing a treat.

"Don't try it, please."

"You can sit." He indicated the bed.

"I'll be sitting all night, if it's all right." Bard stood beside Jori and leaned against the wall to show he was comfortable.

Jori angled toward him. His open vest flapped to the side.

"Once, I followed two Tanyu after they visited, all the way out of town. They never noticed."

"They noticed."

"I was wearing a servant's outfit."

"They noticed."

Jori huffed. "Thank you for ruining my great achievement, Master Tanery."

"I would notice."

"Point made."

A knock on the door meant that drinks had arrived.

Jori leapt off the chair. "Drienne!" he cried, opening the door and snatching up the bottle and two glasses before the girl even came in sight. "What a marvelous lady you are! Thank you, love."

"It was my pleasure, Lord Calthwaite."

At this, Jori shot Bard an astonished face, eyebrows raised. *Lord Calthwaite.* "This will be all," he said to her. "You've been wonderful." And he closed the door.

With practiced ease, he opened the bottle and poured two glasses, offering one to Bard. The dark red liquid smelled sharp and warm at the same time. Unpleasant memories jumbled in with the scent. Wine wasn't offered in Tánuil but Tibor Wat, the Torithian captain, had drunk it all the time. He swallowed and watched Jori down a large gulp before sipping from the rim. The taste wasn't bad. Grapes and herbs.

Jori refilled his glass and then held it out to Bard in a toast. "To exciting dreams!"

"How about no dreams? Help for the Kingdom? Something like that."

"This is supposed to be a fun moment, not a political one. Don't be yesterday's wet clothes!"

Bard tried out a few expressions, but none seemed to fit. He always found himself dampening other people's fun with caution, but wasn't *now*, of all times, the moment to toast to Kiria's success? The list of duties stretched before him, as long as the night—contact Firian, set watch over Jori while he slept, check on Chetana. He'd forgotten about that last one, or maybe he'd just put it off, since Chetana didn't like him very much. Kiria cared about her, though, and she'd been gone ever since Bard arrived. He needed an update from her too.

"Still here?" Jori asked, snapping his fingers.

"Yes. To... you," Bard said, clinking the glasses together. That would do. He'd be Jori's advocate, even if he didn't advocate for himself.

Jori beamed. "What an enlightened choice!" he cried, and tipped back the glass.

An hour later, after the bottle was gone and jovial stories turned sad by memories, Jori crawled into bed. Fuzz clouded Bard's mind as he settled cross-legged next to him on the blankets. *Shouldn't have done that.*

"Your eyes are cloudy," Jori said, sitting up again to peer at him. "Can't hold your drink, I guess." He sighed and flopped back down. "It's more impressive my way but more fun your way."

Jori didn't seem any more sober than Bard was.

"Maybe I could sneak out after all," Jori slurred.

"Just go to sleep." A hint of bitterness laced his tone. There would be no sleep for Bard tonight.

As soon as Jori closed his eyes, so did Bard. He had only minutes before the Kepron was unconscious, vulnerable to attack.

The responsible thing would be to contact Chetana first. He shifted his hips, bracing himself, and looked for her mind. It was subtler than other Tanyu, quieter. Location was more important, but he didn't sense her to the west.

Where else would she have gone? North, to chase after

Kader? He checked. Not there either. She couldn't be further east than they were, or, at least that was highly unlikely. South? What was south? He cast his mind in that direction.

The pit of his stomach hollowed out the longer it took to find her. Had Belik killed her? How could he tell Kiria? Then, a whisper, like sandalwood. That was Chetana! He moved his energy in that direction—almost due south—and the nothingness around him melted into a small room crammed with people, mostly older women. Though they looked nothing like one another, they acted like family, or perhaps an army, standing together in tight knots, others seated so close they were practically in each other's laps. Most of their attention focused on Chetana, who stood in a place of prominence. One scan revealed that Daelon wasn't there.

Who were these people?

Many of the women were well-muscled and all of them had shrewd expressions, like wild animals. Though some regarded Chetana with interest, others held open hostility for her. The uncomfortable quiet made it seem as though Chetana had just finished speaking.

"How is she different than they are?" asked one woman in the small crowd. "She fraternizes with them."

"We have the Talent as well," Chetana explained. "And we aren't Tanyu."

Someone spit. Bard heard the noise but couldn't see who it was.

"Yes, but we don't have relations with them either." The woman's tone was pointed. Chetana didn't quail, but her jaw hardened.

A white-haired woman, apparently the oldest in the room, raised her head. "Why have you really come back?"

"To ask you to help us," Chetana said in a low, measured way. "Your skill is needed in this war."

"It's a coup!" someone shouted.

"You have always wanted to end the Tanyu. Here is your opportunity."

End the Tanyu? What was Chetana a part of?

"It would be the illusion of victory," said the oldest woman. "Rumors state that there was a Tanyu in the palace even before—"

"Shh!" A woman with blonde dreadlocks, who must have been beautiful in her youth, jumped to her feet, head cocked as though listening.

An almost ritualistic silence fell over the group.

The dreadlock woman nodded to the oldest one, Chetana momentarily forgotten. "One's here," she whispered.

"I would never bring..." Horrified understanding entered Chetana's expression the moment before she looked straight at Bard. The vision of her was doubled, eyes open and closed. "Why were you spying on us?" she hissed.

Bard's heart thumped erratically. "I wasn't! I wanted to see how you were, what you were doing."

She deflated and rubbed her lips together. "Your timing may have cost us allies," she murmured. Then, more loudly, "Daelon's alive, but I couldn't get to him. Is that what My Keeper wanted to know?"

"Yes," Bard said hurriedly, wanting to ask about the group of women but sensing that the longer he stayed, the more danger he put Chetana in. "Let me know... anything else."

"Go," said Chetana bitterly. "I might be able to save this."

Bard didn't need further prompting. Who was Chetana associated with that would want to end the Tanyu? He looked down at Jori and fished a red seed from his pocket to stay awake. These women didn't sound like the best allies, but the Keepers could use whatever help they could get.

33

KIRIA

It was a common dream—at least, versions of it were. Big tropical leaves and rocky trails opened up to a place where she could see an open field far below where people practiced their powers like magicians. The colors were rich, like the colors of a storybook. A dark-haired girl shot light from her hands. The ground seemed to move with sparring partners and the air was alive with people flying. Everyone wore black.

This was the Tanyuin Academy as she'd imagined it as a girl.

At the edge of the huge clearing stood a magnificent castle, its size distorted to be both near and far at once. Mysterious caves and rivers and monsters prowled the forests around it, but the warriors were not afraid. No, they were too powerful. A boy shapeshifted into a bear as he faced off against his opponent, but, as he charged, his quarry vaulted over him with a quarterstaff, never touching the ground, but instead perching on its tiny end like a vulture, perfectly balanced.

The dream shifted its details, but the core was the same. Darkness would come over the scene any moment. Kiria felt it as surely as an ache in her chest. But the ache wasn't only for the coming darkness. Longing overtook her as she saw these people who so clearly *belonged*. These people with their strange gifts belonged together. They weren't abominations; they were magic. She couldn't remember why that made her sad, but it did.

To take advantage of the last sliver of light, she rose from the ground, as she had done with Firian all those weeks ago. At the thought of him, he appeared as though summoned. Quiet, intent, floating in front of her. The grass and wet leaves shook beneath them in the breeze.

The pang inside her intensified and eased all at once. "Firian, I..."

He came closer, nearly touching now, blocking the scene below with his body. They looked at each other, not speaking, and as she looked, his face changed. The expression was slow to catch at first, but the warm tenderness she'd first seen melted away, leaving his eyes hard and lifeless, full of fury and disgust. His carved lip curled. Looking at him became like looking into the face of all her mistakes, her failures, every bad thing she'd ever thought about herself since she was young. It withered her as she choked on her own thoughts.

"Stop!" she said, but the word was small and died on the air.

"No."

The voice wasn't his. It was baritone, like Firian's, but the timbre wasn't the same.

Anger replaced her shame and she stood up straight. Her feet touched back to earth. The choking sensation from a moment ago hadn't gone away.

"You think you can kill me?" she asked the thing in front of her. "Wait till you see who I am!"

Her form stretched and fell away to reveal Firian's instead, an even more perfect replica. The change was immediate. She could breathe again as the Tanyu wavered. "Leave me alone!" she said in Firian's voice.

Consciousness was returning. The barrier to the real world

felt thinner. Knowledge that Firian was still, in a strange way, her protector, her talisman, infuriated her. She shook off his form and peeled open her eyes.

A dark room in Rantoul. One side of her face was cool from the autumn chill. Even the shapes of furniture weren't visible in the gloom. She might as well not have opened her eyes at all.

Rolling over, she cast up a desperate prayer for dreamless sleep.

"WAKE UP, DARLING."

Kiria snorted and shot upright in bed, her mousy hair falling over her face. Pushing it out of her eyes, she squinted into the face of Jori, who crouched next to her bed. "What's the matter? Who let you in here?"

"The guards, of course. They're doing their job beautifully."

She let her shoulders slump as Jori's expression registered. He didn't seem upset. It was as though yesterday hadn't happened. She, on the other hand, was in an acrid mood. Her night was filled with dream attacks and the second meeting with Emeric had not gone as she'd hoped. He had even delicately suggested an "alliance," which could only mean marriage, but not before he asked to see her Beauty. He did it all with pristine manners, making it sound almost as though it were Kiria's idea. Nothing was suggested outright, but rather alluded to as a possibility. She suspected it was so he could have deniability in the morning. She'd left in a fury. "Is Haved alive then?" Bard must have checked last night.

"Alive and well."

"Ah!" she breathed. Warmth rushed into her heart and she clasped Jori's outstretched fingers. He rubbed the top of her hand, grinning. She should have stayed up later last night to hear the news from the Watchman. She'd just been so frustrated with Emeric and so afraid that her hope would be dashed again, that Haved would be confirmed dead. But Bard was right. She should have trusted him.

Realization crashed into her. This meant the Charäkhni would stay firm in their decision not to help the Western Kingdom. They had none of their own deaths to avenge. The bitter, horrible irony of it!

Some of Jori's merriment seemed forced as he stood. "You look dreadful."

"I just woke up," she muttered. "Why did you wake me up?"

He held up one finger. "I got up early and hate to be alone."

"Isn't Bard—?"

"Two, Mayor Emeric has invited us to the racetrack."

"This early?"

"After breakfast."

"I'm the Keeper. I decide when breakfast is." But she was awake. Actually, now that she noticed the warm sun streaming in, it was a marvel she had fallen asleep at all. All night, she kept forcing herself to wake up to defend against attacks, but it looked like she'd gotten a few hours of sleep after all. Now, they needed to make progress on gathering their allies.

She took Jori's hand as he helped her to her feet. "I'm glad you're doing better today," she said.

He waggled his head from side to side, a smile tugging at his mouth even though there was something strained about the motion.

She tugged on a robe. "Now get out of here." As another thought came, she touched his arm before he could go. "Tell Royce to have Emeric invite his second-in-command to breakfast with us."

Jori cocked an eyebrow curiously. "Anything for you, love," he said breezily as he exited.

Moments later, she followed. When she reached the dining area with her guards and serving girls, Emeric was already there, as was Jori. Bard was not. The two young men sat on opposite sides of the table, leaving the chair at the head for her. This morning, Emeric had on a deep purple waistcoat and fawn-colored trousers, all immaculate.

Emeric rose from the table when she entered. He inspected her quickly but thoroughly. She frowned a little as she took her seat.

"Good morning, My Keeper," he said. "I trust you slept well."

"Yes. Almost too well, it seems," she replied, adjusting her skirt. "I don't usually sleep so long."

"I'm glad my residence could provide comfort to you." He sat as well, tilting his chair just enough to stretch out his legs as he had the day before. If he had settled his boots on the table, she wouldn't have been particularly surprised.

Despite his politeness, she didn't trust him. His words were too practiced, too perfect. The only time he'd said anything that revealed the man beneath were his suggestion yesterday that she pay him a substantial bribe for helping her.

"Yes, well... I believe I requested that your second-in-command be here too?"

"He'll join us at the racetrack," he said. "I'm sure the Kepron told you what I have in store for you today? If you should wish to go, of course."

"I can stay no longer than a day, and we have important things to discuss," she said.

"We'll make time for it, though," Jori said.

A plate of cured bacon and orange slices was placed before her. Her mind was still spinning with the news that Haved was alive. Wouldn't Charäkhnem want to fight against the people who had *almost* killed her? To back out of the conflict now wasn't good.

She picked up an orange slice with her fingers. "Have you given any more thought to what I said last night?"

Their conversation had circled in diplomatic spirals until she became too tired and frustrated to try for more headway.

"I've considered it," he replied, ordering more coffee for himself.

Kiria noticed a picture in the dining room that she'd overlooked before: an illustration of Cúron, her mother, and Aylmor, each standing with a protective arm over their heirs. Kiria looked a little too cherubic in the painting, with wide brown eyes and brown curls. Her hair had never been curly, and the expression of astonished earnestness was rarely on her face at that age. She'd be more likely to set her jaw when she felt stubborn or grin when she beat the boys. Jori, she realized, wasn't in the picture at all. Atty was there, the picture of young justice, and Kader, who, despite being so much younger, looked almost as tall as she was.

Was this how Emeric saw her? Just a young girl out of her depth, despite being the only Keeper left?

She refocused on him. "*How* have you considered it?"

"Carefully."

A dimple of laughter appeared in Jori's cheek.

Kiria was not laughing. "I hope you came to the conclusion that you misspoke yesterday."

"On what matter?" Emeric's coffee arrived. "Thank you, Drienne. I only want to serve you and your image, My Keeper."

Jori snorted, his amusement turned derisive.

"I don't appreciate being mocked," said the mayor, shooting a dark look at Jori. "In fact, you would do well to humor me." His eyes flicked briefly to Merrick and Lilith who stood guard opposite him. "If I do not overstep my bounds, I would suggest that to both of you. Given the current circumstances, it appears that I have the ability to make an independent choice for the good of Rantoul."

Kiria felt his point building to a terrible conclusion. He didn't need her; she needed him. "We will take back the Kingdom—"

He cut her off. "If you treat your smaller cities well. I have a powerful voice at this table. Perhaps the most powerful."

A cold silence blanketed the table.

Finally, after Emeric attempted a few casual bites at his breakfast and failed, he said, "My Keeper, I'm not suggesting anything extreme, only that you demonstrate your commitment to the Western Kingdom as well. There are some who think you have abandoned us." Kiria recalled the carpenters sent to the poorer half of Rantoul just last year to rebuild houses after the river had flooded. "The Tanyu's announcement has many of us on edge. Since you've come to the forefront of politics, things have been especially... unsteady. I hope you will forgive me for being frank."

"I always value honesty."

"Good. So I—"

"But if you're suggesting I'm the cause of the unrest we've experienced and that I have to make it up to you somehow, you're mistaken. By virtue of my crown, you owe me your loyalty. I'll compensate your soldiers fairly, but I won't give you extra gifts, extra bribes, to fight for me. You are not my Keeper. I am yours. The only question that remains is whether you will keep your position as mayor of Rantoul."

His skin blanched, and his brows dipped angrily. "My Keeper—!"

"Will you fight for me, or take the Tanyu's bribe?" Her blood sang. She wasn't used to making ultimatums. Her way had always been peace, but war demanded a firm hand. If her kingdom didn't rally around her, all would be lost.

Even Jori stopped eating for a moment to watch the two of them. After a too-long pause, Jori broke the silence. "We aren't going to the racetrack today, are we?"

"Only stopping by," she replied, "to meet the new mayor."

Jori had to wake up poor Bard before he got many hours of sleep. They were leaving Rantoul, and he needed to contact several other cornerstone cities in the Western Kingdom to determine their loyalties. The pull of independence and payment was strong. Master Belik had known which strings to tug. How had it been so easy to sow discord among her own people? Belik's version of independence would only be in name. If anything, it freed Brithnem from their part in helping other cities. It didn't free the cities from helping Brithnem.

Kiria took another bath even though she was clean already, knowing she wouldn't see a tub for a while. Freshly clean, with her few belongings packed, courtesy of her serving girls, she waited on the ground floor of the tower, ready to leave.

Her guards, as well as a few from Rantoul, stood in the foyer with her. The new mayor was on his way to see them off. Calix Blackwater was his name. He was short and bearded with a quick smile. Kiria liked him, at least upon first meeting him, though he was initially reluctant to replace Emeric. The younger man was popular in certain circles, he said. Kiria wasn't surprised and didn't care. Calix promised to support them in the war, as they ought to have done at the beginning. That was enough.

Jori tripped down the stairs faster than safety allowed. She feared he might jump on the banister. Outside the palace, it was bad form, but she'd seen him do it dozens of times on the coronation tour. Landing in front of her with a hop, he earned a glare from Royce. "Bard's coming," he said.

"I figured he was."

"When I went to wake him up, he was muttering something about a cat fighting a war game. I admit I waited to see how it would play out." He sighed dramatically. "I'm sorry to report that the story didn't go anywhere interesting. So much wasted potential. You know how I love a good story. Said something about buttons, incoherent sounds... Not sure, really. I've never heard someone talk so much in their sleep." Kiria had heard Bard a couple times herself, and she had to agree.

As though on cue, Bard appeared on the steps, rubbing his eyes but moving sure on his feet.

"You look a vision this morning," Jori said, holding out his hand to Bard, who ignored it.

"Everything sorted?" Bard muttered. Lack of sleep weighed heavily on him. He kept blinking his bloodshot eyes and rubbing them with his frozen hand.

"Yes," Kiria replied, "we're ready to go as soon as we say goodbye to the new mayor."

"New mayor?" Bard perked up at that, then understanding dawned. "He was pretty pushy."

"And insulting," Jori supplied.

Bard cleared his throat. "So, who should I contact today? Where are we going next?"

Kiria wished they could contact Kader, who was braving this ordeal without them, but she had to trust that Bard's word was good—that Firian had taken care of his safety.

"Oh," Bard said, "I heard that Daelon is alive."

Kiria's face split into a smile. "Oh, thank goodness! Is he still in the city? Is Chetana with him?"

Before he could answer, Royce leaned forward and spoke in an undertone. "The mayor of Rantoul has arrived, My Keeper."

She turned to see the man approaching, wearing a more sedate version of Emeric's flashy clothes. His face was fresh and he was beaming. With effort, she wrenched her thoughts from Daelon and onto the task at hand. "Mayor Blackwater," she greeted.

"My Keeper! We're sorry to see you go so soon."

"It's a matter of utmost urgency. It can't wait. You'll bring your troops no later than three weeks." That timeframe sounded so long, so many days of the Tanyu establishing their dominance in the capital, but they couldn't return much sooner than that from Charäkhnem. Despite Haved's being alive, breaking the strongest personal link to the Western Kingdom, Charäkhnem *had* to help them. There were rumors that the Tanyu would come with a second wave of warriors. Her only hope was to overwhelm them with numbers, and the neighboring kingdom would help her do that.

"I'll scour the logistics and inform you of our earliest meeting time," Mayor Blackwater said jovially.

Jori raised a brow.

"Within three weeks," Kiria repeated.

"Of course, My Keeper, and you will be there also?"

"We have a few more crucial stops," she hedged.

"To be honest, My Keeper, you might encounter a similar attitude in other cities as well, if you're going to collect allies."

Her heart felt hard in her chest. "Why do you say that?"

"Emeric is an ambitious man, but not a unique one."

Kiria's mind flashed to her decision not to jail Emeric, but only to depose him. Though clearly ambitious, he didn't strike her as a violent person.

Calix continued. "From my understanding, many Watchmen have received the same story about you. I don't know how much is true." He nodded in a short of apologetic shrug. "And perhaps more will think it kind to offer help in exchange for surety."

"Surety?" she said drily.

"Money. Promises."

She regarded him, trying to parse out the truth in his face. Was he as mercenary as the others he talked about? "You've always been a good member of the Western Kingdom. We will compensate your soldiers fairly, and continue to support you as well. But when my kingdom is in trouble, I expect cooperation."

"And you will get it from us. I just hope you find others as willing as we are. But you're a shrewd leader. I trust you'll get it done. Just don't expect the road to be easy."

She pursed her lips, thinking of the royal portrait in the dining room. "My road has not been easy, Mayor Blackwater." She turned to the rest of her group before facing the mayor again, who was still smiling, whether to appease her or because he was glad of his new appointment, she wasn't sure. She let out a breath, exhaustion seeping into her bones again. There was no time to determine everyone's motives or change everyone's minds. They had a job to do. "Thank you for your hospitality," she said, "but now we must be going."

Minutes later they were on the road again. Jori rode up beside her on his borrowed horse. He got by far the largest horse —an enormous mare with feathered legs—because he offered to ride with Bard, who lay slumped against Jori's back, trying to sleep. She didn't ply him with any more questions about Daelon. Just to know the Amir was alive was a tremendous relief, especially after she'd come to expect only bad news.

"Don't look so glum," Jori said softly, looking down at her from his tall mount. "All politicians are terrible."

"I'm a politician."

"You're a *Keeper*." He scoffed. "If you were a politician, I wouldn't be able to stand the sight of you." A mischievous smile quirked his lips.

"Do you think other cities will help?" The idea that she was alone in this war left her feeling heavy, as though she were dragging a weight, even when she wasn't actively thinking about the coup. It wasn't possible, was it?

"No, probably not."

She frowned. "No?" she demanded.

He flourished a hand. "Men are pigs. Women too if they're politicians. Everyone wants what they can get, and Belik is offering more than we are."

"Besides justice? Loyalty? Avenging the deaths of the Keepers? Probably saving the lives of the Amir?"

Jori's expression darkened. "I don't know what to tell you, love. I've suspected for a long time that it doesn't matter what we do."

She stared at him in disbelief. "Jori Calthwaite, how could you say something like that?"

He shrugged. "The sooner you believe it, the sooner you can try to enjoy the rest of your life."

"Which will be short and violent if we don't get back the throne."

"I wish it were different. I really do." He reached down to pet his mare's neck. His gaze shifted away from her in a way she recognized. This had been the look he had after his father died. He was slipping down into one of his dark moods. "I'd love to see myself with gray hair and grandchildren. I'd be magnificent! But I never really thought I'd get there." With a final pat, he took up the reins with both hands again.

"You will." The voice was Bard's. He straightened uncomfortably in the saddle. "You will. You're the Keeper's heir. You can't throw your life away."

"It's already gone." Now Jori's tone matched his morose attitude. No smile lingered anymore.

"Jori, you need to help your brother, yeah?"

Jori snorted.

"He would have helped you."

That made Jori still, though he didn't respond.

"So, yeah, come on. Don't be a coward when your kingdom needs you."

Kiria could hardly have said it better herself.

"I'm not a coward, but I'm not a fighter either, you leech." Jori's soft retort held no vitriol.

Bard lowered his voice to a whisper. "I know you dream about him."

For a moment, Kiria thought she should leave and not overhear.

Jori's eyes settled on the reins in front of him. "I dream about a lot of things," he muttered automatically, barely audible over the steady clop of the horse's hooves.

"It's chaos," Bard conceded, almost to himself. Rallying again, he continued, "But you're not a coward. You set off fireworks inside—"

"That wasn't me."

"You were inside when someone else set off fireworks. You challenged the fastest foot racer and bet on yourself. You snuck past guards that one night just to get a haircut!"

Kiria raised her eyebrows. Jori had told him that story? Evidently, he'd left out some details. Apparently sensing her look at him, Jori twitched his shoulders in a halfhearted shrug.

"You can do something. Don't pretend you can't," Bard finished. "You're the king of Slug."

That made Jori laugh. Just for a moment, but it was something. He looked behind him to acknowledge Bard's point. "I *am* the king of Slug." The game he'd invented as a child had inevitably burned with the palace. It was the last thing all three of them had done together before everything went to hell.

"No one knows the palace like you do. You've got Atty, yeah? Haved's out there. Kiria's right here." He gestured to her riding beside them. "So don't give up or I'll stop being your Sentry and finally get some sleep." He sighed at the very idea, a sound almost like a groan.

"You can sleep, darling," Jori said softly. The acidic pessimism had left his tone. Thoughtfulness creased his brow as Bard leaned forward again and closed his eyes. Jori needed some space to think, and Kiria was happy to give it.

Bard would stick by her side. She had allies who would die for her—he'd already proven that. A swell of gratitude filled her throat. Now if Jori could let go of despair and take up the responsibility passed down to him, she would feel stronger, ready to take on the Tanyu, ready to face her allies and her enemies.

34

FIRIAN

FIRIAN TOOK a deep breath as he tried out different environments in the Unreal.

This exercise of switching backgrounds normally calmed him, but the tension of knowing what he was about to do boiled inside him, insistent. His Tanyuin allies were almost all inside Brithnem, trapped in the cage with the beast while he was running north. Yet, against Master Belik, they would fight for him anyway.

Around him, a realistic depiction of the palace Main turned into the Torithian beach. Dust and salt mingled in his nose. Squinting up at the sky, he frowned. It was too bright here, with light bouncing off water and sand.

The beach melted away into a blank room with black walls, similar to the one he had created with Kiria once. This time he left out the large black throne. Let the outcome of this fight determine who deserved that.

A bead of sweat trickled down his temple.

Almost sunrise.

The others were set to meet him any minute. Fighting was

the part he understood, the part he could do. But his conversations with Belik and Bard played over and over in his thoughts. Once he had the upper hand... killed Belik, an idea that still felt surreal and somehow wrong, then what?

The Tanyu meeting him today expected Firian to take the throne, not to fight only to give it back to Kiria. Doing so would feel like another betrayal to them. And Kiria had left the immediate area to chase down her own allies and keep her group safe. She couldn't step in immediately and rule in Belik's place. Someone had to do it in the interim.

Why not himself? Power's familiar voice called to him.

Panels of the slick, black room turned over, like scales on a snake, revealing dark purple undersides. The pattern of turning panels took his mind off his uncertainty for a moment. Not long enough.

Breath stuck in his chest. As much as he would enjoy lording over the Western Kingdom—*the Western Kingdom*—would he be able to hand over the crown when it came time? The seductive lure of power had made him do horrible things before.

Kiria was the one who deserved the throne. Bard was right about what he'd said so calmly in the cellar. She wouldn't share with Firian, not after everything he'd done. She was willing to give herself up, to lose her reputation, all for the sake of the Kingdom. She'd worked hard to make it better. But he'd worked hard and sacrificed to rule too.

A crease formed between his brows and the rotating panels stopped, leaving the walls half purple and half a solid, glinting black. They couldn't rule together, but he couldn't see a different solution.

Shaking his head, he dispersed the dark room with a thought. For Belik's crimes, he would pay. He could figure out the rest later.

For a while he would reign in his place, just long enough to restore order. He would cut a deal with Kiria in exchange for executing Belik.

He longed to spend time with her, and all his traveling had pulled his mind again and again in her direction. She needed time to heal from their last interactions, to mourn her dead without his interruption. It's what she would have given him.

He should have seen this coming. How was he so blind to the danger Belik posed? Kiria shouldn't have to mourn anyone. He shouldn't have to track down his Tanyuin Master to kill him. None of this should have happened.

He expelled a hard breath.

What place would suit their mission best? The palace hallway. The carpets, the potted trees, the multi-paned windows... They would remind him what was at stake.

The sun was rising.

Beside the potted *sachion* tree, Vardalt appeared. He was a Master Firian had spent little time with at the Academy, an older Khelê man with a shock of white hair running even through his dark beard. His features lumped together, low on his head, which made the span of his scored brow look uncharacteristically large. Light from the mounted lantern near the tree cast flickering shadows across his face. A glint in his eye was the only indication that he was relieved to see Firian alive.

Firian nodded at him, feeling the familiar cold press of the metal crown against his forehead.

Makai came next, dark and inscrutable, but waiting for Firian's command. Others materialized silently around them. As though bound by clandestine silence, a few wordlessly looked to see who else had chosen to join Firian over Belik. Firian and Tesni had agreed not to give away any names until this moment. Several participants in this overthrow looked pleased to see each other there, comrades on the same side. The hallway, which had always held only Kiria, felt crowded. Firian's chest felt tight, but he couldn't say why.

"Master Belik betrayed me, the Tanyu, and the Western Kingdom—all of us," he said, addressing the miniature army. They reacted with fury and disgust at the mention of his name, brows lowering, grunts of assent. "Today, we'll set it right. I am still the Tanyuin Head." He regarded the room of people he had known, all standing at attention, Masters and Learners alike, primed for the fight. The group numbered about twenty. Not everyone he and Tesni had talked to—Tesni herself was missing —but enough to end Belik's life. "I know you risked yourselves to join me. Thank you."

Makai stepped forward and gripped Firian's forearm in solidarity. Others nodded, grim but purposeful.

"Stay out of sight until I find him. He shouldn't have time to prepare."

"As you would have it, Master Kess," came a few voices. Usually the response sounded rote, but there was a poignancy in the way a few of them spoke the oft-repeated line now. *As you would have it.* It was loyalty, a spoken declaration. Master Vardalt caught his eye before he, like the others, obediently vanished one by one like steam on the air.

Firian cleared his throat. To demand allegiance was one thing, but this was voluntary, and it felt different. No time to consider it.

Though he was tempted to wait until Tesni arrived, enough warriors were here to continue.

Firian flexed his hands open and closed once, and then looked for Belik's mind. It wasn't difficult to find. It felt natural, like an old wound. In the silence of it lurked all the things he'd once told Firian as he grew up, a muted chorus of advice and condemnation and guidance and praise. These words made up Firian's life. What would happen when they were gone?

Firian squared his shoulders. He'd be better off, that's what.

His old Master turned to him with a deliberate, hostile stare.

"We've been through this," Belik said. "I assume you haven't killed any more royals. Are you coming back?"

But Firian didn't answer. He stood, muscles tensed, glaring.

Belik's eyes flashed to Firian's right and left, just past his shoulders. His allies must be arriving one by one.

Firian waited, motionless, as he felt more of them arrive, letting the full weight of Belik's predicament settle on him. But Belik's hostility didn't increase. It didn't turn to fear. If anything, it thawed into disappointment.

"Do you see it?" Firian spat, a Master to a Learner.

One eyebrow rose. "This display? Yes."

Firian's blood ran hot at Belik's attitude. Did he want to die?

"Go." The single word sent Firian's Tanyu hurling themselves forward. Light and dark and weapons and wind rushed past him. His skin zinged with the current of them, all in the Unreal at once. He felt weightless, all-powerful, alive.

Belik disappeared behind the crowd of attacking Tanyu. The air shimmered above him. Holes ripped in the fabric of space almost made Firian look away. There was everything and nothing there. Just like the Unreal itself. The eyes couldn't reconcile it, kept trying to fill it with something reasonable.

From down the hallway came a wave, improbable, huge, crashing toward them. Portraits and plants swept with it, ripped from their positions by the force of the fire water. It filled the space, almost to the ceiling. The grating roar made Firian's heart skip with panic. The wave would drown them all. In the darkness, where there was no air…

Firian shook himself and dismissed the counterattack,

though he saw a couple Tanyu flinch. The hall was back to its original form, all pristine detail, down to the dust motes that floated in the meager light. A company of Tanyu couldn't be shaken so easily.

His warriors kept coming. Firian hadn't seen Belik since the moment of the attack. His form was invisible behind all the Tanyu on Firian's side. Maybe it was invisible altogether.

"Back!" cried Makai in his deep voice. The others obeyed. In the space they created, Makai conjured a thundering flame. It was a good tactic to force Tanyu to show themselves, if they had become small or vaporous for example, or at least to move. But there was no physical sign of Belik.

Firian still sensed him, clear as sunlight. Kaori, a boy he'd known since he arrived at the Academy, looked back at him uncertainly. Should they continue?

Then Belik was back. He leapt from the shadows with a light that made the fire seem dim. It screamed. That was the right word for how bright it was.

Despite some of the other Tanyu being disoriented, the fight ramped up again. Belik against all the others. Glass flew, bodies stretched and bent, weapons sought to crush, slice, stomp, burn. The Tanyu were in a frenzy.

When the attack continued, Firian's muscles tightened. What was taking so long? He would have attacked with them if not for the fact that the Tanyu needed Firian alive to take the throne, for however short a time. His hands trembled with the desire to rush forward. No matter his tricks, Belik couldn't overcome twenty Tanyu at once... could he?

New Defender Kaori fell back, bleeding and then blinking out of existence. There was something oddly final about his movements. Kaori, who always talked too much at meals. Was he...? Minet, his girlfriend, barely old enough to join them for the campaign, glanced backward at the body and roared, doubling in ferocity. Then she fell too.

Defender Fox, Master Vardalt...

Belik was killing them in the Real. In the palace. Firian's body went numb. They'd exposed their identities too soon. Had Belik recognized them all?

"Go! I've got this!" he shouted. "Get out of here! Everyone!"

A few looked at him in confusion. "We're with you," someone insisted. It was the white-haired woman who had attended Firian's first meeting with the Tanyuin Head. She was in her late thirties now, hearty and dangerous-looking. Master Jerica. That was her name.

Firian caught a glimpse of Belik behind her. All their attacks kept going through him like water. He flickered in and out of view, materializing solid to land a blow to one of his attackers. This time the attacker was Jerica. She clutched her chest as blood seeped through her clothes, dripping red down her hand. A good Tanyu, she straightened and tried to shake off the illusion. But then a new stab wound—a phantom knife—sliced through her and she jackknifed back before lying still. Firian thought he heard the echo of a far-off scream.

"Get out!" he yelled again. "All of you!" If there was a chance that Belik didn't know everyone's identities, then they might be able to return to the Real and escape before they were caught.

They all began to disappear, all their tricks and stratagems fading into the air like smoke, leaving just the two of them. Belik and Firian. Alone again.

Belik pursed his lips, apparently concerned about nothing but Firian's lack of foresight.

Firian cursed himself. He should have known. He should have thought things through, but he had been so angry, and the cause had been just, and he'd lusted for victory in these days when he'd had none.

"Firian." Belik said the name gently.

Firian realized suddenly that he didn't want to be the one to do it. He wanted Belik to be gone, but he didn't want to look at his face and snuff out his life. Like Sias. Like Jovan. But now necessity demanded it.

He closed his eyes.

The first hint of fear glinted in Belik's expression as Firian slid into the Second Level. Belik met him there, the only person who could. He appeared in the empty expanse, holding one hand up to halt him.

"We talked about this," he continued. "You won't do it. You had the chance before. It's all right."

Belik spoke as though he sensed Firian's pain and were trying to comfort him. Firian almost yielded to the permission to stop. Steeling himself, he reached deep as he had before, feeling the blood beat in Belik's heart, his veins. He felt the breath held in Belik's lungs. And he pressed. He pressed with all the crushing force he could summon. A whirlwind of darkness swept him up as he directed all his power into Belik, breaking him from the inside. His throat felt dry as a bleached bone, but he kept going. More. More.

But there were no screams for mercy, no panicked curses, nothing but a faster-beating heart. The tree of his life wouldn't split under Firian's tidal wave. It only bent, pausing like a held breath, and then returned to normal.

Exhaling, Firian opened his eyes again. Belik stood before him, panting as though he had just run, as Firian was.

He was alive. How could that be?

Firian had killed over forty people at once with his terrifying ability. Why not Belik, the man who deserved it most?

Belik sighed just enough to be noticeable. At least he had frightened him.

"Proximity," Belik growled, triumphant.

At the word, Firian finally realized his own gory limitation. Belik's nearness to Firian's allies had ruined this attempt and cost several their lives, but that wasn't what he meant. *Proximity.* The killing ability would only work at close range. Firian would have to go back to Brithnem.

35

FIRIAN

W**ITHOUT HIS KILLING ABILITY,** Firian and Belik were evenly matched. Firian's heart charged in his chest as he met Belik's level gaze.

He drew himself up like a diver about to plunge off a cliff, sucking in breaths to fill himself with strength. His hands were fists, his muscles taut.

But the space in front of him was blank. Belik had vanished.

"Belik!" he roared. How could he abandon this fight? Belik was the worst kind of gory criminal, but he was no coward. "Belik!"

Firian ascended to the First Level again. Nothing. His arms shook. All of his allies had disappeared when he told them to, though a few ghostly bodies lay slumped in the palace hallway, slowly fading from view. He felt like he was choking. "Belik!" he tried, but he knew the Master was gone. Even his ears felt hot from the shock and horror and rage. With a yell, he exploded the scene in a commotion of glass and fire.

Reality came back to him. He was jogging, though he hardly knew where he was. He glanced at the position of the sun, the rocks and pine trees around him. Still going north. But still two days away from Brett. Now that wasn't enough time.

The ruse of the Kepron's finger wouldn't buy him any extra days now. He'd tried to kill Belik, and the Master might get his revenge on Brett, who had nothing to do with this conflict. Firian fought for breath, still choked, still moving. His mind whirled.

As soon as he collected himself, he told the Tanyu who had revealed themselves in the Unreal attack to get out if they could, to act penitent if they couldn't, and wait for reinforcements. Tesni appeared with them, frantic to hear news, since she'd been called out at the last moment to stop a skirmish with citizens outside the palace. In that position, she couldn't slip into the Unreal without being noticed. All for the better, since Belik didn't connect her with the attack. At least there was one ally who might be able to help him in the future.

The killing ability didn't work at this range, but he had other options too. There were still Tanyu at the Academy who were loyal to Firian. Sentries too. As soon as he confirmed Brett's safety, he would gather them.

A pull behind his sternum drew him forward as though he were a fish on a hook. He barely slept. More than once he had no idea how he had gotten where he was. Maybe he slept as he walked. He knew his feet were bleeding now, but as long as he hurried, it wouldn't matter.

Plans and fears swirled like a nightmare through his mind as he traveled as fast as he could back to Raewhith. Time wasn't on his side. He would ensure his sister's safety and then go to the Academy to muster whoever he could to march down to Brithnem.

Brett, Academy, Belik. That was all.

Most of the time. All these hours alone made him think

more about Kiria too. Bard confirmed she was alive and heading to Charäkhnem despite that kingdom's reluctance to send troops to help her. She was tenacious, hopeful in the face of hopelessness, as a Keeper should be. Even on his behalf, for a while. He wanted to see her, to talk to her, to comfort her. He wanted her to comfort him.

Their last physical interaction had broken something inside him. He wasn't worthy of her, and that knowledge cut almost as deep as Belik's betrayal. He was just Firian. Not a legend, not capable of swallowing the world. He was a boy with certain skills and certain weaknesses. She had known him far better than he had known her.

The days of travel, despite their speed, slogged on as though time had slowed or he was dragging all his recent history with Brithnem behind him. His thoughts and legs were heavy.

But he wasn't helpless. Others might not see him with a crown, but he could still save his sister—he had to believe it—and then kill Belik. Before, he had hesitated. Before, he had acted rashly. Now, he would be ready. He would think through every strategy the Master might use to protect himself, and he would overcome it. Even as Firian Kess—no kingdom or mythology—he could accomplish that.

He reached Raewhith well after dark, slipping in like a shadow. His town smelled the same as it ever did, like herbs and dusty fruit and faint smoke. Few lanterns lit the pathways, and jogging down the road set his teeth on edge. This place felt too much like the Unreal when someone else had taken control of the environment. Nothing felt solid, yet stores and houses rose up around him, everything in its place.

No one stirred but the night guard. Firian spotted him sitting at the crossroads that led to the watchtower, his bearded head lolling forward. It could have been the slight breeze through the pines, but it sounded like he was snoring.

Firian's house was right over that hill. *No, not my house.* With barely a thought, he bypassed the front door and went instead to the window of his old bedroom. Since his father was a glassmaker, they had some of the best windows in town—the toughest to break into, his father had said. As a boy, Firian had studied those windows, partially because he wanted to know how they worked, and partially because he wanted to break out of them. He never quite managed to figure out how to open them after they'd been locked on the opposite side. His father didn't use the same technique as the palace with its soldered, many-paned windows. Those he could figure out. The memory brought something warm into his chest as he worked.

Peering through the panes, he saw what looked like an empty room, but Brett could have just walked out, or be staying in a different part of the house. In any case, he wasn't sure where she lived if not here.

After examining the glass for a minute longer, he ran back to the garden, hoping the small stash of tools was still there. It was. He pulled out a simple iron bar with a flattened end, fighting back a wince at the memories it stirred, and brought it back outside his old bedroom. He pried off the strips of wood holding the window in place. Once that was done, he could pull the window down from the top, opening like an inverted door. He hopped onto the pane, now horizontal like a high step, and dropped inside.

"Brett," he whispered. The musty room felt unused. "Brett!"

His old dresser still sat against the wall, and his bed with its yellowing blankets. The sight didn't bring memories of fear like he thought it might. Instead, he looked back at his younger self as he would a different person, someone he cared about for a while.

Brett wasn't here. Where was she, then? Had she moved out with her husband, returned from the war?

He exited his room. For a second, he stood before his parents' door, which lay opposite his. Sounds used to come from this room, painful things. He laid his fingers on the door handle, feeling oddly like a child dared to enter a haunted house. Even then, he wouldn't have turned down a dare, though his stomach roiled with nerves. Never once had he opened this door, but now he had no time.

Brett, Academy, Belik.

He turned the handle and stepped inside, not bothering to be quiet. It was a plain room, similar to Firian's childhood bedroom, though a little larger. In the center, his parents' bed was barely big enough for two people, and there was a partially etched windowpane leaning against one wall next to a dark jug sitting on the floor. The room smelled a little like vinegar.

"The devil!" came his father's startled voice as he sat up in bed.

His mother gave a whimpered cry as she woke too.

"Where's Brett?" Firian demanded.

His father squinted into the darkness. Apparently, his eyes hadn't adjusted as Firian's had, because he said, "What? Who are you?"

"Where is Brett? I need to know," Firian repeated. He must have looked menacing as a black shape in the doorframe.

"Who is that?" he demanded again. Did his father not recognize his own son's voice?

Firian's face went hot with angry frustration. "It's Firian."

A momentary pause. "What's wrong? Why are you here? Is something wrong with her?"

His confusion was a good sign, at least. If Brett was dead, it happened recently enough that their parents didn't know. Alive, then. "She's in danger. I need to find her."

"Oh!" said his mother, almost a sob.

His father let out a furious breath as though steeling himself and swung out of bed. "You'd better be gory sure about this."

"I am." Firian's voice was steel. He fought the instinctual urge to step back as his father grabbed his coat from its hook.

"Is it something to do with the capital? Is that what you have her mixed up in?"

That his father knew anything about that was surreal. These were different worlds. Then he scoffed at his own naiveté. Of course they knew—this was world news, and Brett was in danger because of it. He didn't answer his father's questions. "Where is she?" he asked instead.

"I'll take you there," his father growled, lighting a lantern on a hook and taking it with them.

Firian frowned. This was the closest thing to kindness his father had ever shown him. The one thing, maybe, that they had in common was Brett. Neither wanted to see her hurt.

He walked with his father out of the house. They were alone in the night, the breath of the autumn wind whistling around them. The two of them walked abreast, his father refusing to meet his eye openly. Furtive glances shot apprehension into Firian's body. He tensed his hand and realized he was still holding the piece of metal he'd used to pry the window open. Good, he could defend himself if he had to.

Will he hurt me with no one around?

Firian studied his father's profile, scowling and lamplit. In Firian's dreams, he was always enormous, with energy that went far beyond his form, as though he could poison the air around him. His footstep, his voice, were enough to make younger Firian hold his breath. His father was a tyrant, calling down judgment whenever he saw fit, without anyone powerful enough to stop him.

Now, in the darkness, his father looked frail, unworthy of

terror. There was a humanness to him that he hadn't seemed to have before. His voice was just a voice. His body just that of a man aging prematurely because of his unhealthy obsessions.

Neither spoke. Their footsteps—his father's shuffling and Firian's sure and quiet—made the only noises.

All his life, Firian had tried to become the best, and even now as Tanyuin Head, conqueror of cities, his father still treated him as though he were insignificant. There was nothing he could do to earn this man's respect. Why had he been trying at all?

Unbidden rose the image of Kiria's distraught expression when she'd entered that farmhouse, the salty taste of her mouth. All along, she had held the answer that could free him from the self-doubt that had plagued him all his life.

He didn't have to demand admiration from others. He needed to *be worthy*.

The simple truth of it, as he regarded his father's sneering profile in the night blackness, hit him like a revelation.

"There," said his father, pointing to a house as small as his own. "Don't let her get hurt!" An implied threat laced the words, but he was no longer terrifying. He was just a man, a broken part of Firian's broken past.

Firian grunted acknowledgment and sprinted to the house, not looking behind him.

No lights shone in the windows. He would contact the Tanyu after Brett was safely by his side. Who knew if the warrior was waiting here in the shadows? It would be easy enough to blend in, disappear. Firian himself had done it many times.

He pounded on the door. No one rushed to open it. Firian breathed once, twice, ten times, before someone answered. It wasn't a Tanyu in black. It was a shirtless man in his late twenties with a light beard. "Who are you?" he grumbled, leaning on the door jamb and squinting through eyes closed from sleep.

"I'm here to see Brett. Is she here?" Maybe he should have snuck into this house too. He pushed past the man, who tried to stay him with a hand on his chest. The man—Brett's husband, hopefully—was strong. Firian squared himself at him. "I'm Firian Kess. Let me in."

Frowning, the man stiffened but let his hand drop.

"I'm her brother."

"I'm her husband. What are you doing here?" His eyes were fully open now, wary, as though Firian might strike at any moment. Something protective flashed in his intense gaze.

A child started to cry in the dark recesses of the little house.

Gaius. Firian remembered the man's name now. Brett had told him her husband's name once. He had fought in the Torithian War. Where, Firian couldn't remember. Now that the Tanyu were public enemies of the Western Kingdom, how could he not resent the Academy?

"I'm here to save her," Firian said.

From the shadows, Brett appeared in a nightgown, holding her son Sabir, who still sniffled but had stopped crying and was now playing with the frayed end of Brett's braid. "Firian!" Her eyes rounded in fear.

Confusion shot through him. Had she been warned about a Tanyu who might take her life? But then he understood. Brett didn't fear the Tanyu. She feared *him*.

For some reason, Firian had assumed that his reputation had spread all across the world, except in Raewhith. His little town would stay the same, think the same thoughts about him that they had when he was a child. But even they weren't immune to the terror that accompanied the name Firian Kess after both his overthrow of Archer's Point and then the battle at the Academy.

A chasm opened inside him as he looked at his sister's face.

In it he saw horror of his actions. Maybe she even thought the murders in Brithnem were his fault too.

Gaius moved protectively to his wife, moving her slightly behind him.

Cutting off his own roiling thoughts, Firian asked, "Has any other Tanyu stopped by here recently?"

"There was one that would sometimes go to Father's house..."

"No others?"

"No."

Relief crashed into him. Brett was safe. A wave of exhaustion hit him in the darkness, pouncing like an animal. How long had he gone without sleep? He wavered but righted himself. Hopefully none of the others noticed.

Gaius leaned forward. "Why would other Tanyu come here?"

Brett adjusted Sabir on her hip. He was getting big. "Before the end of the war, Firian had one of the Tanyu check up on us sometimes to make sure we were all right," she explained. There was a slight tremor in her normally strong voice.

It wasn't the whole truth, but it was correct. Firian had checked to make sure his father didn't hurt Brett or his mother. The Tanyu he posted in Raewhith hadn't been able to detect any abuse, but Firian was no fool. He knew it still happened out of sight, but at least he wasn't leaving visible bruises and black eyes anymore. Small comfort.

"Are they supposed to check up on *us* now?" Brett asked. Her unspoken questions were loud. *Why are you here? Why... why... why...*

"No." Firian scanned the dark corners of the room behind Gaius. "Light some lanterns."

Brett's husband didn't move.

"Do what he says," she breathed.

He fixed Firian with contemptuous look and exhaled before obeying.

"We heard you were in Brithnem," Brett said carefully. The first light flared in Gaius' hands and washed over her high cheekbones.

At her comment, Gaius cut a dark glance at him. Which lies had they heard?

"Can I talk to you alone?" Firian asked.

No." Brett's husband straightened.

Although Firian appreciated Gaius' protectiveness, it was a nuisance now. He didn't acknowledge the man. He could posture as a soldier all he wanted. Firian and Brett went further back.

Brett searched Firian's face. With her, he could tell the truth —some of it—and learn what she knew. And if they could be by themselves, he would feel less alone. Everyone he trusted had been peeled from him like skin from an onion. He was smaller now, and he needed his sister.

"It's all right," Brett said, reading his look. She passed Sabir to Gaius, who looked completely befuddled at her confidence.

"I can't let you do that," he said.

"You'll be right out here, love," she said, giving him a kiss on the cheek before turning away.

Firian followed her to her bedroom, where she lit a lantern. Square, painted wooden pictures hung from the walls in a geometrical design. The subjects were bright, most with high contrast and tropical patterns. They reminded him of the views in Torith. He hadn't given much thought to how beautiful they were at the time.

The door creaked as Brett closed it partway, stopping it intentionally so it stayed ajar. Crossing her arms protectively across her stomach, she turned and gave him a complicated look. When had they last been alone?

I was eleven. The thought struck him hard. So many years...

"Someone's threatening you," he began.

"A Tanyu? Father doesn't visit—"

"Not him." The mention made him want to spit.

"Why? To get to you?"

A chill spilled down his spine. "Yes."

Brett sat on the edge of the bed. She was barefoot. "Firian," she began carefully, "what happened in Brithnem? The stories I've heard... I don't want to believe them. I defended you at first. But then we learned about Archer's Point. I hope you didn't do that for us, out of some sense of duty. The vandalism doesn't matter..." She trailed off, shivering, pain and the echo of fear etched in her features. Stray hairs stuck out at odd angles from her braid. No longer meeting his eyes, she fiddled with the ends of her hair. "Lord Thraddock. Was that you?" She grimaced at her own lap.

His heart stuck in his throat. Did she already know the answer? Could he keep her from the horrible truth? It didn't matter that someone else's hand had been the one to end the Lord Ruler. They did it on Firian's order. He felt sick.

When he didn't answer, she took a shuddering breath. "What happened in Brithnem?" she asked again.

What happened in Brithnem? He hardly knew how to answer. "What have you heard?" He settled next to her, gently, slowly, with no hint of threat.

"That you killed the Keepers. That the Tanyu have been ruthless, killing anybody who opposes them, not letting anyone leave the city. But then we heard that someone else had been crowned, and that you'd run away with the Second Keeper. It's been madness, all these rumors. Some of them have to be true, but I hate it. Someone the other day asked if you could kill people just by looking at them." She half laughed at the absurdity of it. "That was a friend I'd had for years." Past tense. Her expression grew serious and sad.

"I didn't kill the Keepers."

She met his eyes. Nighttime chats to stave away fears. She dropped her voice. "Weren't you planning to? You were in charge of everyone, and they marched on Brithnem. What happened?" She rolled her eyes upward in a plea. "Everyone thinks you can murder with a thought!" Her words escaped as though she'd held them inside for a long time. "Some people treat us like pariahs."

Sweet Brett, having friends turn on her, because of him? He had no idea how to respond. Finally, he said, "I'll use it to save them, save the capital. I'll kill Belik."

She didn't look impressed. Always, she'd been strong enough not to be ruffled even by the biggest news. Now, she held him like an anchor.

"He went against my orders."

"I don't know what's going on," she admitted helplessly.

"Master Belik is the one who killed the Keepers. He tried to kill Kiria." It felt natural to use her informal name with Brett. "She's still alive." Was he asking Brett for advice? It felt like it, all of a sudden.

"But you came here."

"Belik said he'd kill you if I didn't leave," he confessed. "I had to check. And I'm going to the Academy after this to get ready to face him."

"But aren't the Tanyu fighting with Belik? Is anyone on your side?"

"There are some."

"You're going to kill the new leader?" She said the words as though they were in a foreign language.

"Yes, I will."

Tears glistened in her blue eyes now. "And then what?"

The echo of Belik's words struck a natural frequency inside him that snapped his attention to the question.

Her voice fell until it was barely audible. "You're killing so many people. I don't know you anymore."

Each of the faces of those he killed returned to him. It was no wonder Brett looked at him the way she did when he showed up at her door.

"This is what I was afraid of," she whispered.

She didn't add it, but Firian heard it anyway. *You're worse than Father.* His ribcage felt like bars closing shut. He could hardly breathe. He longed to protest, to justify everything he'd done, all the life he'd taken. *It was to protect you and Mother and Kiria and Bard. It was to secure the safety of the Academy. It was to win a war for Brithnem. It was to free slaves. It was to gain respect.* They all felt like lies, and the faces of the dead felt like truth. He could spend his life making amends and still fall short. He could have the admiration of the whole world and still not be worthy.

Where could he go from here? Was there no way to redeem his future?

Despair threatened to crush him under its black weight. He felt nothing and then... everything. He took a couple hard breaths like forcing water through a hole far too small, and then he collapsed over his knees, shaking violently. Not only did he see the faces of the dead, but Kiria's and Bard's too. He was bound to them and could feel their pain. He *was* their pain. Bard never would have left the Academy and been attacked if not for him. And Kiria...

He choked on a sob, close to vomiting with the need to cry. Everything that had been wound so tightly within him was unraveling, and all the reality he had held at bay with the force of his running and running and running rushed back in. He couldn't stop himself. Tears streamed between his fingers as he held his face in his hands. He couldn't gather enough breath.

He was broken, totally and irreversibly.

Sobs came thick and heavy. He was the Tanyuin Head. And he was crying to the point of being sick, bent in half over his legs next to the sister he had loved and had utterly failed.

He remembered her words when he first entered the Academy. She had been so proud of him.

But he didn't even have breath to apologize.

When the storm inside him abated to an emptiness, he felt her cool hand on the hot skin of his back, motherly. He let himself breathe, feeling that hand on him. Finally, he couldn't excuse himself anymore. He wiped his nose with the back of his hand and sat up. His eyes were hot and stinging when he upturned them to his sister's, the mirror of his own.

No forgiveness shone in her gaze, but the fear was gone and some of the understanding between them had returned.

"What should I do?" he asked, swallowing.

"Besides eat and sleep?" She shook her head. "It's obvious."

"What?"

"If the Second Keeper is still alive, you have to get her back on the throne. You have to find relatives of Lord Cúron and Lord Atael and reestablish the Three Keepers. That's what you have to do." Her tone was like a general's and her eyes flashed. As she returned her hand to her lap, a brief but intense stab of regret passed over her features.

Firian didn't have to tell her that the Keepers could sentence him to death once they were back in power. That, or sentence him to a lifetime of imprisonment. He'd pushed away the implications of his decision to fight for Kiria for as long as he could, but he couldn't deny the truth any longer. He and Brett both knew what the outcome would be. One way or another, if he did what she said, both his life and the Academy as he knew it would end.

Brett twisted her marriage ring, a version of his own nervous tic. Firian stayed very still, his heart aching.

"I know," he finally said, "and I will. No matter what happens, I'll make things right again." Tentatively, he took his sister's hand in his and gave it a gentle squeeze.

This final act for Kiria would be his last chance to do something truly worthy. Maybe, in the end, someone could love him in honor of what he had done, even if it was too late for him to experience it.

36

FIRIAN

BRETT CONVINCED Firian to spend the night before confronting the Tanyu in charge of Raewhith. "You're tired. You need to be in better shape." She used her motherly wiles until he came around to her way of thinking. Gaius didn't seem surprised.

Firian told Gaius to push their bed into a corner without windows, and to stand guard directly beside her, armed with multiple weapons. Brett insisted on holding the baby in her arms in case the danger was as real as Firian thought.

So he slept a few short hours in the front room, planning to wake early to meet the Tanyu who expected him to check in once he arrived.

Even that brief sleep was plagued by dreams. He and Kiria walked together through Charäkhnem. He'd never been there, but it was clear that Kiria wanted to show it to him. It was the kind of thing they might have done when they were together, before there was so much violence and hatred. He created the scenery and she directed him to place a turret there, a road going that way.

She wasn't really there. Dream Kiria was different than real Kiria, like the difference between looking at a person and viewing a painting. She acted like herself in the dream, but all the while he knew he was imagining impossibilities.

Beside him, Kiria smiled at one of his creations, a fruit stall that was a modified version of one he had frequented growing up. Instead of plums and potatoes and carrots, it sold fanciful jeweled grapes and made-up versions of lemons and apples in all shades.

He kept adding detail the longer they stood together. It was never right. They were never right.

Battered coins exchanged hands. The seller had bitten his fingernails to the quick and tiny hairs stood out on his knuckles. Dream Kiria whispered to him, "Almost everyone has dark red hair, not black."

He made the change in an instant. Delight lit up her face at his work. They moved on from the fruit seller, strolling down an empty street that curved out of sight through walled buildings. The air smelled like grilling meat and heavy flowers.

Kiria took his hand. There was something so easy about the gesture for her, as though this version of her had done it a thousand times. That she held his hand didn't surprise him—it was his dream, after all—but his own reaction did. The sense of intimacy grew like a knot in his chest. This was something different, not the heated passion of a kiss, but the comfortable love of a loyal friend. He squeezed her hand gently, the knot hollowing inside him.

They turned a corner into a large courtyard crisscrossed with wooden beams. The pergola cast shadows across the ground and across their faces, obscuring Kiria's expression in darkness. She went stiff as a statue beside him. When he looked up, the light and the warmth became like a bath with his head held underwater. His hand suddenly gripped nothing but air.

Above them hung dozens of bodies, dangling by their necks from the beams. Their arms and legs were bound as though they were encased in monstrous cocoons. They swayed gently in the breeze. Ropes without bodies, like tenantless nooses, hung in the empty spaces.

Firian knew each blank face. These faces had stared at him in dreams before. Sais Jairon, Amir Salaar, Master Jovan, Lord Ruler Thraddock... They were all there, but now there were many, many more. Atty Calthwaite hung closest.

Someone uttered a sharp cry and Firian knifed upward in bed, dread uncoiling in his belly. In the early morning light, Brett's home came into focus. He let out a breath and ran a hand over his face. Just a dream. Not even an attack, just an ordinary nightmare.

Rising, he checked on Brett. She must have finally given into sleep after a long vigil. Gaius and the baby were there too, all sleeping peacefully in each other's arms. Relief turned into an odd kind of longing.

Going to confront the Tanyu in charge of Raewhith would likely mean having to kill again. He didn't want more hanging figures, didn't want to hear another last breath because of him. And what if this were an ambush? It wouldn't surprise him. Belik had sent him all this way to protect Brett. He had to know Firian would protect her, one way or another. Nothing less would have torn him away from Brithnem.

A vengeful part of him, small but sure, was glad he was up to the task of stopping whoever was threatening her. Just because he didn't want to hurt the Tanyu didn't mean he wasn't glad to know that he could. He had the power to use his prowess for good this time, but his gut still twisted with apprehension, not for his physical safety so much as for the magnitude of the task in front of him.

As he left the house, he found a plum and a cup of water on the counter. When had Brett had time to put them there?

Despite his title and his training, despite everything, she still seemed better than he was in so many ways.

She knew the truth before he explained it. He had to fight on Kiria's side, no matter what came of it for himself. Bard had said it too, but Firian had pushed the consequences of that thought out of mind, focusing only on being Brithnem's hero.

He plucked the plum off the counter on his way into the gray morning. The watchtower wasn't far. That would be the Tanyu's primary location, where he would expect Firian to arrive.

Firian had reached forward to sense the Tanyu's presence only once as he raced back to Raewhith. Without his killing ability, he did it mostly for his own sanity. He would confront the man when he arrived and not before, then he'd find out any information the Tanyu had to give on Belik, on Brett, on the Academy.

Tracing the steps he took as a child when he was tested for the Academy, Firian strode to the watchtower. He had no crown, and even his black top had been shredded in the tunnel, so he didn't wear full Tanyuin garb. But he was a Tanyu through and through. This person's leader, whoever it was. The Tanyu's mind hadn't felt familiar.

He met only a few people on their way to fields or workshops. Most eyed him as they passed, but no one challenged him, though someone must have recognized him. Raewhith was small. Everyone knew everyone.

His attention went immediately to the top of the tower when it came in view. That was where he'd taken his first flag. He hadn't planned to, exactly. The Watchman—woman, in that case —had stared and stared at him. He wanted decisive proof of his victory, so that's what he did. He ripped the little flag off the wall in front of her eyes. The hint of green in his office was supposed to remind him of Brett, but it usually reminded him of the rush of taking control. That same adrenaline coursed through his veins now.

In minutes, he passed through the doors. Once inside the watchtower, he sprinted up the stairs on silent feet to find the landing where he had met Master Makai all those years ago.

Firian arrived at the office he remembered so well. Behind the desk sat a formidable Tanyu Firian didn't know well, Master Gallevions, dressed head to toe in black, including the signature long jacket. Gallevions did something high level at the Academy, but he hadn't taught any classes Firian knew about. Belik oversaw him. A mistake in hindsight to give Belik so much unchecked authority. But Firian couldn't have known earlier how big a mistake.

The man had dark hair, gray at the temples, that fell to his broad shoulders. One hand rested on the desk near a shallow dish holding a couple items of jewelry: a ring that looked like a marriage band and a locket wrapped in several links of chain, amid sundry loose beads. The skin on that hand looked much darker than the rest of him, though the fingernails were light. At second glance, Firian saw it was completely covered by Khelê tattoos, even more completely than Atty Calthwaite's hand had been.

Gallevions looked up when Firian entered, as though he'd been expecting him. His face blanched, though, and his heartbeat pulsed visibly in the side of his neck. No other signs of strain. "Master Kess, I was told you might come."

"Gallevions."

The presence of a Sentry was intense, suffocating.

Bastard. He'd put one on himself, probably at Belik's urging, to protect against Firian's killing ability, which finally worked at this close range. Fine. At least he stayed somewhere predictable. Firian didn't want to kill him, but if it came down to Brett or Gallevions, the choice was obvious. One more rope.

"Were you told I would stop you for threatening an innocent woman?" Firian asked, equally composed. He picked up a round bead from the jewelry bowl and rolled it between two fingers. It was blue and ridged and reminded him of Kiria. Brithnem color, lantern shaped.

Surprise registered on the Master's face. "Innocent woman?" he repeated. "I'm keeping peace here."

Firian couldn't help but sense the man was being sincere. But he'd thought that before. "Are you always here, in Raewhith?"

"I'm the peacekeeper, the Tanyuin presence, and I'm the Watchman when the posted guardian can't be here."

"Who's the guardian?"

"Master Gerand. She comes every week or so. I report to her."

So Belik had only told a half-truth. Of course he had. Gallevions didn't plan to harm Brett, but Master Gerand would. She had always taken Belik's side in everything. But with a Sentry on Gallevions now, he couldn't report to her. "How often do you report?"

"Every other day or so."

Firian quirked a brow. "Even with a Sentry?" It was impossible to break through Tanyuin Sentries, as he well knew.

"The Sentry has only been in place for a couple days," Gallevions replied, not truly answering the question.

The barrier had to lift periodically, so he and Gerand could communicate back and forth. That would be when the order might come to harm Brett.

Firian furiously considered his options. Belik often lied, but didn't often make idle threats. Brett could be harmed physically or in dreams. Firian could defend her against both, but if he stayed to defend her from physical attack, that prevented him from going to the Academy and confronting the root of this problem: Master Gerand, who no doubt had plotted with Belik to have Firian killed far from the capital. The Academy would have more manpower than this to use against him, but he had to try. He'd come this far. For Brett, for Kiria. Dreams it was, then. He could monitor Brett's dreams from afar. Which left only the issue of immediate physical harm. Master Gallevions was the most likely to carry out that order, even if he seemed innocent now.

Firian eyed him. He'd seen too much death already, and more was to come. Gallevions was a big man, but Firian could subdue him if he were careful, leave him tied up, away from any means of escape. He'd eventually be found, even if it took a few days.

Protect Brett in dreams and then run to the Academy to retake power from Gerand. It could work.

Then the solution came to him. "Gallevions," he said, "leave everything. We're going to the Academy." Another person didn't need to die today.

37
———

FIRIAN

Returning to the Academy was like returning a ghost to its body, intimately familiar but lifeless. Its dark walls loomed among the pine trees. The needles whispered under Firian's boots like friends. With most of the Tanyu gone, it lay especially quiet.

Strength hummed through his arms. This was the place he had fought and clawed and honed himself into a weapon. Belik may have come up with backup plans or traps, but Firian refused to be caught by surprise.

Two brown-coated men, low to the ground, peered furtively through the trees at him and Master Gallevions following behind. Border patrollers—at least, what was left after most of them marched to Brithnem with the rest of the Tanyu. Firian shouted their names, and they stood, recognition dawning in their faces.

"Master Kess," the one named Soto acknowledged, hurriedly giving an awkward half-bow. His eyes darted to Gallevions. The Sentry, and therefore Gerand, would know that Gallevions had broken rank by coming back, but that was a small issue compared to Firian's return. On the way, Firian explained in a few words that the story Gallevions had been fed was slander. He never betrayed the Tanyu. Belik was the real offender.

The other patroller, Burrell, tried to look as if he weren't surprised to see Firian walking through the woods wearing something other than a Tanyuin uniform. "We didn't know you were here."

"I didn't tell anyone." Firian suddenly missed his crown, which he'd left in the tent outside Brithnem. It was gone for good now, unless he took it back from Belik, who'd inevitably stolen it. "Go back to your duties."

The patrollers were just turning away when he stopped them again. Burrell had new bruises and cuts on his dark face. In his haste, Firian hadn't immediately noticed.

"What happened to your face? Did people come for the tribute?" His inner protectiveness over the Academy reared up again, as natural as a second skin.

"A couple days ago, after the news that most of the Tanyu were down in Brithnem," he explained. "A raiding party. We took care of them."

"Wasn't easy with how few of us are left," Soto added.

The treasure store hidden within the Tanyuin Academy had propelled thieves to search for it even before the Academy's location was public knowledge. Now their riches and secrets were exposed, vulnerable. Firian should have expected this, but the news still stung.

He gave the men a curt nod. Questions about whether any of the money had been transported to make good on Belik's promises died on his tongue. These patrollers wouldn't be the most reliable source of that information. "Good," he said instead.

They nodded back and disappeared into the woods, talking together in undertones.

Firian and Belik had brought most of border patrollers with

them to Brithnem. They provided brute force, like the Torithi-ans. What had he expected to happen at the capital, after all his forces marshalled there? Had he really thought the Keepers would relinquish power bloodlessly?

Now, at least, he could try to make it right.

Firian nodded permission for Gallevions to leave too. On the off chance the Master joined Gerand after hearing the truth of what happened, Firian had made it perfectly clear what would happen if he chose the wrong side.

Alone, Firian approached the main entrance. No need for secrecy. Master Gerand, who currently monitored the Academy, would know soon enough that he had returned.

He paused before the huge double doors, something aching behind his sternum as he looked at the worn wood he'd touched so many times. Setting his jaw, he pushed them open and strode into the fountain courtyard. It was eerily abandoned. Water splashed in the stone basin below the high chandelier.

Before he made a conscious decision, he found himself bounding up the stairs to the room he'd shared with Bard for so many years. He hadn't set foot in it since Bard abandoned him.

No, not abandoned. His mind leaned into the well-worn ruts that claimed Tanyuin superiority above everything, and he had to work to wrench out of them. The Tanyu weren't always right. He wasn't always right.

Silencing his thoughts, he slipped into the room. It smelled faintly of cinnamon and sweat. So, so familiar. Bard hadn't packed his things before going. Good. That meant there were still Tanyuin clothes in the dresser. Firian actually breathed a sigh of relief when he pulled a long-sleeved black shirt from the top drawer. A token fell out of it and clinked onto the floor.

When he bent to pick it up, a small object caught his eye, mostly hidden in the shadows of the dresser. Bard's wooden figure of Corso, the great Tanyuin warrior. Bard had lost it right before Firian killed Sias Jairon and became the new Tanyuin Head. He'd be so glad to have it back. He shoved both the figure and the token in his pocket before shucking off the shirt he'd found in the cellar and replacing it with the Tanyuin one. It fit all right, despite being Bard's. Maybe a little small.

He yanked open another drawer and another. A boot knife, and then... A smile spread over his face. A jacket. Putting it on, he felt like himself again, as refreshed as if he'd slept peacefully all night. He jogged his shoulders, adjusting the coat, feeling its comforting weight. He was home.

His reverie halted abruptly. He wasn't here to stay. He was here to gather whoever was left and take them down to Brithnem to fight for Kiria's throne. After that, there would be no Academy, at least, not as he knew it. Without Belik or Bard or dreams of power and respect, what was left here?

He allowed himself a moment to breathe. So much hadn't changed—the bunk, the courtyard, the patrollers—but everything else had. Everything under the skin had decayed, and Firian felt a tremendous sense of loss. A part of him was dying. Maybe all of him. His life couldn't be long now without identity or purpose. Once he got Kiria back her throne, that was it. If he survived his confrontation with Belik, she'd have to punish him to legitimize her own reign, and probably order the dissolution of the Tanyuin Academy. And could he blame her?

He cleared his throat and sucked in a deep breath. It wasn't time to think about this. He'd never been sentimental. Now would be the worst time to start.

Master Gerand. She would be the next obstacle. She and Belik worked closely together, so she wouldn't freely hand power back over to Firian. He'd have to take it.

THE GUARD AT THE DOOR, Master Shanson, let Firian into the Head's office without question. Either this was a trap, or some still recognized him as the rightful Tanyuin Head. Or they were afraid of him. Hopefully, he wouldn't have to use his killing ability now, but he reached back for it all the same, soothed by the fact it was there at his command.

Master Gerand sat in the chair behind the desk. An extension of Belik's power even here. Firian glared. Gerand's black jacket looked pristine on her shoulders and she had pulled her hair back, as she always did, into a severe knot at the back of her head. With her light skin and thin lips, it was a wonder she was Amir Chetana's sister. Khelê never looked alike. At least their severity seemed about the same.

"Firian," she said as he entered, pretending to look down at some paper or other that lay next to bright remnants of flags. She said it as though she were the schoolmaster and he were a student. Her eyes were unfocused on the desk in front of her. She knew better than to ignore his presence in the room.

He scanned what he could see for weapons. There could be several behind the desk, and she wore one in her boot like he did, if she kept the same habits as a few months ago. He let the stillness he had cultivated so meticulously consume him. He felt his hands, his legs, the air around him, and felt a part of it all, completely in control. His mind raced through scenarios, detached, as though they were strategy simulations.

Command her to gather whoever was able to fight so they could march on Brithnem and retake the capital.

No, she would warn Belik. Maybe she was doing that now.

Expose the evil of Belik's betrayal to win her to his side.

Impossible. Gerand had always been a weapon in Belik's hand, even before Firian had traveled with her on his first trip to Brithnem, when he'd been so eager to prove himself, and didn't realize he was merely a pawn in the Academy's game. Belik's game.

Imprison her and set a Sentry so she couldn't relay information.

Multiple people would have to stand guard and there was always the possibility that she could escape as he had. They shouldn't risk the manpower either.

The truth came into focus like a beam of light narrowed into a point. He had to kill her. He saw no other way.

"I knew you'd be here, sitting at my desk," he said, taking a pen off the desk, nonchalant.

"I've kept the Academy ready for you." The words were careful. Now she watched him openly, wary but unafraid, following the movement of his hands as he flipped the pen around his fingers.

"Not many left here, but thank you."

"What are you doing back?" She cocked her head, just slightly. "I heard you turned your back on the Tanyu, right after giving us the possibility of true greatness, all because of that princess." Now she couldn't keep the sneer from her voice.

That broke down quickly. "Keeper," he growled. She sounded just like him. "And Belik turned his back on me."

They let the silence stretch thin. "I would have killed you for that," she said. The words were quiet and distinct, unapologetic.

"You're speaking to the Tanyuin Head," he said in the same tone.

"Former."

"I'm not dead yet."

She pursed her mouth disapprovingly.

Belik had implied that Firian could live if he stayed out of Brithnem. But that couldn't be true. Firian was too much of a liability. He had to be contained. The point of light tapered into laser focus.

Gerand had always been meant to kill him if—*when*—he returned.

Firian flexed his jaw. Belik had woven nets around him, tighter and tighter—Brett, Kiria, Bard, Gerand... Even Tiev had been used as a pawn against Firian in the beginning.

He let calm sweep over him again. He had to think clearly. Yes, they had him in a trap, but he was a different kind of animal.

"We both know what's coming," Gerand announced, "so at least let's be civilized." She finally emerged from behind the desk and set two chairs opposite each other. She sat in one almost carelessly, except for her rod-straight posture, inviting him to take the other.

He could kill her now, but she was right—this was a better test of strength, a more decisive win. How could she be so confident going against him? Hadn't she seen him kill the Torithian who escaped? Was she planning to team up with Belik against him? For a split second, his heartbeat skittered, but then he set down the pen and sat opposite Master Gerand. This shouldn't take long.

Firian didn't close his eyes as he slipped into the First Level of the Unreal. He recreated the Head's office where they sat, finishing it to the last detail in a breath and overlaying it with what he saw. This was a tricky move. It would be easy to believe in the environment, since he was essentially seeing it with double vision—Real and Unreal. He changed one fastening on the desk.

"Do you see it?" they asked in unison. Firian gave Gerand a poisonous smile. Answer enough.

Right away, he felt sick and saw flesh begin to drip off his bones. After a flash of horror, he fought back the sensation. Firian shook his hand as if slicking off water. Skin flew from his fingers, leaving only bone at the tips. He met her gaze in a challenge. They were just warming up.

He healed his hand with a thought and stood, flashing around the room like a ghost, everywhere and nowhere. Gerand tracked him with her peripheral vision, not deigning to move her head. Belik didn't appear.

Why had he given Gerand this opportunity when he could have simply killed her while she sat in his chair? Always the desire to prove himself. The knowledge spread like heat across his body. Even as Tanyuin Head he hadn't outgrown the compulsion. Well, he was here now, and he'd do what he had come to do.

This was his time to show off. He duplicated himself five times, painstakingly creating unique movements for each. They all eyed Gerand.

He'd never used his copies to fight before, only intimidate and confuse. Might as well try it now.

One of the duplicates rushed toward her, knife in hand.

He fell through her onto the stone ground as though she were a ghost. A second Firian cocked back an arrow aimed at her head. If this also went through her, then she might not believe in the Unreal enough to hurt him, staying one foot in the Real. If that were the case, he'd have to shock her into belief, but then the fight would be over.

The arrow flew.

It embedded itself deep in flesh. But... it wasn't Gerand. Sitting in the chair across from him was Kiria, horribly gored by the arrowhead.

Stifling a cry of horror, he made the apparition disappear. Gerand's presence was only felt now, not seen. Where was she?

The bloody vision of Kiria stuck to his mind as it had stuck to the worst parts of his imagination over the past days, the fear that that might actually happen, and that he would be powerless to stop it.

He had to focus. Shaking his head, he assessed the space again. It had turned dark, not recognizable as the Head's office anymore. Two of his duplicates had disappeared with his concentration, leaving three. The one on the ground now lay sprawled in an explicit embrace with Maya, the girl he'd been seeing earlier that year, the *katah* student from the opposite hall. His stomach turned. Master Gerand would stoop to *this*?

More visions cropped up like memories, dizzying in their speed, none of them flattering. All featured Firian. There he collapsed from exhaustion, there he scowled at Bard, there he bled from a failed Unreal fight against Belik. It was mesmerizing and sickening all at once.

With effort, he banished the parade of images. Like a dust mote in the corner of his vision, he saw movement in the Real.

Just in time. Gerand leaned forward in her seat, fast as a striking snake, and pulled the knife from his boot. It seemed to happen very slowly and very quickly at once. The slight pressure, there then gone, against his ankle sheath. Her lips pulled back over her teeth in a focused snarl. There was an air of not only hatred, but desperation, in the expression, an admission of how much she feared that he would win the fight after all. The blade flashed dully in her hand as she pulled it back.

Automatically, Firian flung himself sideways to the ground, reaching for the Second Level. As it came to him, pulsing with life and breath and blood, other figures came into focus. More knives. Gerand was not alone.

Of course not. Why would she gamble her life on such long odds?

One, two, three more. In the room now. Firian's concentration wavered. Who were they? He had seconds, maybe two, either to kill the newcomers or to identify them and maybe give them the chance to live. Which would probably mean that he would die instead. Kill or be killed.

He propelled himself backward, out of Gerand's reach, giving himself another moment to decide, to think. His only weapons were his body and his mind. And that was enough.

Master Gerand flew forward at him, flanked by three others.

Firian sank down again into the Second Level, swathed in the calm darkness there, so at odds with the regret that already choked him.

Gerand hardly made a sound as she fell dead, burst from the inside.

Breathing hard, he angled up on his knees. As he watched blood dribble from Gerand's mouth, a strange mixture of relief and horror surged through him.

He remembered, as though he'd heard it beneath water, a man's scream. All four of his opponents sprawled across the floor of the Head's office, terrified expressions on their frozen faces.

Master Gerand.

Master Shanson, the only male.

Master Smyth.

Defender Ya'minat.

Firian didn't know any of them well, but the Academy was small, so he recognized them. The women were probably Gerand's students. Weapons littered the ground near their bodies. A growing pool of blood from Smyth's eyes and ears overwhelmed one dagger like a rising tide.

He'd won, but it barely felt like it. The afterimage of himself failing again and again, trying with rabid intensity to be worthy, admired, loved, left a taste of steel in his mouth, as though he were bleeding too. And Kiria. Would he really be too late to help her?

He pried the knife out of Gerand's dead grasp and replaced it in his boot with a shaking hand. The room tilted.

Brett is safe now. The thought should have comforted him more, but he just wanted to curl up on his side and shut out the world. The smell of blood filled the room. He couldn't sleep here. And someone would have heard the scream. Despite his depleted energy, he had to finish what he came to do.

He gripped the desk to haul himself up, eyeing both doors to make sure no one else came in. His vision sparked, blackened. Sucking in slow breaths of the contaminated air, he steadied himself. Behind his closed eyelids, he stumbled and rutted and cried. Kiria bled.

Firian opened his eyes and looked at the lifeless body of Master Gerand. *Katah* Master indeed.

TEN MINUTES LATER, per Firian's order to the man who answered the scream, all remaining Tanyu gathered in the fountain court-yard to hear him speak. It was mostly Learners between twelve and sixteen, though there were a few Defenders and Masters in the crowd.

Firian stood on the second-story balcony, looking down at the small crowd of a few dozen. Gallevions stood tall among them.

Not enough.

He'd bring Sentries too, who weren't present, but he knew Belik would summon Tanyu on mission whom he'd worked with as a Strategy Master. Who knew how many would come to bolster his position in the capital? Belik was always thinking of the next move. Had he thought of this, too?

Firian rested one scarred hand on the low railing. "Tanyu," he began, "Master Belik has betrayed me, betrayed us, and painted the Academy in a hideous light by killing the Keepers. His evil must be stopped. Master Gerand plotted with him, so I killed her." He didn't mean for the statement to come out quite so threatening. A few of the Learners held their breath, all movement stopping.

Here came the part of his short speech that made his mouth dry, almost unwilling to form the words. "I require every able-bodied Tanyu over the age of sixteen to be ready to march in two days." Sooner would be better, but securing enough supplies and food took time. More than two days he wouldn't consider.

There was a stir among the black-clad figures below. Others, like Erron, his former hall master, looked at him steadily.

"The younger ones will stay with families in Tánuil."

An outraged cry from one Learner.

Firian leveled his gaze at him. "Yes, without Masters and Defenders to protect it, the Academy will be open to attack, but this is about more than the fate of this fortress. It's about the fate of the nation, and of who we are as Tanyu." He felt Bard's figure of Corso in his pocket, a talisman. "We must defeat Belik."

The range of expressions revealed that most eagerly agreed with his conclusion, but there were some who glared questions, waiting for the end of his statement to dissent. Belik had fierce ambition on behalf of the Tanyu; others did too. Firian himself would have balked at this announcement just months ago. He would have been a fool to think that all Tanyu would blindly go along with him, now that Tanyuin loyalties were split between himself and Belik.

"Excuse me, Master Kess," said one bold Learner. "Didn't we go to the capital to retaliate against them for attacking us? Isn't that what we're doing?"

The Tanyu next to the boy elbowed him hard.

The crowd went blurry, then focused, then blurry again. Firian gripped the railing. "They've paid for that already," he answered. "Everyone who attacked us has died. No one else has to suffer, but Belik is still ruling like a tyrant."

"Master Kess," said Erron, seriousness etched onto his large features, "may I ask a question?"

Firian inclined his head. Erron had always been fierce in the Unreal, but was ordinarily a silent presence otherwise. He hadn't come to Brithnem the first time because he could do more for the cause through dream warfare, and some Tanyu had to look after the younger ones.

"If we defeat Master Belik, will you also order us against the Second Keeper? Reports say she's still alive." His words were stiff but intentional. Wariness, like defiance, shone in his gaze. Something told Firian that if he were heartless enough to send Tanyu after Kiria, Erron would refuse.

It was a bold question. Inside it was the true one. Who would sit on the throne at the end of this? Were they fighting for the Tanyu or for Kiria? Everyone looked to Firian for his answer.

Pride in Erron's mild defense of Kiria, and apprehension about the other Tanyu's reactions to what he was about to say, roiled inside him. If he said this, then he made his position public, and probably doomed both himself and the Academy.

It's right, though. It's right.

Kiria's voice, Bard's voice, struggled to find purchase inside him. He'd wanted power and respect for so long—all those things that Gerand had showed him trying to get in those horrifying vignettes. Now, he gave more and more of it away.

He cast his eyes to the chandelier and over to the rows of rooms lining the second floor. Who would he be without this place?

Then he thought of her on the throne when he'd pledged his allegiance. She loved the Kingdom in a way he couldn't, saw the good in it despite the way it treated her. She sacrificed for it and labored to make it better and to make herself better for it.

Maybe that's what love was. Not torrid kisses in the dark, at least, not only. Maybe it was this—giving up a part of himself because he knew she was worth it.

"I will not order you against the Second Keeper," he finally answered. "She deserves to rule, so we're winning back the Kingdom for her."

38

KIRIA

OTHER KINGDOM CITIES had mixed reactions to Kiria's call for aid. More of them acted like Emeric than she'd expected. A few responded right away that they'd come, but most of those were small—too small to turn the tide on their own. Their tenuous alliance with Charäkhnem provided the best hope of overwhelming the Tanyu with numbers. Also, the prospect of seeing Haved again energized them all.

On Kiria's other trips to Charäkhnem, she had only heard of the Book of Names. She'd pictured an artifact, a bound book like a copy of the Sacred Scroll, housed in the enormous palace somewhere, but it wasn't an artifact. It was the palace itself.

Haved Ganesha ran her fingers reverently along the polished bronze wall scored with thousands of names in unreadable characters. It was beautiful. From floor to ceiling were listed names upon names, going back for generations. Here and there a name had been blotted out, a deep score covering the foreign letters.

In the center of the room were benches where several people now sat, chanting the names like prayers. They didn't wear a uniform, like the high-collared robes of the Amir. These people seemed to be palace staff, priests, soldiers, and even common citizens. One or two did as Haved did with her guards, touching the letters as they slowly strode the circumference of the space. Doorways on either side led to similar rooms.

Even with Kiria, Jori, Bard, and her coterie of guards, the room didn't feel small. She sensed awe coming from all of them, even Jori, who pointed to one of the scratched-out names. "What did this person do?"

"Unspeakable things," Haved replied, not looking at him.

Jori raised his eyebrows at Kiria.

Haved continued to look at the wall as though searching for something.

"Are you in here?" Kiria asked. "Is your name in the Book?"

"Of course," she answered sharply, as though the question offended her. "The Book of Names is not only for the dead, but for the living. They all live on in memory."

"Except that guy," Jori muttered, pointing to another unintelligible marking.

Bard shot him a warning look. Jori shot him a look back that said he didn't need to chastise him.

"Here." Haved stopped. Kiria's group stopped too and looked where she was pointing. It was a set of new markings, fresh, at least by the sharp edges that hadn't worn away by so many people touching it.

"What does it say?" Kiria asked.

"Atael Calthwaite." She said his name slowly, including every syllable with downcast eyes. The silence grew palpable.

"You added his name," Kiria whispered, running her fingers along the strange letters etched in the bronze. *Atael Calthwaite.*

Jori stared with a hard set to his jaw. Bard blinked a couple times and looked furtively up at Jori with concern written on his face. He moved a little closer to him and Kiria, pretending to get a better view.

"I insisted," Haved continued with a sad calm, "so he will always be remembered."

Kiria swallowed against the lump in her throat. "Thank you."

"Am I on here?" Jori asked, trying for levity.

"No."

He frowned. "Why not?"

Haved looked at him. "The Book of Names is for all the people of Charäkhnem, so they will not be forgotten. We value life, but cannot list every name beyond our kingdom."

"I feel that I'm moderately important," Jori huffed, crossing his arms.

Kiria laid one hand on his forearm. "You are. Atty's on here because of Haved."

Jori relaxed at her touch and nodded, giving up his feeble fight.

As they left the Book of Names, she caught him touching his brother's symbols. They passed through a vaulted doorway into a large corridor with molded trusses.

Haved drew close to Kiria as they walked under the arches of the palace. Her coal-lined eyes held concern. She had bad news.

"What is it?" Kiria asked.

"I wanted to show you the name, so you would know I loved him."

"I know you did."

Haved's eyes became glossy for the first time. What must it have been like for her to wake up next to her new husband's dead body? Kiria didn't want to think about it. The idea made her feel sick. She missed Atty too.

"The king will not help you."

"What?" Kiria stopped walking. "What do you mean?" She hadn't expected the refusal to be so abrupt, now that they had come all this way.

"He will not send soldiers to liberate Brithnem. Now that I

am returned, he will dissolve this alliance completely." Her tone was matter-of-fact, but there was a hint of apology in her gaze.

Kiria felt like someone had punched her. She pictured Charäkhnem settled between the two mountain ranges. Without trade access, the Western Kingdom was essentially cut off from Erad. Without military support from their neighbors, they might not be able to stand against the Tanyu. No one was coming to help her. She was on her own.

How had everything fallen apart so quickly? She couldn't speak.

"Amrit and I have both spoken to our father," Haved continued, smoothing the front of her gold-laced russet gown. "He will not be moved."

"Let me speak to him!" Kiria insisted.

"He will not hear you if he does not hear his heir."

Anger grew like a bubble inside her chest, pressing from inside. "He will hear me," she said with a dangerous edge to her voice.

In her peripheral vision, Jori opened his mouth but wisely closed it again.

"I can get you an audience," Haved said, "but he is like stone. He thinks I was placed in danger, and so he does not feel kindly toward the Western Kingdom." She raised her eyes again. "I have tried."

"And I will try again," Kiria replied. Haved's jaw, square and dark, regal, was set in resolute apology. "We need you to make a decisive victory."

From somewhere nearby, the sound of trickling water echoed through the arches of the palace. "I have done what I can, and I keep trying. For Atty. But he will not be moved," she said again. "The king did not know his kindness." She swallowed and looked away again.

"When can I have an audience?" Kiria asked.

"I will ask him. I have told him about the way Atty treated me, so he allows us to talk"—she gestured to Kiria and those with her—"but I do not know when you may talk to him."

"Tell him I will meet him at sunrise," Kiria said. "He can move any other appointments." A Keeper of Brithnem was not an option, but a necessity, if one demanded a meeting.

Something hardened in Haved's look. Her strength was always beautiful and mysterious. How did she manage to be so collected? "I will tell him so." The princess of Charäkhnem was not one to be denied either. "I will have my servants lead you to your chambers. It is late, and your meeting will be early."

Kiria briefly clasped Haved's hand in thanks before she traced the familiar steps back to her guest room.

Jori waved the Charäkhni servants away once they reached Kiria's chambers. "I know where my room is," he said, barging into Kiria's. He turned to Bard, whose eyes looked shadowed with exhaustion and concern. "You don't need to stay."

"I don't know where to go," Bard replied. He looked at Kiria and bunched his mouth to the side apologetically.

"I'll show you in a minute." Jori and Bard would have to stay in adjoining rooms, if not the same room, because of their arrangement with Bard watching Jori's dreams.

Once the servants had left, Jori turned to Kiria. "Charäkhnem isn't going to help? This is ludicrous!"

"Yes, it is, but I'll have a meeting with the king."

"*Shear Ganesha*," he said, as though explaining something she hadn't thought of. The king was famously immovable on most issues.

Exasperated, she sighed. "Yes."

"No one's helping us."

"No." The weight of it lay heavy on her too. Her list of allies, once so grand, had dwindled to almost nothing. She wasn't desperate enough to call on Firian, but she was close.

"I wasn't surprised before, but this is getting ridiculous," Jori muttered. "We were nothing but good to Haved. She was one of my favorites. And we need them." Jori scrunched up his face, looking first at Bard and then aimlessly around the room as though searching for a solution. "Normally, you know, I wouldn't care," he continued. "But this is Brithnem, the palace!" He waved his arms, looking for words. Exhaling, he let them drop. "Atty."

She nodded.

He scratched his eyebrow. "I hate this, you know."

"I know."

"I hate politics and princes and alliances and laws."

That last one brought a grim smile to her face. "I know."

His jaw jutted thoughtfully. He looked like he was about to speak, but he just stood there, breathing and thinking. He turned to Bard. "Do you think there's a tattoo artist still available tonight?"

39

KIRIA

KIRIA LEFT ALL the guards she could spare for Jori and Bard, who still hadn't emerged from their room when the gray light of dawn began to melt into golden shafts of light. She wasn't sure who was sleeping and who was awake. Keeper tattoos generally took a long time, and Jori started late. Tattoo methods might be different in Char Visil too. That is, if he ever went through with it in the first place.

The thought of Jori getting a painful tattoo almost made her laugh, but she couldn't deny she was proud of him. If he actually did it, that would be a monumental step for him.

The throne room was practically empty when she arrived for her meeting with the king. A guard announced her and opened the golden double doors to admit them. At the end of the gallery stood the tall dais with its large throne. King Ganesha sat robed in dark red, with the golden eagle stole over his shoulders. Amrit and Haved sat at the smaller thrones at the foot of the steps. Had both been required to come, or were they here to support her? She nodded gratefully at Haved.

Just before the steps, she stopped.

"Lady Kiria," said Shear Ganesha from his throne, "you requested an audience." There was a clear note of annoyance in his tone. He used the least formal way to address her that didn't breach protocol. He adjusted the golden stole on his massive shoulders.

"I did. King Ganesha, my capital has been occupied by violent usurpers. The other two Keepers were killed, and I only just escaped with my life."

The king looked unmoved, just as Haved had predicted. He knew this story, but how could he not care?

"This evil action cannot stand. I need your help to restore the three Keepers."

"You have your own kingdom," he replied. "Why do you need mine?"

The muscles in her shoulders tightened. "They do not have the strength, but your kingdom is mighty."

He cut her off. "They refuse to fight for you, so why should I?"

He knew the truth, then, that many of her soldiers wouldn't help. Her face felt clammy. "They are being manipulated by the Tanyu. They need to see the strength that they still have in their Keepers. If you come to support me, they'll follow my leadership again."

The king pursed his mouth as he gazed down at her. Why did he have to sit so high?

"The Keepers," he began slowly, "are the descendants of those who salted our land and killed our people."

Kiria's mouth opened in disbelief. "That was many generations ago." Why was he bringing that up now?

"We do not forget those who have fallen. For us, the past is still here."

"Father." It was Amrit. He twisted in his seat to look up. "That is true, but Lady Kiria is not guilty of those deaths or the broken parts of our land. We have also been friendly with the Western Kingdom."

"Until now," the king finished sternly.

"If I hold no ill will toward the Kingdom, then you should not," Haved replied, eyes flashing. Her will could match her father's.

The king ran one hand down the golden pinion of the stole. "We gave you an opportunity. We even gave you our most precious gift, and you squandered it."

Heat rushed to Kiria's face. "Atty loved Haved," she said, dropping the formality. "He loved her more than life itself. And he was kind. He never would have let anything happen to her. A Tanyu snuck into their room and killed him as he slept. He didn't see it coming, or else he would have stopped it."

"Incompetent guards, it seems to me."

Kiria wanted to scream. "This enemy is well-trained and ruthless, willing to strike in the dark. That's why we need you. We can't take them on our own."

"Listen to her, Father." She had never been so happy Amrit was there. As heir to the throne, his opinion had to hold some sway.

"If your own people will not fight beside you, there is nothing to fight for," said the king. "If your enemies are as dangerous as you say, then you may stay one more night in the palace. No longer. Then you must leave Char Visil and handle your own war."

Kiria felt sick. The black fabric of the mourning cloth felt tight against her wrist. "Atael's name is in the Book of Life," she tried.

"I do not scorn his memory, but that name was a gift for my daughter, and I will not fight for his dissolute brother and an untrained girl."

For a moment, she was speechless. She couldn't feel her

hands. Then words started to rise up inside her like a battle cry. "If you will not fight beside me, then I will fight alone. I would fight if I were the only one left. I am the Keeper of Brithnem, and whether or not they believe in me, I believe in them. I will die to get justice for them, if I have to. I think you know what's right, King Ganesha, and I think you fear losing someone close to you." She glanced at Haved. "I've already lost people close to me. So you can hide behind your insults. I'll show you who we really are." She didn't wait to be dismissed.

The red and gold throne room all but disappeared before her eyes as she stalked back out the doors. Haved was right. Her father would not be moved. He thought so little of Kiria and the Western Kingdom that he would rather cut off their alliance completely than honor the agreement they made such a short time ago.

The morning didn't become bright after all. Blackened clouds covered the whole city like smoke. By the time she reached her room again, the sound of pattering rain was echoing through the walls.

"My Keeper." Vayci rushed up to her when she entered. Kiria took in the room in an instant. Guards were moving purposefully, Candrae looked close to tears. Although nothing had been disarranged, there was a manic feeling in the air. "The Kepron has disappeared."

"What? Jori?" This was not the time for him to run off somewhere. "Have you checked with any tattoo artists?"

The door opened behind her. Bard looked relieved to see her. "Oh, you're back!"

"Yes," Vayci answered. "Master Tanery told them to look there first."

"And he's not there?"

"They didn't find him."

Kiria tugged at an earring. "Have you checked the kitchens?"

Royce appeared in front of her. "Yes, My Keeper, but we're trying to be discreet."

"I was sleeping," Bard said miserably. "I thought he'd be back later and then we could switch."

"So you don't know if he came back to the room."

"I don't think so, but…"

Kiria stopped. Something had seemed off, as though an essential fixture was missing in the throne room besides the king's compassion. Slowly, the pieces came together. The last time, King Ganesha had had a Tanyuin bodyguard standing behind him. Now, the black figure was gone.

Kiria whirled toward Bard. "The bodyguard!"

His black eyes went wide. Despite never having been to Charäkhnem before, he clearly understood.

"Go, check where he is," she told Royce. The guard was out the door immediately.

"He won't be here," Bard said. He was no longer sad, but serious, looking down with darting eyes as he shuffled through options.

"Okay, what do you think happened?" she asked. Bard had been trained as a Tanyu. He might know.

"If he took Jori, he'll take him to Brithnem."

"He won't—?"

"I don't think so. If Belik controls Jori, he has the biggest game piece. Except for you. He's trying to get you all. And you're the biggest threat to him. Jori's just easier to get alone. It must have been convenient to take him instead of you." His ideas made sense, although his words came out piecemeal. "He'll use him as leverage."

Kiria addressed her serving girls. "We're leaving today. Pack our things." The rain pounded against the window. Fitting. Jori always said he liked rain. Was he out there now? Did he get a tattoo marking him as a Keeper? She knew from experience that it hurt for a while afterward. Were they hurting him?

"Do you think the king had anything to do with this?" Viktor asked in an undertone, looking down at her.

Bard jumped in. "He would have no reason to side against you."

"He said he won't fight for us," Kiria said.

"But to actively go against you is something else." Bard was right. "It wouldn't make sense. I think his bodyguard worked alone."

"So, he just heard from Master Belik and ran?"

"Tanyu are loyal. They're always Tanyu first." *They*, not *we*. He paused, but didn't take back his statement.

Her mind spun. "When's the earliest Jori could have been taken?"

"An hour after he last saw you, maybe? He said he was going out, and I thought he would bring a guard. That was stupid, yeah?"

"Not stupid," she stopped him. "He should have. He knows what's at stake."

Bard rubbed the back of his head, sending his already disheveled black hair spiking in new directions. "I thought so. I've been trying to talk to him."

"It's a losing battle, sometimes." She tried to smile.

"He really was going to get that tattoo." Finally, when Jori was accepting his place as a Keeper, this happened. Could the timing have been worse?

The door opened without an announcement. Royce was back. "The Tanyuin bodyguard is gone. The king is furious."

Kiria put her fists on her hips. "How did he not know before? Doesn't his bodyguard follow him everywhere?"

"The man who filled in for him said he had terrible food poisoning, but then he wasn't in his room. No one can find him."

Viktor cursed under his breath, then shot an apologetic look at Kiria. She didn't mind. She wanted to curse too. "We're leaving," she said.

Bard stepped before her, serious. His expression made her pause. His face was set hard, lines around his eyes and between his brows. He thought she was going to argue. "I'm going to tell him what happened," he said, leaving no confusion about the *him* he was referring to. "We need him."

Movement swirled around the two of them—Kiria and Bard—as she considered his words. Firian didn't need to know how vulnerable they were, how much danger Jori faced. Helping Kader was wonderful, but couldn't this opportunity prove too tempting for him? "We don't know where he is," she stalled.

"I do," Bard countered. "He's farther west than we are. He could stop them before they get to the capital."

"No. You said it. He's always a Tanyu first." If only they could count on Firian to come down like a hurricane and deal with this threat... but she'd been down that road before. The very idea sent her heart beating harder.

"He's on your side."

"But he knows an advantage when he sees one," she said, getting angry with Bard now too. "Who can say if he'd give us Jori or not? I can't risk it."

Firian had helped them since the attack, by protecting Kader, by saving Bard... For those things, she was grateful, but Belik was still alive. Couldn't Firian have killed him already? Months of standing up for Firian when he ultimately betrayed her still stung like salt in an open wound. If there was the slightest chance he'd take advantage of Jori's predicament, she wouldn't ask for his help. Firian could continue to help them from afar if he wanted to, but she wouldn't rely on him. She had trusted in his goodness too many times.

Bard spoke his next words carefully. "You don't have a lot of options, you know? And I think he would help you. I know he would."

"I've thought that before." She turned away and started directing Candrae and Vayci as they packed. Tears streamed down Candrae's face. Kiria set a hand on her shoulder. "We'll find him. He'll be fine," she soothed, trying to believe it. That Jori was gone hadn't fully penetrated her thoughts. She couldn't dwell on it, couldn't process it. All she could do was act.

When she turned around again, Bard had disappeared.

40

BARD

WITH JORI, waking up was an adventure. Yesterday, when Bard squinted his eyes open, Jori's head had rested on the edge of the bed like the family dog had done in Enderin. Jori sighed with disappointment and told Bard he was just getting to the good part of the story. At least Jori didn't mind his rambling. Two days before that, a high, rattling roar sounded through Bard's dreams. When he'd finally sat up, Jori was sitting on the floor near the foot of the bed, rolling marbles ("I said the floor was uneven!") It was hilarious and odd. Before that, Bard's hand hit something cold and hard. He recoiled and found it was a porcelain plate with a scone on it. Jori was nowhere to be found. It was a delicious scone.

Despite the unpredictability, Bard was glad to room with someone again, or many people, as it was when they were on the road. When Firian had moved into the Head's office, he'd left Bard alone for the first time in his life. Growing up, he roomed with multiple siblings and eventually just his older brother Jac. At the Academy, he roomed with Firian. Then nothing. It was a bit lonely.

This morning, it had actually been morning when Bard

awoke. Feeble rays of sun filtered sideways through the pouring clouds. That was when he knew something was wrong.

Now, as he reached their room, he pictured where Jori and the Tanyu might be. If he was taken as early as they feared, then they'd never catch up following in a straight line. Not with this many people. Not with the Tanyu's head start.

He shoved their belongings into their trunks. His clawed left hand slowed him down. Most of the time, it didn't bother him too much, but mobility had never returned. He hadn't realized how often he used his left hand until it was useless.

Where they had gotten trunks, he wasn't sure. Why were they so heavy and big? He wouldn't mind leaving everything but a jacket and snacks. He couldn't take on the Tanyu by himself, though. Master Jovan had worked as the bodyguard for King Ganesha for many years. Bard cringed at the memory of their first meeting. Master Jovan, a mountain of a man, had crushed the top of his foot just to make a point. Bard was eleven, and classes had been extra difficult for a week afterward. He limped everywhere. This bodyguard probably wasn't much different.

Firian could do this. Bard's chest felt like coiled wire. Firian would just have to think and he could free Jori, or he could rescue Jori without killing the man. You know, if he could avoid it.

Jori would be in far more danger once he reached Brithnem. Maybe Master Belik would do to him what he had done to Bard. He tried to swallow and couldn't. Instead, he scrubbed his eyes with bloodless fingers before closing them.

"Fir!"

Firian appeared immediately in the blackness, blending in with his Tanyuin uniform. "Hey. How's Kiria? Everything all right?" His gaze was piercing, his stance confident. It was good to know that some things stayed the same.

"Kiria's fine. But Jori... Jori's been taken."

Firian's dark brows lowered. "Taken?"

"We're in Charäkhnem. The bodyguard must have heard from Master Belik. He's gone, Fir, and Jori's gone too."

"To the capital?"

Bard gave a quick nod.

"Gore," Firian breathed. "Where are they now?"

"I don't know. I'm not great at locating people unless, you know, unless there's a *katah* or something." He had been careful not to create a *katah* with Jori, despite focusing on him so intently. It was difficult to do both—focus and not get too involved. After knowing what it felt like to break one off, even a weak one with an evil Torithian, he couldn't take it, not with all their lives hanging in the balance. He'd known for a long time that he had one with Firian, but hadn't said anything. The truth felt embarrassing. Surely Firian had figured it out himself by now. He was reckless and ridiculous and cruel sometimes, but his grasp of the Unreal was the best Bard had ever seen. It was probably the best anyone had ever seen.

"I have a group with me now," Firian said, changing the subject. "Sentries and some of the Defenders we left here. I have the Academy again. Master Gerand was running it for Belik. I took care of that. I'm headed back."

The words spilled out of him. Bard struggled to make sense of it all, to place the ideas into a pattern. "Sentries, that's good. Are you saying you're still at the Academy?"

"Yeah. Leaving today."

"Can you go ahead, help us take care of this?"

His lip curled, just a little. Not a good sign. "The Sentries were eager to go after I told them... I told them what we talked about, that the Keepers are sitting on the thrones at the end of this. Some of the others put up a fight, though. The Academy's divided, but I did what I could. I'm taking most of them with me."

"Nobody you can trust to watch everything, yeah?" Bard supplied.

"I'll look. I'll try to find someone who can lead them down while I go ahead." Exhaustion passed across his eyes for a moment, turning his light skin gray. But only for a moment. Firian could be wrong, but he was always tough. Bard wanted to be that tough, but he felt the opposite now. Hope of rescuing Jori before he reached Master Belik was dwindling. Even if Firian did find someone to lead the reinforcements, could he go fast enough to intercept them? Bard realized he was worrying his lip.

"Bard." Firian's tone was serious.

"Yeah."

"I'm taking everyone, everyone but some of the younger Learners." He looked in Bard's face with an odd expression. Understanding dawned. The Academy would be left completely undefended. Once this was over, there might not be an Academy to come back to. It would be gutted.

Bard's heart twisted, but not for the building. He'd already given that up. For Firian, though, doing this meant giving up who he'd been before. His identity was linked to the Tanyu, to the Academy. No one took more pride in it than he did. To Firian, the Academy was home.

"I think that's good, yeah?" He touched Firian's arm lightly.

"It better be," he said in a low voice. "Are you going after them too?"

"We're leaving now."

"And Kiria's with you."

"She's fine, yeah." He checked himself. She had the same gray expression as Firian these days, trying to stay positive in the face of overwhelming odds against her. "Well, except everyone's turned their backs on her. Charäkhnem won't help us. Even a lot of the Western Kingdom."

Firian's gaze went dark and threatening, as it did before a fight. "No one's backing her?"

"Just a few people. I'm not sure if it'll be enough." He wrung his hands. "Firian, this isn't good."

Firian lowered his shoulders and lifted his chin. At moments like this, it was hard to believe Firian could ever be beaten. This was the Firian who had defended Bard against cruel classmates, who had spent sleepless nights practicing, ignoring Bard's advice to rest.

"She'll win," Firian said. "She has us."

His words were threaded with that old confidence. Bard straightened. It was the kind of comment that would set up Jori for a smart remark. He'd toss his hair and grin and say something like *Can't lose then,* or *One-man army, that's me.* Probably something wittier.

They would save him somehow. At the Academy, Bard had practiced coming up with moves, countermoves, and backup plans, real and imaginary. He'd always had a knack for it, at least in games. Real life was a different matter, but his mind still spun, ideas sluicing through his mind. Two Tanyu and a Keeper could figure this out. They had to.

"Yeah," Bard agreed. "They have us."

41

KIRIA

THOUGH THEY MOVED AS FAST as they could, the trip back to Brithnem seemed interminable. A dream-like slowness coated everything. Days felt like sleepless nights. Kiria's very bones were exhausted by the time they were halfway there. Bard, on the other hand, seemed to have manic energy now that he didn't have to stay awake at night and sleep during the day. His dark eyes filled with fire at any mention of Jori.

Today was another chilly one. It kept raining off and on as they rode, lifting no one's mood. The horses were slogging through mud since the roads had gone soft. They were worn out too.

Kiria sheltered under a canopy quickly constructed by her girls. Viktor helped them to get it attached high enough on the tree. Sighing, she tightened the black strip of fabric around her wrist, absently remembering that her aunt had Original Harmony, the Ability that allowed her not to be hurt by the elements. Well, the rain didn't hurt Kiria either, but this delay made her antsy. Still, they couldn't make the horses go any further without a pause. A stream ran nearby where they could drink and chomp dying grasses.

Bard scampered up close beside her, huddling under the square of fabric. He leaned out from its shelter to shake some of the wetness from his hair. Rainwater still streamed down his face and neck as he turned back to her. "I've heard from the capital," he said in a hurried undertone.

Her eyes went wide. "Is he okay? Did they do something to him? Did they get the Little One?" The questions poured out of her as she thought them. To hesitate was to lose her nerve. Was it possible that Jori had reached the city already? Her limbs went cold with dread.

Bard nodded quickly. "It's... not good." He held up his hands. "He's alive! I mean, but Master Belik is telling the Watchmen of other cities that he has Jori, that he caught him running away from the Kingdom. You know. It's all the things he said about you."

A coward. A traitor. Yes, she knew, and so did everyone else in the Western Kingdom. "Did he reach Brithnem already?" She calculated the time and distance in her head, as she had many times along the journey as she bobbed along on her horse. Only at a steady gallop could he have reached the city walls. Keeping that up in this chilly rain seemed impossible.

"I don't think so," Bard replied. "Right now it's just the announcement that they have him, but I'm pretty sure they'll do something to make you turn yourself in. You're the more important one, yeah?"

"Politically," she admitted.

"Yeah, exactly." Looking down, he rubbed the back of his head with his knuckles. "Kiria, I thought we could stop him from getting all the way there..."

"I hoped so too, but we couldn't have gone any faster." She couldn't keep the bitterness from her voice. She was shattering from the inside. If Belik demanded her life for Jori's, what could she say? As a friend, she would go. She had to. But as a leader, she couldn't leave her people under the control of this monster. Her heart thumped painfully in her chest at the thought. *Please, don't let it come to that...*

"No. Well..." Bard said, tilting his head. "I called someone who could."

A current jolted through her. Hope. "Bard, you called Firian?"

"It's life and death!" he cried. "And I thought he could intercept them. He could still be on his way."

"Here?" Then she realized it was a foolish question.

"To Jori," he said. "Maybe I shouldn't have mentioned it. I don't know if he was able to break away. But I asked him to go to the capital if he could. He was still north of the mountains when I talked to him..."

Her hope deflated. "He couldn't break away? What could be more important than this?" She sighed and slicked wetness from her hair. "I told you not to tell him."

Bard set his mouth in a determined line and stood straighter, puffing out his chest. "I had to do anything we could to save him."

If she didn't recognize the attitude as her own, she would have gotten angrier. "Is he coming in time or not?"

"Between the two of us, we'll save him," he said, evading the question. *Us* meant the groups—Kiria with Bard, and Firian on his own. "I just, um, wanted to tell you, in case he did it. Rescued Jori, I mean. And I've been thinking about what to do, now that... with everything that's happened."

"Tell Firian, apparently." She pursed her mouth. "Have you been telling him everything?" She knew the answer before Bard gave it, and her heart gave a twist. Part of her felt betrayed but another part had a new, irrational, foolish hope.

"Most things," Bard admitted.

She clenched her teeth against the wet cold and her annoyance. *But what if,* said a small voice inside her, *what if Firian can save Jori?* Firian would follow through with whatever plan he had in motion anyway. Why not help them too?

Glancing over at the horses still munching grass and the soldiers refilling their waterskins, she made up her mind. She'd give him five minutes in the Unreal, ask him to help them. Bard was right that it could mean life or death for Jori, and there was nothing she wouldn't do for him, even confront Firian again.

"I've been thinking about how to retake the city," Bard said quietly, bringing her attention back. "It doesn't have to be with Firian. Do you want to see my ideas?"

"Go and get them," she said. "We'll leave soon and I'll have a look."

With a nod, Bard jogged off into the rain. It pattered against the awning like an irregular heartbeat. She'd only have a moment alone, not enough time to contact Firian. *Tonight,* she promised herself. *I'll do it tonight.*

THE NEWS from Brithnem got worse as the clammy day went on. Bard communicated snatches of information as he gathered them—Jori had given up all of Kiria's plans, and therefore any diplomacy was off (as though it had ever existed.)

Kiria didn't believe it. She couldn't. Jori would never give them up, and he had to be getting close to the capital but couldn't have reached it already. Their efforts couldn't have failed yet.

Kiria's party stopped only when the horses and riders began bobbing with exhaustion. Despite their desperation, they had to regroup in the morning.

Alone, she couldn't help remembering how Firian seemed never to get tired, fueled by urgency in whatever he did. That, and many other things, made him a formidable enemy, but it also meant that he might be able to help Jori.

She wrapped a blanket over her nightgown and strode out of her tent into the shelter of nearby trees. On the way out, she waved at Viktor, who waved back. Her mind and body felt fatigue, but anxious energy kept her moving. Moisture dripped off the leaves above and landed, cold, in her hair. Maybe the worry would wear off if she just paced for a while. Maybe she wouldn't keep picturing and hearing all the things the Tanyu were doing with Jori at this minute. Sucking in a breath, she pressed her palms to her eyes until she saw red.

Poised before the Unreal, Kiria tensed. Firian was on the other side.

At first, all was dark—the nothing, rainbow dark of the Unreal. What was she doing here? Was she really going to Firian for help?

Kader, she reminded herself. *Bard. Jori.* All people he had helped or saved or spared after their own connection had been severed in the farmhouse. After creating an intricate deep purple dress to wear, she felt calmer.

He appeared easily, as he always did, details filled in. She scanned him to see how well she'd imitated him earlier during the dream attack. Same broad shoulders, black outfit (though tighter this time), scarred hands, dark hair and brows, bright and questioning expression in his blue eyes. He seemed both disarmed and still dangerous, if only because of his hyper awareness, the life that seemed to pulse at every nerve, making the moment crackle with possibility. Surely, she hadn't mastered the *force* of his presence. It hit her low in her gut.

Whose side are you really on? Always, always, he had his own agenda, but her mind kept inclining toward its old ruts—the insistence that maybe he could be good.

She swallowed the thought.

"I heard Bard contacted you," she began.

"He did." The question burned between them. Why was she here? A tinge of relief edged the words, and she knew that it was because she wasn't furious this time.

"He told you what we're doing? That... Jori's in trouble?"

The blank space around them transformed into tower ruins, the style reminiscent of ancient Haelben, the society that ruled the land long before the Western Kingdom. They stood on a stone platform surrounded by crumbling battlements and, below them, trees. One lantern hung on a ring bolted to a partially standing wall. Its light spilled over the area where they stood, staving off the night darkness. Above them were stars— more than she'd ever seen in a real sky. They crowded together in glowing, swirling clusters like cream in coffee. Haved would love this.

"Yeah, he told me about Jori."

She snapped her head down at the sound of Firian's voice. *That* was why she was here. To save Jori. It was desperately practical, not personal. Every word they spoke, though, prodded at her wound.

Was this setting meant to be romantic? The idea, now that time was so critical, repelled her. *Not now.*

"Have you gotten any closer?" he asked.

"Not close enough," she admitted. "We need... someone faster."

His jaw flexed. "I would, but I can't."

Her heart sank. "Can't?"

"There's snow on the mountains."

"Bard told me."

His eyes glimmered at that, searching. "If you want me to intercept the Tanyu before he reaches Brithnem with Jori, I don't think I can. And I—Did Bard tell you?"

"What?" Apprehension crawled up her spine.

"I'm bringing people down from the Academy."

"Who's left?" she exclaimed before he finished.

"Not many. Some Sentries. But I'm not bringing them for Belik. I'm bringing them for you."

She narrowed her eyes. "Killing Belik would have been helpful for me. Right now, all I want is to see Jori safe." She wanted a bit more after that. Taking back the Kingdom. But hopefully she could do that on her own, without having to rely on someone who'd hurt her so deeply.

She sighed, letting go of a bit of her armor. "I heard you helped Kader, though. That was... thank you." She shook her head. "Why did you leave so quickly? If you're telling the truth, you could have stayed to prove it." *Maybe*, she wanted to add, *Jori never would have been kidnapped.*

"I will prove it. But I had to go. Remember Brett?"

"Your sister."

He nodded, sinking down cross-legged. "Belik said he'd hurt her if I didn't go back to Raewhith. So..." He looked away.

"Is she okay?" Kiria liked Brett the one time they'd met.

Firian raised his eyes again.

She sat across from him on the shadow-dappled ground.

"She was all right when I checked on her. I did... what I could." He tossed hair out of his face, worried lines creasing his brow.

"I'll send a patrol that way to make sure she's not harmed. She doesn't deserve for that to happen." Someone was bound to be close to Raewhith, too far to help in her fight now. There were odd patrols in every Kingdom-controlled city.

Firian smiled, a surprised, genuine, hopeful thing.

Her pulse skittered and she adjusted her sitting position.

"Thank you," he said.

She waved off his gratitude. That gravity between them pulled at her, even as she fought against it.

"You can't reach Jori in time?" she asked. "I thought you could do anything."

His face fell, expression darkening. "No." The syllable was bitter. Firian always overestimated himself, but he couldn't do this thing she asked him to do, she needed him to do.

"You're not bringing your soldiers down for us, are you?" she asked flatly.

"I am. I'll show you."

Familiar words. For a moment, she was torn precisely between thanking him for helping Kader and telling him off for all the times she'd believed in him and he had failed her, preferring selfishness to love.

She had loved him, but he had never loved her. Not truly.

She had to get out of here. Firian couldn't help, and that was that. Her company would move out soon.

The warm night tempted her to stay, but she had to get out, rush to Jori's aid if she possibly could. She, at least, would do all in her power to save him, no matter who reached the city first.

"My soldiers might attack yours if they see them coming," she said, standing up. "I won't stop them. You're planning something, Firian. Surely, you can understand that I can't trust you."

A muscle ticked in his cheek. "I'll show you," he said again, this time more sincerely.

"Show me you can help Jori," she said, mimicking his inflection. "Show me you can stop Belik. Show me you can do the right thing for once!" Unexpected emotion flushed her face with heat and balled her hands into fists. The past few days had been so utterly frustrating.

He stood and a moment of uncertainty passed between them, something awkward during which no one spoke. The brightness of the stars made the black sky look blue.

She'd said what she needed to say. Of course she wanted him

to demonstrate that he'd help her, to swoop in, rescue Jori, and then disappear from their lives, but it was all wishful thinking.

Finally, he said in a quiet, low voice, "Kiria, I—"

But something hit her in a gasp, scrambling her breath and thoughts like a high fall would do. Was she falling off the tower? Collapsing to the ground? Had she been stabbed?

One second, she saw Firian, concern in his eyes.

The next, red behind her lids.

And the next, nothing at all.

42

BARD

"Bard!"

He jumped as Firian's enormous form invaded his dream, sudden as light shining in his eyes.

"Kiria!" Firian said before fading to a picture version of himself.

The jolt had been too sudden. Bard was awake, heartbeat thudding quick and heavy. He pried his eyes open, though there was little to see in the darkness, just sketched outlines of bedroll, pile of clothes, sack with supplies, and the lightened sliver of the tent flap. The smell of stale bread still lingered on his fingers, and heavy drops still splattered on the fabric of his tent. He couldn't have been asleep long.

Kiria. The name returned to him after floating free for a second. He gripped it tightly in his mind, repeating it to himself as he rolled out of bed. *Kiria, Kiria.* Something was wrong.

He pulled on a shirt and stumbled outside in the direction of Kiria's tent. Merrick, standing guard outside his own, asked no questions when he passed.

What could it be? Was Jori...? No, Firian's message would have been different. He would have been more careful. Kiria must be in danger. Maybe a dream attack? But, if Firian knew about it, why wouldn't he defend her himself?

As consciousness pieced itself together inside him, reality came into focus. Fear clung to him as he picked up his pace, jogging now.

Viktor, standing by Kiria's tent opening, gave a confused smile when he saw Bard approach. "What is—?"

"Kiria. Is she all right?" Bard's words came out breathless, frantic. He pushed past the guard with his cold metal armor and peered inside. Invasive move, normally, but he had to know. He had to see for himself that she was all right.

The tent was frustratingly dark. "Kiria!" he called, louder than he'd spoken before. "Kiria, are you here?"

A lump of blankets came into focus and he cast himself toward it, feeling for her shoulder to wake her. His hands went deep into the soft folds and hit nothing solid. Bard's entire body went frigid. He patted down the length of the bed. Nothing.

When he turned, he met Viktor's eyes. "Where is she?" Bard asked. "Did you see her go?"

"The necessary."

"Where?"

"Over there." Now Viktor's tone held more professional seriousness. He followed Bard as he ran into the forest in the direction the guard had pointed.

"Kiria!" Bard hissed.

"Lady Kiria," from Viktor.

Nothing nothing nothing.

Kiria never snuck out for fun like Jori did. She was gone, taken. A noise like a frustrated animal escaped Bard. *Jori, now Kiria? No!*

Royce, his eyes steely with urgency, appeared beside Viktor. "Kiria's gone," Viktor explained, his voice almost lost in the haze of Bard's thoughts.

Desperate, he cast his mind in search of Tanyu. There!

Bard was moving before the conscious decision to run after her. The Tanyuin mind was retreating fast, much faster than Bard could sprint, or the guards could run beside him. He halted, bark spraying up at his sudden stop. Willing enough presence of mind to think, he stood still a moment, panting with terror. His own breathing obscured his ability to hear if there were fleeing hoofbeats, but it only made sense that Kiria would be taken by someone with a swift retreat.

"Horses, horses!" Bard cried as he turned around. Could he ride without tack? Getting the saddle and reins situated would take time, and they had no time. He wouldn't be fast that way, at least.

The mental signature of the Tanyu was just a blip on the edge of Bard's awareness now. He focused on Kiria instead. Maybe she would sense that he was trying to contact her. Maybe she could tell them where she was going.

But they all knew where she was going already. He might even compromise her safety more if she gave information. The Tanyu would be sure to figure out Bard was trying to access Kiria in the Unreal, probably before she did.

Bard found Firian instead, forgotten after the initial shout in his dream. "They have her," he said. No background, not even a body. Just voice. "I tried, but I think by the time we get the horses..."

A roar from Firian that mirrored Bard's own distress.

Jori and Kiria.

With both of them, it was no longer leverage Belik had, but power. The Master could kill them both and be done with it. Were they torturing them now? The memory of Firian's beaten body coming back from additional "training" filled his chest with dread. If that was training, what would Belik do to someone he really wanted to hurt?

Bard grabbed a cold saddle with numb hands. Time had gone hazy.

If Jori and Kiria died, there would be no defense against Belik, besides Firian. They could get revenge, but nothing could put this tragedy right.

His mind spun impotently. Voices rose around him, and fragments of rescue ideas circled like refuse in the waning tide. The kidnapper was too far away by now. They would chase, but they wouldn't find Kiria. Fear, icy-fingered and cruel, gripped Bard's throat. This night meant his friends' deaths and the end of everything Bard had been fighting for. Unless, unless...

The night passed in a delirious frenzy that left Bard shaking and cold and hopeless. By the time he and the soldiers returned to camp, it was well past midnight. Words had become empty of meaning. Something about meeting first thing in the morning. Plans. Trying... something.

Even though exhaustion had him gasping and seeing light bursts in his vision, Bard couldn't sleep for a long time after they returned. What if he had jumped out of bed faster? What if he had taken a horse to begin with? Could he have stopped this attempt to take Kiria? Belik wanted to kill her and Jori, probably even make a spectacle of it so anybody who still had the courage to resist would cower. What if they were both tortured and killed and he never saw either of them again? If he had tried harder, looked after them better, would they have lived?

He pressed his face against the pillow to stifle the sound of his racking sobs.

<hr>

BARD LIFTED himself up on his elbow, yawning and scrubbing his hair with his free hand. His eyes were sore from crying the night before. Sunlight against the walls of his tent seemed to insist that there was hope. His mental protests against that stupid notion sounded grumpy rather than despairing. A tiny improvement. The air smelled like leaves.

Today, he would come up with a plan to rescue them. He wasn't much of a Tanyu, but he was a Tanyu, and he had people on his side. Corso did more with less.

On the ride toward Brithnem, he tried to keep his mind busy. Over and over, he ran through the cities and towns that had agreed to back the Keepers in battle. The list of *no*'s rang louder —Charäkhnem, and even Carradoc, held hostage by a few Tanyuin plants inside the fortress. Belik's promises won over some, and fear of the Tanyu silenced others. Another, smaller group also refused to help. Through his few checkups with Chetana, he learned she had tried to contact some sort of group who hated Tanyu so much that they refused to come on the grounds that they were working with Bard. After that, he didn't ask her for any more updates, afraid she'd blame him for the lack of backup they had.

At Bard's request, Viktor mapped out the city gates and palace layout. Royce described the original guard rotation before the Tanyu attacked. He learned more about the system the Western Kingdom employed for ships coming into the docks... Anything he thought would help in formulating a plan to free Kiria and Jori, assuming Belik held them prisoner for a while before killing them.

That was all before lunch.

By then, the wetness in the yellowing trees had evaporated, but the ground still sank slightly with each step. Bard stared at the little sandwich he'd made with their provisions, wrapping his fingers around it to keep the dried meat from falling out.

Shouting cut through his thoughts. Some of the guards had spotted movement. They leveled their swords at an area of thick trees. "Come out!"

Bard lowered his sandwich and rose to investigate.

From the foliage, a figure emerged with raised hands. A woman. Most of the guards relaxed their weapons.

Bard couldn't believe it. It was too much to take in at one time. Kiria was gone, but Chetana was here. Bard's last glimpse of her in the presence of those warlike women flashed through his mind, but they weren't with her now. He walked forward like someone in a dream. Others looked at her with the same confusion. After everything that had happened, she could have been a Shee nymph here to tell his fortune and he would have been equally surprised.

Then he saw who she brought with her. Bard barreled forward, crashing into Jori, holding him in a fierce hug. The Kepron's hair hung dirty and he smelled sour. His loose shirt and embroidered vest were smudged and torn, with loose threads tickling Bard's nose. He squeezed tighter, and Jori squeezed him back. Neither let go for a long moment.

"You're alive!" Bard managed. "You're back!"

"Of course I am, darling," Jori said into his hair with the same cavalier attitude he ever had. Only the hoarseness of his voice and the slight tremor suggested that anything traumatic had happened.

They let go of each other. Jori looked around at the gathered crowd. "Where's Kiria? If she's sleeping through this, she really should have anticipated—"

"She's missing," Bard said, blinking to clear his vision.

Alarmed, Jori turned back to him. "What?"

"They took her."

"The Keeper is gone?" Chetana asked. Bard had all but forgotten about the Amir. She must have rescued Jori on her own. When things settled down, he would ask them what happened. She began talking urgently with Royce and the other guards.

"When?" Jori demanded.

"Last night."

"Then let's go!"

Several of the servants went back to their duties. One asked if they could get Jori anything. "Nothing but a clean shirt and a bottle of wine, but that can wait," he replied.

"You're going to have to tell me everything that happened," Bard said carefully. Would Chetana be able to rescue Kiria too?

Jori's gaze hooded, but he set his jaw. "I'll need that glass of wine first."

Bard gave him a flat-lipped nod.

"And a snack."

"I can get that for you!"

Jori caught his arm. "Let someone else get it. We need to get Kiria and, until then..." His thought faded, but Bard warmed with the feeling that Jori wanted him beside him. "We've got to get going. Quickly."

Bard nodded swiftly, urgency lighting up his body again. "Yeah. As fast as we can."

"Then"—Jori clapped his hands, looking around imperiously—"let's not stand around." It was a performance, but one Bard was grateful for. There was too thin a layer that separated them from falling apart. Theatrics at least allowed them to put on a mask and carry on with what needed to be done.

Bard called over Candrae. "Food for Jori, please. On the road."

She nodded and disappeared to find some rations.

"Good of you," said Jori, clapping him on the back. He poked his arm. "You'd be proud of me. I got the tattoo." He rolled up one sleeve and lifted up the front of his shirt to show it off. The tattoo covered his chest and scrolled down one arm, the arm where Atty had chosen to have his. A raincloud poured into a goblet covered in a design like the one on Kiria's back.

"Looks good, mate," Bard said. "What does that mean?" Down Jori's arm, all the way to the back of his hand, beautiful script in an old language replaced the traditional swirls and points. *As elithäma kemai.*

"*May it rain hope always.*" He flexed his hand open and closed, watching the old letters move.

"From the Sacred Scroll?"

"My favorite part."

Jori still hadn't pulled his shirt down. "Wait," said Bard, "is that...?"

Jori gave a small, crooked smile. At the base of the goblet were four tiny letters, a throwback to their final night in the palace together: SLUG.

43

BELIK

Of course it was Chetana. Belik dismissed the messenger from the room.

Tanyu could have had both the prince and princess, but now he had only one, all because of Chetana and her terrorist friends in Original Plan. Was he twenty again? This felt too familiar.

At least she'd rescued the boy and not Kiria. The princess would arrive in Brithnem under heavier guard within a day.

Predictably, she'd chased after Jori, and then, like the teenager she was, had wandered off alone. And some people still thought she was fit to rule a kingdom. Well, finally, Belik would show them.

Consolation for the support he'd lost in Master Gerand. They'd been partners for years, allies at least, though they didn't get on personally beyond their shared mission. It smarted to lose the Academy, though. Another thing he'd have to put back together after all this was done.

Jori was useful, impactful, but Kiria was his perfect hand at cards. It would be simple to kill her, but better to use her first, briefly, to tie up his loose ends. If everything went smoothly, the prince and their allies would surrender themselves, and Firian, mustering feeble forces against him, would abandon his little army of Sentries and Learners.

Simple.

He stumped over to the door, where Nedi and Shiro waited on the other side. "Make sure the arena is ready by midday tomorrow, and invite citizens to come see something that concerns them."

Too few people had the acuity and tenacity to chew on a problem for years and, when they discovered the solution, stomach the actions necessary to make it happen. Belik had no such problem.

$$44$$

KIRIA

Kiria woke in darkness. Her head throbbed in time with her nausea. Faint breezes played around her wrists and ankles. She was moving.

Trying to shake the haze from her mind, she fought to remember where she was. Her own caravan wouldn't treat her this way, slung uncomfortably over something that bucked beneath her—a saddle. The horn of it dug into her ribs. A rough, warm body pressed against her other side.

She moved her head slightly and the rough weave of burlap touched her cheek.

They'd taken her.

Her heart thundered and her speedy breathing huffed against a fabric gag, warm and stifling. She could barely suck in enough air through it to feel grounded.

Twisting her wrists in their restraints, she felt around for anything within reach that she could use to get herself free.

Despair threatened to settle like mud in her stomach. She swallowed down the acid that rose up in her throat. Belik now had her and Jori. That left only Kader, who was still underage. No one could rally around him the way they could rally around her. Even Jori had followers. He'd started to embrace his destiny right before...

Fighting to keep her breathing even, she took stock of the situation. She was taken. Jori was taken. As far as she knew, Kader was still free.

She couldn't let them take her behind the palace walls. Tanyu controlled that entire area. It would get progressively harder to escape the closer they got to the capital.

She hadn't moved enough to alert the rider that she had regained consciousness. Her breathing had changed, and she had stretched her fingers, but those were small clues, difficult to notice on a cantering horse. She cast her eyes down. Maybe there was an opening to see the ground, get a sense of where she was. Nothing. A string around her neck held the bag in place. No light meant no vision.

Not knowing how long she'd been unconscious proved a new problem. She couldn't calculate how close they were to Brithnem. Would they stop before they reached the city walls? If they did, then she could try to find a way to free her ankles and run.

With consciousness came greater pain. It built quickly as though making up for lost time. Her ribs, pressed against the saddle horn, spiked with agony every time the horse moved. Her legs flopped uselessly to one side, chafing the ties around her ankles. Over everything was a blurriness not due to hurt or exhaustion. Thoughts wouldn't stay in place. They blinked in and out like fireflies. Some kind of drug?

Hopelessness gripped her. There was no reason to keep her alive now. They must only be taking her to be murdered somewhere public. Firian knew she'd been taken, didn't he? She only remembered part of their conversation in the Unreal. Was he close?

But she heard no scuffle, and the horses didn't stop until their hooves beat on the stone streets of Brithnem.

No one took off her mask or restraints when they arrived. Instead, she was hoisted onto someone's broad shoulder and carried roughly into a place that smelled like cool mold. A hint of garbage tinged the clammy air.

She didn't struggle. Without a way to run or fight, all struggle would harm more than help. Iron squealed. Something rough scraped across stone.

When they threw her down, she landed on her bruised ribs and couldn't hold back a cry of pain.

"She's awake," someone said. An accented male voice she didn't recognize. "Let him know."

"Don't you want to see?" a new oily voice suggested. His salacious tone sent frost to her limbs. She lay very still.

"We're supposed to bring her intact," said a woman's voice, high, though commanding.

"I didn't say we'd break her apart," said the oily one querulously. Kiria felt a large hand run from her knee to her ankle, almost as though it were petting an animal.

"Shut up," snapped the first male voice.

"You're not curious?" the oily one insisted. "You don't want to see the famed Beauty?"

A moment of hesitation. "Show us, then."

The woman huffed. "I can't leave you alone with—"

"Go tell Master Nedi we've got her," sneered the oily one. "Don't worry. We just want a look. She'll be here for you."

After a snip by the back of her neck, a flash of indistinct light and cool air washed onto her face. She blinked a few times before her eyes focused. A hand rolled her roughly to face upward, her arms twisted awkwardly beneath her. Three people stood over her, dusty from their ride. Around them, she didn't see the main dungeon of the palace, but the little used rooms—

more exhibitions now than actual prison cells—beneath the arena.

Her throat felt dry as chalk as she took in the three looming above her, two men and a woman. The woman wore black and she stood with the knife-sharp gracefulness of a Tanyu. Her bobbed hair was sleek and black and her coloring looked as if she might be from Bosha in the Eradi Desert. The men's heads were shaved. Both of them. Torithian. Somehow this made her anger and panic worse.

The taller man's lip curled. "That's it?" It was the first man, with the accent.

"Maybe it's hard to tell with all her clothes on," said the oily man, stooping down to run his fingers over her.

She screeched into the gag, rolling away from him. But he could move and she couldn't. She squeezed her eyes closed and felt something warm slide down her temple. Was she crying? All her thoughts followed those fingers, tracing their path, flinching away from them, expecting them to rip her nightdress open.

"That's enough," said the woman.

Kiria kept her eyes shut. When the searching hands disappeared, she lifted her chin. It was such a tiny gesture that she was probably the only one to notice. That was all right. The defiance felt almost mechanical, but she needed the reminder. They would not break her. She would escape and free Jori and take back the Kingdom. Or, if she could not, she would fight until the end. She would die with ferocity and dignity.

Squeal and scrape and silence. Something dripped far away.

Even during the attack on the palace, and after her father was killed, and she watched the Torithians go down as Firian defended her, death was a concept, a thing far away. Now it was a monster in this old cell with her, threatening to choke out her breathing and turn her existence into a fading memory.

She struggled to her knees. Was there anything sharp in here to break her bonds? All the old stone, more sandy than gray, looked smooth, and the iron bars had no sharp angles.

Soft bootsteps sounded down the hall. When the owner of the boots appeared, he was far larger than his quiet approach suggested. He was one of the tallest men Kiria had ever seen, although maybe being on her knees had something to do with that assessment. He had pale skin, a large nose, and large hands. He wore all black.

The sight of the Tanyuin clothes made her heart constrict. Something about it was insulting, wrong, as though the world were askew. During the attack on the palace, she had seen no attackers. Here was one standing in front of her, in league with Torithians. She glared.

After entering the cell, the Tanyu angled his head down to her, his small eyes squinting. Without ceremony, he stood her on her feet. She could have weighed as much as a cat. She barely kept her balance. Lightheadedness and her bound legs acted against her.

He pulled the gag over the back of her head and out of her mouth. Her hair mussed crazily, loose ends tickling her cheek. Part of her wanted to spit at the man, but she had to weigh her options before doing something drastic. Besides, between the gag and lack of water, she had no saliva.

"Kiria Arioc," he began in a voice like gravel. It was one of the lowest she'd ever heard. "That is your name." It was a question, though he didn't phrase it that way.

She didn't currently look like the image on new-minted coins or the wooden figures of her sold in Grand Market Square. Standing as straight as she could with her head swimming as it was, she lifted her head and glared levelly at him.

His hand shot under her jaw, rough and squeezing, catching her breathless in its speed. "Answer me." The scariest thing might have been his lack of anger. This man gave no clue about what he was going to do. Could he kill her so dispassionately?

"I am," she managed, wrenching her chin away.

"You are going to die, Kiria Arioc."

The words bounced off her awareness. She could not let them in. She would not.

"But you can still save your followers, few as they are, if you give us the location of the Kepron."

Which one? Did they know Kader was alive, and only needed him to eliminate all Three Lines? Or did they mean Jori? Impossible hope welled in her. Had Jori saved himself? Had Firian saved him? Every scenario that spun through her mind seemed too improbable to contemplate.

"We don't need you in order to find him, but you can reduce his suffering if you help."

She jolted away from her brief spark of hope back to the cold eyes of the Tanyu. She stayed silent, tasting rebellion on her tongue. She was the best hope the Kingdom had of restoring the Keepers. The thought should have bolstered her, but it made her feel so, so inadequate.

"Where is the Kepron?" The huge Tanyu kept still, but a simmering violence radiated from him.

Shaking, she kept silent.

The Tanyu's enormous hand sped forward again with the deadliness of a snake and caught her around the throat. Her head crashed against the cell wall. Her feet couldn't keep up and they buckled under her. For one panicky moment, the Tanyu held her entire weight by her neck. As she struggled to get her legs under her, he said in the same low, even tone, loud in the silence, "I told you to answer my questions."

Surely her nightdress was trembling with the speed of her frantic heartbeat. "I won't." Her voice came out choked and raw.

Red pain exploded in her left eye socket. The back of her head cracked against the wall again with such force that her hair must have become matted with blood. The Tanyu retracted his fist. "You will when we're done with you."

45

FIRIAN

Firian's boot sank into half-frozen mud. At least snow wasn't blocking his visibility as it had a few days before. He, along with his ragtag group of Tanyu, Sentries, and border patrollers, had finally reached the southern foothills. Almost due south was Brithnem, where Belik had Kiria.

Maybe he should have left everyone and run to help her. Even so, he wouldn't have been able to get there in time. It would take a few days with or without the emptied Academy trailing behind him.

Her eyes. God, her eyes as she looked at him. She thought he could do anything. He'd started to lose that belief in himself.

Would that Kingdom patrol still protect Brett just in case something happened to him? Doubtful that Kiria could have communicated that order so quickly. No, she'd been taken while they spoke together in the Unreal. But she'd cared enough about his family to offer it.

Firian stopped dead, his breath stuck in his throat. He could feel the tendons in his neck and the veins in his fingers. Panic. That could only mean...

He lunged into the Unreal.

When he spotted Kiria, she stood Beautiful, high in a balcony of the arena with her arms bound behind her, wearing nothing but a thin nightdress pasted to her body with sweat. A purple bruise blossomed over her left eye. She held her chin up, but her mouth trembled and her eyes were wide.

A small crowd had gathered below on the sand. The shadow of the great statues fell over the people, but the sun beat down on Belik and Kiria. They stood out like a glare on water. It was hard to look at them, but impossible to look at anything else.

Belik stood before her, saying something about giving her what she deserved as a coward and enemy of the capital. Then Firian saw Belik's knife. Was he really going to kill her?

"In exchange for her life," Belik said, not loudly but clearly enough to be heard as his voice bounced off the arena walls, "I will accept the surrender of Jorrim Calthwaite. In exchange for her pain, I demand that Master Kess abandon his small resistance."

This show was some twisted test of loyalty? What did Belik think would happen? That Firian would give up the fight?

His breath came choppy. He was too far away. He couldn't get there to help her. He was too far away. *No, no, no!*

Belik spoke louder, but Firian didn't hear his words. Instead, his gaze was locked on Kiria's panicked one. She knew the same thing he did. Whether or not Jori surrendered or Firian disbanded the dregs of the Academy, Belik would kill her.

He felt sick.

Belik held the knife idly against her face. Her chest rose and fell frantically and tears started spilling down her face as he pressed the blade into her lip.

"Kiria!" Firian called.

She looked at him. He changed the background to Shifra, something that might be comforting to her. In a flash, she stood in front of him on the wooden planking, holding his hands so tightly that the knuckles grated together. Her eyes pressed shut and her breath hissed through gritted teeth. "I can't do this," she managed.

He squeezed her hands back. "You can. Be brave."

Tears coursed down both sides of her face. He wanted to hold her, to comfort her, but he didn't come closer. With her Beauty and the clinging nightgown, any move toward her could be seen as an unwanted advance. "I can't," she repeated, her voice hitching as she braced herself.

In the distance, screams echoed over the water. Her screams. His stomach twisted into a ball. "You can push pain into the Unreal. It helps. You just have to believe it completely."

She grimaced again.

"Believe it," he ordered.

She was crying. "Help me. Distract me."

He watched her helplessly as she tried to do what he asked. He could run his hands up and touch her through the clinging nightdress, and then her body would be underneath his as they clung together, the only sound in the darkness their own ragged breathing.

But that wasn't what she meant. Not now, not with him. He dismissed the fantasy with a desperate curse, holding more firmly to her hands.

"Look!" he said, shifting the setting to Brithnem. Brithnem before any of this had happened. The city glittered below them in the sunlight, as they watched the city from an imagined height. Happy people walked the streets, new statues bloomed at the crossroads... He even put some of the people she'd lost far below. The palace was intact, flags flying in the ocean breeze. "Look!"

She opened her eyes. Blood dribbled from the corner of her mouth. It disappeared at his will.

"Be brave," he said again.

Her eyes devoured the sight. He held her hands tightly. Was this all he could do? He'd never felt so useless.

"See, there's a statue of you." He let go with one hand to point.

She laughed, but it was like a sob. She was trembling all over. Maybe she didn't want him comforting her, but no one else could do it. Maybe she still blamed him for everything. It didn't matter. Anything that helped her get through this torture was welcome for now.

He couldn't swallow the lump in his throat as she ground her teeth together again and squeezed her eyes shut. Blood appeared on her chin, painting a streak of red across her light skin.

If she died here, with him...

He couldn't think about it. Again, the blood disappeared, but her grimace remained fixed. She was trembling. *Gore.* She opened her amber eyes. With one hand, he cupped her face and smoothed away the new tears with his thumb. He couldn't help it. "Be brave. You can't give up now."

"I don't think I can." Her broken voice rose barely above a whisper. She had nothing left.

"Sometimes courage just means lasting. You can do it." He shook her hands, trying to bring her back to him. Her mind was clearly on whatever was happening in the arena. He refused to look. Rage and sadness already threatened to consume him. He was the only one standing on Kiria's side, helping her through the pain.

She looked into his face with gleaming eyes. "I can last. I can do it," she said, like a mantra. "Just stay with me."

46

KIRIA

When it was over, two Tanyu—the big one who had interrogated her and the woman with slim green eyes and black hair—threw Kiria back in her cell under the arena. She collapsed, shuddering violently. Blood pooled under her face. Revulsion paralyzed her. She ached to know the extent of her wounds, but couldn't bear the thought of touching her face. Belik had carved deep into her lips and chin, saying something about taking away her Beauty. It was all a trap for Jori and Firian.

She had to get up. Her mouth was filling with blood. She had to get her face above her heart. A strange breath of air touched her teeth in new ways, outside to inside. Crawling to the corner, she propped herself against the wall and spit. The trembling hadn't stopped. She felt cold and sick and afraid and alone. But she was alive. Barely.

Blinking a few times to clear her mind, she made fists as tight as she could, driving her nails into her palms to distract herself from the pain in her head. *Bind it. I have to bind it.* The black scrap of mourning fabric still wound around her wrist, but it would not be long enough to tie around her head. There wasn't much extra material in her nightdress, but it did go to her knees, so there was room to rip off the bottom without compromising what little modesty she had left.

Images of the arena assaulted her like a physical thing. She had been with Firian in the Unreal, but she had been in the arena too. Despite her best efforts to remain stoic, she writhed and screamed under the torture of having her face ripped open. For a split second, she had considered that it might not be so bad to die.

Sometimes courage just means lasting.

No one watching in the arena or hearing about her situation from afar could help her. Firian was her only choice, and she had clung to him like a drowning woman in rough waters clings to a floating board. And she had outlasted the storm. This storm, at least. But she wouldn't last much longer at the rate she was bleeding.

She spit again and tried to get her eyes to focus. It took her five tries before the delicate red-stained fabric finally gave when she tried to rip it. Her strength was all but gone. The dress tore unevenly but she was past caring. Sweat coated her skin, slicking the silk. Everything took so long, but a tiny part of her was grateful to focus on the repetitive movements of trying and failing to get the fabric to stay.

In the forest, she had known this method would help the wound on Firian's back. Would it work the same way on her face? At least it would stall the blood, and it was all she knew to do.

Besides observation, of course. She scrutinized each face that came in range. According to Bard, Firian had gathered some of the Tanyu against Belik, and when Kiria's forces took back the city, she wanted to be able to distinguish any good Tanyu from the bad.

With her face bound, she allowed herself to lean back—not too far, or else her mouth would fill with blood again. Her shuddering had begun to subside, leaving occasional violent jerks in its place. She was too tired to strategize, to do anything beyond surviving. But sometimes that was courage too.

47

BARD

Kiria, tortured in the arena? It was unthinkable. Bard winced as Firian left, the news still sending shocks through him. Firian, who hadn't seemed to notice he had blood on his fingertips, said he had left her sleeping fitfully in her cell. She was alive, but oh! who should be put through that?

Determination flamed through Bard's veins. He squinted through the thick shafts of sunset light at the others. Royce could help, rallying the other guards. He knew the inner workings of the palace and the walls—Bard hadn't stopped asking him questions about it. Jori would join the cause of saving her, but his talents didn't lie in anything that seemed immediately helpful. His status as a Calthwaite was something, as well as his knowledge of the passages that the guards didn't watch over. He had a little working understanding of the seedier parts of town as well, if that came up. So there were a few things. Chetana was valuable asset, although her full set of skills was still a mystery even after hearing the story about Jori's rescue. The serving girls would do all they could, but they weren't fighters.

They might meet allies nearer to the walls. Would those armies be decimated already? A lump formed in the back of his throat. As soon as Kiria was taken, a sure voice had told him, *Bard, you knew it! You knew that following Jori the most obvious way would lead to trouble.* The voice sounded like his mother, with a tinge of Jac's ridicule. But they were right. He had known it, but had worried so much for Jori's safety and the pressure of time that he'd ignored the warnings in his mind and run forward with the others.

Now Kiria was in the hands of Belik. Tortured, Firian said. He hadn't gone into detail, but he hadn't needed to. Tanyu were marked by their imagination, and in that way, Bard was no different from the others.

Bard pulled his mount alongside Royce, who wore full armor, silver and sleek, with a sheaf of blue fabric across the shoulders. The ends of the fabric barely looked worn from all this riding. Bard, by comparison, felt grimy, his yellow shirt stained with sweat under his arms.

"Royce?"

The older man turned to him.

"Do you already have a plan to save Kiria when we get there? Did Chetana talk to you?" Ever since returning, the Amir avoided Bard when she could. She must have blamed him for ruining the chances of Original Plan helping them any more. But he hadn't known who those women were when he'd gone to check on her. How could he have?

"It's war," Royce replied simply, with a hard expression on his face. "We'll wait for our allies and then we'll strike."

"We can't do that," Bard said quickly.

Beside them, Jori rode abreast, interest and concern written deeply in his dark brows. "Is there news?" he asked.

Bard turned to him. "Kiria..." He stopped, although he should have kept going. The truth, though, was not much better than the horrible guess hanging in the air after his silence.

Jori paled. He looked immediately older, with dry lines forming across his smooth skin.

Bard soldiered onward. "She's alive. She was... tortured in the arena."

Jori's lips fell open in a silent, horrified sob, like a backward gasp. The skin around his eyes grew taut. "She's alive?"

"She's alive."

"Did the Watchman announce it?"

"Not yet. And you know we can't trust the Watchman. Belik will have gotten to him a long time ago."

His expression clouded. "Then how do you know?"

"Firian told me. You know the... connection. He witnessed the whole thing, but he isn't at the city yet either."

Jori clenched his jaw. "You *know* that he's telling you the truth?"

Bard put a hand over his heart. "Yes. Absolutely."

Sadness replaced Jori's hostility and he slumped a little in his saddle. Normally he rode tall and glorious, smiling despite his own pain to lift up other people. Bard was finally starting to see how he could one day be a Keeper too.

Bard turned back to Royce. "We can't start a full-out war until we have Kiria back. She'd be the first casualty. They'd kill her for sure. The people need to have someone they can put their hope in."

"They aren't putting enough hope in her," Jori remarked.

"The leaders aren't. We don't know about the citizens. I think more of them will be on her side, yeah?"

Jori cracked a smile. "Yeah. Hopefully! So how do we get her out?"

"I was hoping you would help me with that." He shifted his attention back to Royce, who rode with an impassive expression. The glittering of his eyes, however, told Bard that he was listening intently. "I'll consult with you too, and Chetana, if she'll meet with me. She has to. This is Kiria. Together we'll make a plan."

"Look at you, the general!" Jori wrapped the reins around one hand, leaving the other free for gesturing. He lifted one eyebrow until it disappeared into his hair. He was teasing, but a serious air permeated the words too. Was it pride?

"I don't have a glass of wine," Bard said.

"Make it a bottle owed."

"Deal."

CANDRAE AND VAYCI split a piece of paper and wrote in tiny, cramped handwriting while Bard and Jori sat at the edge of the bed and conspired. They'd add the ideas to the pages Bard had given Kiria, which they'd found afterward in her tent.

Jori's ideas were endless. Many of them would never work in real life, but he put them forward all the same. He had the imagination of someone who spent his life in the Unreal, except that his ideas weren't for war but for play. The fresh perspective sent Bard's mind spinning through new corridors, as though he just learned that Indisfate players could stack their pieces three high.

A single lantern hung from the center of the tent, casting a dimly glowing haze over everyone inside. They had all ridden until the horses were panting and covered with sweat. Jori had immediately climbed a tree against the soldiers' protests, to confirm that they were in sight of the city. The palace, he reported, wasn't on fire anymore. Bard did his best to usher him inside the shelter of a tent while the guards stood protectively at their posts.

It was late, and Bard was exhausted too, especially knowing that he was back to the duty of monitoring Jori's dreams, but this was too important to put off. He could always chew more of Viktor's dried seeds to keep himself awake. A few cities had vowed their support, but none of them would likely arrive outside the capital walls for several days. They had little help to rely on but themselves.

"Could we release an animal outside her cell to scare away the guards?"

Candrae's eyebrows rose and she scribbled something on her paper. Kiria's serving girls had been desolate but this task directed their efforts to something more helpful. Bard saw grim determination in their eyes.

Bard didn't say that getting a terrifying animal would be more trouble than help. Instead, he nodded. "What else?" Jori's words were like building tools. Some were bricks and hammers and beams, while others were wild decoration or wheels that would never fit on the edifice Bard was trying to build.

"Seduce the guards."

"Yeah, that would take longer than we have," Bard replied, as though considering the suggestion.

Jori gave a roguish smile.

Bard ignored it, looking down as he rearranged the strategy board again in his mind. "What else?"

"Flood the cell. Make them move her. Or we could go to the arena dressed as Tanyu and replace the guards. Do you still have your old clothes?" Jori picked at the front of his loose shirt, where his tattoo was etched underneath.

Bard shook his head quickly. They had been in the palace when it burned. "They'd recognize me. And you."

"I was thinking about Viktor."

"He has a huge tattoo on his face. He wouldn't fit in my clothes anyway. He's too tall."

"Well, he would *fit*..." Jori gave a short, hoarse laugh.

A tiny smile curled Candrae's lips, though she didn't look up.

"All right," said Jori, smoothing his shirt down in a fussy manner, like someone about to address a much bigger audience. "We go in as doctors to check on her."

Bard shot a glance at Vayci, making sure she wrote that one down. She nodded back at him in confirmation once it was done.

"Was that one good?" Jori asked, catching Bard's silent conversation.

"Maybe. Yeah." He scrubbed the back of his head with his knuckles.

Jori hadn't needed a doctor, since he was never tortured. Chetana and Original Plan had waylaid the Charäkhni king's bodyguard when he grew complacent near the city walls. The worst Jori had endured were days and nights of relentless travel, bound and gagged, with his fresh tattoo aching and itching. That, and the fear of inevitable death, which was enough torture for anybody.

Bard suspected that Jori hadn't told him everything, especially about Original Plan, but he had been specific about the conditions of his kidnapping, so Bard didn't pry. All he knew was that the group of women refused to help the Keepers beyond freeing Jori, and Bard had a sinking feeling that their decision to leave was all because of him.

"Or," Jori said grandly, "we could tunnel below."

Candrae started to write. Bard subtly shook his head no.

"What about that thing, that blocking thing you Tanyu can do? Blocking the mind? Would that stupefy the guards? I bet you could do that, dear. You're very good."

Bard blushed at the compliment. "No." He'd never trained as a Sentry, although he knew he could block someone's access to the Unreal if he tried. Being a Sentry was the opposite side of forming a *katah*—the painfully mind-numbing side. "That's not how Sentries work."

Jori snapped. "Sentries! That's the word."

None of Jori's ideas, Bard noticed, involved Firian. Bard could feel Firian getting closer, although he wasn't positive about his location. "Firian's coming, you know. He might be able to help."

Jori bit his tongue lightly, a clear message that he hated the idea. If that weren't enough, his gray eyes stormed at the mention. When Bard waited, Jori sighed and ran his fingers along the bedspread as though checking for dust. "He's on his own side, love. Surely you can see that. I will suggest nothing that has us count on *him*."

"But I could—"

Jori set a firm hand over Bard's useless one. "Not if I can help it."

Bard cleared his throat when Jori let go. It was foolish to ignore such a big player as Firian, but Jori had reason to dislike him. There was still a chaos of ideas that Bard could gather into strategy. "Then what else?"

48

KIRIA

THE SAME THING happened the next day. This time the cut was to her cheek, deep and horrible. Firian appeared again, transforming the Unreal into backgrounds to distract her. He offered her tarts and strawberries, took her to see glassblowers and to meet imagined versions of her past heroes. The statues in the Main became walking people she could talk to, lanterns around the Amiran Academy turned different colors, mirroring the ones along the wooden pathways of Shifra, the grassy plains of Enderin housed improbable animals, stars shone above, water below... And then she was left in her cell again, alone, and cold with the autumn and feverish terror.

Because of the pain, Kiria hadn't slept, though she felt weak from blood loss. Thirsty too. Cool water going down her throat —she fantasized about it but got little. She could hardly drink anyway. Her mouth didn't move correctly. As much as possible, she kept her whole face still so it could heal, binding it with the cloth when she could bear it. One day, she wanted to talk again without slurring. The awful scars were unavoidable. But they didn't concern her as much as everything else.

Was Jori really all right or had they killed him? Was anyone coming to rescue her?

She'd done her own inventory of the cell and the door, to see if she could escape by herself. Unless someone came to assist her, it was nearly impossible, as far as she could see. The best option for her to escape alone would be when they took her from the cell to the arena. There were so many more variables then, and she kept her eyes open for all of them. But before they took her out of her cell, two Tanyu would come—she learned their names were Enktuya and Nedi—and tie her arms behind her before they marched her into the arena. She had her voice and her feet, but barely. Even if she could run, where could she go that would be safe?

Her conclusion, and the best plan she had, was that she would escape from the two Tanyu however she could and run to a hiding place. It didn't matter what it took to get there. A fleeting indignity was worth the prize of freedom. Once she hid, hopefully behind a locked door, she would...

Here, her mind stuttered. She would wait until there were no sounds, perhaps in the deep of night, and get out of the palace to meet up with her caravan. Right?

Remembering Firian's and Bard's strange sleep schedules— each for different reasons—part of her knew that there would never be a time Tanyu weren't on guard, especially if she were missing. If she contacted Bard about her location, that could help, but that plan relied on his knowing which Tanyu were trustworthy enough to help her.

Kiria had tried to contact Bard, but it took so much mental effort that she hadn't been successful yet. She barely had enough presence of mind to pray. Hopefully Firian updated them all. He was the only one who truly knew what was happening to her. Despite Firian's kindness through the torture, she hadn't granted him a lasting place on the list of those she trusted. Being in the Unreal did soothe the pain—Shifra and an unblemished Brithnem, her own palace halls and her room in the morning—but the smart of his betrayals hadn't completely left her.

In the desperation of her pain, when she forgot she was a Keeper and had only one thought—to make it stop—she wouldn't have prevented him from embracing her. In fact, she'd welcome it. Anything to distract from the arena. In the past, his strong arms had felt safe. She could pretend they were back in that time, just until the blade was put away and the Tanyu's insults and demands subsided. But he hadn't done anything more than hold her hands, and she'd initiated that, squeezing with all her might as though he were the only thing anchoring her to this world. In the dizzy, shaking rush that followed the torture, she wondered why he hadn't held her, hadn't kissed her, pressing his body against hers so she could lose herself. Part of her was glad. It meant she could have no qualms about going back to him if she had to endure another day.

How many days? Her eyes welled. Carefully, she rubbed the tears from her left eye before salt could dribble into the wounds.

It isn't over.

The temptation to give up hovered around her like fog. She told herself again, told the darkness smothering her, the same words.

It isn't over.

In a hum that was more sound than buzz (since she couldn't fully close her lips) she began the anthem. It was the same soaring song they'd played at her coronation, the same song she'd played badly on the lyra for captured fireflies. This was her song. These were her people. She would make it through this and restore the rightful Keepers to their thrones. Violence and manipulation and cruelty would not have the last word in the Western Kingdom.

Her hoarse song got louder. Let them hear her defiance. The small part of her, like a ghost, that hovered above this moment, above this pain, welcomed anyone who would listen.

And someone did. Two people.

One was a young Tanyuin woman with a reddish-brown braid down her back. Her coloring was like Haved's, except that this person was lithe and coiled, rod straight and thin, as though she were made only of bone and strong sinew. Kiria had never seen her before. She wasn't in the usual rotation of guards.

The other looked unmistakably like Candrae, *her* Candrae, except that her long golden curls now looked dusty brown, like Kiria's, and she wore a nightdress reminiscent of the one Kiria wore as she sat looking through the bars of her cell.

Kiria blinked. She hadn't hallucinated, except perhaps to see flashes of light or moving shadows. Her Talent was too weak to let her get Lost in the Unreal. So what was this? She gazed at the pair—the Tanyu had one hand on Candrae's shoulder, and Candrae's tear-filled eyes were locked on Kiria.

Kiria was afraid to speak and break the spell. Or maybe this was a rescue effort that relied on her silence. Her ragged song of rebellion faded away.

The second guard standing watch leaned toward the new Tanyu. "If you're here to clean up, Tesni, don't bother."

Tesni, the Charäkhni Tanyu with the braid, replied, "Then let's move her. Just because we can take the smell doesn't mean we have to." She gestured to Candrae, whose changed hair was mostly obscured by a hood. "I found a servant who can do it for us."

Had they taken Candrae too? A scream of protest welled up inside Kiria but she forced it back down. They weren't treating her like a prisoner. And the only reason they'd have to hurt Candrae is if they knew it would hurt Kiria to see it. She clung to the dim hope that they didn't know their connection, pressing her thumbnails into the sides of her fingers. Meeting Candrae's gaze, she gave what she hoped was a heartening look.

"Are you here to clean too?" her guard cried to someone out of sight.

"Yes, sir," came an unfamiliar male voice. "These cells over—"

"You shouldn't be here."

"But I was told—"

Tesni cut in. "Tell them that we're moving her." She began unlocking the bars.

The other Tanyu didn't budge. "Master Belik said not to move her to safeguard against escape." Doubt bled through his words.

Tesni drew herself up to her full height, which wasn't much. "You think she'll escape on my watch? Look at her!" She flung one hand toward Kiria, still sitting, weak, against the wall. "I've already posted another Tanyu at the entrance. So you can keep your gory thoughts to yourself." At that, she turned away from him and finished unlocking the door. After a final appraising look, the other Tanyu disappeared. Kiria didn't even see him leave.

Through the whole exchange, Candrae stood silent, watchful as a spirit. If they truly were just moving her, then why was her serving girl here? The sight of her made Kiria's chest ache. Her own torture had smothered hope inside her, as though everyone else had died too. Here was a sliver of home, coming without comment into her cell.

Kiria still didn't dare speak, and wasn't sure she'd be able to anyway. The cloth made it difficult to breath, much less talk.

Candrae approached her, falling her one knee and kissing her filthy hand. "My Keeper," she said quietly, with tears in her voice. "We're going to—"

As Candrae spoke, Tesni pressed something soft and suffocating against Kiria's nose and bleeding mouth. Kiria thrashed once, and fell into nothing.

SOMETHING STUNG KIRIA'S cheek and she woke up grimacing, which didn't help the pain. As the room where she lay materialized around her, she found that she wasn't in her cell, or in the arena at all. The air smelled fresh, like trees and salve, and there was soft fabric over her arms. Her face felt cold. She was in new clothes in a new space and there were faces over her. With light behind them, she couldn't make out who they were.

One dove for her, kissing her uninjured cheek.

"Stop!" hissed a voice. "You'll hurt her."

Kiria didn't mind at all. Jori and Chetana. Jori was alive, and they'd both come back safe.

"You're awake," said Bard's glad voice. "Try not to move."

She gave a little nod, but it was hard not to smile or cry at the shock of being back. How had she gotten away? Scraps of memory felt more like dreams than sensible parts of a plan.

"Were you really singing the anthem?" Jori asked, his face growing clearer as her vision adjusted. The same as ever, he didn't seem to be injured or maimed. Royce and Viktor stood in the room too, along with Vayci and two other guards who had traveled with them. Chetana held a pot of fragrant salve.

She nodded again. Bard and Jori gave matching grins. "That's my girl," Jori said, swallowing hard. His face looked puffy.

For the first time, Kiria wondered what she looked like. Everyone stared as though she were an apparition. But she didn't want to ask and she didn't want a looking glass. Another sting surged through her lip and cheek.

"Where's Candrae?" she managed without moving her lips.

Jori looked grim. Kiria's breath halted. Had something happened to her?

Chetana cut off whatever response Jori was about to give. "She's not here yet." She dabbed more cooling ointment on the cuts.

From the corner of her eye, Kiria saw Vayci wringing her hands.

"She still there?" Kiria asked, still keeping her mouth still. Candrae had been dressed approximately like Kiria. They couldn't have meant to *switch* them... Master Belik and the other Tanyu who regularly watched her cage would have caught on immediately. Candrae would be dead already if that were their plan.

"Not in the arena," Bard explained. "She should be on her way to us." He and Jori shared a look laced with concern.

"It's a little complicated, and not what I would have liked," Chetana said archly, "but you're here now, and safe. You need to rest."

"Yes, safe," Jori echoed meaningfully, touching her arm through the blanket spread over her.

"You'll need to apply this to your cuts twice a day for the next two days, but you'll heal," Chetana said, closing the pot of salve. "We should leave her to rest."

"No," Kiria said. The word felt wrenched from her. She didn't want to be alone.

Jori seemed to catch her meaning. "I'll stay."

Her neck and shoulders relaxed as Vayci said, "I'll stay too."

Chetana placed a soothing hand on Kiria's hair, cradling the top of her head as though she were a child. "Just don't let them keep you up," she said, running her thumb once over her forehead. For a moment, genuine love shone in her eyes. Kiria returned what she hoped was an echoing look.

As the guards took up their posts all around the exterior

circumference of the tent—it was her old tent, she noticed—Bard looked uncertain whether he should go or stay.

"He came up with the plan to save you," Jori said quickly, following her eyeline.

"We did," Bard amended, though there was a flash of pride about him.

Kiria held out her hand to Bard, who took it and squeezed gently.

A smile softened the corner of his lips. "I'm really glad you're back. Seriously, I can't say. You know, we were worried. I can't even believe what they did to you." His eyes gleamed. "I'm so sorry. They're not all the same, you know. I just…"

Jori patted his back, not taking his eyes from where Kiria lay comfortably on the bed. "And you were singing the anthem," he said, a punctuation mark to Bard's apology.

"I couldn't do much else." It was freeing not to have a bandage around her face and the constant taste of blood. Chetana's mixture stung, but in a healthful, healing way. "Is anyone else here? The armies?"

"Not yet," said Bard, "but it'll only be a few days before most of them get here."

Disappointing news, but not the worst. She was in no shape to plan a battle today, anyway. Tomorrow would be a different story. She could already feel her body recovering just by lying down. And the best thing of all was seeing her friends and family still very alive.

"We already have some strategies laid out for when they get here," said Bard. "It's a combination of what we talked about and a bunch of other ideas. Mixed together, I think they can work, yeah?"

In this half-delirious state, she didn't know if she could remember all their allies or make sense of what best to do against this unprecedented enemy, so she tucked the question away for tomorrow.

Her next question felt frivolous, but had to be asked. "Do I look like myself?" Not once had she traced the lines of her face since the first demonstration in the arena. It had been too painful and she was afraid of what she might find.

She looked to Bard for an honest reaction. The Tanyu just bit his lip.

"You're beautiful as always," Jori said, dipping to kiss her forehead.

Not an answer. She sighed. Well, there were more important things. She was Keeper with or without the face she'd grown up with. And she had a kingdom to take back.

49

BARD

IT WAS such a relief to sit with Jori and Kiria together that Bard almost forgot his worry. Almost. He never truly let it go.

Tesni and Candrae hadn't come back and the thought of the serving girl flushed his face with concern. The plan had been mostly his idea. Candrae was about the same height and build as Kiria, and they needed a decoy for the Tanyu to follow while a Kingdom soldier friendly to their side brought Kiria back to the camp. It was imperative that the Tanyu not follow her *here*.

It was a temporary solution anyway. As they talked, Viktor was checking to see if Jori's underground party hall had been compromised. If it was safe, then they would all move there, better hidden, once their allies found them.

Jori counted off with his fingers. "So, we have the soldiers still alive in the city, a handful of Endrian soldiers who are coming tomorrow, six Kingdom towns, and ourselves."

"That's it," Bard confirmed. Endrians weren't required to come, but some had volunteered to repay in good faith all that the Kingdom had done to help them during the past years' raids. Jac might be with them. Did his brother even know which side

Bard fought on? "And the Tanyu on our side, like Tesni," he added.

"Yes, well, there aren't many of those, are there?"

Bard drummed his fingers against the side of his chair. Firian's troops were coming, Sentries and all, but the Brithnem guards had the order not to let him near the Keepers. *Well, he's not here now.* "Maybe more than we think," he went on. "Firian's coming back."

"He'll fight on his own side for his own reasons," Kiria said. Her speech sounded slurred since she tried not to move her mouth. The deep wounds on her lips and cheek had closed overnight, but she still sported wicked red lines. One began on her upper lip and pierced all the way down to her neck. No matter how she healed, one side of her mouth would be left twisted.

"I think he's for you," Bard insisted.

"Then he can show it." Her tone was steely, but there was a vulnerability in her eyes that said she really did want him to.

He couldn't blame her for her skepticism. Bard had known Firian most of their lives and he had trouble sorting out his motivations sometimes.

"And Belik has Tanyu, Torithians, and all the towns he coerced into helping them," Jori finished.

"And a couple that went willingly, remember?" Kiria said wearily. "Most are staying out of the conflict, though."

Bard's thoughts drifted to Haved and Atty and the Charäkhni king. "At least the fight's on a smaller scale, I guess," he said.

"It should be on a bigger scale," Jori grumbled. "This is our lives and our kingdom." His face brightened with a sudden recollection. "I never showed you my tattoo!" Standing, he lifted his shirt to reveal the image of a rain falling into a goblet. The color of Jori's design looked redder than Kiria's black one. Maybe they had different ink in Charäkhnem.

She winced good naturedly, waving for him to stand farther away. "I'm so glad you got it! We weren't sure if you made it to the artist or not."

"Oh yes. I made it." Jori beamed.

"What'll happen when you get old and fat?" she teased.

"Me? Never!"

"That's what drinking does."

"Bigger canvas."

"This design is complicated," she said.

"Like me." He touched the side of his face with two fingers in a gesture of pathos. Dropping his hand, he added, "It hurt worse than that hail storm. I had to keep thinking of happy, fluffy things to maintain my dignity."

Bard chuckled.

A head appeared through the tent flap. "My Keeper," said Chetana, "they're back."

Relief flooded Bard as he, along with Jori and Vayci, bolted for the door. He felt as if he'd been holding his breath until he heard the news. The worst aspect of the plan to rescue Kiria had been risking Candrae's life. He knew it was a risk, but she was willing and the best person to do it. Chetana had wanted to begin the inevitable war instead, to overwhelm the Tanyu after more of Kiria's allies arrived. But that would have meant bloodshed, so much of it, and no guarantee of success.

War was coming—Bard wasn't denying that—but it didn't have to come now, and it didn't have to come with so many casualties. He hoped. Remembering the black pit of horror he felt after snuffing out the Torithian captain Tibor Wat, he doubted he could ever do it again. Certainly not to other Tanyu. Happily, Jori had chosen his plan over Chetana's, and she had yielded, calling him "My Keeper" for the first time.

Tesni and Candrae waited in another tent—they only used three now, to be less noticeable. Tesni stood, all in black, her face set and alert. Candrae sat on the side of the bed, hunching over her knees, trembling slightly.

Vayci ran to her, lifted her chin, and hugged her. Candrae held on tight. A slight but unmistakable odor of human feces rose from Candrae's clothes.

"I'm so, so glad you're back!" Bard cried, resisting the urge to hug Tesni as well. She'd never acted affectionately toward anyone, that he knew of. Tesni regarded him warily. Bard knew what she might be thinking. *Traitor. Defector. Boy who turned his back on his own.* He'd accepted that the Tanyu might not love him. Hopefully they were beginning to see why he left and why he ran to Kiria for help.

Once the hug between Candrae and Vayci was over, Jori took a knee beside Vayci and looked Candrae in the eye. "You were very brave, my girl." He took her hand gently and squeezed it. "We're indebted to you." Candrae looked abashed, wide-eyed and filled with emotion.

Movement at the entrance signaled Kiria's arrival.

"My Keeper!" Candrae exclaimed, as though she were glad for something else to focus on besides Jori's piercing gray eyes. "You look so much better." At that, she fell into weeping.

Vayci embraced her protectively and the others left them alone to wash up and compose themselves. The whole group headed back to Kiria's tent, which was the biggest.

"Kiria, this is Tesni," Bard said, almost adding, *She's a Tanyu.* But that was obvious. Her poise and black outfit made Bard keenly aware that he wasn't wearing his.

Tesni inclined her head to Kiria while keeping her eyes on her.

"I'm glad you came," Kiria said. "Is Candrae all right?"

"She will be. She wasn't hurt." Her tone was flat, though whether from her business-like composure or distrust, it was hard to tell.

Firian's unspoken name sizzled in the air, crackling in their ears like static.

Two guards parted the curtains and allowed them all inside. One followed them in. The group stood in a tense circle—Kiria, Jori, Bard, Chetana, Tesni, Royce representing the guards.

Bard's Tanyuin training guided his attention to all the potential weapons. Tesni must carry a dagger in her boot—they all did—and Royce had a sword at his side. Jori and Kiria were weaponless, and so was he. As the clearest link between Brithnem and the Tanyu, he felt the weight to speak. But how could he, with all these important people here? He looked to Jori, who met his gaze.

"Well," Jori declared, clapping his hands, "isn't this a fun party? We were just in the middle of counting our allies. I hope we can count you." This last comment was directed at Tesni.

"I'm against Master Belik," she replied. "He supplanted Master Kess."

"Which means you're for us," said Kiria, casting a warning look at Chetana. Suspicion didn't leave the Amir's face, but the rigidity of her jaw softened. "You've made it clear by how much you risked to help me escape. I'm deeply grateful, and I'm grateful that you took care of Candrae."

"She's very fearful," Tesni said.

"She won't be going on any more missions, so it doesn't matter, does it?" Jori added. "I thought she was brave. Not sure if I'd do that." He stretched his back so he stood taller and turned to Kiria. "No, I take it back, darling. You know I'd do anything for you."

Kiria gave him a smile made lopsided by her cuts. The small gesture tugged at Bard's heart because he knew it was true. They'd each do anything for the other. If only their eyes would dart to him too.

"Tesni," she said, "once you swear loyalty, you're welcome to stay in our camp."

"Are there others like you, who could get out?" Jori asked the Tanyu.

"I said there were," Bard answered, his dark brows ticking downward, but only for a moment.

"Will they?" Jori revised.

Tesni's frame had relaxed a fraction since she'd entered the tent. Bard sensed less threat from her now, not that there was ever *threat*, exactly. Just excessive wariness on both sides. "We've been staying on the inside to gather information. I expected most of us would strike from there when there was a coup."

Three voices spoke at once to correct her. Bard faltered in astonishment when he realized the others deferred to let him speak. "This isn't a coup," he explained. "Kiria belongs on the throne. Belik usurped what belongs to her. To both of them. Kiria and Jori."

"How does the Tanyuin Head feel about that?" Chetana asked in a dangerously measured voice.

There it was. The unspoken name.

"Whose side is he on?" Chetana looked as fierce as any Tanyu Bard had seen. Her dark eyes flashed and the patterned septum ring in her nose shone like a war trophy.

"Yours," Bard answered. Their time in the cellar had convinced him of that, and every time they met in the Unreal afterward solidified his belief in his friend.

Chetana tipped her head at Tesni, prompting her to answer.

"Hers," Tesni said, looking at Kiria.

Bard was suddenly aware of Royce standing with them, shifting his weight as though to beg Kiria's attention. She granted it, but said nothing. No change in her orders.

"We want peace," Kiria said, addressing the group and looking them in the eyes one by one. Despite wearing a simple dress, plain face, and struggling to speak around her wounds, she looked like the Keeper she was. "We all want peace for Brithnem, as little killing on both sides."

"Master Belik is ready for you," Tesni said, sounding remorseful now.

Ready? How? Did Tesni know more than they did about his plans?

She continued. "There are four ships due in the port today to drop off new soldiers. I don't know all his plans—he only confides in three others—but I know he has allies coming, and he plans to crush you before you get into the city. Especially since the last plan failed to turn up the other heirs." She gestured to Kiria's face without embarrassment. "Or Master Kess."

The news affected them all instantly. Bard wasn't surprised, but still felt his chest tightening. Kiria stared at Tesni, not in challenge, but with a burning sort of courage. Chetana took in a slow, deliberate breath, and a muscle ticked in Jori's temple. The skin around Jori's eyes constricted and his pupils went small from fear. He still stood in his insolent way, but it was obvious that he'd never been around war. Bard's small taste in the storeroom of the Academy was more than he'd ever wanted to encounter in his lifetime.

"Now Belik will kill them on sight." Chetana's words were more of a statement than a question.

Tesni nodded, eyes narrow. "When are your forces coming?"

Kiria held up a hand to stop anyone else from answering. "We'll only give information as necessary. We're working for a solution that spares as many Tanyu as we can."

"Master Belik won't negotiate away his power." Everyone knew Tesni was right.

"I'm not talking about negotiation," Kiria replied. "But surely more Tanyu don't approve of Master Belik's methods."

"There are some, yes. He purged several already who made attempts on his life. He would have done the same to me if he'd known. Many of us still consider Master Kess the Head, not Belik."

"Well, now you aren't following him, are you?" Jori said. "You're following us."

"She still hasn't pledged her allegiance," Chetana observed icily.

Kiria lifted her chin. "There are two sides to this war," she said, her gaze fixed on Tesni. "For the Kingdom and against it. Keepers or Tanyu. Firian hasn't demonstrated his side clearly, but he will take one. I need to know that you are on ours."

Bard watched Tesni's hands, so capable. Royce seemed to tense beside him.

"We can't work with Tanyu," Chetana said abruptly, and then shifted to Tesni. "Thank you for your help, but we know we can't expect any more from you."

"Chetana," Kiria chided. "We already do." She gestured at Bard.

He fought not to fidget under everyone's renewed scrutiny of his Tanyuin background. "Yeah," he said. "We're not all the same. Some of us see the injustice of this. You need us. At least, we could be helpful."

"Already are," Jori added. "Honestly, I think it's a relief that we can count on some Tanyu. I always hoped they weren't all murderous." He said it lightly, but there was a pointedness to the words that made Bard feel bolstered.

Tesni didn't take the comment kindly, but fell neatly to one knee before Kiria anyway. "I swear loyalty to you and the crown."

"Let's rephrase," said Jori, stepping in. "Repeat after... her." He gave a theatrical flutter of his fingers to Kiria and stepped back.

Tesni repeated the traditional oath, with an addition. "I swear to serve my Keepers, Kiria Arioc and Jorrim Calthwaite, and my country, the Western Kingdom, to the best of my ability, regardless of danger and should I betray them, may the punishment be death." She rose, stern but resolute. "I'll be glad to see the thrones restored."

"So will I," Kiria said, motioning to Royce. "He'll show you where you can rest and wash."

Once Tesni was gone, Bard leaned over and spoke in an undertone. "Did you forget the words?"

Jori pretended to be affronted. "I never forget things. Also, yes." He winked. "At least I'm trying."

50

FIRIAN

Endrian forces, though not many, had arrived in Kiria's meager camp. At least that's what Bard had to report. He seemed antsy. Jac must be among the numbers.

Firian peered through a break in the trees. A couple other small Kingdom towns had swelled their numbers too. A little colony of tents barely hid among the full yellow and orange trees of the Gray Forest.

Though firelit guards were stationed around the perimeter, the camp looked woefully tiny considering what it was about to attempt. This was Kiria's army, barely a few thousand, and yet she planned to fight despite small chance of success. *Justice*, he could almost hear her say. He couldn't help but be impressed.

Tanyu are coming, he reminded himself. Sensing the final conflict drawing near, he'd told his Tanyuin allies inside the city —those who lived—to figure out a way to get out and meet them. Bard said he had plans for them. The way Bard talked suggested he was one of the main figures in charge of strategy. Maybe Indisfate was directly related to strategic ability. So far, though, Bard's plans had succeeded. Kiria was safe.

Per Bard's instructions, Firian had contacted Tesni and

explained how to rescue Kiria. It was risky. A non-Tanyu took the real Kiria back to her camp, while Tesni drew all the attention with the serving girl posing as the Keeper. Firian never should have doubted it would work.

Bard had also said that Kiria hadn't fully warmed to the idea of accepting Firian's help.

"She said you'd have to show her," he'd told him, eyeing Firian with a curious look, a sort of sympathetic challenge. A look like he'd given him in the mansion's cellar. Bard believed in them both, but his belief had always been bigger than Firian's.

So he would show her. As he told Brett, he was on Kiria's side. No matter what happened, she was the one who deserved to be on the throne of Brithnem. She could establish justice over tyranny. His mind gave a little skip. He couldn't think about what would happen next to him or the Academy.

Firian mapped a trail of blind spots away from the guards. His black clothes would give him away as a Tanyu , even if they didn't recognize him as Firian Kess, the Tanyuin Head. Night shadows would be his salvation.

He had to appeal to her directly. If he went to Bard's tent or approached the nearest guard, there was no telling if the soldiers would let him near her.

Let. He hated that word.

He could get to her if he wanted to, but he also wanted to avoid conflict. The point of this exercise was to prove that he was on her side, after all. It would be hard to prove that if he had to fight his way to her.

Firian's own troops—if he could use the word—waited about fifteen minutes away. Sentries and Defenders and remaining Tanyu, all that were left at the Academy.

The memory of Kiria's pain tore through his gut. He hadn't known she would be tortured, but *that* was why he'd emptied the Academy. To keep her from pain and to help her get where she belonged.

Was she all right now? Her wounds had been terrible, but she had gritted her teeth and survived. Since she met him in the Unreal during her torture, she hadn't come again. Now he was actually here and could do more than comfort.

Belik's words in the arena had come back to him piecemeal. At the time, he had blocked them out, trying to avoid rage in favor of whatever care he could offer. Belik's demands for Jori and Firian in exchange for Kiria's life twisted like a familiar knife. The words sounded like Firian's own. *Just give yourself up.* He felt sick at the thought. Had he really said that and considered it mercy?

He was closer now, assessing the guards. Extra stood in front of a couple tents. Kiria and Jori. It had to be. Both tents were light blue, Kingdom blue, with dark purple edging and smudges that could be scrollwork along the top. One of the tents was a little larger than the other. He'd go there.

It was surrounded by many other shelters, almost at the center of the camp. Moving into position, he started edging between tents, avoiding the light of fires that punctuated open areas. A medley of smells ran thick through the air, campfire smoke and sour body odor and tanned skins used for new tents and melted cheese over the fire. His fast steps were silent.

Just in front of him, almost colliding, an Endrian soldier came out to take the air. Without thought, Firian reached up and silenced him—a painless cutting off of blood. He frowned and stepped over the limp body. The man would wake with nothing worse than a hangover.

Finally, he slipped into Kiria's tent, not through the proscribed opening, which was heavily guarded, but underneath.

A large bed sat in the middle of the dark space. A hint of firelight shadowed through the tent, playing over Kiria's sleeping form. Furtively, he approached. She didn't use her Ability as she slept. It wasn't the sumptuous silks and furs given to the only remaining Keeper that captivated him—it was the artless, defenseless, mussed countenance of the girl. Her mouth was open. Her hair was wild. And she'd never looked so beautiful.

He wished she could sleep without his interruption. For a few breaths, he took in her peaceful expression, careless of the danger around her.

She rolled over. Two wounds came into sharp relief, one on her cheek and the other dragging from her lips to her neck. Anger and pain shot through him at the sight. He had held her hands...

Maybe he gave an audible breath. Kiria jerked upright. Immediately, her eyes locked onto him.

He managed half a smile. He didn't expect a smile back.

"Firian! What are you doing here? Guards!" she shouted.

He stayed. His plan depended on it.

Moments later, after being thoroughly searched, he was tied tight to a chair, his wrists chafing against each other. He faced the big bed with blue and purple coverlets, and Kiria stood before him. She watched him intently, still in her night clothes. In the chaos and speed of his arrest, she hadn't bothered to change either her clothes or appearance.

"Why did you come here?" she demanded, eyes burning.

"I came to help—"

"Into my tent," she clarified. The words' edges blurred under her injury.

"I needed to speak to you directly, and I didn't know what your orders were... about me."

"They were going to arrest you."

That's ambitious. He almost said the words aloud, but now was not the time. His mission hung by a thread. She could reject his help completely, refuse to let him get involved, and then his decision to empty the Academy would be in vain, and her own mission might fail.

No, he would help her anyway, if not openly, then secretly.

Behind her, one of the serving girls lit a few candles by the bed to give the space more light. Judging from new shadows flickering over Kiria's face, the other girl was doing the same thing behind where Firian sat.

There was something like relief in the rigid lines of Kiria's body. He felt it too. At last, they could confront each other directly. No matter what happened, at least they would know where they stood.

She shivered.

"My jacket's over there," he said, indicating with his eyes.

She wrinkled her nose skeptically, but then moved toward the long black jacket the guards had taken from him.

When she pulled her arms through the sleeves of his coat, he had to remind himself that her wearing the jacket wasn't a concession to their earlier relationship, but defiance in the face of it. She didn't look like a Tanyu—she was too soft, too idealistic —but she did have a Tanyu's core of strength, tempered hard like cooling glass. She gazed down at him with those heart-breaking scars and his gut twisted. She was a queen.

"You could have spoken to me directly," she said softly. Her forehead was lined with concentration and anger.

"In person," he said.

"Okay. What are you here to offer? Can you kill Belik for us?" she asked, pulling the coat closer around her. The dirty hem dragged on the ground.

"I can try."

Kiria gave both the guards behind him a meaningful look. Her busy fingers did the buttons up the front of the jacket. Firian followed their movements with his eyes, realizing he could look at her like this for a long time, watching her do simple things. And world-shaking things. Eating strawberries or talking to Brett and then deposing a tyrant. He could picture her talking to his sister.

"Could you distract him?" she resumed.

"Yes. I can get to him."

"Can you?" There was a challenge in the words.

"I can," he replied. "We're the only two who can go to the Second Level."

She stuffed her hands in the jacket pockets. "The Second Level?"

"It's an advanced level of the Unreal." He twisted his bound wrists behind the chair to settle them more comfortably. "Trust me. I can manage it."

Trust. How much had she told the others about their encounter in the farmhouse that night? That had been their last time in person. Firian's demand that she give herself up for the safety of her people. The memory made him sick with shame. If he hadn't been so stupid, none of this would have happened. The Keepers would still be alive, and Kiria would still be in his arms. But he couldn't take it back now. All he had was a purpose, and a purpose had to be enough.

Kiria cleared her throat to freshen her tired voice. "We might be able to use you, then. But let me be perfectly clear," she said, touching her lip with a knuckle and checking it for blood. "My allegiance is with the Western Kingdom. It is not with you. Don't think that I'll make an exception for you because of our *katah.* You know exactly how far I'm willing to go to protect my people." She was leaning closer now, glaring at him with amber eyes.

He did know. He knew better than anyone else how much she would risk for her people's safety. At his insistence, she'd nearly sacrificed her body and reputation. And later, he had stood with her through the pain of withering torture. Despair had shone in her eyes both times, but she hadn't broken.

He didn't quail as he looked back at her. Then something between them softened. Everything in the room, besides the two of them—her standing, him sitting—blurred to hazy edges. His gaze dropped to the cut on her lip.

She blinked, cleared her throat again. "What's this?" she asked, drawing out Bard's wooden figure of Corso from his jacket pocket.

"It's Bard's. It goes with his Indisfate set. He was looking for it."

She closed her fist around it protectively. "He doesn't have his set anymore."

"But he'll still want that back."

After looking at the figure's bearded face, she guessed, "Corso?"

A corner of Firian's mouth lifted. "Yeah."

"Hm. I'll make sure he gets it." She put the piece back in the pocket. Did she plan to keep his jacket? Where was Bard now? "You still haven't said why you needed to meet in person," she continued, picking up the thread. "You could have just offered your help some other way." It was a challenge. Would he admit to doing all this in order to win her back? But it wasn't that simple anymore.

The moment stretched, her implied question singing like the aftereffect of song's last note.

"I brought an army with me," he said. "They're yours."

She straightened again and froze, motionless, but in a way that made it seem like she would suddenly start at him. If only she would. If only she would see him like she used to. All of him. All the ugly parts, the selfish parts, the proof he laid at her feet now...

"To do with what you want," he continued. "It's Tanyu, civilians, Sentries..."

Her forehead knit together, her expression unreadable. She searched his face.

Instantly he was transported to another time when she'd looked there for the truth and hadn't found it. They'd sat on the wooden walkway in Shifra, surrounded by the colored lanterns she loved. He had longed to kiss her, and she had searched his face, trying to discern his love or loyalty. He'd failed at both.

"I'll see where they fit in," she said, her manner businesslike, but her fingers playing with the buttons. "But I can't let you go with them."

Emotion lodged in his throat. He'd expected this, but the reality didn't make it better. He nodded stiffly, wishing they were alone instead of being watched by so many others.

"They're still all yours," he repeated. "They're waiting for you about fifteen minutes northeast. You need to take back the throne. Just tell me what you want me to do."

Something lit up in her eyes. It was only there for an instant, and then her calculating expression was back. "We'll find a use for you."

A strange swell of pride bloomed inside him. She had become the confident leader he knew she could be. She had outlived Belik's torture. She was powerful. She had the Tanyuin Head tied to a chair. A bolt of desire, low and hot, shot through him as he gazed up at her. He dropped his eyes to her bare feet. Neither of them had time to revisit what had once existed between them, and she'd made it clear she didn't want to.

The jacket swished against the ground, it was so long on her, as she turned to yet another guard near the door. "Keep Master Kess under guard until we're ready to move tomorrow." She cheated a look at him that revealed she knew it was still Firian's choice to remain shackled.

He flexed his wrists, testing the restraints. It wouldn't take long to undo them, and it wouldn't be difficult to control the room even without being untied. But he'd respect her order. If he didn't prove how serious he was about helping her, she wouldn't use his prowess to take back the Kingdom. She might even order his incarceration early. Or execution. How many knew the extent of his crimes? But, with odds this slim, his participation could mean the difference between victory and defeat, especially with Belik at the helm.

"When was the last time you ate?" Her voice shook him from his thoughts. It was gentler than before.

He raised his eyes. "Yesterday."

One of her eyebrows twitched upward.

"I needed to get here quickly."

"And eating would slow you down?" she asked, her shoulders relaxing a little.

A tiny smirk threatened to spread over his face.

His eyes must have given away the smirk despite his effort because she looked away. Though composed, she had the smallest tinge of fear in her expression. Wavering balance on the edge of a cliff. "See that he gets food and water," she instructed.

Firian felt the rope tying him to the chair release as it was cut, though his wrists stayed bound. Two guards gripped both his arms roughly and heaved him to his feet. He held still under their control, though his instincts roared to break free. As they marched him out of the tent, he cast another look at Kiria. Her arms were crossed in that long black jacket, and she didn't look back at him, instead calling over one of her serving girls.

Helping Kiria regain her rightful place on the throne, doing something that could begin to make up for all the times he'd failed, was its own kind of freedom.

51
_____

BARD

CONCENTRATION AND HAZE MADE Bard's head pound. Jori's dreams always had a dark blur of unreality. He didn't have the least bit of the Talent, but none of that was his fault. Bard tried to focus on what was happening while remaining aware of possible threats. Chetana and Tesni and the nearby capital meant a constant faraway buzz of other minds, but nothing invading Jori's sleep.

Jori walked—or floated, it was hard to tell—along the edge of the palace roof. He held his arms outstretched, bobbling gently from side to side as he tripped along. In the way of dreams, it wasn't the gardens with the Amiran Academy far below but the roiling sea. Narrow warships had sailed right against the palace walls, tapping against the stone with every wave. The movement didn't seem to damage the ships at all. Every ferocious face tipped upward to watch Jori as though they had come so close only to watch him fall. The tenor of the dream wasn't terror, but a balance of levity and tension, like a hard knot of anticipation. Nerves for something long put off.

Would he jump into the churning sea? Crash onto the waiting decks and wake up?

Then Bard saw himself, waving for Jori to get down off the edge. The dream Bard held out his hand to help him down onto the safety of the roof, which looked similar to the one Firian had created when they'd fought—almost a plaza, with pavestone paths patterned through patches of improbable green grass. Maybe Firian had actually gone up there at some point. Bard never had, and he lived in the palace for weeks. But he didn't have Firian or Jori's penchant for troublemaking.

It wasn't unusual for Bard to see himself in Jori's dreams. He'd become almost a fixture, playing small parts in the strange things that happened. Kiria frequented the scenes too. And Atty.

As Jori approached dream Bard, steps appeared, leading him even higher until Bard had no chance of reaching him. The steps materialized just before Jori placed his foot. This development seemed to distress him but he couldn't turn around. Something drew him onward. Dream Bard was small now, and the waiting ships looked like toys. The stairs, nearly invisible as they drew him up into the clouds, widened so that Jori could have lain down across the length of them three times. Creatures appeared on them, fantastical things, and people shuddered in and out of vision like flashes of shadow. The steps took on the quality of being indoors, and haunted.

Something was at the top, and the top was drawing nearer. Bard tried to see what it was, but the entire dream was so murky, and he couldn't see anything that Jori wasn't experiencing. The effort squeezed Bard's headache tighter. He took a couple slow breaths to clear his mental vision through the pain.

It wasn't something. *Someone* waited at the top.

Who? The question was invasive. But then, so was watching someone's dreams. Bard's curiosity made him breathless.

A long, fur-covered lizard slunk past Jori's legs and disappeared off the edge of the step, into the nothingness outside the dream. A large square of light lit an opening at the top.

Please reach it. Please reach it. Dreams had an annoying way of ending right before the exciting revelation.

A violent shudder ran through Bard.

Jori took two more steps.

Another shudder shook Bard, and he realized that the sensation didn't come from inside him but from the real world. So he wouldn't find out what Jori wanted so much.

He took quick stock of anyone nearby who might want to attack Jori in the dream space, found none. Exhaustion made returning to the Real like swimming through custard. His eyes felt sticky as his lids fluttered open. He cracked his neck. All night, he sat hunched over Jori's sleeping form. His back and head ached. It was easier to ignore when he had entertainment. Most nights he even laughed.

He squinted into the face of Kiria. Two guards flanked her. Her expression was serious but not alarmed.

"Firian's here," she said softly.

The revelation rushed in at the same time as her words. When he guarded Jori, his concentration was all-consuming. He hadn't realized that he had boxed out even his awareness of Firian, which usually waited just outside his own consciousness. Still recovering from dream logic, Bard hadn't noticed that Kiria was wearing a black Academy coat. What did that mean?

He couldn't hold back his smile at the news. "Where is he?" he whispered, slowly rising from where he sat on the big bed. "Is he here with the others? I told you he'd come."

She didn't answer either question. Instead, she tipped her chin toward Jori. Dusky brown waves of hair flopped over the arm where he rested his head. One bare shoulder blade peeked above the fine sheets. His face, turned toward them, had the seriousness of dreams.

Despite his new excitement, unable to stop himself, Bard yawned. Jori just looked so comfortable.

"I want you to choose a Sentry for him," Kiria said. "Someone we can trust."

Bard fought the urge to pump his fist in silent exultation. He could finally sleep again! Part of him would miss the odd sort of companionship that came with guarding Jori's dreams. "Wells, for sure," he said. "He's trustworthy. He was my friend back in Tánuil." And he hadn't needed to guard Kader for several weeks, ever since Firian convinced Belik that the boy was dead.

"We should take this conversation outside," Kiria whispered, indicating for the guards to precede her. "We'll wake him up."

"I mean, I doubt it." Bard shared a look with Kiria.

Her lips rose in a small smile. "He's hard to wake up," she agreed. Walking back to her own tent, she instructed one of the many guards to locate Wells and give him his instructions.

The soldiers seemed to multiply around Kiria and Jori as new troops arrived. The new mayor of Rantoul had sent some soldiers, though it looked a poor showing. Skirwith and Redshore too.

Enderin had sent volunteers to help as well. Only a few hundred, and Bard hadn't had time to welcome them. Casual questions revealed that his older brother Jac was among the volunteers. Bard's eyes darted among the firelit tents to find his brother's stylish black hair and confident attitude, but of course there was nothing. Jac was sleeping, most likely. What time was it, anyway?

He could find Jac in the morning, if he wanted to. He did want to. It was just that the last time they'd spoken, Jac had confirmed Bard's fears that his family held a grudge against him for being on the wrong side of the brief Tanyuin War against the Kingdom, the precursor to the war they were now about to fight. Home had evaporated like smoke with Jac's words, but Bard loved him anyway.

No time to worry about that now.

"Firian's under guard," Kiria said, resuming where they'd left off.

"You know that's—"

Kiria cut Bard off with a look. They both knew that Firian's killing ability made guards obsolete unless there was also a Sentry. Even then, keeping Firian in chains was difficult.

"I need to tell you something," she said.

Her seriousness filled Bard with nerves. Was someone hurt, dead? Was he in trouble? He ran through what he did over the past day. Nothing she could criticize, unless she wanted him to use her title, or never disagree with her or tease the royals.

When they reached the illusory safety of her tent, she turned toward him. Firian's jacket, too long for her, dragged in the dirt. Bard's mind roiled with questions like the ocean in Jori's dream.

"Oh," she said, "this is for you." She produced the figure of Corso Bard had lost back at the Academy.

He took it from her, beaming. It was in perfect condition, the miniscule knives crossed in front of the hero's chest and everything. "No way! He had this? Where did he find it?" It had been months since he last saw it, a piece of home. All his homes.

"I know you're excited that Firian's here," she began, "but I'm seriously concerned. We both know what he is, but there may be more that you don't know."

Kiria swallowed, circling her wrist with her fingers. "Right before all this happened, Firian... gave an ultimatum. Me for Brithnem."

"What?" Bard whispered. He knew something bad had happened between them, but he hadn't realized *this*.

Her eyes dropped and her voice grew smaller. "I couldn't tell anyone, or he'd take the city. I thought I could save it. Everyone would think I'd run away with him, but it wouldn't matter if everyone was... safe." Her lashes fluttered with memory.

The figurine felt heavy in Bard's hand. No wonder she didn't want him telling Firian what they were doing, even after he'd helped Kader get away.

"I went," she continued. "I thought it was the only way. There's a... farmhouse... in the outer edge. We met there." Her eyes looked glassy and faraway. "I thought he'd take me away, like a prisoner of war. What else could happen? He'd demanded the trade of my life." The words snagged on emotion. Her brows lowered, lines forming between them. "But he let me go back." She looked up at Bard again. "That's where I was. I wasn't taking a walk. That's how I knew Tanyu were outside the city."

That night, Bard had known about Firian's presence too. No one had listened to him until Kiria appeared, looking like she'd witnessed a murder. Horribly ironic, Bard realized, since that happened just afterward.

"That's why I keep pushing back," she said. "Firian can say whatever he wants, but I can't believe him. Why do you?"

An unexpected question. It clung to him uncomfortably. He considered. Hopefully there was room both for comforting Kiria's terrible, legitimate pain, and the possibility of Firian's redemption. Bard had always assumed there was. Well, not always. But since Firian saved his life, yes.

"He's ashamed," he said, remembering the cellar. "Maybe he acts brave around you, but..." Bard shook his head. "He is brave. That's not my point. But not in every way. He's afraid there's no hope for him, that he started all this, and he can't end it, and he hurt you... and me." He didn't realize the truth of the words until he heard them coming out. "He knows you won't take him back, and I don't think he expects you to keep him around after this. I think..." The truth formed clearly in front of him and stole his breath. Sickness surged through his stomach. "I think he expects to die."

Kiria's lips parted in surprise. They shared a fraught silence.

"What would happen to us if he did?" she asked, her voice

barely above a whisper. Her eyes were shot through with concerned determination.

Images of Tibor Wat sent bile crawling up Bard's throat. Everything had moved so slowly after Firian, in the pirate's compound on Torith, had shouted, "Now!" Bard extricated himself from the captain's mind, pulling pieces of himself out like sinew through teeth. Bard's life had replaced some of the captain's own, unbeknownst to Tibor Wat. A *katah*. A death sentence. It took Bard long enough to complete the job that he'd put Firian in extra danger. Happily, his friend was a good fighter. Otherwise...

Bard didn't leave his room for four days. Then he got news of Tiev's death, Lost in the Unreal. Four became five. He felt nauseated and cold, plagued by thoughts of the captain. He'd been a horrible man—stealing young men and women, forcing himself upon them—but he'd once been a child too. He had parents somewhere. And Bardhon Tanery had snuffed out his life. It was something he would never willingly do again. Even during the Kingdom's attack on the Academy, he had only injured, not killed.

He took a breath. When he spoke, his voice came out fractured. "Firian never *declared* a *katah* on us. It just... happened." It was the intention, the dismantling of another person's reality, that killed them. "So we would live. We would just be weakened. But..." *But I don't want him to die.*

Kiria nodded thoughtfully. "You can see him before you get some sleep," she said, cutting off any further discussion. "It'll be a short night. We're moving to the new location just before dawn."

That couldn't be far off. The darkness outside had the heavy, muted quality of deep night.

"I'm so sorry he did that to you," Bard said.

Her returning gaze was level, sad and regal. She didn't look like the Keeper he'd met at the beginning. Now, she bore the weight of the Western Kingdom. She was its tradition and royalty, everything standing in the space between her people and domination by the power-hungry sect of Tanyu. She straightened her shoulders.

Bard bit the inside of his lip, hesitating. Then he opened his arms to her.

She breathed a small laugh and took his offered hug.

Both feeling bolstered, Bard went to find Firian. It didn't take him long. The pull of Firian's mind made itself clear once Bard was focused on him. Again, no black hair appeared among the tents as Bard made his way. *Jac is asleep, and besides, he's not looking for you.*

In the quiet, Firian's voice filtered through the walls of a tent, listing names of Tanyu that Bard knew. He moved the flap aside to enter. Firian sat, bound, in a chair, and Tesni stood beside him. They both wore black. It was almost like being back at the Academy, except for the flip of power. Behind Firian stood three guards, and in front of them stood another, carefully writing down the names in a list. Could Firian really have done that to Kiria? Yes, in his desperation, he could have. But Bard saw a new aspect to his friend now. Something settled, determined, not frantic.

Firian lifted his head as Bard entered.

"Hey, Fir," Bard said, grinning as he held up Corso.

Firian's eyes brightened. "She gave it to you?"

"We had a talk, yeah."

Firian closed his mouth. Maybe he guessed what they talked about. "I tried to get here sooner," he said.

"I'm sure you went as fast as you could, mate."

"I did." He nodded toward the guard with the list. "Tanyu are going to meet us in the new shelter. I told them all to get out while they could."

"How many?" Bard was already adding calculations to his strategy and backup plans.

"Thirty-one."

The number fell heavy. So few. Bard nodded quickly, scratching the back of his head with his stiff hand. "Okay."

The movement caught Firian's eye. "How's the hand?"

Bard raised the useless hand in question, little better than a stump, and shrugged. The fingers had never uncurled since the cellar. It was a nuisance, but Belik's attack could have left him dead instead, so he was grateful.

"Who else?" prompted the guard with the list. "You said thirty-one."

Tesni gave another name. Firian gave the next.

"I'll see you later, yeah?" Bard said, turning to go. He didn't want Firian to feel alone among people who hated him. "Are they just gonna... keep you like that?"

Firian narrowed his eyes, a grim joke in them. "It looks like it."

"Okay, well..." He wanted to stay and talk, to thank him again for saving his life, for dropping him off to help Kiria. He wanted to see if his guesses were right about Firian's fears and expectations. He wanted to talk about his conversation with Kiria and see if Firian was still ashamed of his actions then. But those weren't topics for a greater audience. Later, he would see if they could get more privacy.

Tesni provided the name of another Tanyu inside the city.

"I'll be back, then," Bard said as he left, feeling the unsaid things like gnats in the air.

The sensation vanished almost as soon as he got outside. Bard didn't have his own tent. There weren't enough tents, for one, and for another, he and Jori slept at separate times so they shared. He headed back there. Now that sleep was imminent, he was so eager for it that he moved faster.

A mental buzz grew as he got closer and went in. Wells sat cross-legged on the ground, his eyes slitted open as though in a trance, his thin frame perfectly still.

A pang of regret lanced through Bard. He'd made Wells relive some of the horrible memories of being a Sentry, but he stood by his suggestion. Wells was trustworthy and would keep Jori safe.

The Kepron lay just as Bard had left him. Had he ever reached the top of those stairs?

Suddenly awkward, he realized they were both going to sleep at the same time. Should he make a bed on the floor? The idea of stripping off blankets and constructing something new filled his limbs with exhaustion. Jori only took up one side of the bed. And he wouldn't mind. He'd probably just make a joke about it in the morning.

Bard quietly took off his shoes and lay down on top of the blankets on the other side. Glorious comfort soaked into him as he laid his head down on the pillow. His upper back still groaned from the hunched position he'd held earlier, but now that he was lying down, his spine seemed to stretch. His limbs sank into the deep blankets and in seconds, he was asleep.

$$52$$

KIRIA

KIRIA FOLDED FIRIAN'S JACKET. They'd just arrived in Jori's underground shelter again. After reconnaissance, it seemed not to have been discovered. Alone in her quarters, she felt the fabric with her fingers. A guard had informed her that Firian had thirty-one Tanyuin allies inside the walls. It was nearing nightfall now, and only seventeen had reached them. Eight were killed trying to leave, and six were unaccounted for. Seventeen. The number sounded so small, despite the fact they were some of the very best.

The remaining towns had sent their troops as well, but even those were small to summon a decisive victory against an enemy like this. All throughout the day, she kept getting reports of more cities coming to aid Belik. The Tanyu apparently had members in most large cities, and in every nation. Belik was leveraging that pressure now, using his influence with the older generation of warriors to come help him. Kiria's camp had no strong numbers, but the estimates of Belik's power were growing all the time.

It became clearer and clearer. The time to act was now.

She set down the jacket in a corner, the smell of sweat and

pine coming off it. After a pause, she bent and fished in the pocket, where she'd felt something small as she'd interrogated Firian. She held it up to the light. It was a tiny blown glass bead about the size of a fingernail, Brithnem blue. Its shape, round with minute ridges, reminded her of the lanterns in Shifra. The trinket struck her in a way few objects did, as though she recognized a piece of herself in it. What was Firian doing with this?

Unwanted feelings bubbled up as she observed the tiny lantern bead, its workmanship so fine. Glass, that was going to be Firian's profession if he hadn't been recruited to the Academy.

She stuffed the bead away, only realizing afterward that she put it in her own pocket instead of his.

Firian himself was kept in another small room with nothing but a guard and a Sentry. He had a small but crucial role to play in the plan that she and Bard had laid out. Right now, Bard was communicating to the leaders of the different groups in the main room.

To highlight her belief in working with Tanyu who proved their loyalty, she had urged Bard to give the presentation instead of her. He wouldn't give all the details in this briefing. Those would go to individual groups. Only he and she would know the whole scope of what they planned to do.

Straightening her dress and putting on her Beauty, Kiria exited and followed the sound of Bard's voice. The tingling change was less comfortable than before, her scars stretching as a result. They felt much better today, though. The bruises on her ribs and face were dull, and the pain in her cheek wasn't as piercing. As much as she longed to be alone to process everything that was happening, Bard needed her presence for support.

She emerged into the main room. Bard stood on a crate at the far end, overlooking a sea of heads. Endrian soldiers in brown leather armor, Brithnem guards in gleaming metal, Tanyu in black. Heads turned toward her. The presentation momentarily stalled as exclamations resounded around the space. People touched their neighbors' shoulders to urge them to look. Was it her Beauty or her new scars calling up this response? Probably both. Now she had many reasons for people to stare. The storm of whispers slowly died down as she took her place near Bard's platform.

"Yeah, as I was saying," Bard resumed, "most of the Tanyu will remain here..." He outlined the plan with fewer stutters or stops than he tended to use, his lilting voice clear as he addressed the crowd. From where she stood looking up at him, Kiria could see an occasional tremble or extra blink, but Bard was doing exceptionally well for his first time speaking to a large group. Kiria even saw Chetana at the opposite end of the room, nodding in sincere agreement. Bard gestured and nodded and answered a few questions at the end mostly with, "That information is only for the people it directly concerns."

"Thank you. That's all." He stepped off the crate, and the crowd, dismissed, started moving around the packed space. Several people craned to get a better look at Kiria. Others immediately began directing their men and women what to do. Some vented the questions Bard wouldn't answer at each other instead.

"You did very well," Kiria said softly, leaning toward Bard so others wouldn't hear.

He gave a wide, closed-mouth smile. "Thank you."

Two male figures pushed their way through the mass of bodies to talk to Bard.

"Well, that was sexy," said Jori once he was free of the tangle of the crowd. He dusted off his embroidered purple vest with exaggerated care.

Bard barked an uncomfortable laugh, but his demeanor

changed when he saw the person beside him. "Jac," he breathed. Then, stronger, "Jac!"

Bard's brother. He'd mentioned him multiple times but Kiria had never seen him. Jac had light brown skin like Bard's, and black hair, though his was tamed into an attractive coif instead of Bard's wild spikes. He wore the uniform of an Endrian soldier, brass-studded leather over a coat of mail. He stood a little taller than Bard and didn't seem to have Bard's charming humility. Jac's attention ricocheted from his brother to Kiria and back again. Finally, his black eyes settled on Bard, though it looked like it took some effort to keep them there.

"Hey!" Jac greeted, giving Bard a one-armed hug.

Jori raised an eyebrow at him, assessing. Then he pointed between the two of them. "Brother?" he asked.

"Yes," Bard confirmed. "This is my brother Jac. Jac, this is the Keeper Kiria Arioc and this is Jori Calthwaite."

"Also a Keeper," Jori said, shaking Jac's hand and tapping his chest where the royal tattoo lay beneath. "Almost."

Barely disguised amazement shone in Jac's eyes. He looked again at Kiria in disbelief, though whether it was because of her Beauty or because he couldn't believe his brother kept such high company, it was hard to tell.

"It's a pleasure, an honor," he said, unsure.

"I'm happy to meet you too. Bard has done great work for us," Kiria said, deciding the amazement was a good thing. Bard could stand to get more credit.

Jac turned once more to Bard, taking him by the shoulders and shaking him. "I'm proud to be here." Leaning closer, he said, "I wish Mum and Dad could have seen that. And Edom and Rissa and everybody."

Bard's dark eyes shone tearful and a line formed between his brows as he looked into his brother's face. He gripped Jac's arms.

Words started to form but never fully materialized, his mouth twitching, opening, closing. He nodded instead.

Jac laughed and pushed him playfully away. "I've got to get back," he said, taking a furtive look around. Kiria could have sworn he was checking to see if people noticed who he was talking to.

"Will I see you again?" Bard asked in a rush. "I mean, I have to talk to the different leaders, but..."

"You know where I'll be!" Jac called, absorbed once more into the crowd.

Bard's question sent an ache to Kiria's chest. They all didn't have much time left. The plan they'd concocted began in earnest tomorrow afternoon. One day. That was all any of them had before the battle really began.

53

KIRIA

OF COURSE it was Jori who suggested the party. Word spread as quickly as if everyone were Tanyu and could speak mind to mind. The large space all but emptied as everyone took an hour to get ready.

Kiria wasn't sure she wanted to be around so many people the night before they were going to put their plan into action. Her stomach was in knots as it was.

She couldn't keep strategy out of her thoughts. It swirled around like an unholy brew. Any time she paused, thoughts she didn't want came rushing in. The pain of the knife digging into her face, which still stung to the touch. Firian bound to a chair with a look so complicated that she couldn't unravel it to reach the end. The faces of all those they'd lost, and the faces of those she still had to lose.

Maybe the party would be a welcome distraction after all. In the days of Shane and Mari Calthwaite, armies traditionally held huge parties before campaigns. Only recently had the tradition started to fade. Even her father, General Rhet, had learned to dance for such occasions. They were a time of abandonment and gratefulness and joy when there was bound to be a scarcity of those soon.

The underground rooms weren't decorated—Jori complained pleasantly about the fact as he directed the placement of small platters of food—but the light of the torches looked friendlier than it had weeks ago when she and her coterie had hidden there from Belik's forces. Barren but inviting. Well, not barren for very long.

People began to arrive again in droves. Some soldiers abstained from the festivities so they could guard the entrances. She was thankful to them, but also glad to see the Kingdom soldiers, Endrians, a few Sentries, and even Tanyu. Several of the Tanyu greeted her respectfully when they entered, treating her as they would a general.

The room grew hot with all the bodies inside. She shed her soft jacket and wore only a sleeveless blue dress—the nicest one she had with her. This was her last moment to forget about being practical, if she could. The dress had frothy tiers of light blue skirts edged in silver embroidery. The back plunged, as most of her dresses used to do, highlighting her Keeper tattoo, the swirling, sharp-edged pattern of black that ran from the middle of her back to the nape of her neck. Candrae had twisted strands of her hair up into an elaborate knot so the entire pattern would be visible.

Kiria, with considerably less skill, had tried to return the favor, pinning up Candrae's wavy locks, now brown instead of golden. Already, Candrae's hair was falling out, strands trailing down her neck as she talked to Vayci near the hall that led to Kiria's room. Kiria had lent them two of her own dresses. They fit the girls imperfectly, but their eyes shone with excitement nonetheless.

Endrian soldiers in only their shirts and breeches began to play a lively tune on pipes and drums. Unlike so many others, who jumped up to dance, she couldn't rid herself of her worries so easily.

Bard looked like he felt the same way, chatting seriously in a corner with the commander of the Endrian forces. He could talk to some of the leaders tomorrow morning and that would still give them time to prepare, but he had used his hour conversing with the different groups, checking times, counting soldiers, tracking down friends from the Academy. His energy was up, despite the long night he'd had the day before.

From somewhere in the crowd, Jori emerged, his cheeks already pink with drink, and grabbed Bard's arm, dragging him toward the center of the room.

At first, Bard frowned, apparently peeved to have been pulled away from his conversation.

"You can't be solemn all night. There's dancing to be done," Jori said, then stopped. "Look, look!" He leaned down and pointed at something across the room.

Bard and Kiria followed his eyeline to two dark-skinned young women, laughing and talking beside the musicians.

"You know what they're talking about?" Jori asked.

Bard looked confused. "No, do you know them?"

Jori grinned wickedly. "Maybe I will later, but I'll wager they're talking about you. In fact, I know it. I know things. Look!" he repeated. He shifted his voice to a higher register. "Have you seen that Tanyu over there?" He laid a self-assured hand on Bard's shoulder. "Oh, the handsome one?" he made the other girl reply. "That's right. I hear he rescued the dashing Kepron. He's practically a general. So talented, and so good looking!"

Bard put his head down and pulled away half-heartedly, smiling. When Bard wasn't looking, Jori eyed him warmly.

He fished Bard back in with one arm and talked lower in his ear, almost too quiet for Kiria to hear. He was still mimicking the girls across the room. "Oh, if only he could hold me in his arms!"

Bard grimaced before his grin turned wider.

"Oh, darling," said Jori as the second girl, "he's too important and brilliant to dance with you. Can you imagine him coming over here?"

What he said next was lost in the noise of the crowd, but Bard blushed deeply as Jori stood straight again, his raised eyebrows showing he was satisfied.

A touch on her arm made Kiria startle. She spun to face a Tanyu she didn't know, a stern girl with bright red hair cropped short. "Master Kess has asked to speak with you, My Keeper."

Kiria's brows lowered. "Right now?"

"He said it's about tomorrow."

She sighed and followed the girl back through the labyrinth of passages to the room where Firian was kept.

The girl opened the door. Viktor trailed Kiria to the room and entered with her, standing dutifully by the door.

Firian sat in the chair in the middle of the room, no longer bound. In fact, he slumped forward, knees wide apart, hands clasped, head bowed. When she came in, he stood quickly.

Her heart hammered at the sight of him. His presence had always undone some of her composure, though she wasn't sure why that was still true.

"Is everything ready for tomorrow?" he asked. He didn't have the heat in his gaze that had characterized their interactions before the palace attack.

"Everyone knows the plan. All that's left is to do it. May God be with us." She raised her eyes to the ceiling. A familiar ache returned like a wave. She couldn't relax tonight, not with everything at stake and the final stand so close.

Firian drew his lips into a serious line. She looked away from them as he lowered his voice. "Belik put a Sentry on me. I just told Bard a minute ago."

A lump lodged in Kiria's throat. She'd learned a lot about

Sentries lately. They blocked others from the Unreal, but Firian had said something about another level below the Unreal. Would Sentries prevent him from getting there too? "Does that mean you can't do it?"

His usually arrogant manner faltered and his eyes dipped to the floor, darting as though he had dropped puzzle pieces there. "We tried to locate him. Lev Aramin is his name. But his mind is out to sea."

"Out to sea?"

"On a ship," he explained.

They couldn't reach the Sentry in time, not without expending soldiers she couldn't spare. Her expression hardened. "You'll still try it," she commanded.

He nodded once, without argument. Fire without light. Almost hopeless.

She took a step forward. "Firian," she said, lowering her own voice to match his, "you are the most dangerous person I know. So be dangerous."

The slow intensity of her words made him raise his eyes to hers again, and a smirk tugged at the edges of his mouth. He pulled his shoulders back and stood tall. "You know I will."

"I know you will," she echoed.

The warm moment between them froze quickly. She was getting too close again. *Again!* Would she never be rid of him?

"Is that all you had to tell me?" she asked.

"No one's broken a Sentry before, that I know of." Though his confidence had returned, the words still felt like a confession. He could fail.

Regardless, he was their best hope of finding and eliminating Belik. "That was true of a lot of things, before you came along."

"Dangerous things," he said, apparently comforted by the idea.

Though he didn't step closer, she remembered the times he had. *Dangerous things.*

"Yes," she replied curtly, eager to get out of the room. "Let one of the guards know if you need anything else."

He breathed in as though he wanted to say something else, but then he just exhaled slowly.

She turned to go and remembered her Beauty and the tattoo on her bare back. Her skin flushed warm.

"My... Keeper," Firian said. Had he ever called her that before? It didn't feel like it. She turned. "I'll get it done. Good luck tomorrow." He clamped his mouth shut and nodded, as though biting back other things he wanted to say.

"You too." She paused. Though she kept reminding herself that she couldn't trust Firian, he was helping her. He'd effectively saved Kader by faking his death. He'd brought troops to her aid. It felt wrong to keep him always locked away—in the Academy, in her mind, in this room. "Do you have any other clothes?"

His brows darted downward. "Why?"

"You read the Scroll."

He nodded.

"Do you remember the party the founders had before the war started?"

"In Shifra."

"Right." Maybe she had told him about it too. She had been so giddy with excitement when they'd visited the fortress there together. "Since we're... taking the Kingdom back tomorrow, Jori started up a party in the common room."

"You did look dressed up."

She didn't respond to the comment, even though he said it more innocently than usual. Firian would have to prove himself with more than a couple weeks of good behavior. But he wasn't a prisoner, not really. She looked back at the guard by the door.

There was another one just outside. "Get some of Jori's clothes and bring them here for Master Kess," she said. Though Firian was more muscular, they looked as though they'd wear approximately the same size.

"I have this," Firian protested as the guard left the room.

"Have you ever been to a party?" she asked, eyeing his dusty black shirt and pants.

"Yes."

"I don't know. You never let yourself relax." She could have been talking about herself lately. "Go ahead and change. Everybody's in there. I'll tell the guards it's all right."

Kiria relayed the message to the guard as she left with the Tanyuin girl. Tracing the dark path back to the party, she mulled over his new information. His ability in the Unreal was crucial to their success against Belik. She didn't understand everything about Sentries, but if Firian felt that he couldn't break through, maybe something terrible would happen if he tried too hard. He wasn't the kind of person to do things by halves. He wasn't afraid to die.

She emerged into the main space in a burst of sound and laughter and music and light. The room had gotten even more crowded than before. People had to walk sideways to thread their way through the mass of bodies. The smell of bubbling cider and meat and sweat hung heavily in the air. A raucous burst of laughter came from beside one of the bracketed lanterns. Every other light was intricately patterned, casting a multi-colored glow over the party. A small group of soldiers were placing bets on the comparative abilities of the Brithnem and Endrian troops. Their glittering eyes and loud voices as they held up their coins told Kiria they were already drunk.

Kiria made her way through the crush to the guards at the steps leading out, to make sure they knew that Firian was invited just like everyone else. Most of them didn't like Firian, but they didn't need to. They did all need to work together, though.

Everyone seemed to be having fun, but Firian's news troubled her, interrupting even the lively music trying to caper into her thoughts.

"So sour!" Jori acknowledged the female Tanyu with a wink as he drew Kiria with him into the throng of dancers. People pressed against her on all sides, moving to the beat. "This is your chance to relax, you know," he said once they were within arm's length of the musicians.

"I thought you were talking to Bard." She had to yell to be heard. Jori should just leave her to her thoughts for once.

"Here. Stay here." He disappeared and returned with something strong in a cup. "Drink this."

"You'll make a terrible Keeper," she said, thawing toward him.

He shrugged. "We all know that."

They shared a look. Then Jori's gray eyes turned impish as he started waving to the rhythm of the drums. She rolled her eyes as he took her free hand and shook her arm. Tension seemed to fall from her body as he made her dance like a rag doll. Once she was loose enough to start dancing on her own, Jori caught her in his arms and they whirled around the floor. She tripped a little as they spun. He'd always been the better dancer.

She pulled away to sip the drink he'd given her, half of which had already spilled. The bubbles rushed to her head immediately. When was the last time she'd eaten?

Jori was already dancing with someone else, and then she was too as the sparkling tune shifted into a different song, a familiar drinking ballad. Jori clapped and leaned heavily on Bard, who had reappeared. Although his voice was pitchy, Jori launched into a lusty rendition of the song. Volume made up for accuracy. His enthusiasm drew those around him to sing too. Even Kiria sang, glad that the others drowned out her voice. At first, Bard didn't join, as though he'd never learned the words, but then he came in on the repetitive chorus. Jori sang at the people around him, men and women, as though it were a competition he was winning.

When the song came to a warbling end, everyone cheered and clapped and threw back the last gulp of their drinks. Kiria laughed and did the same.

"You can sing. You can sing!" Jori told a few people around him who'd carried the tune better than he had.

Another song began. Some moved off to get food while others joined the dancers. Through the crowd, Kiria caught flashes of Firian walking along the side of the room. He'd actually taken her suggestion. He wore dark gray pants tucked into his Tanyuin boots, and an embroidered vest of dark blue over an off-white shirt. The white made his skin look tanner than usual. Rather than wearing it as Jori usually did—open and dissolute—he had buttoned the entire vest. The result made him look like a prince.

His too-straight posture was the only detail that gave away his discomfort. Otherwise, one might think that he owned the room and had suggested the party himself.

Stomping, not in time with the music, caught her attention. A small group from Erad hunkered together, slapping their thighs, stomping, clapping, in a dance they all knew by heart. They whooped when an Eradi Tanyu joined in.

When she looked back at Firian, Bard was by his side, beaming and chattering. Firian's expression softened, more at ease.

This was a night to forget what lay ahead, to delight in what they still had right now. Everyone had their own ways of doing that. Some arm wrestled, others danced, others drank or flirted or sang or laughed. But there was no talk of strategy, no dour expressions. Tonight they all had each other, if only for one more day.

Kiria went back into the midst of the dancing. She was instantly face to face with Jac Tanery, who looked abashed to be dancing with a Keeper. She danced with them all, even Viktor, who had eventually switched duty with Merrick so he could participate in the fun. When she looked over, Jori had joined Bard and Firian, all with mugs in their hands. He'd lifted up his shirt to the neck to show off his royal tattoo. *Incorrigible.*

Every time she spun around, Firian drew her eyes, but he didn't always meet her gaze. He was having fun of his own that didn't include her. She half expected him to stalk forward through the crowd and dance with her when the music slowed, but he made no move toward her. The more glasses she had, the more she wished he would try.

Jori began to lead another chorus, beckoning for Bard and Firian to follow. Jori had never liked Firian, so it pleased her to know he was trying to get along with him. To her amazement, Firian danced. He instantly caught the attention of some of the younger female soldiers, who eagerly danced beside him. Kiria kept one eye on him as she jumped and kicked her feet to the beat. Firian caught onto the steps quickly, and pulled many partners close, but not any one person for long. Not that it mattered.

When the song ended, Firian clanked his mug against a few others and drank. His smile afterward was everything. It made her heart skip with its openness and boyishness. It was the smile she'd wanted to see from him since the moment they'd met. It wasn't crafty or seductive or arrogant. It was a short glimpse beneath the mask. This Firian had a family, had friends that cared about him. This Firian could be different. The dimpled grin was gone in a flash, but it burned in her memory like an aftershock.

He turned his eyes to her, and she realized she was staring. She looked away. Her plan to help him have fun and to be more accepted into the group had worked—miracle of miracles! Still, a small part of her, a secret part, had hoped he would talk to her, not about the coming battle, but just to talk. It had seemed inevitable. He'd always had his fixation. They. Together. But seeing him like this, giving her space when she didn't act interested, reminded her of what she had loved in the first place. He was still dangerous, but now, it seemed, he might be able to show kindness too.

She took a break from the dancing to eat from a stack of buttered bread. She couldn't afford to relive feelings that had brought her nothing but pain.

Firian left early, while the moon was still high outside.

Kiria stayed, even when the music slowed down and leftover food was brought out when the new plates were gone. She laughed until her lip split open again. How long since she had laughed? Too long, she decided.

She ran her gaze over the remaining people, a fraction of those who had crammed the space earlier. Bard was still bobbing joyfully to the music with his brother and a few others. A couple kissed in a darkened corner. Two servants had begun to clean up dishes.

Jori sidled up to her, looking at the others. "Oh, love," he sighed. "I sincerely hope we don't all die tomorrow."

$$54$$

BARD

WHEN BARD finally steered Jori back to his room after the party, the buzz of a Sentry already surrounded the Kepron's mind.

Wells wasn't sitting in a corner as before. Sentries didn't need to be close to the people they guarded, but they did need to get their assignments in person. Connecting to the Unreal in healthier ways wasn't something they could do after a while. It was all static.

Won't be long, though. Former Sentries could be free to live their lives without taking shifts at their old, mind-numbing job. If Bard's plan worked. If they all lived.

Familiar worry descended into his thoughts. Jac believed in him now. The knowledge had made him as buoyant as the wine. His home, which he'd felt slip further and further away with every passing day, was his again. But now his brother's life was at stake because of his plan. This had to work. They had too few allies to regroup if his scheme fell through. An ache twisted his stomach.

"Don't you look grim!" Jori exclaimed, poking Bard's face. "No grim... grimness. Is that a word?"

"I think so."

Jori tried to toe off his boots but they were on too tight. Giving up, he bent over, stumbled, and managed to undo the laces. "Your brother, he's not so bad."

"I didn't say he was bad, did I?"

"Brothers... are good," Jori concluded.

Bard chuckled, though his heart ached for Jori, who didn't have one anymore. "I like mine."

Jori fell into bed, gathering the covers up over himself. "Won't they all be jealous?" he said, curling up on his side.

"Hmm?"

"I took the strategist to bed after the party."

Bard's cheeks flamed.

Jori laughed at his expression. "I'm sorry, I'm sorry," he said, then disarmingly patted the blankets beside him. "Come here."

Maybe it was the bubbles still floating through Bard's head, but he did. Kicking off his shoes, he laid down on top of the blankets like before. Jori tucked up next to him and threw an arm over his chest. It was surprisingly comfortable. Feeling someone next to him reminded him of home, of sleeping three to a bed when he was a child in Enderin. It was nice to be held. It was nice to be held *by him*.

"There you go," Jori murmured, kissing the back of his head.

Bard hummed, feeling strange and relaxed all at once. He hadn't wanted to find a different room where he would be alone. Not tonight. Jori must have seen it written on his face.

Tentatively, he reached for Jori's hand with his good one and held it.

"Did you know you have a freckle on your ear?" Jori asked, barely audible, his breathing deep and slow. He was asleep before Bard could answer the question.

55

KIRIA

KIRIA STARED at the darkened ceiling, trying to summon prayers. The fizz of hope from Jori's party was wearing off—that buffer between her and the inevitable conflict beyond. She touched her lip and rubbed her fingers together. The split had apparently closed, because her hand felt dry.

Had she thought of everything? In this breathless wait before the battle began, her courage felt small.

Whispering into the dark, she repeated to herself the sacrifices and losses she had already endured. Compared to those, the task ahead became manageable. She could stare it down and see it through.

Candrae and Vayci, exhausted from the excitement of the night, slept nearby, ready to help her in a second. Her whispering might have already woken them up, but she knew they wouldn't grudge her for it. The Western Kingdom depended on her. Her body sagged with the weight, but sleep wouldn't come.

A soft knock rang at the door. Royce spoke through the crack as he opened it. "Amir Chetana," he announced.

"Let her in," Kiria said, sitting up and fumbling for a way to light the candle by her bed.

Vayci stumbled to her feet and helped a guttering flame appear as Chetana strode into the room with a bundle in her arms.

"My Keeper," she greeted in a gentle voice. "I thought you would still be awake."

"I was having trouble falling asleep," Kiria admitted, trying to puzzle out why Chetana had come. She hadn't been at the party, but that was no surprise.

The Amir set down the bundle on the bed. Layers of clothing and armor. It was difficult to make out all the details in the gloom except for the impression of gleaming blue and silver. "For tomorrow," she said. "I asked if I could bring it to you."

"It looks perfect." Kiria indicated for her to sit. Something was clearly weighing on Chetana too.

Candrae was awake now and standing beside Vayci.

"Do you want privacy?" she asked.

"No, that's not necessary," said Chetana, waving her hand.

"What's going on?" Kiria folded her hands in her lap and turned to her former advisor.

Chetana's posture was immaculate with her strong neck and imperious gaze. A slight crease appeared between her brows. "I owe you an apology, My Keeper."

"For what?"

"I underestimated your judgment. More than once. You were right to put your trust in Master Tanery. He has clearly demonstrated his loyalty. Kiria, I..." She pursed her lips and took Kiria's hand. "I never doubted your intention, but I doubted your strength, your ability to lead. I'm sorry for the ways that I have sown that doubt in others. You've fully shown your capability to be the Keeper of the Western Kingdom."

Kiria squeezed her hand. "There's nothing to forgive. You always considered the Kingdom before devotion to its leaders. I want more people like you around me. And I'm glad you've finally come around about Bard."

Chetana gave a wan smile. "I have... difficulties... with the Tanyu."

"Don't we all," said Kiria drily.

"But you," Chetana resumed, looking intently, "you deserve all the love and loyalty of your people. You are worthy of their devotion."

Kiria's forehead felt tight. Chetana said the last sentence with such conviction. *Worthy.* She'd fought to be worthy enough to lead the land and the people she loved. The layers of her sacrifices had started to confer that title on her, but to hear it from someone else's lips... She swallowed the rock in her throat. She couldn't respond.

"I was your advisor, but you are the one who has taught me. I have always striven to be worthy of love," Chetana began. The word *striven* made Kiria miss Daelon. Chetana wasn't able to contact him directly when she tried to go back to Brithnem, but rumors said he was working as a slave for the Tanyu. "My sister..." She cleared her throat, forcing out the words. "My sister and I grew up in King's Heights. Bastard children, both of us. We had no one but each other. And we... we loved each other." Her voice broke as she talked about Gerand, but she quickly recovered her queenly composure. "I thought she loved me. Our mother died when we were young, so we were left alone. You went there. You saw how different we would have been from everyone else."

Kiria pictured the sea of traditionally Kingdom-looking people with pale skin and dusty brown hair. Their suspicion of her had spilled into violence quickly. As far as Kiria knew, they were still angry because she had worked with the Tanyu to defeat the Torithians, and they didn't trust how quickly she had ascended to the throne.

Chetana continued. "Gerand fit in better than I, but we were both outcasts. We needed each other. We found a... small group of other Khelê to belong to, out of the public eye. They didn't mock or persecute us. They said we had Talent, and they fostered it. We both became strong in their ranks. Their goal was to dismantle the Tanyu, because of the ways they'd strayed from their purpose. I was devoted to that task. And then our invitations came to be tested at the Tanyuin Academy. I dismissed mine immediately. I think I burned the letter. But Gerand was lured by the glamour and power she perceived in it. So she went. We fought." Chetana's pained expression became abstracted. Lines pulled around her full lips. "We fought. She thought I should be glad for her, but I couldn't forgive her for abandoning me. Life with Original Plan was a hard one, and we had no other family. Now I don't know whether or not she still lives." A fraught silence fell.

Kiria's mind spun with the pieces of Chetana's life. Pieces clicked into place like machine parts. She had Talent that she'd used for Original Plan, a group Kiria had heard of in passing, always in negative terms. In reputation, they were just shy of a terrorist organization. And Chetana's *katah* with Master Belik. That must have happened as a result of something she was doing with that group. Daelon resulted. The depth of that history was more than she felt equipped to fathom. And then Chetana had turned to God and to serving the Keepers.

Chetana adjusted her face and pressed Kiria's hands once more. "I don't tell this story to unburden myself, but to demonstrate what you have shown me. Without you, my young Keeper, I would not know what unconditional love looks like. You love the unworthy."

Kiria wasn't sure which "unworthy" one she meant.

"Thank you," Chetana concluded with the seriousness of a

prayer. The candle flame danced over her lace septum ring as she dipped her head.

Kiria's face felt hot. She hardly deserved such heartfelt confidence. Only Kiria knew the extent of her own weakness, how she nearly broke under torture, how she still sometimes thought about Firian despite all her good judgment, and how she was so, so afraid of tomorrow.

But she was a little less afraid now.

When she found her voice, she said, "You give me strength too, Chetana." Abandoning the protocol that the Amir so carefully maintained, Kiria leaned forward and grasped her in a hug. The bruises along her ribs protested against the contact, but when Chetana held her like her mother used to, the sting was worth it. Tears slid from Kiria's tightly shut eyes. She savored the warmth and breath of the Amiran woman who had endured so much.

Time seemed to spill into the space between them when they broke apart. Only hours left now. Maybe that was part of the reason Chetana had come. Time might be running out for all of them. They had to say what needed to be said. More tomorrows weren't guaranteed.

Kiria's grip on Chetana's brown hands grew tight.

The Amir extricated her fingers and laid one palm on Kiria's head, softly chanting words from the Scroll. "*Greatness is found in service and majesty in love. Remember a heritage of evil but a future of hope.*"

Kiria nodded stoutly. *A future of hope.*

Happiness pulled at Chetana's mouth as she stood to leave. "*God supports the just man's cause—*"

The Scroll game. Kiria smiled. "*—and dawns upon him light in darkness.*"

56

___

KIRIA

THE NEXT DAY was cloudy and a little cold, even into midday. Kiria tightened her grip around the small scroll she had just sealed. Her wishes, should she not make it out of this conflict alive. Really, there were only two wishes, that the struggle for justice in the Kingdom continue and its three thrones be restored.

After some thought, she had named a third cousin—the only relative she was sure was still living—to be her heir. Her cousin had married a wealthy merchant and moved to Hinter, north of Enderin, far enough from the fighting to be safe.

Merrick, armor-clad, took the roll of paper from her and tucked it neatly inside a pocket. Kiria's heart beat a dull thud in her chest. The leather tunic beneath her own armor left her plenty of room to breathe—she had checked when Candrae and Vayci helped her put it on—but it felt as though it were shrinking.

She nodded a thank you at the guard.

Most of the others had already left to their positions. No more soldiers from Rantoul or Redshore, Skirwith or Tarryall, remained in the bunker. Endrian troops were gone too. Bard had left early to check on the Sentries. Some of the other Tanyu remained, and a small company of Kingdom soldiers that would go with Jori. They'd arrived just yesterday. She didn't ask them how they got past Tanyu at the gates. Others had been waiting outside the city for Kiria to arrive, since it was safer outside than inside now. Firian was here too, still deep in one of the smaller rooms. As soon as Sentries blocked the mind of Belik and his inner circle, he would leave as well.

Chairs had been set up in the main room in a few short rows. Leftover from last night, the smell of tart and savory food tanged the air.

Boots hitting the hard floor of the hallway signaled the arrival of Jori. He was dressed in armor similar to hers, except that he had no swath of blue across his shoulders. The thin plates of metal moved soundlessly with him. Most armor Kiria had seen looked bulky but Jori still managed to look lithe and dashing. His smirk as he approached told her that he thought the same thing.

"I know," he said, holding up a hand and then transitioning into pinwheeling his arm as though testing it out. "I look amazing."

"Did you take time to do your hair?" she asked, squinting at his perfect, dark waves.

He drew his hand through it. "Always best to be prepared." Despite his cavalier attitude, she saw the same edge of fear in his eyes that haunted her own thoughts.

"Speaking of that," she said, "we need your heir."

"So soon?"

It took discipline not to roll her eyes. She gestured to the guard. "Merrick will keep the names safe for us. I don't think we'll need them, but we have to be ready, just in case." She tried to keep her tone light. "I'm sure you'll have no trouble at all finding a girl you like after you're the Keeper, but we have to be prepared now, like you said."

"Hm, yes." His gaze darkened. "Who'd you choose?"

"Third cousin."

"I'm sure I have one of those. Does it have to be family?"

She considered. "Normally, but we're running low on them." They shared a look full of memories of Kiria's mother and Atty.

"Does it have to be a man?"

Her eyebrows shot up. "No." If they were abandoning the idea of bloodlines, then they could abandon the idea of two men and one woman.

He considered his fingernails. "Haved. I choose Haved."

A smile crept onto Kiria's face. "Jori, that's perfect," she breathed. "Write it down and seal it. Then..." *Then you can go.* But she didn't want him to leave yet. He looked strong and brave and she was so proud of him. "You'll do wonderfully," she said instead.

Someone handed Jori a slip of paper and a writing utensil. He scratched out the words, looking from her to the paper and back. When he was done, he rolled it up as she had and sealed it, giving it to Merrick for safekeeping. "I have no doubt," he replied, settling his hands on her shoulders, "that you'll make us all proud."

"I love you," she said, voice breaking.

"I love you too, darling." They couldn't wait any longer. Kingdom soldiers were waiting for Jori to arrive. "I'll see you in the Main!" he called as he let two guards usher him away.

When he was gone, she took a deep, calming breath. This was it. Now it had really begun. At the thought, her sadness and fear started to crystalize into something more, something different.

Since the attack on her home, she had run and hid and

planned. No more. Now was the time for action, for justice, for her to shove the tyrant off her throne.

Tesni approached. "Master Tanery just said the Sentries are in place, My Keeper."

"Good. Thank you."

Moments afterward, Kiria found Chetana praying in a separate room, their time not yet come to leave. She joined her for a short while, then checked compulsively on the Tanyu in the front room and with her army preparing outside. Bard was next. It was difficult to contact him, but a good way to use the remaining minutes. He reassured her that everything was ready.

Finally, she strode down the hallway to Firian's room. The guard outside opened the door when he saw her coming. Firian sat on the floor, bent over one outstretched leg, limbering himself for the task ahead. He raised his eyes to her and came slowly out of the stretch. As ever, he wore the black uniform of the Tanyu. No jacket. Dust from the floor clung to his pants as he stood.

"Are you ready?" she asked.

"Yes." His blue eyes blazed with the intensity he'd always had, but there was a softness now that hadn't been there before. Strength and passion but no chemical lust. Either he had figured out a way to break off the Sentry, or he was confident he would find one.

"I assume you still have the Sentry." She wasn't strong enough to sense whether or not it was on him without trying to go into his mind.

He nodded, a faint note of frustration bleeding through.

"My sources say Master Belik spends most of his time in the front wing of the palace, near the Main."

"I'll take care of it."

"Sundown," she said. "You'll have ten minutes."

"I understand," he replied, tightening a cloth around his

hand with his teeth. It was black like the rest of his clothes, but he wore it much like a gesture of mourning.

They would lift the Sentry on Belik's mind only for that long. One of their only advantages was their Sentries that could hinder communication on the enemy side. Ten minutes would provide Firian a window to use his killing ability. If he could break through or disable the Sentry on his own mind.

Kiria frowned.

Catching her look, he raised a questioning brow.

"Can you do this?" she asked intently, matching his stare.

"If anybody can," he replied.

He was right. So much of their plan hinged on someone who she didn't want to trust. The new foundation he had built in support of her instead of against her was still a tumbled ruin, but she could see its outline. She sighed, then gave a curt nod.

"Be brave," he said softly. His baritone voice cut through her thoughts, steadying her. He met her eyes. Strength and, if she didn't know better, admiration shone in the depths of them.

"Be dangerous."

A smile tugged at his mouth, crinkling the corners of his eyes. His effortless confidence bolstered hers. The leather jerkin under her armor didn't feel quite as tight. "As you would have it, Kiria." With that, he cracked his neck and swiftly left the room, silent as a shadow.

More pieces moving on the board.

She watched him go. He moved as someone who completely inhabited his body, knowing its every facet and point of balance.

She'd never heard him say her name like that. Soft, yet distant and respectful. Something definitive had changed in him since the attack. It was in the line of his jaw and the level of his gaze. He still had the awareness of a predator, but not the razor-sharp edges.

Tanyu were beginning to settle into their seats when Kiria

returned to the main room. They spent no time shuffling or adjusting like people did in the Main, she realized. This pool of black figures simply took their places like frozen figures in a pantomime. She was transfixed. Without any external signal, they closed their eyes as one.

Hopefully, the presence of so many Tanyu would draw out some of Belik's from beyond the wall. Kiria's allies would be ready for them.

Seconds ticked away. Soon, her army would march on Brithnem.

Be brave.

Be dangerous.

<hr>

KIRIA ADJUSTED THE FOREARM GUARD, tightening the strap that held it in place. Around her marched Kingdom soldiers and allies from across the continent. The force, to her, looked huge. Thousands strong. But she could see the end of the marching mass of armored bodies, and before them lay the walls of Brithnem, tall and thick and guarded by expert Tanyu and ruthless Torithians. Her blood went hot as she spied moving figures above the massive Abrecan Gate.

Her army wasn't quiet or subtle. Their boots whisked through the charred grasses of the outer edge, armor gleaming in the sunlight. In the absence of many traditional generals, Royce had taken charge of soldiers' behavior and cleanliness. He was with Jori now, along the northern edge of the wall. Jori needed him more than she did, having no combat experience and going into the heart of enemy territory—territory that rightly belonged to them.

Flexing her wrist, she forced her squeezing heart to slow. They would all do their best. No one could ask for more.

The army stopped. She, in the middle, couldn't see how much land was left between her forces and the gate. Enough to avoid arrow fire. Chetana stood somewhere out front. Too bad Kiria couldn't see her. The latent power in her former advisor would make her a terrifying foe.

"My Keeper," a soldier murmured reverently, offering her his hand.

She hadn't noticed them bringing the platform forward. A square stand made of planks lay at her feet, lined with men and women ready for combat.

She took the soldier's hand out of courtesy as she stepped up. Her veins hummed with life and something almost like gladness. Gladness—a word that belonged to Chetana and Daelon's vocabulary. Appropriate that it should come to mind now. Once she stood in the center, six soldiers lifted the platform and muscled it onto their shoulders. Brief vertigo rocked her, but she spread her feet and laid a hand on the sword at her hip.

For a long minute, she didn't speak, just stood there feeling like the statue of her ancestor Mari in the Main, gloriously beautiful, armed, and resolved to get her kingdom back. All her life had sharpened to this point. She would drive forward until victory or death.

The dark figures pacing the walls stilled and the line of them grew thicker as more climbed to see the Keeper held aloft. Could any citizens also see her? Hopefully they did and knew that hope was coming.

Finally, she spoke. "My name is Kiria Arioc," she cried. The scar stretched across her lip but she didn't slur. "Second Keeper of the Western Kingdom. I have a message for Master Belik, the pretender, the murderer, the usurper who took my throne."

A breeze blew across the seared fields, ruffling the stray hairs pulled free around her face. Its gentle hush revealed just how quiet everyone was. In the mass of people, no one made a sound. It was like being in the Unreal.

"Surrender now," she demanded, her voice rising above the silence. "Surrender, or we will take the city back by force."

She had considered many other things to say—addressing the torture, the manipulation, the way no citizens could speak against Tanyuin rule—but in the end, she had decided on those words. That was the heart of it.

"You have one hour," she called.

The soldiers lowered her down. The figures above the gate began bustling again, faster this time. She couldn't hear anything they said from this distance, but her threats had galvanized them into action, at least.

One hour.

It was enough time to hurry from the palace to the Abrecan Gate, enough time to send troops from other stations along the wall, enough time to focus Belik's every thought her way. Having Chetana in front would hopefully solidify that.

It was enough time for the others to get into position while everyone turned their attention toward her.

57

BELIK

THE DULL CRACKLE of a Sentry slammed into Belik's mind. It was like cutting off air. His eyes shot to Nedi, Shiro, and Enktuya, who stood nearby in the Main, and they confirmed his suspicions. All of them had Sentries.

Shit. "How many others have Sentries?" he growled. "Find out."

Shiro disappeared to obey.

Like a new wound distracts from a duller one, the Sentry removed his *katah* with Chetana. He hadn't actively used it in years, but it festered in his mind, always a thought away from rekindling. Being so angry and yet having to be so careful had made him tense, always. That tension shifted now. The difference was slight, but it pushed some knowledge he hadn't realized a moment ago into relief. Chetana was here. She was in the army marching against him.

Of course she was. She was a warrior, and had chosen her side. His heart beat furiously in his chest. He should have dealt with them all sooner.

There was one primary reason not to attack the princess right away after he found her cell empty. Everything in his blood wanted to crush her decisively, to tear away the feeble hope that Firian and the people of Brithnem still clung to. But if he waited, he could flush out all her allies, destroy them at once. No lingering, petty attempts to unseat the Tanyu from their rightful place. This way, when he killed her, she wouldn't be a martyr, but a final note in a song that would never play again.

Her forces were approaching the main gate. A frontal assault. Always so gory predictable. Well, he could work with that. Early estimates from the walls suggested they were seven thousand strong. Not bad considering the offer he'd made to all towns in the Western Kingdom—money and autonomy. Very few people could resist such a potent combination. Especially when the alternative meant marching into death at the behest of a young girl who'd betrayed them all by running into the arms of the enemy and leaving her people vulnerable. His version of the story had spread, and no one had the facts to deny him. It was close enough that it had the smell of truth.

Seven thousand, and now Sentries. It was the Sentries that bothered him, more than an army's-worth of weapons.

Sentries meant that Firian was back from the Academy. Several Tanyu—traitors—had defected to Kiria's side, trying to leave the city. That should have tipped him off. He hated killing Tanyu, but what could he do? They were like Firian's spineless friend who left after the Academy was attacked. A liability.

Something gnawed the pit of his stomach. Not fear, but anger, frustration, disappointment. He'd said he would kill Firian on sight if he returned. The idea didn't thrill him, but he would stay true to his word. Sentries also meant that there were more than the seven thousand that met the eye.

Even if Kiria did have more people on her side, she couldn't win. They'd wear themselves out against the gate as more and more people sailed to help the Tanyu. It was more of a nuisance, though, like untangling a knot he thought he could cut clean through.

A Tanyuin woman approached the foot of the dais. "The Keeper's allies have reached the Abrecan Gate, Master Belik."

He grunted. "And?"

"She demands your surrender within the hour."

That actually brought a laugh to his lips. It came out humorless and grating. That girl dared to defy him so openly? The girl who had quivered and cried and screamed in pain in the arena? This was her last gambit. He was sure of it.

The buzz of the Sentry coursed along the line of his mind, whining incessantly. Already he couldn't stand it.

He flexed his jaw and faced the Tanyu. "Send all the Torithians and soldiers to the walls." Raewhith and Imlin and Archer's Point and myriad others whom he compelled to be there, to earn their place in his new world. The new world he was supposed to share with Firian. But it was better this way. Better alone. Attachment only made one weak.

"As you would have it, Master Belik," the Tanyu said, turning to go.

"And set up chairs in the Main."

"Of course, Master Belik."

Belik could throw all those forces at Kiria and not even use the Tanyu to defeat her army. Most of those he would keep inside the palace for now, the deadliest weapon and a precious resource. But Firian had Tanyu as well, and they wouldn't keep quiet in this fight. Better to address them head-on.

An hour? Maybe this battle could end before it began.

It would be a short fight. Kiria and Chetana would die, along with all their allies, and he would rule unopposed.

58
———

JORI

Jori felt like a hero in a book. Or, he would, if he weren't wedging himself between two muddy wooden planks like a child hiding from its nurse.

Armor was distinctly overrated. He'd suspected it already, though he couldn't deny its aesthetic appeal, but now the verdict was clear. Too clunky. Too hard to move in.

"Isn't this exactly what you were expecting?" he hissed at the trailing group of soldiers behind him, flashing them a grin.

Nobody answered. Spoilsports.

A small pang of regret lanced through him that so many people knew about these places now. He was giving up the best hideouts, after all. Parties, escapes, stolen kisses, places to be alone... He would just have to find new ones. He had the nose for it.

The armor protested as he finally squeezed himself inside. Turning around, he assessed the relative fitness of the other soldiers. They weren't pudgy, but some of them had manly barrel chests or women's breasts that he doubted could fit through the opening. Not that he was complaining. He bit his lip and drummed his fingertips together. "I'm sure if you just..."

The nearest man tried once to get through, failed, then crashed into one of the beams with his shoulder, pushing it aside.

"Marvelous," Jori said. "Just what I was going to do. Of course, we should also be quiet."

"*You* should be quiet," grumbled the soldier.

"That's hardly the attitude." They should be grateful that someone could lead them onto the palace grounds through undiscovered ways. *Undiscovered until now.* He sighed.

They'd been struggling on for two hours. The sun was setting. They'd come from the north, past the wall, the Maze—a neighborhood he frequented, inhabited by a colorful cast of poor and unsavory characters—then through Soldiers Way, and were nearing the palace itself. It wasn't easy taking a group of eight, even if they were the palace elite, through back ways secret enough to hide them. No Tanyu accompanied them, so Belik and his ilk wouldn't read their minds, or whatever Tanyu did exactly, though Jori could think of one he wouldn't mind having near him.

That morning, he'd woken up with Bard Tanery's hair in his mouth. It was wonderful.

Jori dropped his voice. "It's up here," he said, pointing down an earthen shaft. "Down and up."

His chest gave a twist of apprehension. They had nearly made it. He, Jori Calthwaite, had led troops to the enemy's doorstep. He smiled, even as his heart darkened. The end of his expertise lay straight ahead. As soon as they emerged into the cell of the Amiran Academy, his job was over. Then he became just the black sheep of the Calthwaite family, standing there in borrowed armor, suddenly a liability. If Kiria were here, she would say something lovely to him. Maybe that he wasn't alone. But he was. At this moment, he was.

I hope you appreciate what I'm doing for you, he thought to

Atty. The memory of his brother galvanized him, and he wiggled his fingers to get feeling back into them.

Kingdom soldiers followed him deeper into the darkened tunnel, less regular than the official escape tunnels for the Keepers. There must have been some forbidden love story involved in its making. That, or smuggling. Jori hadn't used it for much except escaping his lessons.

The soldiers' skepticism about this route followed him but he slicked it off like water. He had one job, and he was going to do it. Feeling blindly above him, he detected a handhold, something more solid than the fragrant, loose dirt they crawled over. *Stupid armor.* Though he had to admit, he was devastatingly handsome in it. Gripping the handle, he pushed upward. The trapdoor stuck, leaving a sliver of fresher air trickling from the room beyond.

He considered his options. Something was blocking the way, so he'd have to call out. Was an Amir in there, or an enemy? He tried to squint through the opening but saw nothing. He felt dashing, but that was as far as his skills went. He couldn't fight a Tanyu or a pirate. The dim memory returned to him of a frustrated tutor explaining that it was strategically better to have the high ground in a fight. This, he concluded, was not the high ground.

"One of you lovely people want to take a stab at this?" he said, stepping back. Royce stepped forward.

Surely, Bard wouldn't have put them willingly in danger. It must be only an Amir in there, if anyone. Maybe someone friendly, like his frustrated childhood tutor. Jori clasped his hands behind his back and smiled encouragingly back at the other troops, though they probably couldn't see him in this gloom.

Royce laid a strong forearm against the trapdoor and pushed. He managed to get it wide enough that they all could see a piece of furniture balanced on it, its legs pushed to a tottering angle. Shuffling feet hurried over to right it. Long grayish-blue robe. The face came next.

"Daelon," greeted Jori, relief washing over him, "how are you?"

JORI WAS wrong in his first approximation that the air in Daelon's cell was fresher than the air in the tunnel. It was not.

A sour tang in the air made him scrunch his nose as he emerged from the trapdoor in the floor. Daelon had graciously moved the desk out of the way to let them up. The Amir grasped Jori's upper arm to haul him inside.

After his initial surprise and happiness at seeing Jori alive, his face was a mask of worry. "How many of you are there?"

Jori looked at Royce, who had come up first. "Eight? Nine if you count me." Looking around the space, it was abundantly clear that the foul-smelling cell could only hold perhaps two more people, unless they wanted to start stacking on top of each other.

Powerful memories of his own tutor returned to him. Jori, age eight, told to sit still and memorize figures. Age nine, presented with world maps. Age ten, quizzed on passages from the Scroll.

These books, this dust, those high-necked robes... He stiffened as though there would be a test. This, he supposed, was the test. He smoothed the place where his collar would be, though now it was just dirty leather and metal.

Daelon's brow creased. "You're taking back the city," he said in a quiet voice.

"You catch on quickly," Jori replied.

"With eight? I hope there are more of you." Then, an afterthought, a realization. "My Keeper."

Jori's heart flopped over at the title, though he couldn't have said if it was from pride or apprehension, or just the sense that someone else should have that name instead of him. He cleared his throat. "Yes, we plan to storm the capital and overwhelm them with eight soldiers. Me at the front. That should frighten them."

Daelon didn't even smile. "Where are the others?"

"Kiria and all them? They're safe." He hesitated and revised. "They're alive. We have more troops but no time to explain it all. Right now we need to get out of this room."

The lines across Daelon's forehead deepened. "I can't open the door. They jam the locks when we're not needed." His handsome scholar's face looked suddenly gaunt.

Jori squeezed his arm. "We'll get you out. Right, Royce?" He craned back to the soldier before leaning again toward Daelon. "He's a war hammer. You'll see." He winked.

Hope kindled in Daelon's eyes, small but firm.

Jori called quietly down the secret tunnel. "All right, lovelies. Stay there for a moment."

"How did you know that was there?" Daelon asked. "I didn't know about any passage."

Jori's eyes roamed over the tiny space—cot, desk, candle, Scroll. *Really, how could he not know?* But some people, he'd learned, weren't the same kind of curious as he was. They walked over mysteries without looking into them, looked at mysterious substances without tasting them. Well, he'd done that last one too many ill-fated times, but at least then he *knew*.

He turned his longsuffering attention back to Daelon. "Fate, love."

Royce had finished investigating the door, testing his massive shoulder against it without crashing through.

"Need a lock pick?" Jori asked. He wasn't particularly good, but he'd learned a few things.

"No," Daelon answered for the soldier. "The lock is jammed, not regularly locked. Otherwise, I could open it from the inside."

"Ah, yes."

After much fuss and altogether too many armored bodies wedging through the tiny space, someone managed to get the door open. Actual fresh air flowed in. Jori nearly moaned with relief. He took a long whiff of it and stepped toward the opening. Something closed like a vice on his arm. Royce.

"You stay here."

"Really? After all that?" he whispered back, but the soldier was already gone into the shadowy colonnade with its ever-lasting white lanterns. Jori and Atty had tried to put one out once. Amir Parohim, Cúron's severe advisor, had caught them, Jori on Atty's shoulders. The two of them had been consigned to nothing but lessons and kitchen cleanup for three days after.

Running a casual hand through the muddy hair that had been so perfect earlier, Jori blinked away the sharpness in his eyes.

More soldiers climbed up through the floor, improbable as a magic trick, and carefully filtered outside.

So that was it, then. All Jori was useful for. That, and being a charming figurehead. Staying alive, that was his job.

He blew out a breath and looked out the door. It seemed odd that there weren't Tanyu everywhere. After the attack, he'd alter-nated thinking about the palace as a silent tomb and a crawling anthill. Silent tomb it was, then. The Kingdom soldiers didn't reappear. Some of them were supposed to do reconnaissance to get Jori to safety, and who knows what else. Well, Bard knew. He came up with the idea. Damn, he was impressive. And shy. *Focus, Jori, focus.*

Jori scanned the horizon, just like when he waited for his

father to come home from one of his trips. His longest journey had been to the Tanyuin Academy. He'd been gone almost two months when Jori was seven. Jori and Atty had been so jealous, and they'd missed him. That was a long time for a kid. The Academy's location was a close-kept secret then, so all that time must have been spent misdirecting him and blindfolding him and who knew what else. In retrospect, it was stupid for their father to go at all. But he was a good Keeper and was trying to do some helpful diplomatic thing, no doubt.

A speck of black on the horizon caught his eye. Clouds made dusk come on more quickly, so the sea already looked inky. Could be a wave. Jori blinked, in case the speck was in his eye. No. The little object didn't move. There were more than one, he realized. Four. Four ships.

He straightened, pushing himself away from the doorframe. Daelon and three soldiers had stayed with him—keeping him alive, that was their job too. They looked at him now with alert curiosity. Viktor peered through the doorway toward the ocean. From his reaction, he saw the vessels too. "We weren't expecting more help to come for Belik, did we?"

"No, they were all accounted for, we thought," answered another.

This wasn't good. If the strangers docked at the main port, that was uncomfortably close to where Jori and the others were now. He licked his lips, trying to wet his suddenly dry mouth. "Do we know those ships?" Their sails and flag were still shrouded in gloom.

"No. We have to tell the others to shelter in place until we can see what we're up against."

That sounded reassuringly competent. At the insistence of the others, Jori backed away from the door. There was nowhere to go, so the back of his knees hit the dingy little cot. His blood sang too loudly to allow him to sit.

A familiar face appeared outside. Royce. "We've opened the doors and confirmed that the upstairs is empty."

"There are ships inbound," said Viktor.

"We saw them. We should still have enough time to move the Keeper to a more secure location without being seen."

Jori needed to end up *inside* the palace. That was the deal. Preferably the Main, where the thrones were, if Belik wasn't already in there himself.

After all this talk of Belik, it was strange that Jori had never seen him with his own eyes. He pictured him like some half bestial warrior with impossibly broad shoulders, a wicked glare, and clawed feet. All with the Tanyuin uniform of black on black. Not a lot of creativity there. Jori didn't know what he would do if he saw Belik in person. Would he strike out, despite his woeful lack of military training? He'd want to, that was for sure. He'd want to flay off his skin and put out his eyes. The very thought made him shiver away from the gruesome possibilities his mind concocted. He could hear Kiria's voice ringing in his ears. *We aren't that kind of leader.* Or something like that. But Belik did deserve to die for what he did.

"If we go out through the tunnel," Jori said, "there's a way to get back to the palace." He pointed two fingers in the air and zigzagged them around each other. Apparently, his visual demonstration wasn't helping. "But that way is known by more people." He gave a little shrug, glancing back out at the sea. Four ships had become nine.

"We have a clear view from here to one of the servant entrances," said Royce. "If we take your way, the ships could already be here with reinforcements."

A cold thrill ran through Jori at the idea of running through the gardens, completely exposed. "These are Tanyu, you know." The warriors Jori had idolized as a kid. It would be much easier if there were separate names for the good and evil Tanyu. That they all had to be called the same thing played havoc with his childhood memories. Should they be good? Should they be—

"We know," Royce replied grimly. "But it's a short distance, and four of us will cover you."

He bit back a joke. "All right. Do I run flat out?" He might have finished middle of the pack on the beach with the racers, but surely that wasn't too bad...

"Flat out."

He knew the door they meant. It led to a small private kitchen attached to the formal dining room. Next door was the Main. That didn't feel very safe—more like running into the jaws of a bear—but he ran his thumbs over his eyebrows and prepared to sprint. *Stupid, stupid armor.*

Turning to Daelon, Royce added, "If you can, lock the door behind you when we leave." He counted down on his fingers. Three, two...

And they were off, Jori pumping his arms and keeping his head down as he vaulted over furniture and low hedges. The plants had grown wild around the edges with lack of tending. Chest heaving, he and the four soldiers surrounding him reached the side door. The soldiers laid hands on their sword hilts as Royce reached for the handle.

Across the garden, a dark shadow flew by, too big to be a raven. Jori's insides turned watery, the ghost stories of his youth welling to the surface like oil. The side door was partially obscured by a teardrop-shaped tree. One of the soldiers pressed Jori behind it with one rough hand.

Something clanged close by, metal on metal. Someone had seen them.

Jori was dragged inside the dark kitchen. It smelled like stale bread and pickling spice, but he couldn't see anything. Someone gripped the front of Jori's breastplate and pulled him down to the ground. Dizzying terror made him almost lose his balance.

Their barely controlled panting sounded loud in the room. Jori held his breath, trying to count the number of others in the room, but it was no use. The cacophony of breathing was too haphazard.

They waited and waited and waited. Jori's legs burned with the effort of squatting so long. No one spoke.

With renewed vigor, weapons crashing against each other sliced through the dark. It sounded like a battle out there. Jori knew little about battles, and had only seen the one black shape. Could one or two Tanyu do so much damage to the remaining soldiers? His mind whirled around and around, in a nightmare. He had no facts to ground him except that he was in this kitchen with Kingdom soldiers, he couldn't see, and the plan relied on his not dying.

Someone near him stirred. The movement made Jori jump.

"Tanyu are distracted," a low voice breathed. Royce, probably. "We need a room with better—"

The door flung open, deafening and bright. All four soldiers were on their feet in an instant, swords ringing out of their sheaths. Jori looked up at the intruder. It was a middle-aged man with dark skin, his eyebrows high with the excitement of discovery. He held a bloody knife. Jori felt the food from yesterday's party rising in his throat.

Royce pulled the intruder inside—*inside?*—and slammed him against the wall. He rested the tip of his blade against the man's exposed neck.

That was when Jori realized he wasn't wearing Tanyuin black. The outfit was gray and orange, lightweight for the weather, with a leather jerkin on top and a metal piece guarding shoulders and neck.

"Who are you?" Royce demanded in a hiss. If Jori hadn't been nearly afraid enough to wet himself, he would have appreciated the sexy impressiveness of the moment.

The man tried to jerk out of Royce's grasp. Viktor stepped in to make sure he stayed pinned to the wall. "We come from Galve, in Somul."

Jori struggled to picture a map. Must be a small town. It wasn't on the list of allies that he knew about. Outside, clanging continued. Someone screamed.

Viktor closed the door. Though Jori squinted against the darkness, he couldn't see what was happening anymore.

"Whose side are you on?" came Royce's stern baritone.

Small, huffed sounds of struggle echoed before a response. "We bring Tanyu," he said, "and you—"

His next words cut off in a strangled gasp of surprise.

Jori crouched back on his heels, away from the sound. Had Royce killed him? Did that actually happen?

"Lock the door," Royce commanded.

Jori said, "It's easy to—"

"Then bar it. Block it. We can't have any more getting in. Where is the Keeper?"

"Here." He felt faint. A coppery smell mingled with the cooking spices.

"Belik has more soldiers inbound. We'll stay here for now and make sure you're safe."

"Yeah, we'll make sure nothing happens," added Viktor.

Like killing someone in front of me? Jori's eyes had adjusted enough to see a lumpy dark shadow by the wall where Royce and Viktor stood. He laid a hand on his chest, trying to stop panting. No luck. This was already the scariest thing he'd ever done, and they weren't finished yet.

59

FIRIAN

THE APOTHELIN RIVER flowed under the city wall to the south. There was a checkpoint there, probably for trade, but it was still the weakest point in the city's land defenses.

Firian eyed the place where the river met the wall from his position among the trees. There were two guards, both on the same side of the opening, clearly talking to each other. Kiria's forces must have arrived at the main gate. His chest felt full at the thought of her in the middle of that army. It wouldn't be enough to take the city. They all knew that. If he took too long, if the other parts of the plan didn't work, then even the Tanyu who had sided with him wouldn't be able to save her. They'd be over-whelmed. Seventeen was such a small number when Belik had the force of everyone else on his side.

Firian couldn't fail.

He ran back through the trees, a black shadow among deep-ening shade, to test the water. The river ran though his hiding place before running to the Kheltor Ocean. The water frothed and glided, its noise a liability and a blessing. He dipped his hand into the swift-moving water. Frigid. And deeper than it looked. He regarded it sternly, his insides balling into a fist. Not the entrance he would have chosen. But he couldn't tell Bard now. He couldn't tell anyone anything. This damn Sentry was a bigger worry even than the cold river. No one had ever broken a Sentry.

Could he?

A faint light glowed in his tight belly, something pure. He would try. For her. And she was right—he could be dangerous when he needed to be.

He fell into familiar breathing patterns that magnified his calm, his presence, his ability to shove physical reality aside in favor of the making of his mind. He stood at the bank and pulled out a bag lined with wax from his pocket. Then he stripped down, the cool breeze playing across his skin, telling him about the cold rushing water splashing his feet. All his clothes fit in the bag. It wasn't heavy, but would it be enough to tip his equilibrium in the water?

He gripped the mouth of the bag in one fist and packed those thoughts down into darkness. Maybe the monster within would eat them up. *I am the Tanyuin Head*, he chanted to himself. *If anyone can do it, I can.* And Kiria's voice, *Be dangerous.*

She'd had the tiniest glint in her eye when she said it. She believed he could do it.

Sucking in a deep breath, he plunged in.

The cold hit him like a body blow. Everything was moving. Freezing water covered every inch of him. He bobbed his head to the surface and gasped. But he couldn't let the guards see once he got out of the tree line. The forest was already thinning. The lights of the palace glimmered through them against the blue and orange of the setting sun. He had to go under.

He mentally ticked his progress as he floated from one tree to another. Ten counts. Measuring the distance from initial visibility to a place within the city safe enough to emerge, his heart dropped. Two hundred counts at least.

If anyone can do it...

His bare feet had already gone numb. He could regulate his body, control his thoughts and his breathing. The flow of the water pressing against his bare skin became only sensation, his panic stuffed safely away. This was just another element he could conquer. He shut his eyes. No up, no down. Only one moment and then the next.

An undertow sucked him down a moment sooner than he planned. Out of tree cover now, he had no choice but to clutch the bag, hold his breath, and let the violent water bear him, lungs burning, into the city.

FIRIAN COULDN'T STOP the violent shaking and explosive coughing when he thrashed out of the river. His head barely stayed above the freezing line of water. In the dark, it almost felt as though he were still under, still sucked underneath with no light and no air. He pushed himself, arms scooping hills of water, to the side. With trembling muscles, he drew himself up on the bank and rolled onto his back.

He was in a warehouse built over a narrower part of the river. Crates filled most of the space, perfect to hide from prying eyes. Firian curled up into a sitting position, still clutching the bag with all his clothes. He heard nothing but the slosh and rush of his own ears. He popped his jaw to clear the water. It took a few tries, but he finally felt a slight sensation like a bubble bursting, and cool water leaked from his ears down his neck.

Still, he heard nothing. No one stirred among the crates. It was late enough in the day that whatever workers normally filled this building had gone home. The racket he made gasping and coughing and spluttering hadn't alerted anyone. He breathed deeply and coughed again.

That was it. He hated water.

He stood shakily to his feet and dripped over to a more hidden place among the crates to slick off his body and put his dry clothes back on. After a few pushups to get his frozen blood moving again, his head started to clear. He was in Brithnem and, so far, none of Belik's forces knew. A familiar feeling of empowerment began to warm him as he shucked on the black shirt. He knew it must be freezing but it felt warm against his icy skin. Pants and boots too.

Blowing into cupped hands, he approached the door. The space between the stone wall and wooden door was wide enough for him to spy through. The angle didn't allow him to see the palace, but a street lined with stalls and stores and food vendors. The few people he could see seemed to be closing their wares. Even during war, life went on. There was a quick and furtive quality to their movements, though, which told him that they'd probably gotten wind of Kiria's forces outside. They knew battle was imminent.

He glanced at the shadows. How much time had passed since Kiria made her pronouncement? He couldn't be sure because of the gory Sentry, but he guessed a quarter of an hour was already gone.

Time to get to the palace.

$$60$$

BARD

JUST AS HE had that day in Jori's tent, Wells sat cross-legged with unseeing eyes as he blocked Shiro from the Unreal. His back nestled between the exposed roots of an enormous tulip poplar. All the Sentries were spread out around the forest. It was essential that Belik's forces not find them all together because they wouldn't be able to defend themselves. Their minds had gone to a steady buzz of pain and abstraction.

Bard hated to see Wells like that, but Sentries were one of their greatest weapons. Kiria's side could mess up communication between higher ups, but Belik didn't have that power. Except with Firian, apparently.

Bard bit his lower lip. Not good. But Firian had surprised him before. He'd figured out that horrible killing ability and had also saved his life, so anything was possible. And if not, the soldiers with Jori would finish the job, incapacitating Belik and the four people he kept in his inner circle. At least they'd try.

Bard had been very careful with his language when he spoke to Royce. *Incapacitate*, not *kill*. He knew killing was likely, and Bard wouldn't cry over Belik, but Shiro had been his friend. Or at least an acquaintance. They'd lived on the same hall for a long time. Shiro mostly teased him. He'd been the one to come up with Bard's long-standing nickname "Tawn." Bard didn't think he pronounced Tanyu that differently than anyone else, but apparently Shiro did. Everyone his age called him Tawn except Firian, who thought the name was stupid.

Shiro had been Rian's best friend. Rian, whom Firian accidentally killed in the whirlwind of his mental energy, protecting the Academy from Kingdom forces a couple months ago. When Bard left. He understood why Shiro was mad at Firian, even hateful toward him. Hatred didn't need to mean revenge, though. This took things to a totally unnecessary level of violence.

Some violence was inevitable, especially at the gate, and the thought made Bard struggle against guilt.

Restless, he mentally checked in with Makai who held the rear of the army waiting for Belik's answer to Kiria's challenge. The buzz of Wells' Sentry made pressing through more difficult, but he soon found the Master's mind.

"Anything yet?" he asked.

"Nothing," Makai replied. "Belik isn't going to respond."

Bard knew that. Master Belik was about as likely to surrender as the ocean. But an hour bought Jori and Firian time to get into position. Bard's mind constantly aimed toward them —a reflex—but he couldn't get in touch. Firian was blocked and Jori didn't have the Talent. Neither did anyone around Jori, by design. Bard hated not knowing what was happening, if they were okay. Jori didn't have fight experience. Would he have to fight, despite having soldiers to protect him? Jori was fun and inspiring and kind, but not vicious. It would take feral energy to beat any Tanyu they might encounter, and Bard doubted Jori had that in him.

"Yeah," he said to Makai now, "I know he won't. Just let me

know if something changes, yeah? Have you seen any of Belik's Tanyu around?"

His mouth was dry. Worrying did nothing. He'd spent his whole life worrying. Would he get kicked out of the Academy? What would his family think of him? His family, he'd learned, was proud. And he'd walked out of the Academy himself. There was nothing left but to see this plan through, and get Kiria's crown back.

"No, but they'll come soon." The slightest edge of tension laced his deep voice.

"You'll be all right. Just give us time. Take as long as you can, unless you see an opening." *Unlikely.* "Then take it. We really could use the gate, but time is even more important."

"As you would have it."

Twisting his black Master ring, Bard came back to reality, to the little hollow where Wells stared unseeing. *As you would have it.* Younger Tanyu responded to Masters that way. Bard doubted he'd ever get used to that response to *him*.

After checking the status of all the other groups he could actually contact, which was harder than usual because of the fog of Sentry static in the air, he sat beside Wells. He felt short when he did because Wells sat higher on a cushion. It was the least he could give the Sentries. Their past had denied them the most basic comforts. Bard's good hand curled into a fist at the memory of their lifeless and beaten faces in that hot room underground. Burns and shaved heads and atrophied muscles. Inhuman. Once the shock had begun to wear off, that was the first time Bard thought he might leave the Academy if he could, but he'd thought at that time that he couldn't without becoming a Sentry himself.

A soft sound crackled in the hollow. They waited down an embankment, so no one should be able to find them unless they already knew where to search. Bard looked up.

A Kingdom soldier dressed head to foot in armor stepped down to meet him. Bard stood. The soldier looked vaguely familiar, but Bard didn't remember his name. He wasn't one of the few who had traveled with them to Charäkhnem and back.

Was this one of the soldiers he'd sent with Jori? Was Jori okay? If so, why was this soldier here? He belonged either with Jori or at the gate. A cool prickle danced down Bard's spine. "What's wrong?"

"Nothing," said the man, casting a wary glance at Wells, who didn't stir.

Something *was* wrong here. "What do you need?"

A weapon appeared in the man's hand. Something blunt. No blade. He swung it at Bard's head, but he dodged out of the way in time, gut swooping with confusion and terror.

In the split second that the soldier's arm followed through his motion, Bard scrambled for Kiria's mind, not the easiest to find since she was still honing her skills. Her lavender presence echoed from amid the army at the gate. "Take it," he choked out, hoping she would hear and understand. If he was hurt or killed or taken, she was the only one who knew enough to coordinate all the pieces of the plan. Most of the pieces could move on their own now, but they were crucial emergency measures.

He flung his eyes open again, but something was in them. Pain exploded across his cheekbone. He stumbled but stayed upright, looking for a weapon for himself. Nothing but the small dagger he'd brought. He bounded forward, landing on the man's foot, then hopped back and reached for his knife.

Wells hadn't stirred. Would the soldier kill him?

Desperately, Bard placed himself in front of his friend. His ears rang and the edges of his vision blurred as the soldier wound up again. A dagger was too small. He sucked in a breath to brace himself the moment before another blow hit him and he crumpled to the ground.

61

KIRIA

Kiria scanned the darkening wall again. Now off the platform, she didn't have the best view. Forced to look around armored shoulders, a persistent tug of unease plucked at the nape of her neck.

More and more people had joined the others on the wall. A low sound indicated that crowds gathered just inside the closed gate. Hopefully the citizens living close to the gate would leave before the battle began.

A moment ago, she'd felt as though Bard were trying to contact her, but when she closed her eyes and found her way to the Unreal, he wasn't there.

Half of Belik's time had elapsed. Chetana shouted the update from her place at the front of the central column. Her clarion voice sent chills over Kiria's skin. Chetana was twice the warrior Kiria would ever be, but Kiria stood tall—as tall as she could—in her armor and encouraged the troops around her. She could be brave, but that didn't make the waiting any less terrible.

Every moment that slipped by grew chillier and made her brain churn with awful possibilities.

Movement ahead snapped her back to attention.

Abrecan Gate was opening.

She lifted up on tiptoes to get a better vantage. The huge double doors swung outward, helped by four men. One person appeared in the opening, then two, then three. Many, all in a row. They marched forward, pouring out like liquid and spreading to match the breadth of Kiria's army. None wore Tanyuin black.

She tensed. Was this it? Did this slow march mean the clash had begun? Maybe it just seemed slow with her heightened senses. Her right hand squeezed the hilt of her sword. Wearing it was a precaution, but she didn't know how to wield it in battle. She'd learned the basics on a week when Daelon caught cold. A guard close to her father had taught her the mechanics of swords and arrows and armor. She remembered that swords were much heavier than they looked. Her palm grew slick with sweat, and she adjusted her grip.

There were no cries of pain, no clang of metal on metal. Kiria's heart hammered as the enemy lined up to face her allies. There couldn't be more than the length of three people between the two armies. The dying sun gleamed on shaved heads. Torithians. Anger bubbled in her blood. Faces flashed once more through her mind. She closed her eyes in a promise. The Western Kingdom belonged to Atty, to Cúron, to her mother, to all those they'd lost.

Her fear fell away, replaced with determination, the cycle looping back to courage that grounded her. Master Belik killed her family. He drew Firian further into corruption. He used Torithians on the front lines, but not his own Tanyu.

They had hoped to draw Tanyu from their posts on other parts of the wall, thinning the enemy presence around the perimeter. Bard had insisted that Belik would send warriors to the underground den to flush out the Tanyu there. With the

Talent, they'd be easy to find. Little did they know that there were extra Tanyu, soldiers, and Sentries waiting to ambush and neutralize whoever came inside. Were Belik's warriors still coming?

Maybe Bard had heard something. She closed her eyes, partly to contact him and partly to block out the enemy force in front of her that still streamed through the gate. They filled the streets beyond and all the space between her army and the wall. Seeing it in person was different than looking at plans with Bard. It was visceral and made her feel alive and fragile and strong all at once.

The Unreal was dark. She still didn't have the hang of talking to people without backgrounds, like the Tanyu could, and it was harder for her to find other people's minds. She'd only managed it with three people: Firian, Bard, and Chetana.

The darkness became the palace hallway, the easiest setting for her to conjure. "Bard," she called.

Maybe she was looking in the wrong place, not that space mattered in the same way here. Still, for her, it could be helpful to cast her mind in the direction of the person she wanted to talk to. She came back out of the Unreal and physically turned around.

She tried again. "Bard."

He could be busy with someone else, but he was a Tanyu, and knew to be attuned to her. Her heart was in her throat.

"Bard!"

Something was wrong. He wasn't there. Maybe he had tried to contact her earlier but she hadn't found him in time.

She opened her eyes, her mouth gummy. *Please, please let him be all right.* If Bard wasn't answering, she would organize the battle effort as best she could. Her level of Talent fell short of his, but she would do it.

She faced the army in front of her. The air smelled like

leather and lightning with an edge of acrid smoke. They'd known the task could fall to her. Lifting her chin, she stared at the people who had taken her home and her kingdom, knowing with certainty that she would still be standing there even if she had been the only one to fight.

62

FIRIAN

FEELING HAD RETURNED to Firian's feet and hands, though the black cloth around his palm kept one hand cold. He'd never seen the southern edge of the palace grounds. He'd always come and gone through the main entrance that faced east, toward the Abrecan Gate. Now he stared at the wall surrounding the palace grounds, scanning for Tanyu.

Mon Párinath was wrapped in walls—outermost were the city walls, tall and thick, then the walls around the palace grounds, and finally the walls of the castle itself. He'd breached the most difficult layer. Now came the second.

In the intensity of saving Bard and then his prison escape, he hadn't noticed just how much the fire had damaged the palace. Most of the glass in the windows had blown out. Smoke stains smudged the area above the openings. A pile of black char must have once been an outbuilding. The palace, made of stone, still looked stable, though. The fire damage only made it easier to breach, once he was past the wall.

Firian pushed experimentally against the Sentry again, a compulsion like tonguing a loose tooth. Jarring red pain shocked him. He cursed under his breath.

Proximity, Belik had growled.

The Master knew he was back. The only question was which of them would find the other first.

After scouting the palace wall as quickly as he could, Firian determined the angle that could be seen from the fewest vantage points. No window of the palace faced this section, and the hulking castle itself blocked the view of anyone patrolling the gardens or the seaports beyond. The only danger was someone directly on the other side. That, Firian could handle.

The palace wall wasn't as thick or high as the city wall, much more climbable. Running forward, he vaulted up, catching the wall with two steps before clinging to the top. In one swift motion, he pulled himself up and over. His training took over as he dropped on the other side behind badly manicured trees.

Two figures in black ran past. One continued on toward the gardens but the other pulled up short. Firian stilled. The Tanyu looked around, up at the wall, almost as though she sensed exactly what had happened.

As careful and sure as a wolf on a scene, the Tanyu slowly strode toward Firian's hiding place. No one else was in sight. Firian rushed out from his hiding place, Jovan's drills moving him automatically. A fist glanced off the side of Firian's neck, but he was faster. Fighting felt good. One, two, three. Moves he'd practiced a thousand times. With surprise on his side, the fight was over almost too quickly, now that adrenaline raced through him. He dragged the unconscious body to the thick group of bushes where he had hidden moments ago.

His blood was high now. Youth and power filled him, directing his muscles as he ran surefooted toward the palace to find Belik.

Moments later, he was inside one of the guest rooms in the front wing. It wasn't as large as the one where he'd stayed only a few months ago, but it was similar, though starker. No tapestries hung on the walls, no chairs by the cold fireplace. Firian suddenly remembered the Torithian he'd caught running out of the palace with treasures in his arms. Had the whole palace been looted?

His lip curled. Belik wouldn't mind if it were. The Master depended on the riches at the Academy to pay the cities that wouldn't help Kiria.

The image of Kiria in armor stoked pride in him. Before everything had gone to hell, they'd talked about her future as a Keeper. She'd had such earnest love for her kingdom, despite her personal insecurities about ruling. How different she was now... The resolve in her eyes that afternoon fed his own determination.

He couldn't depend on this room remaining empty for long. Belik wasn't here. But he was probably nearby.

One look out the window told him he didn't have long to find him. Belik's Sentry would lift, releasing his mind and making it vulnerable, but only for ten minutes.

He quieted his blood and breathing, feeling the environment around him. Far away, he heard the dull sounds of conflict. That had to be closer than the main gate, which was nearly an hour away. Something was happening outside, maybe on the shore or in the gardens. He couldn't parse out its meaning. Any distraction was in his favor, but something told him this change meant nothing good. More allies for Belik, probably.

No footstep sounded just outside his room, so he gently opened the door. It swung on silent hinges. A side hallway, not the massive one he was so used to seeing in Kiria's mind. It provided more cover than the window-lined artery that led to the Main.

The nerves in his body were alive. Air flowed around him, bringing scents and sounds that made his skin tingle. Every tremor under his feet told a story.

"...roll of who's there?"

Firian's eyebrows twitched. It was too easy. That was Belik's voice. He froze.

"Well, look!" After a pause when someone else presumably spoke, he said, "It'll be quick." Another pause. "What?" he snapped. "How many?"

Firian inched closer. Maybe he could hear the other speaker.

"Five soldiers," Belik muttered. "From the barracks?"

The other speaker, it turned out, was Enktuya, a girl Firian didn't know well. She was a young Master but kept to herself in the Academy. "They're giving us trouble by the port."

"Then kill them. We don't need distractions. This should be over soon." A sigh.

Belik's voice grew further away. A door closed. Firian's lips curved. *Got you.*

The Master would leave a lookout, but probably only one. Firian dropped to the floor and peered around the corner, quick as the cold current that had borne him into the city.

One. He was right.

Hopping back to his feet, he didn't bother being silent. He made a small sound, like a breath when he needed to clear his throat. And he waited.

The Tanyu was swift, flying around the corner like a swallow. He gripped a knife in his fist, a flurry of winged black.

Firian used the Tanyu's own momentum to grab both his wrists and slam him against the wall, kneeing him hard in the diaphragm. The Tanyu gasped, only managing to give an impotent squeak. His eyes bulged as recognition dawned. Fear edged the anger in that stare.

Firian recognized him too. A Defender named Zhufal, Khelê, about twenty. He smashed the wrists against the wall again to loosen the knife. It fell from the Tanyu's hand, or maybe he just let go. They all knew about Firian's killing ability. Before the blade could clatter on the floor, Firian caught it out of the air and pressed it against the delicate skin at the man's throat.

Firian slanted his eyes across the hall in a command.

The Tanyu peeled away from the wall to walk toward the guest room Firian had just left. Still holding the dagger to the hollow of his neck, Firian wrapped his arm around the man's head and clasped his hand over his gasping mouth.

Even looted, the room provided enough cloth to tie and gag the lookout before knocking him out.

The sun still wasn't down, but it was sinking, marking time. Kiria's ultimatum had to be expiring.

He looked at the Tanyu tied at his feet. How could Zhufal side with Belik and his ruthless violence?

You did.

The unwelcome voice sounded like Kiria. She had been right about him all along.

Firian shoved those thoughts aside. He wasn't the same as he had been. His purpose burned, clear and difficult.

He slipped into the hallway again. No one had raised an alarm. No Tanyu came running. Belik was probably still in that room—maybe Cúron's? Its placement felt familiar, like a smell he couldn't place, but that was probably the *katah* with Kiria, who knew these halls so well.

If he was right, then there would be a washroom or servants' quarters attached. He ran his hand along the stone of the corridor, as if it would give up its secrets. Tanyu might meet in servants' quarters, but not in a washroom.

He cycled through options, picturing the sunken room with the claw-footed tub that the royals had offered him when he came to stay. He didn't remember any opening except for two small ventilation holes, one near the floor and one by the ceiling. He couldn't fit through those, even if he tried. They were barely bigger than a fist.

Was there any way to determine how many Tanyu were in the room with Belik, how many weapons, what configuration? Firian had nothing but two small knives. They were relying on his killing ability. It would only take a bloody moment, but he didn't want to sweep others into the carnage.

If he could reach his ability at all. With it, he could get close to that tipping point and sense how many people there were, their breathing, their heartbeats, the blood in their veins. But he had no access to it. Anxious energy spiked through him. *If anybody can do it...*

He laid one hand lightly on the door handle. He could storm the room, take his chances.

Belik would stand there, unsurprised, immovable as a mountain, staring him down. With his bad leg and the knowledge that Firian was after him, he'd keep as many Tanyu around him as he could until this was over. Tanyu that Firian had known at the Academy, people that had followed him, had admired him, had abandoned him to death when Belik lied to them.

Firian has turned his back on the Tanyu, betrayed you to the enemy so he could screw the princess.

Firian's heart beat too loudly in the hollow of his chest. Yes, he fought for Kiria, but he never meant to betray the Tanyu. The Academy was the only place he had ever belonged. Moments of belonging flashed like sunspots when he was with Bard or with Kiria, but that kind of life was for someone else. That was for people like them.

His fingers closed over the handle. The hall had become darker. Not quite sundown, but close.

In a flash, with his dagger in one hand, he opened the door.

The room was empty.

63

KIRIA

Kiria wandered in the dark emptiness, feeling like a blind woman. Panic threatened to claw up her throat. Bard could do this almost without thinking.

Finally, she felt something, a shift in the air, a new essence. "Tesni!" she cried, wrapping the palace hallway around her again. She'd abandoned that setting after she determined it was too distracting. The blankness that followed focused her mind on the search, but also carved a hollow in her heart. She didn't feel Bard anywhere. His absence weighed heavily on her. If something had happened to him...

Tesni appeared across from Kiria, who let out a breath, grateful to have finally found someone. "Tesni," she said, "can you see any Tanyu behind us?"

"See?" Tesni asked with a hint of haughtiness in her tone. "No, but they're there."

"Okay, can you check that everyone underground is ready for them?"

"As you would have it." She disappeared, leaving Kiria once again alone.

As you would have it. The same wording that Firian used. It must be distinct to the Academy.

She opened her eyes and the dying light seemed flashing bright. She squinted and her heart stuttered. Almost an hour had gone by. Belik's forces hadn't stopped coming, oozing around the edges of her army's formation, only a sliver of space separating the two.

What had she seen of battle? Firian killing the Torithians who assaulted her in Raewhith? An arrow, impossibly, flying at her face? She'd seen her share of pain, but never true battle up close.

All these people, she realized, looking around, were willing to die for her cause. That room in her mind had shut tight, self-protective, but it opened now. She turned to one of the Kingdom soldiers who had lifted the platform. He had dark brown skin, green eyes, and a tattoo covering both hands. She gently touched his metal-clad upper arm. "Thank you," she said quietly.

He looked down at her with a professional expression of care. She didn't know him, but he was with her.

Privately, she thanked a few others, asking their names so she could use them. Appreciation swelled larger and larger within her until she fairly glowed. Having her friends closer would have completed the joy that came out like hurt. But they were all far away, also fighting for her.

The hour elapsed.

A change moved over the crowd, a tensing of muscles and sharpening of senses. Chetana, now by her side, nodded solemnly.

Kiria stepped again onto the platform. Her joints felt like wood but her will was iron. The soldiers lifted her up again. From up there, Belik's army looked far larger than it had from her shorter vantage point. It flooded the streets of her city, a mass of bodies, ready for them if they were to breach the gate.

Her city. City Beautiful.

"The hour has passed!" she shouted. "Will you not surrender to the Kingdom's rightful ruler?"

She waited for a pregnant pause. No dignitary or Tanyu stepped forward to take her offer. If only they would. If only Belik weren't so hard headed...

"Then," she said, her voice carrying over the heads of thousands, "we are at war."

64

JORI

IN THE CRAMPED LITTLE KITCHEN, Jori began to wonder if he would ever race again. His legs screamed from being in the same position. Heroic Keepers—or nearly Keepers, to be unnecessarily scrupulous about it—didn't complain about leg pain when they were hiding. Still, his mind wandered to the sparkling wine he knew the cooks kept on the upper shelves, invisible now in the darkness.

As soon as Jori was sure the conflict directly outside was over, another sound echoed and the fighting renewed. Oh, to stretch! And they still didn't have a tally of who had made it through the gardens and was in here with him. Did soldiers just have a sense of these things?

"I thought you said we were going to move," he whispered, barely above a breath. The idea frightened him out of his wits, but those were leaving anyway the longer he stayed motionless in this darkness. Even his neck had a crick. If ears could be strained from listening too hard, he had that too.

A heavy hand descended on his shoulder. A warning to be quiet. The gesture was so authoritative that he wouldn't have been surprised if a finger had been laid against his lips. He shut up, though his muscles ached and his thoughts became increasingly edgy.

Maybe my legs will be stronger. And my shoulders from hunching. I'll look even better up there on that throne.

But the thought didn't soothe him. Picturing the throne inevitably conjured images of his brother on it, then the importance of this mission came flooding back.

On and on it went, a cycle that seemed to last ages.

Someone tapped his shoulder. Jori snapped out of his daze and the muscles in his thighs whined as he shifted. Questions bobbed to the surface of his mind, but he shoved them down. Keep quiet, they'd told him. They were the experts here, the ones making sure he didn't get killed.

Biting down on the words he wanted to say, he attempted to stand. A grunt escaped him. His legs spiked with pain. He stumbled lightly into the nearest guard, who caught him around the waist before he fell.

"Are you all right?" came the soldier's voice, too quiet to distinguish, almost too quiet to be heard.

"Fine." In the dark, he winced, flexing his feet to ease some of the tension in his muscles, like touching a bruise.

Dim light leaked over the shapes of bowls and counters and hanging utensils. There was the sparkling wine, glimmering on the top shelf as always. *I'll come back for you. We'll celebrate.*

He turned to see the soldier in the doorway leading deeper into the palace, who nodded curtly and opened the door wider. Still limping, Jori followed in the midst of the soldiers. Three of them, he now saw in the light of the dining room. Stoic Royce, Viktor with his flower tattoo, and one he'd just met before he led them through the back ways into Daelon's room. What was his name...?

Jori stopped short. Half of the long dining room table where he'd shared so many meals had burned completely away. White ash coated the floor by the main door. Near Jori, the room looked the same, everything in its place, down to the centerpieces, now holding crispy dead flowers. But the table ended in a jagged black rent. Jori's chest squeezed tight. He counted the chairs. No, he hadn't been mistaken. Jori and Atty usually sat where the table now looked ripped apart. *Don't think about metaphors.*

The warm, acrid sting of smoke still coated the room.

"Rather exposed, isn't it?" he whispered, eyeing the door to the magnificent hallway feeding into the Main. It looked warped. Did the lock still work?

He knew he had to be near the Main when they were victorious, so he could immediately resume the throne, settle the concerns of the people, wave and smile. All while his guards secured the symbolic location. The Main was such a big space, though. Tanyu probably swarmed it now. He pictured it all black with a portrait of that gigantic creature Belik instead of the wonderful statues.

Royce put his big blond face next to his. "Is there a secret way to the preparation hall attached to the Main?" To his credit, he didn't even grimace at his own suggestion that Jori knew the palace better than he did.

Jori mustered a smile for him. "Not through here, no, but there are a couple." He held up fingers as he listed, "Outside ledge, chimney (which I don't recommend), or the space between the generals' office." When Royce looked blank, Jori tutted. "Don't tell me you haven't noticed."

Royce's gaze narrowed to a glare.

"It's the shared opening with the light." Attached to the Main, on the north side, were two small rooms—the antechamber where royals waited for big events, and the head general's office. A window-like aperture between the two rooms opened near the ceiling, carving out a space that also looked out into the Main, like a missing puzzle piece connecting all three. When Jori, age twelve, had managed to get up there, he found a cold candle covered in dust. In the past, it could have been a signal or extra light source. He didn't particularly care, and had moved it to the side to continue exploring.

The soldier shared a look with the other two. They seemed to like Jori's idea, or at least they considered it better than the chimney. Through the generals' office, they wouldn't have to cross the ominous expanse of the Main until it was time.

A sound scraped outside the door. Tanyu were usually quiet as cats. Jori's blood froze. His legs, still burning, didn't feel ready to run.

Now a muffled sound, like someone talking behind thick walls. The soldiers drew closer to Jori and backed him up to the kitchen door. There were no windows in this room, either to see outside or into the hallway. Helplessness ate at the edges of his thoughts. He glanced at the ravaged table, briefly picturing the soldiers hurling it to the side to shield them all.

The noise grew louder, everything magnified in the stillness. A persistent murmuring. Now that it was closer, it sounded almost familiar, though no word was distinct. Words still didn't form as the voice passed within range of the dining room. Jori's guards laid hands on their weapons, shoulders rising, feet spreading. This would all be very exciting if it weren't so terrifying.

Then Jori's face went bloodless. He couldn't feel his fingers, and it had nothing to do with that horrible wait in the dark kitchen. Shock jolted through his core as he heard something he recognized. The quality of the muffled voice broke through in one indistinct syllable, and he knew.

The Tanyu had captured Bard.

Jori's mind suddenly filled with static and, floating like an island in chaos, one solid idea. *This cannot happen.*

He stumbled once against the table as he shot out of the room.

65

BARD

RAGGED, brown-tinged Brithnem flags waved like ghosts as Bard got closer to the Main.

He was conscious now, gagged, wrists bound in front of him, but no Sentry. They knew there was no point in blindfolding him. He knew exactly where he was going. They were taking him to Belik. The Kingdom soldier who'd betrayed him walked on his left and a male Tanyu he'd seen before but did not know walked on his right.

What those two didn't know—hopefully!—was that Jori and Firian were in the palace somewhere too, waiting for their moment. Bard felt the pull to think of them as though it were a physical thing, but he leaned away from that worry, focusing instead on a less incriminating thought. The news that he'd been taken. If Kiria knew, then she would understand how to proceed. She could ignore any false message Belik might make him send.

Because Belik must want him to send a message. That, or reveal the parts of his plan that he didn't already know. Otherwise, Bard would have been killed already.

Twisting his wrists, pressed backward farther they should be because of his clawed left hand, he sensed Kiria's mind. It was in chaos. Was she all right? He couldn't sense anything clearly. She didn't have the calm mental center of a Tanyu, but he battled on, searching for purchase.

"Kiria! I've been taken."

A fierce sting lashed across his eye where the soldier had beat him. Pain dragged him back to the Real. The Tanyu glared at him, knowing exactly what Bard was doing. Masking his distress about Kiria and the others, Bard gave him a bloodshot glare right back.

"You know this isn't right," he said through the gag. It came out as a slurred murmur of indistinguishable sounds.

The Tanyu ignored him.

"It isn't right!" His heart was beating hard now. The Main was close. He didn't want to be afraid, but the last time he'd seen Belik, the Master had hurt him. He didn't remember most of the details, but flashes had come back to him in the past few weeks. Blood from the floor seeping into his hair, piercing pain in his back as though he were being pulled apart, Firian's white face filled with horror. And of course he had his useless hand to show for the encounter.

Bard turned to the Kingdom soldier, who looked pale and shadowy. "Kiria is fighting for you," he said. "Why would you do this? Did Master Belik promise you something?" Without magic, no one could understand what he said, but it felt good to say something. If he distracted them with his babble, then he could find another sliver of an opening to try Kiria again. Or, if he couldn't do that, at least he could take stock of the Tanyu they passed and gather information. It occupied his mind and pressed out the horrible voice that said he wouldn't make it out alive. If he could just—

A figure bolted from the room just behind them. Bard

turned in time to see arms pumping with speed, close wavy hair streaming behind. Kingdom armor.

"Here!" Jori yelled, disappearing in the opposite direction.

No! No, no! He was supposed to be hiding. He wasn't a fighter. There was no way he could take on a Tanyu. Even Bard had learned moves that could incapacitate Jori quickly. Why hadn't he stayed hidden?

Three Kingdom soldiers followed behind. Viktor's Khelê tattoo shone black on his cheek as he sprinted after Jori.

Bard was going to race with him on the beach. They'd talked about it that morning, Jori flashing too many coins for a bet. Bard couldn't match it, but Jori grinned anyway, keeping the bubble of the fantasy intact. Neither mentioned the unpredictability of the next few hours. They would race. That was that.

Reality was slow to dawn. Jori was creating a distraction. For him. *You're more important!* he wanted to shout, but the gag and situation stopped him.

The Tanyu pointed. Another materialized from the shadows. "Get him! That's the Kepron." Without a word, the Tanyu obeyed, moving with animal speed and grace.

Bard's heart felt like a stone, but as everyone looked to the place where Jori disappeared, he crushed his heel into the bridge of the Tanyu's foot. Ducking and twisting from between his two captors, he turned to run back down the hallway.

With a tilt of vertigo, the purple patterned rug rushed up and smashed him in the nose. A solid hand pressed his face into the ground. Bard couldn't even turn his head. For a panicked second, he couldn't breathe at all through his gag. Judging from the boots in his peripheral vision, the Tanyu held him down. He ripped Bard upward by the hair and cracked his face down again. Bard's eyes streamed with pain.

The Tanyu whispered a few foul curses in his ear before

hauling him up again. Blood streamed from Bard's nose into his mouth when he stood.

Where was Jori? They knew he was in the palace now. Did he have any chance of surviving? Bard didn't want his final memory of him to be his stupid, sweet bravado.

A shove to his shoulder got Bard moving again. The huge carved doors of the Main loomed before them. They opened and Bard felt his connection to Kiria, to Jori, to the others, all snapping away. His eyes darted around the huge space. He'd only been in this room once before, when he offered to help Kiria find an end to the war. All three Keepers had sat on the dais. Only Kiria had believed his sincerity. Hopefully that trust would pay off.

Now Belik sat on the platform, not on a throne, but on a plain chair like the many set up in rows across the mosaic floor. Shiro, Nedi, and a young woman he didn't recognize stood beside him. Wells had been guarding Shiro. Had they killed him? Could Shiro access the Unreal now?

Tanyu in black uttered soft noises of surprise or effort, some twitching like dogs in sleep. Someone cried out, slumping to the floor, her chest impossibly slashed open.

Bard felt sick, but also fascinated. If his plan worked, then the Sentries were bouncing from mind to mind at random— with the exception of Belik and his enforcers. Bard had never heard of such a thing killing someone, but the pain would be incapacitating for a while. Without access to the Unreal, Belik would just see the scream of pain as an ordinary battle loss.

As Bard drew closer to the steps and saw Belik's glare more clearly, he became eleven again. The Master looked as he always did, no added crown or finery—just the black outfit of a Tanyu and a hawk-like awareness behind his glasses. Wide-eyed terror clawed at Bard. He trembled with the effort to keep it at bay.

"Good work," said Belik, his attention slicing to the Kingdom soldier. Bard feared for him. He was in a room full of Tanyu—some guarding Belik, others fighting in the Unreal, still others patrolling the blown-out windows. Any one of them could kill him in a blink, and Belik was ruthless enough to order it.

The same realization must have filled the soldier himself, because he went paler, his skin like paper, though he kept his perfect posture. "Master Belik," he said, "I've only done this to ensure safety for my family. I apologize that they haven't always been sympathetic to... your cause. But we just want to live in peace. I need your word that this will be done." His throat bobbed as he said the words.

Belik pursed his mouth, his expression unreadable. "You would like them out of the city?"

"Yes... sir."

Belik's lips twisted at the word.

From below, a cry of pain split the air as a Tanyu grabbed his head and wavered in his seat. The soldier tensed at the noise.

"We'll see it done," Belik said. "The Tanyu aren't monstrous, as you've been led to believe." He nodded once to a female Tanyu standing by the opening that had once been a glorious, multi-paned window.

Even with the armor, the relief in the muscles of the soldier's back was obvious. Bard tried to catch his eye as he walked away, but the soldier refused to meet his gaze. Now, at least, Bard understood.

It was almost dark outside. The Sentry would lift soon, giving Firian ten minutes to use his killing ability on Master Belik. Bard scanned the space as subtly as he could, but saw no sign of Firian. He didn't think he would. Was he here? Was it even possible to break off a Sentry through mental will? His skin tingled with apprehension.

"Master Belik," the Tanyu holding Bard said urgently, "Jorrim Calthwaite is in the palace."

Belik's focus locked onto the words. "Here? Where?"

"We saw him just now."

"Saw him?" Belik stood, ready to issue commands.

"Tanyu are on it. It shouldn't be long."

Bard's breath hitched, only a little, involuntarily. It was enough to swivel Belik's attention on him. He glowered thoughtfully before leaning back in his seat. "What idiot put you in charge?" he muttered. "I hear that you are. In charge." His gaze dipped to Bard's clawed hand. "So this is what you'll do. Bring a chair for him." Shiro did. "Sit," Belik said.

Bard sat.

"You will tell them all that the prince is dead. He was found in the palace. His half-cocked plan got him killed."

Bard's blood beat so loudly in his ears that Belik's gravelly voice barely made it through. He huffed out a breath, clearing his nose of blood so he could breathe more easily. No one took his gag off. He wasn't supposed to argue.

He shook his head.

No one would believe the message if Belik sent it, even if he tried to disguise himself as Bard in the Unreal. Maybe a Watchman couldn't, but a Tanyu could tell the difference. It had to be Bard himself.

"This isn't a negotiation," Belik said, holding up one hand to stop the Tanyu from beating him again. "Jorrim Calthwaite is dead. He was found in the palace."

The words echoed like a nightmare song.

"No," Bard managed, speaking as distinctly as he could through the cloth. His lips tasted like salty blood. "He's alive."

"Tell them now, word for word, with no additions, or we'll kill you. As a traitor, you deserve worse."

Bard's brow furrowed as he looked at Belik. Suddenly, he realized that he wasn't afraid of death, if it meant he could help those he loved. He'd faced death before. After all his worry, almost every terrible thing he feared had happened. Yet here he was, still breathing, still defending his friends. Not terrified anymore. Just... a little afraid.

If he refused to tell the lie that Jori was killed, then the Tanyu would kill him instead. But if he gave the message, they might keep him alive. Kiria might already know that Bard was taken, and would know that the information was coerced.

She wouldn't give up hope even if she believed the message. She'd had plenty of chances to do that, and had chosen to continue.

Another moment meant another opportunity for freedom, for Jori's ridiculous heroics to mean something.

May it rain hope always.

The slice of sun sank below the horizon.

Bard set his jaw, a hard lump forming in his throat, and nodded.

66

FIRIAN

The room was empty.

Firian's mind spun. He hadn't heard Belik leave, but he had been stowing the lookout Zhufal so maybe that masked the sound. His gaze flicked to the dying light. Kiria and her army were fighting now, and he had minutes before the Sentries lifted to give him access to Master Belik.

He didn't need to know exactly where Belik was. All he needed was proximity. He'd never tested the range of his ability, only that it worked when the targets were close. Belik had to be close by, probably in the direction of the Main, unless he had a good reason to go somewhere else. He would walk the paths Chetana took, probably without realizing it.

He turned on his heel and returned to the bedroom where Zhufal lay unconscious. There was no time to go searching for Belik, and the more Firian moved, the more risk there was he would be discovered. His body tensed with the familiar longing for a fight. That would be so much easier than what he actually had to do.

Silently, he shut the door behind him. His feet sank into the plush carpets, untouched by the fire. The feeling stirred a dim memory of being with Kiria. He couldn't remember what they were doing, but the memory was good. He burrowed into the feeling, leaning into the sensation of being seen, comfortable, enough. The memory turned inexplicably into a single moment at the party the night before, of her smiling. It was no more than a flash, her hair floating around her in a dance, a huge grin radiating her joy. Despite her scars, despite the danger, despite everything. Defiant joy.

His chest filled with tenderness. A new, brilliant pain. Her story would continue. He would make it so. His story, on the other hand, balanced on this knife's point, this single moment. Past it, he saw nothing.

Purpose flowed through him like air, like blood. Fortifying. He could break off the net of pain that hovered over his mind.

He stood in the center of the room, drawing strength for the task.

The light dimmed like an extinguished candle. It was time.

Skipping the tentative prodding, he dove straight in, hurling himself against the Sentry barrier. His hand flew to his mouth to stop a scream as he stumbled back a step. With effort, he righted himself. A violent shudder didn't soothe the searing pain in his head. The room pooled with black spots.

Firian sat on the edge of the bed. A human was creating this, so it had to be breakable. He gritted his teeth and tried again.

The shock of pain stole his breath. His whole being recoiled from it, like a hand jerking back from hot metal. His chest rose and fell with frustration. This was just like what happened in Belik's cell. It was probably the same poor Sentry, recaptured after Firian helped him escape. What more could he try?

His eyes rose to the window. Seconds slipped away. If he broke through the Sentry, he still might have to get closer to Belik for it to work. He had no time to lose.

He flung himself against the barrier. Again and again. He

tried it in motion, lying down, slowly, quickly. He tried bringing the Unreal to him instead of going to it. He tried bleeding ordinary thoughts into the region of the Talent until they melded like dreams. He tried testing his endurance against the pain as long as he could, until he felt blood vessels bursting and skin melting away from the coke-hot heat. He was sand and the Sentry was a furnace turning him to liquid nothing.

He opened his streaming eyes on the bed, curled on his side, covered head to foot in sweat, nausea blurring his perception. His body, inside and outside, throbbed with overexertion, like torn muscles. He pressed one hand into the soft blankets and eased himself up. The room spun and he choked back the urge to vomit on the floor.

After one steadying breath, he tried again. Again, the impossibly strong force flung him down like a child's toy.

A shadow crept by the toe of his black boot as a stream of cold sweat ran from his neck down his back. He raised his face to the window. That split-second image of incandescent joy faded. Ten minutes had come and gone. He was too late.

67

KIRIA

Kiria's whole body was in pain, and she hadn't even fought yet. The helmet cut off her peripheral vision as Chetana and several other guards ushered Kiria away from the center of the army. There was a spot where she could watch and command, they said.

The center of the army felt safer, somehow, than this movement toward exposure.

Already, the buffer between her and the gate had thinned. She could barely think. All was motion. Battle sounded more glorious than this in stories. She hadn't believed the shiny veneer, but she hadn't understood the truth either. She wasn't a Keeper; she was a girl surrounded by jostling elbows and sharp blades. Moving feet had wakened choking dust that clogged her throat and dimmed her vision. Desperately, she dragged her cause back to mind, holding it in cupped hands like a bird in a storm. *Justice. My family. My friends.* The only part that made sense were the faces of the people she loved. She could fight for them, and nothing else.

The brunt of the attack would come from the front, and they expected Belik to send Tanyu to try to surround them. That was the reason Kiria and Bard had reserved some of the few Tanyu on their side to watch the rear of the army. But even in the center, screams reached her, the chaos of battle, the great surges forward, the madness of blood.

She needed to check for Bard one more time.

Guards surrounded her so closely she felt squashed between them. She gripped her sword and closed her eyes. It took her maddening seconds to get any sense of him. A cool wash of relief swept over her. Now, she realized the fear she'd bottled that he'd been killed. Other fears too, but she didn't open the bottle.

"Bard!"

They were nowhere together, suspended in a blank space, feet grounded only by will. Her elation faded when she saw Bard's expression. Devastation and fear pinched his black eyes.

Her flesh crawled. She didn't know what she feared most.

"Jorrim Calthwaite is dead. He was found in the palace."

Her breath was stolen from her chest. Her mouth and nostrils opened wide, but her gasps brought in no air. Her mind converged on one barely articulated word. No. *No no no. No!*

The last of her air expelled in a whispered scream. "No!"

Bard gave an odd quirk of his brow before he disappeared. Strange. On most people, it would be a casual apology. But not here. She grasped that tiny detail as if it held truth itself.

She couldn't lose Jori. She couldn't.

Did Bard mean he wasn't dead? The hope was like grasping a vein-thin root to stop from falling. But any hope was better than none. She would grasp at anything.

She opened her eyes. Chetana and the guards around her pressed even closer than before as they neared the edge of the army. She was almost thankful, since her legs barely kept her upright. Something was different, though, in the mass of bodies around her. *You have to care. Don't give up. There's life on the other side. You can think about Jori later.*

Jorrim Calthwaite.

That was what Bard had called him. She frowned, her whole face tight. Her mind moved sluggishly. It kept snagging on the news. *Jorrim Calthwaite is dead.*

Bard wouldn't call him Jorrim. Hardly anyone called him that. A new sliver of hope cautiously reared up.

Exclamations cut through her thoughts. She looked up. The bodies around her faced the wrong direction, all looking behind her. Thick horror coated her as she turned.

From the tree line came a new force. It wasn't a few Tanyu—frightening enough—but a new army. Not one of theirs, it sported a blue and black gonfalon. More were coming through the trees, but the mass of people looked huge, large enough to completely surround them. *But all of Belik's allies have come already*, she thought stupidly.

Obviously, he had more.

The new force quickly arranged themselves, shouting orders, as though surprised to see the conflict already underway.

She would have to fight.

Reckless rage surged through her and she screamed an inarticulate battle cry. It ripped through her chest and lashed her throat, drowning her fear. *Bring everything you have, you bastard, you murderer!* The Unreal seemed to merge with the Real, as though she could rise into the air like Chetana in dreams and rout entire armies, leaving nothing but scorched earth and a legend of vengeance.

Before her mind buzzed to blankness and battle fury, she reached for the Tanyu who were their allies to come and help. In her inexperience, she couldn't muster contact fast enough, but she shouted orders into the emptiness where they all waited to hear from her. Maybe they would hear.

Her feet started to move as the charge began. A slow dream with dark tree shadows.

Dark.

The bloody sky had no sun.

Her army just had to hold out a little longer. Firian had his window to kill Belik. He could do it with a thought. Without Belik driving the Tanyu, they could find victory. She sent up a prayer with no words. If Firian didn't succeed, it would be up to Royce and the others.

If Bard was right, then Royce, Viktor, and the other guards were gone too. Firian was their best chance.

Jorrim.

Pieces fell together. Bard's silence and then *Jorrim*. He'd been taken, told to say it that way. Did that mean Jori wasn't dead? Did that mean *Belik* wasn't dead?

Bard taken.

Jori alive.

Belik alive.

Then where was Firian?

The scraps of her thought fell away like shredded paper as the first wave of the new army collided against them.

68

FIRIAN

IT WASN'T in Firian to give up. Every nerve in his body burned, and the sun had sunk below the horizon, and the Sentry blocked his access to the Unreal as surely as a stone wall prevented someone from walking through it. But he stood up, shakily, to his feet. He flexed his fingers and bounced on either leg, trying to regain a sense of strength and balance. Killing Belik this way had only been the initial plan. It wasn't the only one that might work.

Zhufal stirred. His eyes opened, meeting Firian's. He didn't try to cry out.

In a second, Firian had crouched beside him and yanked down the gag. "Where did he go?"

Indecision warred in the man's features, though he remained composed. "The Main."

"How many are with him?"

"I don't know."

"Guess," Firian snarled.

"It's not a good place to strike. Most of us are there."

Of course Belik had made the Main a war zone. He could oversee more people from there. Then Zhufal's wording struck him. *Not a good place to strike.* This Tanyu wanted Firian to succeed.

"Why didn't you come before?" he demanded in a whisper, still clutching the gag around the man's neck.

"I couldn't." The simple response carried the weight of Belik's cruelty.

The Master's lesson came back to him. *Fear is the fastest way to power.* He'd been talking about nightmares, fear campaigns, debilitating an enemy, but its application extended far beyond that, it seemed.

"Will he stay in the Main?"

"Probably. Until this is over. I don't know his plans," he added hastily.

Firian replaced the gag. Would others side with him if they had the chance? It was a mildly encouraging thought. "I have to keep you here," he said.

The Tanyu's expression was impassive. He'd expected no less. Once the man was secured, far from anything that could help him escape, Firian knocked him out again to prevent him from contacting anyone and crept back out into the hall. His head pounded from his attempts to dislodge the Sentry, his vision narrowing and expanding. Sweat was starting to dry on his skin and clothes. He blinked a few times, then squatted and peered around the corner.

Belik would have noticed the absence of his guard. There was a good chance he knew Firian was in the palace. He had to assume they were looking for him. If that were the case, there would be several Tanyu close by, since they would search the adjacent rooms first. He exhaled an incredulous breath. How had they missed him in the guestroom? He had been vulnerable during those grueling minutes, and yet no one came. Gore, he was lucky.

69

JORI

ROYCE'S GRIP on Jori's arm was a vise. The hold suggested Jori was a wild animal that would bolt at the first opportunity. But he had no desire to bolt at the moment. He fought to catch his breath as he crouched with the guard among garbage. His boots half-slid over nameless foodstuffs ground into the floor, peels and gristle and slimy pits.

Jori's frantic thoughts circled around the smell like a bird of prey. Thala was usually the servant who took care of the trash in the lower kitchen. He kissed her once. Had she been killed in the first attack too? Shame prickled across his skin like insect legs. He hadn't thought of her one time since the palace burned. His mind had been too full of Atty. But more than his brother had lost their lives.

Like Viktor.

After sprinting out of the dining room, Jori had barely caught Bard's eye before careening around a corner. He flung himself with the desperation of someone jumping from a height without looking. There would be no Tanyu because there *could* be no Tanyu.

He was fast, fast enough to beat Bard if they raced on the beach. Royce's daughter, Adelisa too.

Run, Bard! In the split second that he actually saw him, he took in the gag, the binds, and unfettered legs. Bard could run too.

Jori dove down a side stairwell.

Running footsteps followed. *Chuck chuck chuck* tripping down the stairs after him. He didn't look to see who it was. Many people. At least three.

Jori skidded to a halt. This wasn't a dead end, was it? There were rarely dead ends. Panic fritzed his mind and kept his eyes from focusing. They skipped like stones over water.

He turned. Royce and Viktor and the other guard and two Tanyu. No Bard, of course, but his mind had trouble grappling with what he saw.

The nameless Kingdom guard went down first, neck snapped as the Tanyu leapt up, more a predator than a person. The Tanyu landed on his feet. Reality blurred.

Royce and Viktor whirled on the two attackers. "Go!" shouted Royce.

Jori went, a destination finally locking into place. Trash heap. It fed into several areas below the main floor. He wouldn't be trapped. He kicked in the locked cupboard and lunged inside, tripping and bracing himself on his hand. He'd forgotten the short drop.

Through the opening, he saw the armored backs of his guards. Two Tanyu in black faced them.

"I'll cover you," said Royce.

"You go," Viktor insisted.

They didn't argue. Royce wedged his big body through the cabinet door after Jori, keeping his sword pointed at the entrance. His bulk blocked out all light. As it spilled back into the space, there was a lightning-fast movement of feet and steel outside. A strangled gasp and then a hand flopped into the opening, quickly kicked away.

Royce shoved Jori forward through the foul-smelling refuse. The force almost made him fall. Blindly, he ran.

That was a while ago, or a few minutes. It was impossible to tell. At first there were feet, but, after crouching and staying silent in an alcove for another long, stinking while, the sounds faded. It was so completely dark that no one could see them, even a Tanyu, and their special powers didn't work on him, he liked to think. At least they couldn't do that thing with their minds.

Viktor's death replayed in his thoughts. It was so short, so small. It didn't make sense. That's not how people died. They died after saying their last goodbye or a long, valiant fight. They didn't flop to the ground. They certainly didn't die because of *him*. He was Jori, the fun one, the unimportant one.

He smacked his lips quietly. His mouth was so dry he could hardly swallow. Royce's death grip on his arm tightened. He knew exactly where to squeeze, underneath his arm where there was no metal plate to shield him.

"My Kepron," he seethed into his ear, more warm breath than words, "don't run." The words were slow, severe.

Jori had to remember where he was, that this was a place to listen and not rebel against the wrong people. He almost apologized, but the words stuck in his throat. He wasn't sorry for running. He was more than sorry for the other two guards. Those words would ring empty. Instead he looked at Royce, or where Royce must be in this darkness.

They had to get to light. Jori was sick of darkness, and wasn't it more dangerous to stay put in the pitch black? Who knew if a Tanyu was lurking somewhere? They wore black, after all.

"Light," he croaked.

The image of Viktor's hand made Jori lightheaded. A person

couldn't drop like that. It didn't make sense, not after a complex life. The hand turned into the blood-soaked blankets around Atty's ashen face. It could happen to anyone. It could happen to *him.*

He swallowed back bile. The sour garbage smell wasn't helping. He followed Royce without resisting as he guided him forward. "Left," Jori managed in a hoarse voice. They had to get to the Main. That was his goal, and the place they were taking Bard. Whatever happened, he needed to be in the right place when... when this was over, he supposed. Kiria would want him to.

His life had narrowed to a few things: Bard, Kiria, and the intrusive images of Belik's hulking form dominating the Main (imaginary) and Viktor's hand (real).

"What's to the left?"

"The general's office."

70

BELIK

BELIK LOOKED at Firian's roommate, black eye purpling, his only useful hand clenched in his lap. Red seeped through the cloth covering his nose and mouth. After Belik tried to kill him the first time - *had* killed him, but he'd clung to life somehow—he hadn't used the Second Level to kill anyone else. That exertion of his power dulled his wits, made him weak. But he would try it again on Bard once this was over.

He'd misread this boy. He had more iron in him than Belik expected. Hopefully he would fight back, then the others would see that Belik hadn't failed to kill a young boy who by rights should be a Learner, but a worthier adversary.

When Bard opened his eyes, the Unreal flooded back, pure as oxygen. Someone must have killed his Sentry. About time.

In a flash, Belik searched for Firian. Nothing but static. He was still safe.

He was too late to check that Bard had sent the correct message to Kiria, though, so he looked at Shiro for confirmation. He nodded.

"He told the princess and you told the Tanyu in the underground storeroom?" he clarified.

"Yes," Shiro confirmed.

Bard gaped, wide-eyed. Well, one eye was swelling, but the other turned perfectly round. Belik smothered a smirk. *Fight back. Show them you're made of something besides your mother's dinner rolls.* "Yes, we know," he goaded. "Let me be clear. I'm not worried about winning the war. We know almost everything about your plan. And I am the Tanyuin Head." He drew out each word. "My allies will never stop coming."

Tanyu embedded in cities and fortresses all across the continent were at his disposal, like Lord Ruler Thraddock was at Firian's. A simple command, and most of them would force their town to mobilize. One city from the Phlaxtin border was due about now, in fact.

Belik had waited for the princess' army to gather, to feel strong. There were at least two advantages to that: better intelligence and greater opportunity for surprise.

So far, the Sentries had been the only unexpected element, and that rankled. But it was temporary. For now, he could filter his commands through Shiro, who had championed him from the first moment he defied Firian's decision to leave the Kingdom alone. He was young and strong and held a grudge. It didn't matter that everyone knew Firian hadn't meant to kill Rian. Belik threw it in Shiro's face whenever he could. Hatred like that was so useful when harnessed.

It didn't matter that Belik had thought Rian was an idiot who deserved what happened. When survivors told Belik the story, most included that Firian had shouted for the Tanyu to get behind him. Rian didn't. Power like Firian's wasn't something to underestimate.

Enough pining over lost opportunities. He lowered his glasses and picked at the inside of his eye before issuing a few new orders, leaving Bard to stew in worry.

Finally, he returned his attention to his captive. "Take his mask off."

Shiro untied the cloth around Bard's face.

A shift in the quality of sound caught Belik's attention. Actually, the lack of sound. There were fewer grunts and groans and cries from the Tanyu seated around him like an enormous, blind audience. Fights had ceased or been won. A good sign.

Bard gasped and spit. Dark red streaks painted his face. Someone had broken his nose.

"We know the prince is here," Belik said, leaning forward. "He's probably dead. And we know Firian is here. Isn't he?" It wasn't a question. The moment the Sentries blocked his access to the Unreal, he knew, even before his lookout had disappeared from the hall. "Where?"

Bard's stained throat bobbed. His eyes darted to the window where the sunless sky darkened. "He's... He's with Kiria. Hidden in the army." His Endrian voice sounded thick and nasally.

That wouldn't be the worst place for Firian to be, since they were so intent on keeping their one royal alive. But his Talents wouldn't be best served there. He'd carve through armies, but his unique ability couldn't help unless he planned to explode and take everyone with him. No. He couldn't risk his princess getting hurt. Evidence and common sense would say Firian was in the palace, hunting down Belik. Judging from Firian's anger when they'd last met, he'd insist on it.

Before he could speak again, a Sentry electrified his senses. Again, the suffocating feeling. How many Sentries did they have? He barked an expletive. "If you didn't understand before, I don't need you. It will be easier to find him when he's weakened by your death."

Composing himself, he waved a hand for everyone to stand down, not to hurt Bard. Yet.

"We'll keep going until we get to our targets," he continued, keeping his voice more even, "but you can save a lot of people by telling me the truth." He readjusted his glasses. "This war doesn't have to go on. I know we're both tired of it and would prefer less bloodshed."

Bard just gazed back, steadfast.

"Firian abandoned you. He doesn't do what you want. Isn't that why you left the Academy? And now you're protecting him? Why?" Belik felt his blood rise as he laid out the arguments. Based on his observation, this was the way Bard thought, so why didn't he respond? "I'll ask you one more time," he said, "where is Firian?"

Blood ran down over Bard's chin, and his lip curled—barely perceptibly—in defiance.

71

BARD

Bard's eyes streamed from the pain of his broken nose. A cold breeze flowed through the blank windows. The feeling on his skin was like the drafts that snuck through slatted boards back home.

During the party, Jac kept telling other people that Bard was his brother. He overheard him doing it twice. Bard had been trapped on the wrong side of the first conflict between the Tanyu and Enderin's ally, the Western Kingdom, but now he had put it right.

He was where he belonged. If everything he'd done had led him here, it was all right.

Trying to stay calm, he flashed through his options. Physically, he had no chance here. He scanned the space behind Belik. Where was Firian? The room was blurry through his tears.

At least Belik thought that the Tanyu in the underground room were under control. The problem was, they could be. Bard's plan had been to neutralize some of Belik's force in a secure location before the Tanyu on their side left the room and joined the fray. Not as many casualties and more chance of success. That was what he'd thought at the time. Hopefully the ruse was still working.

But now Bard's resources had worn thin. He could offer time —maybe minutes, unless they chose to interrogate him—and perhaps one real message to Kiria or one of the others. To get off the message, he'd need to distract Shiro or, better, get him out of the room. He acted like the only one of Belik's followers who had access to the Unreal. To buy time, Bard would keep Belik talking, focused on him.

You can save a lot of people by telling me the truth. If only that were true. The image of Jori running down the hall threatened to encroach on his new calm.

"This isn't what the Tanyu are supposed to be," he said.

"That isn't an answer."

A shadow shifted behind Bard, maybe Master Nedi. He didn't turn to look. He couldn't lose his nerve. They wouldn't snap his neck, right? Belik wanted to restore his reputation in front of his followers. And he couldn't do that until the Sentry was off him and he could do... whatever it was that had left Bard crumpled in a heap on the carpet. Belik was patient. He could wait for it.

This revelation bolstered Bard. He sat a little straighter. "I know it isn't."

Belik arched a brow.

"Corso fought *for* the Kingdom. He didn't try to take it over, yeah?" He tried to speak slowly, but the words spilled out as though a bottle had been uncorked. He ran through all the games he'd played as a child, the stories he'd heard at the Academy that made him proud to have the Talent. "Naedra defended it against enemies. They were heroes in the Lantern Rebellion. They prevented the rout of the Chrysï. Even Anewa stopped an ambush single-handed. Tanyu are defenders, not attackers."

Shockingly, Belik didn't interrupt, his expression perched between furious and bemused.

Bard hadn't thought he would get this far. "We were never meant to murder and conquer and... you know, control everything."

"You think that's what's happening?" Belik asked, his tone low and flat. "I saw the Tanyu disrespected and I'm not afraid to demand that respect. You ran. So when you say *we* shouldn't control our own gory property, you can leave yourself out of it." Belik's gaze dipped to Bard's Master ring as though he wanted to rip it off. "That's enough. Tell me or we're done with you. Where is Firian?"

Above Belik's left shoulder, a slice of a dark profile disappeared—almost a black spot in the vision or a shadow in the darkening space. It was too high to be expected, in an opening above a large side door. Bard might have missed it, except that he had stared at that profile for nights on end, chewing the seeds Viktor had given him in an effort to stay focused and awake.

Jori.

72

BELIK

BELIK DIDN'T NAME the cat he saw every week in the library, even after it started following him home. Being a two-person household, they had extra food, and his father often ate at the barracks, so Belik began feeding the creature. It stayed with him then, followed him everywhere, the perfect quiet companion. After long days of studying and pre-military training, he'd read with the cat on his chest, running calloused fingers through its soft fur.

It happened the day before Belik turned thirteen. A stray dog killed his cat.

He killed the dog.

That should have been it. Simple arithmetic. But rage and bitter sadness ate at him like acid. When his invitation to join the Academy came a few weeks later, he jumped at the chance to leave everything behind.

He had a feeling he was looking at Firian's cat.

Regret thrilled through Belik, a feeling all too familiar. This boy, Bard, could have been a Tanyu after all, his size and his hand notwithstanding. Belik considered his own bad leg.

"I'll tell you where he is if you call off the fighting," Bard said. "It's getting dark. Your people will..." He caught his breath, looked at the window looking out toward the sea. "Your people will just kill each other in the dark."

The balls on this kid. Unfortunately, he was right. Outright battle wasn't the best option now that the autumn sun had plunged the landscape in darkness. Subtler methods would achieve their aims better. "You're in no position to make demands." If he could reach the Unreal, he'd tell the others privately to contact the army, but that wasn't an option. "I know you have a *katah* with Firian. Find him."

"Lift the Sentry."

Either he liked Bard Tanery or he hated him. Lifting the Sentry meant giving Firian power. But... if the royals insisted on blocking Belik's own mind with a Sentry, what did he have to fear?

"You'll have seconds," Belik said, jutting his chin at Shiro. "It's getting dark," he added. He would catch his meaning. *Stop the fighting. For now.*

Shiro closed his eyes to inform the lone Sentry to halt. They had sent him out to sea with another Tanyu to relay messages. Firian's Sentry would be much harder to track in the vast Kheltor and would be out of range for Firian's killing ability.

Belik tapped against the wall of his own mental barrier. Still intact. Firian couldn't reach him mentally or bodily.

Commanding the armies to stall would take a few extra messages than the one to pause Firian's Sentry. To do it, Shiro descended the steps and found an empty chair.

After a moment of silence, several of the other Tanyu stood from their seats, a hint of stiffness to their limbs. Bard's purple, swollen eyes caught the movement.

"How will I know when...?"

Belik didn't answer. If Bard had a *katah* with Firian, then he'd know without prompting. The presence of the other mind would present itself, not loudly, but clearly, like a breeze.

Bard blinked slowly a few times, growing more abstracted and looking less fearful. It was strange having no sense of what went on in Bard's mind. Unsettling. Belik closed one hand in a fist at his side. Finally, Bard's focus narrowed on Belik again.

"You called off the fighting, yeah?" His voice, less nasally with blood now, had grown small.

"It's black outside," Belik answered.

Bard worried his lower lip. This kind of hesitation usually meant a truthful answer. He didn't want to betray Firian. Belik hadn't wanted to lose the boy either, but Firian had betrayed them all first by choosing the princess over the Tanyu.

After a few more seconds of struggle, Bard released a breath. "He's... coming here. He's close to the east wall now, outside. Not the wall around the grounds, but here, the palace." He flicked his gaze at the wall he described. The broken window acted as an enormous entrance. Though guarded, it seemed a wider opening than before.

Here. Belik heaved himself to stand. "Look into it," he told Nedi. "Bring others with you. Go. Now!"

They obeyed.

Belik limped down the steps. "Bring him." Bard's Tanyuin guard hoisted him to his feet and pushed him after Belik. "Set up a room for dreams elsewhere. Guards where necessary. The rest can go back to their quarters." After a moment, he added, "Remember, Firian has a Sentry, so if you see him, engage."

The Tanyu all around the room began to end their fights and head out.

Shiro approached at the foot of the stairs. "It's done." The fighting had stopped for the night.

Behind him, Bard hung his head.

73

FIRIAN

"Go to the north side of the Main. Room on the north side." Bard's words were so fast they blurred together.

A question had half-formed on Firian's lips before the Sentry slammed back into place. He bit back a cry of pain.

The Sentry had faltered, or else Belik ordered that it be lifted for a moment. Why?

To find him. That had to be the only answer, or else Bard wouldn't have been there, giving him his desperate message. And Bard would only have known exactly when the Sentry would lift if he was with Master Belik.

That small taste of freedom, of success, shocked him as much as jumping in the Apothelin. He started running. He was outside and heading toward the Main from the west, staying close to the palace. From his vantage point, he could see gardens, Amiran Academy, and ocean. This was almost the same path he'd taken a lifetime ago with Kiria and Atty and Jori, when he'd broken them into the Main through a window.

Room on the north side. As he pictured it, its dimensions took shape. Kiria had been there. Firian dimly remembered seeing a door on the far side of the room when he'd gone to the Main himself.

Was that where Belik was holding Bard? He refused to consider the other reason Bard's message had been so brief. No, Belik could use Bard to find Firian. He wouldn't destroy an asset like that while he still needed him.

North side... north side...

The only light filtered up from the Amiran lanterns. Firian pushed aside branches as he moved with all the speed and secrecy he could muster.

As he got closer to the north side of the Main, he craned his neck to see entrances. Were there any unguarded openings? Considering the skeletal jaws of the blown-out windows, he knew they must be watched. The mourning cloth around his hand would let him enter without cutting himself, but it was too risky.

When he stilled, the sounds of people, quiet but distinct, flowed from inside. Tanyu. The sound reminded him of a home he could never go back to, one that never existed the way he thought it did.

If Belik and Bard were in the north room, then he would find a way to get there. He may have missed his window of time to kill Belik with the Second Level, but that didn't mean Firian wasn't physically dangerous. Bard wouldn't have led him there if it were a trap, or if there were too many Tanyu faithful to Belik. He could do this.

He prodded at the Sentry like an open wound, just checking, before curling his lip with frustration and surveying the wall that separated him from the place Bard said to go. It looked solid, no exterior entrances. But high up there were a couple openings, barely big enough to be called windows. More like embrasures. He could barely make them out in the dark.

Brushing spiderwebs off his sleeves, he measured the

distance with his eyes. Too high to jump. Very difficult to climb. Even if he got up there, he could find the space was too narrow for him to fit through. The poor light and angle of the rough stone made judging their width almost impossible. He sucked his teeth. Belik was practically within arm's length, but a wall and a Sentry kept Firian from victory. Bard's life was on the line. If he didn't find a way in, then the Western Kingdom could cease to exist as he'd known it all his life. Kiria wouldn't find justice for her slain family, and would likely meet death herself.

Firian's cheeks flamed with heat. A wall and a Sentry.

Setting his jaw, he bent down under the cover of foliage and broke off a few thick stems from the bushes. They cracked as he split them off and rubbed the sticky sap on his hands. He avoided the mourning cloth, daubing his fingertips on that hand. Once done, he took one last look behind him. No one had spotted him. He wore Academy black, but his famous face would give him away even at a distance. Also, scaling the palace wall just might rouse suspicion, he thought bitterly. He had to be fast.

He inhaled and jumped. Most of the stones had worn smooth with age and angled gently outward, not up to create handholds. He kicked his boots into the grooves between stones and pulled himself up by his sticky fingertips. By the second handhold, the sap was already growing grainy and slippery with dirt. He reached as high as he could. Fewer handholds, less likely to fall.

He clung more than two stories off the ground when his hand slipped. His stomach plummeted. Pain shot through Firian's wrist and shoulder as he gripped with his other hand that had made it through the opening and grasped the other side. His legs nearly seized as they lifted him high enough to regain his hold. The toe of his boot slid free, wavered in sickening midair above the drop. His heart pounded fast, too fast, heavy and thick in his chest. He forced air into his lungs and reached with his other hand. Boots found footing. His muscles spasmed from the strain as he pulled himself up.

It was dark. Shadowy recesses pooled below in what looked like an antechamber, with several doors leading to other places in the palace. One set of double doors was particularly magnificent. Above them was another small opening into a lighted room. The Main, then.

No one was here. Did Bard try to hide him from a search party? Possible, but that didn't feel right.

Firian eased himself through the embrasure, a tight fit, and no way down but to jump.

Something moved in the darkness. A door adjacent to the fancy double doors slowly opened. A blond Kingdom soldier stepped inside. His armor gleamed dully in the gloom, and so did his sword, which he held in front of him as he scanned the small room. Then he looked up. Immediately battle ready, the man widened his stance and brandished his weapon.

"It's me," Firian mouthed, trying to maneuver so his face was more visible. Hopefully the soldier would know him. Even with so little light, Firian saw the moment the soldier recognized him. He lowered his weapon, though he didn't sheath it.

Firian lowered himself down from the little window, and then jumped to the floor.

"Master Kess?" the soldier whispered.

Firian nodded.

The soldier's face grew taut. "Master Belik is still alive. He has Bard. I was part of the team that was supposed to eliminate Belik if he wasn't dead by now, but that's become more difficult…"

For both of us. "My mind is blocked," Firian explained, ignoring the sting of criticism. Belik was supposed to be dead already. "Where is Belik now?"

"He just left the Main, but many of the Tanyu are still here." He cast his eyes toward the darkened door.

Just left? That didn't make any sense. Why would Bard lead him here then? "How many are with him? Did he say where he was going?"

"Only three Tanyu, and Bard."

Firian had handled four on his own before. But they hadn't been Tanyu. Especially not Tanyu he knew personally. Still, it would be easier to take care of Belik when he only had a handful of Tanyu around him instead of a room full of them.

Someone peeked around the open door to the next room. His wide gray eyes took in the situation—Firian talking to the soldier—and he straightened, eyebrows rising. It was Jori Calthwaite.

Firian's mouth opened in surprise and relief.

"The other guards with me didn't make it," the soldier explained. "I have to protect the Kepron first."

"Thought I heard whispering," said Jori.

"Then we'd better stop," said Firian. His mind whirled with a plan. The meaning of Bard's message wasn't perfectly clear, but it must have included helping Jori. Belik just left the Main. He had to be going to a small, less guarded location. The perfect chance for Firian to finally end this and restore Kiria's throne. But now he had Jori to look after as well.

The warmth of rightness settled in his chest as he looked at the others. This wasn't what he'd expected, but Jori was safer with him than with anyone else. The blond soldier looked capable, so he could help deal with any threats along the way.

It was time to be a bodyguard again.

74

—————

KIRIA

Kiria unclasped her breastplate with shaking fingers. A single candle lit her tent, hiding the phantom shadows of the guards that stood in a tight ring outside.

She'd barely begun to fight, feeling the meagerness of her training, when the soldiers around her spotted an opening to spirit her away and fought to get her clear of the melee. The escape was grueling. Enemy soldiers by twos and threes kept appearing to track down their little group. Chetana felled several of them. Protect the Keeper—that was their duty. And they did it. She helped where she could, but her ability didn't stack up to the meanest trained soldier. So many attackers got close, though, spraying her with their blood, before full darkness settled and the battle paused.

Soldiers had put up these small tents while Kiria, Chetana, and the remaining leaders of her army met to talk about the day. She'd contributed, but each word was an effort. They all agreed that they couldn't sustain the same losses two days in a row.

She stacked the breastplate near the small cot, almost losing her grip on it as she set it down. Next, the arm and leg braces, each with buckles. This would be far easier to do with her serving girls, but they were away from here, out of reach of the fighting. Boots, sword belt, pants, leather jerkin, underclothes. Grime and sweat smeared her skin underneath.

She had to get clean, had to wash the blood and noise from her mind. A pitcher of water sat on the floor. It sloshed as she lifted it up and poured it over her head. With the breeze slicing through the tent, the water felt freezing cold. Moments ago, she had been hot in the armor, unbearably hot. She scrubbed ruthlessly at her limp hair, frozen cheeks, and stinging eyes, trying to clear her head.

Both forces had ceased, but not before it was nightmare dark. At first light, the war would begin again.

After all that fury, she'd remained a spectator, protected from the main violence of the battle. It might have been worse to watch without being able to get close. She couldn't help the wounded or hurt the guilty or raise the dead. *Am I a coward?* She gave her face an extra hard scrub, avoiding her new scars. No, she wasn't a coward. They fought to protect her, and she had done what she could.

But her mind was in the palace.

She'd barely caught it. As the fighting began to lessen and messages were being passed back and forth, Bard had come to her again in the Unreal. Even now, it felt like a dream. How much was real? When she'd tried to contact him again to confirm, there was no answer.

"Jori and Belik are still alive," came his frantic voice.

"Where are you?"

No answer.

So she'd been right. Bard was captured and Jori wasn't dead.

Water trickled from the ends of her hair down her back. She let her Beauty fade with it. For the first time since the news, she allowed herself to feel relieved. She held her face in her hands and breathed. Hot tears mixed with the dirty water. She couldn't lose Jori. Her poor, ravaged Brithnem needed his enjoyment of life. *She* needed it.

With a sniff, she grabbed a new set of clothes. No nightdress tonight. She would try to rest, but then her forces needed to regroup, finalize their adjusted plan.

Belik was still alive, and had more allies than they thought.

Firian couldn't break the Sentry, then. She'd truly believed he could. Bard's message hadn't contained any information about him. Presumably, he was still alive, and still near the palace. Bard would have told her about Firian's death, and they both would have felt it.

She laid down gingerly, as though she were covered with bruises, which was only partially true. Right now, her insides felt more fragile than the outside. A knock against the fabric of the tent made her bolt upright, clinging to the thin blanket.

"A visitor," said one of the guards. Not Royce or Viktor, whom she'd come to trust. They were with Jori.

A visitor? "Who?"

"Princess Haved Ganesha."

Kiria jumped to her feet, untangling her ratty hair. "Haved? Here?" Her mind was too full to understand it. "Let her come in."

The tent flaps parted and Haved, clad in a red tunic, strode inside the little space. Kiria's eyelids fluttered with disbelief. Haved might as well have been a ghost.

"Sister," Haved began, her typically stoic expression soft with concern.

"Haved." Kiria gulped back a sob and pulled her into an embrace. Haved stiffened with surprise before holding her tightly, smoothing her tangled hair and rubbing her back. Kiria soaked up the soothing contact. Haved's warm presence was a miracle, or maybe a mirage that would fade once they let go. "What are you doing here?"

"Amrit insisted on your behalf to our father," she said, backing up to see Kiria's face. "He told him that we fight for our own, and that Atael was one of our own. He is in the Book of Names." Her expression clouded with grief, but she didn't pause. "Every day my brother requested an audience with him, and it was granted. Finally, my father agreed, but did not allow Amrit to go himself, only to send an army to assist you."

Kiria was dumbfounded. "An army?"

"Yes, they wait in the forest, ten thousand strong." Haved said it so simply, as though it didn't change everything.

Ten thousand! "I need to tell the others!" About to run out of the tent, she paused. "And you came." It was a question. What wasn't Haved telling her? She wasn't a fighter. It couldn't be as simple as the narrative she proposed. Amrit asked enough times for his father to listen? Kiria doubted it. As Haved had said, the king was like stone.

"Yes." She shut her lips tight after the word. There was more she didn't want to say.

Kiria wouldn't push her. Not after this. "Thank you," she said, "and thank Amrit for his petitions. This... I can't express how much this means."

"The royal Lines of Brithnem deserve the thrones," she replied. A stern kind of smile curved her lips. Kiria ached to return it, but couldn't manage it. Haved reached for Kiria's hand. "Tell your people we are here to help. With us, you will have victory."

And Kiria wanted to believe her.

75

BELIK

SHIRO'S green eyes filled with shock. "Master Belik," he said as they walked away from the Main.

"Yes?" he answered gruffly, glancing at Bard. Did he need the gag put on again? The Endrian's nose and lip had swollen purple. They could offer the gag as a tactic to encourage him to carry out any last commands Belik might have. They'd leave it off.

"Charäkhnem is here."

Belik's attention swiveled to Shiro. "What? Fighting?" Enktuya put a hand on the knife at her waist. He hadn't summoned Charäkhnem. It was too large and complicated. That kingdom's strongest Tanyu had disappeared after failing to deliver the Kepron. He must have known how furious Belik would be, and what horrible consequences he'd face.

"Not fighting yet," Shiro said, "but camped, for the Keepers."

Bard's good eye lightened with hope and he panted once before catching himself.

Belik glared at him and then stretched his jaw. "How many?"

"No one's counted. More than we have, until our other allies arrive."

So Kiria had more bodies to throw at the problem. At first light, their ground forces would be overwhelmed.

Why hadn't Belik chosen a successor, someone to ensure that the Tanyu could fight on, that his dream of a globally respected Tanyuin Academy wouldn't die with him? He knew why. He'd been holding out, waiting for Firian to come around, and then the day-to-day business of securing the city had pushed the thought out of his mind. How did this conflict manage to find all the chinks in his armor?

"We won't wait 'til morning," Belik concluded. "We'll finish this now." In a perfect world, he'd crush Kiria's rebellion and every one of her allies as he planned. Now, speed was of the essence. Time to end this posturing.

"Tell all the Tanyu not to sleep. We're ending this tonight. Targets are the royals first, Sentries second. Send them out, physical and Unreal, and let me know when it's done."

He should have done this a long time ago, but he had to be so gory proud. Sometimes it was better just to finish something and be done with it.

76

JORI

Royce offered Firian a leg up to see into the Main from the candle opening. He didn't take it. Tanyu, or at least that Tanyu, didn't need it.

"I could have done it," Jori repeated.

Royce just scowled at him, one finger to his lips. He hadn't forgiven Jori for bolting and jeopardizing their lives. Jori hadn't forgiven himself either, but Royce didn't need to keep reminding him with rueful looks.

Without a sound, Firian perched on the ledge and looked out. When he stopped moving, Jori's eyes couldn't track him anymore. His black outfit blended into the nighttime shadows above, despite the faint light coming in from the gap overlooking the Main. Impressive. Jori hated that he was impressed. But... damn.

Firian dropped back to the ground as gracefully as a cat. "You said it was full."

"The room, yeah," Jori whispered back. When he had peeked through the opening himself, the Main had swarmed with Tanyu, like one enormous session. Everyone wore black, sitting and standing, except Bard, whose face was all bloody. Jori hadn't gotten a good view of him when he'd run from the dining room. Bard's wrists were bound. Why would they bind his wrists when he had a hand that wouldn't move? The memory of their unnecessary cruelty prickled over his skin. He adjusted his cuffs under the forearm guards.

"There's hardly anyone in there now," Firian said.

"I wonder why," Royce said.

"Three," Firian clarified, staring past them to the general's office with its desk and books and instruments, as though he would find answers somewhere.

Jori was just as perplexed. "You can take three, can't you?" Judging from the way Firian leapt up into the opening above them, and the obvious muscles in his shoulders, that should be no problem for him.

Firian turned toward him, a grim smirk on his lips. He nodded.

Jori shrugged and held his hands out to his sides. *Why wait?*

"There could be more," Royce said.

"He's right," Firian said. "We need to—"

"What?" Jori cupped his hand around his ear, genuinely surprised and delighted. When Firian didn't take the bait, he lowered his hand and merely grinned at Royce, who looked gruff as always.

"We need to find Belik," Firian continued, a slight edge of annoyance coloring his voice. He closed and opened his palm, his demand obvious. Jori handed him his sword. "We won't have another chance like this again."

"Where did all the rest go?" Jori could hardly hear Royce's objection, they were all keeping their voices so low.

Firian's lips pressed into a line.

"Sleep?" Jori suggested.

The Tanyu shook his head, his blue-eyed gaze cutting to the side. "I think they're looking for you."

The room felt suddenly colder. Viktor's arm had just flopped there like it was nothing.

Firian's hand was on his shoulder, giving him a light shake. He didn't offer any words of comfort, but he looked into his eyes. The force of his gaze made Jori understand Kiria a little better. Firian was indomitable.

After a nod to Royce, who laid his hand on the hilt of his sword, Firian went through to the waiting area—Atty had stood right there waiting for his coronation—and opened the double doors into the Main.

Jori squinted against the light. Firian was right. Only three. The Tanyu froze when they saw who it was. Firian Kess, Jori Calthwaite, Royce the palace guard, in that order.

Sweat coated Jori's neck and forehead. A bead dripped into his eye. He blinked it away, hoping it didn't look like he was crying. That would ruin the image of the moment.

Firian raised one weaponless hand, but every eye in the room looked at him as though he had crashed through with a battering ram. "I'm back," he said calmly, "as the true Tanyuin Head. I'll protect anyone who helps me, but I'm going to finish this." The unspoken threat if they decided *not* to help vibrated through the air.

Jori held his breath.

77

KIRIA

KIRIA GOT NO REST. If she fell asleep, Tanyu would attack her in dreams.

So she stayed up, talking to her commanders about the next day, and what they were going to do about the situation at the palace. If Bard was still alive, he was under Belik's control. There was no way to contact Jori, but Kiria was confident he must still be alive since Belik wasn't gloating about killing him. Firian was missing, either dead or trying his best despite the Sentry with no success. Kiria didn't want to admit how much she had counted on Firian to come through. The situation at the palace was tenuous, to say the least.

With the Charäkhni army, Kiria felt much better about their chances outside the walls. It looked like it would be up to her and her allies to breach the defenses and force Belik to surrender.

She ran her fingers through her hair. It had long since dried but still felt grimy. She rolled her fingertips together.

"You should get some rest," said Lanthe, one of the Kingdom commanders, rolling up the square of paper where she'd drawn a makeshift map. Several of her fingernails were dark purple, a shocking contrast with her white-pale skin.

The bearded Charäkhni general eyed Kiria with the same concern. Haved had started at the table with them but had since gone to bed. Kiria didn't blame her.

"I'm fine." Kiria looked at the general. "You have doctors rotating through your camp, right?" Besides twitching and other obvious signs, she didn't know what a dream attack looked like from the outside. Chetana, seated beside her, didn't know either. They'd given their best guesses.

"They are all looking into the tents," the general responded. His embroidered military crest—a golden eagle—gleamed in the dim lantern light. "It has become late and I have heard no reports of attacks."

"None?"

Chetana met her look.

"No, Lady Kiria." The general pursed his bearded lips as though to suggest that keeping the doctors awake all night was a waste of resources.

It was impossible that Belik didn't know about Charäkhnem's arrival. Now Kiria's army outnumbered Belik's own. He wouldn't go to sleep and hope for the best the next morning. He would try to weaken them, intimidate them.

"Please check now," Kiria said, gesturing to a soldier standing near the general. The soldier wore his pointed helmet, even though they were inside. After a nod from the general, he tilted his head and went to do her bidding.

Kiria put the back of one finger against her lip—habit now— but the wound had sealed for good. She turned to Chetana. "What does it mean if Master Belik hasn't sent any Tanyu after the Charäkhni army? Is there any chance he doesn't know they're here? It's been hours…"

"None," Chetana confirmed. "He knows."

The Charäkhni general's expression grew more pinched. Perhaps he was finally realizing something was wrong.

"Everyone has to sleep," said Lanthe.

"Yes, but the Tanyu will overlap so they don't miss any time." She and Bard had discussed this. "What are they all doing?" she muttered. Belik had to see the Charäkhni force as a threat. There was no reason for him to leave them alone. Unless... Unless there was nothing for them to fight for in the morning.

Chetana seemed to come to the same realization. "He's sent them after you and the Keprons."

Cold fear gripped her. "He wants to end this tonight."

"What can we do?" asked the Charäkhni general, shifting as if he would jump out of his seat that instant.

"Can you find out who they've sent? How many?" asked Lanthe, eyeing Kiria and Chetana, the only non-Tanyu with the Talent. Master Makai and Defender Erron sat with them too, recently come from the underground storehouse that now kept several of Belik's warriors secretly contained, but Lanthe avoided their gazes.

"It's not that simple," Kiria said, her eyes straying to an empty seat where Tesni should have sat. She had been targeted first when Belik's Tanyu invaded the space, one of only two casualties there, but sorely missed.

"What if Master Belik were dead?" her commander persisted.

"Then we could claim a victory," Chetana said, "and all that would be left are a few vigilantes. But I don't know that we could do anything in time." As a grim quiet took the room, her gaze turned inward, that all-seeing stare that used to scare Kiria when she was a child.

"We have Tanyu here as well," said the Charäkhni general, as though Kiria's fears were unfounded, "and our troops wait to serve."

"But he thinks he must only kill *two* to destroy the royal Lines." Chetana raised her head. Rage kindled in her expression. "He does not need a war. He needs an assassination."

"Then why fight in the first place?" asked Lanthe, frowning. Her eyes ticked to the cuts and bruises almost everyone sported.

"To show his power." The skin of Chetana's nose wrinkled. "To let everyone know that he cannot be beaten."

"Which means that you scare him," Kiria added, gesturing toward the Charäkhni general. The edges of his eyes softened with pride.

"He's using all his force to search you out." It seemed like Chetana was speaking to herself now. "The order might be countermanded if he were dead."

The look on her face was so singular that Kiria couldn't help but stare. Nerves bubbled up inside her at her tone. Kiria realized she was clenching her teeth.

The Amir turned her cool gaze to her. "My Keeper," she said, "take the Sentry off Master Belik."

78

FIRIAN

FIRIAN DIDN'T WEAR his crown, but he felt the rightness of the place where he stood, as though he'd found a jut of land in a violent ocean.

After announcing his return, a charged silence surged through the empty expanse of the Main. The three remaining Tanyu stared at Firian as though he were a ghost. Jori stood behind him, a clear symbol of Firian's intention to restore the Keepers.

He scanned the corners, the ceiling. If these three refused to help him, he could stop them. But he didn't think he'd have to. None of the three reached for weapons at their waists or in their boots.

"Master Kess?" one said incredulously.

A soft thud drew his attention to the eastern windows. Master Nedi, with more agility than his big body suggested he had, swung himself through the window and landed beside one of the huge statues of the founders. More followed. One, two, three... six more.

Firian's blood raced. He'd worked with Nedi on Torith, commissioned him as head of the Torithian troops after Jovan died, but the Master always had a bloodthirsty streak. He told the prisoners on the slave ship he'd kill the children if they weren't quiet. But Firian would have said the same thing if Nedi hadn't. Despite the bite of Nedi's betrayal, Firian saw his own decisions reflected back at him.

"Master Nedi," he said in a low voice, gripping Jori's sword. The name was slow, conciliatory.

Ignoring him, the older Master pointed and five ran forward swift as bird shadows. One hung back and unslung something from his back. A bow.

The next few moments happened in a blur of movement and heartbeats.

"Down!" Firian told Jori, bending also to exchange the sword for unsheathed daggers. He'd brought two this time.

The archer was far. Too far? No time to think. He flung the first dagger at the archer, missing the throat but hitting center mass, sending the man's arrow wide. It zinged between Royce and Jori before clacking to the ground behind them.

As the five sprinted closer, one of the Tanyu already in the room grabbed the arm of one attacker, simultaneously tripping him. With Firian, then. The enemy Tanyu fought back, kicking the other in the knees and earning a cry of pain. Firian didn't see the rest except as a fast-moving whirl of limbs.

The other four, and Nedi, were almost on him.

Clearly experienced, the Tanyu in front held two small knives in her fists. She had a shock of wavy brown hair that the tie could hardly wrestle back.

Behind her were three others—two Masters and a Defender —peeling off to the sides. They were going to hem him in and probably attack Jori. Nedi took up the rear.

Firian's heart pounded, though he held perfectly still. Fighting Torithians was one thing. Fighting Tanyu was something else.

Two knives. Three around the sides. Nedi at the back.

He had to even the odds. Who was the easiest target? And why did the others in the room just stand there?

Tanyu respected power. He'd give them a reason to pick a side.

He flung the other dagger, though he hated to lose it. One Master, headed toward Royce, went down in a gasp of blood.

The sole Defender, a mustachioed man in his twenties, had the least experience. The Kingdom soldier, Royce, could try to fend him off, or distract him, at least, until Firian could get there.

Firian gestured behind him without looking. "One on your left!" he cried.

Taking the one on the right means I'm open to knives, the one in front and I'm surrounded.

He stared straight ahead, his lethal training battling against his desire not to kill Tanyu. He'd known this was inevitable. Sweat formed in the hollow of his throat. Without giving himself another second to think, he threw himself at the front attacker, sword-first.

She parried with her knives hard enough to jump to the side, roll, and spring up again. The time lost while she rolled, he slammed his boot onto her hand, pinning one knife. She snatched her fingers away when he sprang back to cover Jori and Royce, but he had one of her weapons now, along with the sword. With so many Tanyu now so close, this would be his last throw. He flicked the blade. The Master would dodge, but she'd already given away the side she favored, so he factored that in. Slight right.

He didn't wait to see if the knife hit its mark, instead jumping back toward Jori crouched on the ground. Beside him, Royce fought with strength but no finesse. It would be seconds before he went down.

Firian couldn't spare time to help Royce with the Master closing in on the right. Could he get them closer to each other?

A dagger stabbed the air just over Royce's shoulder as Firian hauled him backward by the collar, toward Jori. With his cloth-wrapped hand, he wrenched the dagger from the Defender's grasp when he tried the same move again. Hopefully that save would be enough to see Royce through the battle.

Holding the knife by the blade, Firian whirled to the Master on the right, arcing both sword and bludgeoning hilt toward him. No contact. Momentum sent him kicking wide, bracing for impact.

With a jolt, Firian's body stopped. The Master had grabbed his foot.

A shock of hot pain knifed into his side. In response, Firian sliced behind him with his sword, an untenable position. No balance. But he got the result. The brown-haired Master gasped and went down, just as the other Master twisted Firian's foot while swiping at the other. Firian hopped in time to stay upright, but the combination of the two Masters somehow managed to make him lose his grip on his sword. It rang and clattered across the floor.

"Oh!" Jori exclaimed as one attacker fell.

Down to a dagger and one foot planted on the ground, Firian ran through his options.

Disadvantages: No control over footwork. Vulnerable. Injured. Advantage: One opponent has no hands.

Leaping toward the Master, Firian brought his knees up, one foot to meet the other, knocking him off balance and breaking the hold on his ankle. When the Master didn't fall, they grappled for a few seconds. *Balance, practice, strength.* The rest was muscle memory. Normally, that would have been enough, but this was a Tanyuin Master, not a brute Torithian. A waver gave Firian an opening and he smashed the Master's ear with the hilt of the brown-haired Master's short knife, recovered in the fighting, finally sending him crashing down.

Jori, still cowering, let go of the Master's pant leg. He'd tried to trip him. Firian acknowledged his help with a nod.

Firian had no time to relax. Royce still dealt with the Defender, now farther away, and Master Nedi had reached them. He lifted a chair – they were close to the place where the haphazard rows began – and set it down hard over Jori's head. That would protect him for a few more seconds from an attack from above, the most likely angle. Using the seat to get extra height, Firian jumped from it onto the Defender before turning to Nedi. The Defender wasn't dead, but he stumbled, disoriented, and the fight against Royce no longer looked like a certainty played out in slow motion. He had a chance.

Nedi, though.

Throw him off balance. Firian ran closer to disrupt Nedi's sense of rhythm but he went suddenly lightheaded. The room rose and fell. Nedi had ducked at the last moment and scooped Firian up over his back.

Nedi wasn't going for him. He was going for Jori, the easier mark.

Panic spiked in Firian's chest. *There are many ways to kill a man.* Flailing his arms, head spinning, he caught hold of Nedi's hair as he fell, sending him off balance, neck craned back. But Firian's balance wavered too. Both fell.

Not on the ground. Not on the ground.

They scrambled to get up. Firian met Jori's fear-stricken eyes. His face was pale, his expression pleading. He expected Firian to save him, to put things right.

With a roar, Firian leapt up. But he didn't land upright. Nedi shoved him down. The Master was so much bigger that Firian couldn't keep his feet. His dagger swung harmlessly in the air as he fell, missing its mark wide.

Master Nedi whirled on Jori. *No no no.*

Firian flung himself forward, hurling the knife. It lodged into Nedi's back. The Master grunted and slowed. Grabbing Nedi's leg to propel himself closer to Jori, Firian spun to face Nedi, shielding the Kepron with his body. No thought, just action. His mind crashed against the Sentry as it dove toward the Second Level. He bit back a scream.

Blood spattered Jori's face. Above them stood Royce, sword in hand, his chest heaving with heavy breaths. Jori, disgusted and shocked, shied away from the growing red pool beneath Nedi's bleeding body.

Royce helped Jori to his feet. The Kepron's mouth kept moving, lips rubbing together as he stared at the motionless bodies on the ground. Most of them weren't breathing. Firian nodded at Royce and clapped a hand on Jori's shoulder to assure him it was all right.

Firian's lower back throbbed and stung. He didn't investigate the feeling. This was for Kiria, and if he were injured or dead by the end, it would still be worth it if he succeeded.

"Where's Belik?" he demanded of the only two Tanyu left standing.

"I'll show you," said one, leading the way. Firian had never seen him before. He was old enough to have been sent on mission before Firian arrived at the Academy.

A direction. Finally! For the first time since he'd left Kiria, he felt optimistic and alive.

"Where are the other Tanyu?" Firian asked, moving fast in case the injured Tanyu in the Main woke and pursued them.

"They're all looking for the Keepers, Master Kess," came the reply with a glance at Jori.

So Belik sent most of his loyal Tanyu to find them while leaving the ones whose loyalty he didn't trust. All for the best.

Once out of the partially burned double doors leading to the main hall, a stab of pain lanced just above his hip. He stalked forward, not breaking stride, with Royce and Jori following. He'd had more than his share of scars.

Now, he felt more like the true Tanyuin Head than he had in a long time.

The end of the hall was doused in shadow. Brown smoke stained the walls and lined broken windows. The decorations Firian had seen so many times before in Kiria's mind were mostly gone. Looted, like that tapestry he'd seen the Torithian carrying when he first escaped the palace grounds.

"He's close," said one of the Tanyu, jogging ahead.

Firian's breath came more quickly. The Sentry still blocked his mind, and the stab wound created a new area of weakness.

"How can we tell which ones are with us?" Royce whispered loudly. His square jaw was set as hard as Belik's. Spots of blood dotted his pale skin and hair but his gaze was level.

"Just stay by him"—he nodded at Jori—"and follow my lead."

One blond eyebrow arched upward a fraction.

The Tanyu who had jogged ahead returned. "If your goal is to get to Master Belik, there are too many other Tanyu with him."

"How many?" Firian cut a glance at Royce, who had told him three.

"In and around the room, maybe twenty."

Firian backed up a step to shield Jori with his body, though they were almost the same size. "Any who could side with us?"

"We can't count on that."

Firian chewed his cheek. *Twenty.* "Belik's there? And Bard's with him?"

"Yes, Master Kess." The Tanyu's eyes shone absent for a second.

Firian knew that look. His brows drew together. "What?"

"You didn't hear it?"

"Sentry," he growled, then brightened with an idea. "Is there a Tanyu with Belik's Sentry? Can you call him off me?"

"He doesn't tell anyone but his enforcers where the Sentry is."

Firian reigned in his frustration. If they stayed in the open much longer, Jori would be killed and, if it were twenty against four, Firian might as well. Not to mention Bard in Belik's clutches. "What did you hear?"

"Belik wants an update on the Kepron."

"Tell him he's dead." Then Firian's breath caught with realization. "Who gave you that message?"

"Master Belik."

"Himself?"

"Yes." The Tanyu frowned at Firian's confusion.

Firian waved his hand. "Tell him. Tell him now. Jori is dead."

His thoughts raced. Belik's Sentry had lifted. Was the Sentry killed? Had the Tanyu gotten to Kiria's camp that quickly? His insides were ice and his wound burned. The other possibility was that Kiria decided to lift the Sentry again. Was this a new gap for him to take advantage of? Was Kiria expecting him to kill Belik *right now*? He had to believe the latter.

If Belik had access to the Unreal again, he could not only communicate with his followers, but also use the killing ability again. And Bard was in there with him. Bard had no further information they could torture out of him, if that was their goal. They wouldn't even need him as bait. Belik's presence was enough to bring Firian to them. Bard was disposable. Firian's muscles tensed.

Now. He had to kill Belik now. It didn't matter that he was outnumbered. If he didn't, then Bard and Kiria would die.

79

BELIK

MESSAGES CAME in at a dizzying rate at soon as the Sentry released. Most were variations of announcements about Charäkhnem coming to Kiria's aid. Belik was no fool. Although he had more allies to call on, they wouldn't have time to react before the princess' combined troops took back the city. His best chance to keep this power was to kill the heirs as efficiently as possible.

So when someone told him that Jorrim Calthwaite was dead, he replied, "Bring me the body." He couldn't gamble his fate.

With Firian loose on the grounds, he wouldn't risk having insufficient protection either. Every Tanyu was on duty, a slim number patrolling vulnerable areas or guarding him, and most searching for the heirs. Fifteen Tanyu stood in and around the room with him.

This excessiveness, he reminded himself with an uneasy adjustment of his shoulders, was temporary. Belik was the lynchpin of their success. He was the visible leader to the people of Brithnem and had more strategic experience than anyone else. That experience had taught him to trust no one. He alone could begin or call off attacks. The Tanyu could continue without him, but their victory—if they found it at all—would be bloody and chaotic. Chances were that either Charäkhnem would overwhelm them by sheer numbers or Firian would assert himself in Belik's place. And who knew what he would do as the leader? He certainly would accede some power to the princess, like he did before.

At least Belik had the Unreal again. Not knowing the reason made him wary, but it felt as though he'd had one arm pinned behind his back, and now he was free to move.

He turned to Bard, who looked back with wide black eyes. Still tied and bloody, he sat in a chair against the wall of the bedroom. This room was in a different wing of the palace from the Main, farther from Firian, and it didn't have as many windows as the larger room down the hall. Even though the expensive items had been stripped from it, and the dead guards of a month ago taken away, Belik knew very well whose room this had been. There was a certain rightness in winning this war from Kiria's bedroom.

"I haven't heard from the Tanyu searching the eastern wall," he told Bard. An absence of any report concerned him. Instead, Master Il'kamarse had informed him of the Kepron's death. Il'kamarse, who was supposed to stay in the Main. It felt suspicious.

"It's Firian," Bard answered simply, as though that were reason enough that they couldn't find him.

The door opened. Tanyu let four servants enter with trays of food. In all likelihood, this would be a long night. Tanyu could work through hunger, but Belik needed them at their best, and not everyone had the same capacity for self-denial as he or Firian.

Daelon was the last to enter. The other three kept their eyes down but his son met his gaze. Belik had given the Amir two choices: die or serve. Most chose to serve.

He snapped in Daelon's direction. "Feed him first," he said, jutting his chin at Bard. "Something from every plate. Quickly!"

Daelon hurried over and the other servants, who had actually been servants, not Amir, during the Keepers' time, gathered around him.

To Belik's annoyance, Bard ate the food Daelon put in his mouth with relish, as though he were starving. It didn't matter. This was the only task left for that traitor to complete. Belik hoped there was no poison to do his job for him.

He checked the Unreal again. Agitation rippled through but no words. He found the mind of a guard outside the bedroom. "What?"

"I think..." He trailed off.

"What?" Belik demanded again.

A sense of shuffled confusion.

Belik brought his notice to the bedroom again. "See what's happening," he said, eyeing Shiro.

The boy nodded and went to obey. Bard's eyes followed him as he chewed a bite of ham.

The door opened and Shiro grunted as he went down, folded from the middle.

All of Belik's senses went on alert. He pointed to several Tanyu behind him to take care of the problem. They moved stealthily and quickly as one, using multiple planes—high, medium, low—and protecting each other's blind spots. At least he'd chosen his guards well.

Belik's ears, both physical and mental, strained to hear what was going on. "Firian," someone managed to tell him, "and Calthwaite."

Belik sent more Tanyu to help.

Daelon straightened to his full height to listen too. He stood a little taller than Belik. He licked his lips. "Father."

The whispered word caught Belik's attention. *Not now.*

The door slammed open and everyone inside saw what was happening. Four Tanyu slumped on the ground, someone who looked like a Kingdom soldier blocking the Kepron against the opposite wall with his body, and Firian Kess fighting in front of them as Belik had never seen except in the Unreal. He was everywhere. It mesmerized him, made his breath stop. The fighting was almost perfect, each movement like a piece clicking into place.

Enktuya blocked part of Belik's view as she moved to protect him.

"Please stop this," came Daelon's voice.

Angry at the interruption, he turned on Daelon.

"Take me instead of the Kepron." The words were low and level.

Belik's heart thudded thickly in his chest. Soon the Kepron and the princess would both be dead. But this moment felt suspended, like the fall before a harsh landing. Why? He raised his lip in a snarl. He could kill both the Kepron and Daelon if he wanted to. But he didn't want to. His son was nothing but a disappointment and a reminder of his failures, but the possibility that this useless Amir could amount to something more snagged his thoughts more consistently than he wanted to admit.

Unless it meant the difference between victory and defeat.

"Bring them both!" he ordered, meaning Firian and the Calthwaite boy cowering behind the larger blond soldier.

The Tanyu must have misunderstood that *both* meant two and not three, because they finally subdued Firian's little band and wrenched their arms behind them. A meaty crack sounded and the Kepron screamed, his shoulder oddly configured in its socket, visible despite the armor. The boy was wearing armor and hadn't been fighting. He continued to grimace, eyes streaming, as Tanyu guided all three roughly by the hair and wrists into Kiria's bedroom.

Firian wrestled against his captors, almost pulling free. His leg hooked back, yanked forward, making the Tanyu holding him jackknife backward. Several Tanyu jumped on top of Firian, pinning him to the ground. With effort, they tied his limbs tightly together, their hands coming away bloody. That was interesting. Firian was injured, though Belik couldn't see where.

Belik crossed his arms. Maybe he should have ordered their quick deaths instead. Normally he would at least have had the Calthwaite boy executed without further fanfare. However, surrounded by reminders of his failures, he wanted something definitive and memorable, reestablishing his dominance.

All it took was a thought.

It didn't matter if he was weak afterwards, as Firian had been. He still had seven guards with him, and several Tanyu in the corridor were beginning to stir.

"So you lied," he said softly to Bard, whose gaze snapped from the captives back to him. "And you too." He signaled to Enktuya and nodded at the traitor who'd told him the Calthwaite boy was dead.

To his credit, the Tanyu didn't protest as his neck was broken. The display made the servants gasp and Jori sob.

Firian didn't register surprise or say a word, but his eyes flashed hatred.

"Father," Daelon pleaded.

"Over there," Belik instructed, ignoring his son.

Many pairs of eyes darted between Belik and Daelon at the word. Nobody commented, but only brought the prisoners against the wall near the fireplace where Bard sat.

His son wasn't the only one whispering hushed comments.

"I'm sorry," Bard said with tears in his swollen eyes.

"No, darling," murmured the Kepron.

"Take *me*," Daelon insisted.

"They all have successors," said the Kingdom soldier stoutly. "This won't end."

Belik's mouth twisted wryly. "And you think anyone will follow *them*?" He scanned the lineup. Firian stared murder at him, but there was something different in his eyes this time. A tinge of imploring. Belik looked levelly back. They both had wanted not to end up against each other. Why was that always the way? Why did everyone betray him?

Belik flicked his fingers. "Kepron first. Move the others out of the way."

"No!" came simultaneously from Bard and Daelon.

Firian fought against the Tanyu holding him, but there were too many and they had him completely bound. Desperation shone in his face. Even caged, he was dangerous. So why did he keep Firian alive? Belik was surrounded by his weaknesses—not only his failures, but also the two people he was most loathe to kill. That kind of attachment could be used against him, as he well knew.

Best to get on with it.

He closed his eyes and focused on the boy blocking his way to power. Dimly, he heard his son begin to pray. Pushing aside all awareness of the bedroom, he made himself in tune with the person before him. He found Jorrim Calthwaite's body in the Second Level, blood pumping violently and breath coming in gasps. Firian was right about their killing ability. It did work even on people who didn't have the Talent. All he needed was focus. He'd almost killed Bard, and Firian had done this many times. Belik could do it too if he concentrated.

But a strong sensation like sandalwood, always in the back of his mind, burst to the forefront, pulling him irresistibly upward. He fought like a swimmer against a current but the pull was absolute. To resist was like closing off sight, not by normal methods but merely by willing it. Couldn't be done. He had hoped never to feel the hateful smoothness of this insistent pull again. But it had to be dealt with. And it finally explained the absence of the Sentry.

Chetana was here.

80

KIRIA

"It's not up to you." Kiria put her hands on her hips. "I won't stand by while you die for me."

"You'd be in incredible danger," Chetana protested, tidying the few items in her tent. Her movements were brisk, efficient, almost too neat. There were no superfluous gestures, all was tight and rigid with nerves.

"I can just open my eyes," Kiria insisted. "I don't have to believe it." *You do.* The words remained unspoken. She gently touched Chetana's wrist. "I want to be there for you."

Chetana straightened and sighed. "I cannot guarantee that this will work."

"But you think it will?"

"I think it *could.*"

Kiria bit her lip, shooing away images of Chetana lying lifeless on the ground. What Chetana needed was encouragement. "No one can get to the palace more quickly or effectively than you. Not even the Tanyu. Belik will pay attention to you. Didn't you say you broke his leg?"

The Amir's mouth tilted downward in a rueful smile. The septum ring settled in the bow of her lips.

Kiria took her hand. It felt like warm parchment. "I'll be right here."

They both sat down on the edge of the bed. "You can't distract me."

"I'll just stand there."

"That will surely get his attention." Chetana tried to laugh. Kiria had never seen her this uncomfortable. The strangled chuckle died away. She squeezed Kiria's hands with both of hers. "Forgive me for what you see."

"Of course." The brittle sound of the candle flame magnified in the silence. Kiria's heart pounded as though she were going to kill Belik herself. Somehow, Chetana had become her rock again. She didn't want to lose her.

Friendly Tanyu surrounded the tent and nearby area, but who knew how many Belik had sent to destroy her? This, at the very least, would give them all a greater chance.

Chetana still hadn't closed her eyes. "Tell Daelon," she said, breathing strangely, "that I... have always loved him."

A hard lump formed in Kiria's throat. She could barely manage a response. "I will."

Bending her forehead down to meet their joined hands, Chetana paused as though in prayer. When she sat up, her face was lined with determination.

"Ready?" Kiria whispered. She wasn't sure that she was ready herself, but she would go anyway. At least once, she had to see the man who had ruined the people closest to her and torn her city away.

Chetana took a deep breath through flared nostrils and slowly closed her eyes.

The setting was clear in an instant, with so many details that it felt practiced. A whitewashed barn. Hay littered the ground and filled the loft above. Bales made a barrier along one wall. Square wooden pillars with peeling paint held up the loft at intervals. In front of them was a warped double door with a complicated lock. The setting sun shot hard beams through thin gaps in the boards. It smelled like dried hay and oil.

Chetana now wore a green dress and yellow shoes. Her curly hair was even shorter. Kiria stayed carefully plain so she didn't attract extra attention. The setting was so convincing that Kiria swam up briefly to the back of her eyelids and spread her hand over the bedspread in the tent to show herself it wasn't real. All she had to do if Belik attacked was to open her eyes, to believe he couldn't hurt her. She might even be able to help, using the tricks Chetana had taught her.

A man appeared by the doors. Broad, medium height, glasses, a pockmarked though not unattractive face. He looked maybe fifty, and he wore all black.

This was Master Belik.

The same Master Belik who had killed her family and friends, taken her home, and threatened her life. The one who had shaped Firian into a killer. The one who had stolen her kingdom.

Her hands were shaking fists, but Chetana barely stiffened at the sight of him.

For a long moment, no one spoke. The fascinated hatred between Belik and Chetana made Kiria's heart beat quickly. She was an intruder here.

The two began walking at the same time, predators circling or dancers beginning a violent routine.

"I see," Belik said, his gruff voice low and commanding. "This was not a good idea."

"I hoped I would never see you again either," Chetana bit out.

"I can find you more easily now. Is it really worth it to try and kill me? That's what this is." The last sentence wasn't a question.

"Yes."

Then why weren't they attacking? They must have been sizing each other up, sensing weaknesses or something. All Belik's attention was focused squarely on Chetana, as though Kiria wasn't worth looking at. She was grateful not to receive such a glare of hatred.

"Your son is here."

Chetana stopped walking. Her face was suddenly ashen. "Where?" The question came out weaker than anything Kiria had heard before. Tears stung her eyes. Daelon.

"With me. In this room."

"You wouldn't—" Chetana cut herself off with a gasped breath. Her elegant hands flew to her collarbone. Then she collected herself, brought down her shoulders. "I see him."

Kiria didn't. All she saw was this barn. Since Belik had come in, even more detail permeated it until it was indistinguishable from a real place.

"He has nothing to do with this," Chetana continued. "You know it."

"Don't tell me what to do with my son!" The shout came out violent and Belik advanced on Chetana.

"He was never your son." Chetana raised her chin, imperious. "You only wanted him to atone for your own sins."

Kiria struggled against helplessness. Did Chetana want Belik to come closer so she could kill him? This didn't look good. Kiria could fight with a blade or turn into a Firian lookalike or levitate as Chetana had done in her dream. But her arsenal of tricks felt pitifully thin.

Belik stood even closer. "I don't have time—"

A scream ripped through the air.

It tore at Kiria's soul. Belik stopped to listen but Chetana didn't seem to hear at all. Only Kiria saw him. It was hard to pinpoint where, but the mirage of a falling boy in pain appeared. He wore Tanyuin black, with dark hair and light skin and eyes squeezed shut. His mouth was open in that dying shriek.

Time seemed to slow to the space between one halting heartbeat and the next.

Firian opened his eyes. They were blue, even in the haze, and fixed on her. She wanted to scream with him, to stop him from falling, to say new words. But all she had was a look. And all it said was goodbye.

81

FIRIAN

THE GROUND FELT HOT. The cheek pressed against it burned with the sharpness of shock. Firian's arms and lungs spasmed, muscles contracting at random. He shuddered as he drew the first mouthful of air into his lungs. Thoughts wouldn't form in his mind. His body could only feel, and it was hellish. It felt as though his head had been split open with an ax. Maybe it had been. If he wasn't dead, he was dying.

Events in Kiria's bedroom settled into his mind like butterflies, landing and flying away and landing again, bright as blood. He was here to kill Belik before he could take the Western Kingdom for himself. This was Firian's last stand.

But he couldn't stand.

He peeled his eyes open and turned his hammering head. Above him, darkness reached as far as the sky. The sight made him dizzy.

He wouldn't get out again.

Kiria had seen him fall. She would know what happened to him, what he'd tried to do. That he had tried his best for her, even if it hadn't been enough. There was no time to show her that he felt ashamed of how he'd used her, or that she impressed him with her courage, or that she showed him what it meant to be a leader. Or that he loved her.

Touching the floor with his palms to ground himself, he rocked upward, determined to stand up. He crouched with his feet under him and stood slowly, wavering.

Belik met his eyeline.

Firian's gut clenched. Belik's scornful look took in all of him, knew all of him, and dismissed it in disappointment. He didn't seem afraid that Firian still had the power to kill him. Or maybe Belik wasn't afraid of death. If that were so, Firian wasn't either. But this time, it wasn't the recklessness of desperation, it was the strength of knowing that his life was as small and large as other lives. The gigantic shadow of his own importance had shrunk into himself. Now he was Firian Kess, just Firian Kess, and he could save the ones he loved.

That assurance brought life into his limbs again and he stood more steadily.

"We both know you can't kill me," Belik said. He hadn't moved from his position opposite Firian. Neither of them created a background apart from the darkness. Each of their bodies glowed as if a light shone on it. "You're too weak." He held up a hand to stop a reply, but Firian still couldn't gather enough breath to say anything. "I know they stopped you only because you're outnumbered. You fought well out there."

Firian dragged air into his lungs, summoning all his strength, which was barely anything now. *Breathe.*

Still Belik didn't attack. Firian's mind spun. He had an opening then, something he could say to stave off the inevitable, to hold off the execution of Jori and Bard and Kiria.

"Then stop," Firian croaked, his voice a ragged, breaking whisper. He could barely see around the pain in his head. There was no way he could use his killing ability now.

Belik gave him a sardonic look and wiped the lenses of his glasses on his shirt as though deciding what to do.

"I could stop," the Master said slowly, not looking at him.

As he waited for an explanation, Firian felt like prey in the sights of a predator. He was the deer with a broken leg, or the rabbit chewing grass without sufficient camouflage. He tried to flex his hand around a knife, any weapon, but his joints only creaked. Breaking through the Sentry and falling, falling in pain had robbed him of all the ability he'd worked so hard to gain.

"I'll make you a deal," Belik said, repositioning his glasses as though he'd just made up his mind.

Firian struggled to keep his attention sharp. "What deal?"

"You're doing this for the princess, yes?" Belik didn't wait for a response. "What if I could give her to you?"

The pounding of Firian's heart just made his body hurt worse. "What do you mean?"

"If you come back"—the words seemed almost wrestled from him—" then I'll make sure you have her. That's my offer. I dispose of the other heirs, all of them, but keep her for you." His stare became earnest. "We could *make* something of the Tanyu, Firian. It's what we've always wanted. I saw you fighting out there. And..." He took a deep breath and leaned back, glaring as though Firian had said something defiant. "And I hate being against each other." He bared his teeth almost as if he were reprimanding himself for the words. "So that's my offer. Gory generous, is what it is."

Belik had said he wouldn't make an offer twice. In some part of his twisted brain, he couldn't let Firian go.

And then what? Firian had given that question a lot of thought. Belik's offer didn't describe something he could live with anymore. It was everything he wanted, and nothing. Now, despite his pain and despite the offer, was the warm certainty of what was right. But, if he played along, could he buy her time?

"Princess," he found himself muttering.

"Yes, Tanyu are almost there. I don't have time to waste, Firian."

"Keeper," Firian said more loudly. "You'd be better off calling Kiria a queen."

The two men looked at each other. Firian's answer echoed through the featureless darkness. He hadn't addressed Belik's offer, but by defending Kiria, he defied it.

Finally, Belik observed his nails, clenching his teeth. His brow creased in obvious anger.

Firian waited for the killing blow. His feet were stronger now. He felt them beneath him. His legs too. His head still pounded, but his body belonged to himself again.

He watched the man who had been his mentor, who had cared for and aggravated him, believed in him and betrayed him. Firian swallowed. And he summoned all the strength he had left, which felt so small, and directed it at Master Belik.

Firian had more experience killing this way. This was a slim chance, but at least it existed. As long as Firian lived, he would fight. All of Kiria's courage and sacrifice for her people would pay off.

Belik looked at Firian again, and Firian felt his own bones and muscles constrict, bending backward. Firian pressed harder through the headache and the pain shooting up his back.

The muscles in Belik's face twitched with exertion. *It's working!*

Firian kept on, throwing the whole weight of his mind toward Belik until he felt the fluttering heart, the straining muscles. His own body felt shredded open, but as long as his mind could focus, he fixated on Belik.

Firian's vision narrowed, blackening to a point. He couldn't breathe anymore. The pressure on his spine and skull and eyeballs was too much. He'd burst apart. He had to give one last try. Hopefully that would be enough.

Kiria laughing at the dance last night and Bard squeezing his forearm and Brett staying up with him until they could fall asleep.

He tried one last time and collapsed.

82

KIRIA

BELIK WAS GONE. Chetana and Kiria stood alone in the barn. The Amir looked at her with dark, skeptical eyes. Kiria didn't know what to say. Had Belik gone back to the real world, refusing to take Chetana's bait? Or had he somehow followed Firian's apparition?

"Belik!" Chetana called.

When there was no answer, Kiria said, "I saw Firian."

Chetana's forehead creased. "When? Where?"

"He fell." She traced his path with her hand. *He was screaming.*

A tiny measure of relief showed in Chetana's face. "His Sentry is gone?"

"I don't—"

Belik's big form appeared where it had before, stumbling once before righting himself. Kiria couldn't remember ever having seen a Tanyu stumble. He was wounded or exhausted. Firian told her about his bad leg, but Kiria hadn't noticed it in the Unreal.

Chetana wasted no time. She glided forward, seeming not to use her legs. Belik's expression was different. He looked at

Chetana as a soldier might look at someone who could help him to his feet. Kiria could imagine Firian looking at her like that.

Chetana raised a hand and touched Belik's cheek. Then she shoved his shoulder so his back was pressed against the wall. Kiria was invisible behind them, intentionally so. The moment was strangely intimate. No words were said.

Chetana planted a fierce kiss on Belik's lips. Belik was a little shorter than she was, and the kiss was almost like a battle in itself.

When she pulled away, Belik was bleeding from the chest. The Tanyu sucked in a breath of disbelief and rage when he realized. As he fell awkwardly to the hay-strewn floor, light slicing across his body, he glared at Chetana, who held a blade in her fist. Then the glare lost its luster. His limbs settled horribly, small movements, into permanent positions. The barn itself seemed robbed of breath in the silence that followed.

Chetana turned around to face the place where Kiria stood unseen. The Amir seemed to know exactly where she was anyway. Her dark face was drawn and bloodless. She took a shaky step and stopped as though she couldn't go any further. Instead, she stood rooted to the spot, her gaze falling to the ground.

Kiria came back to the Real and squeezed Chetana's hand. Chetana still didn't open her eyes. Her mouth hung slack and a concentrating line formed above her nose.

"Chetana." Kiria shook her lightly with her free hand. "Chetana."

The Amir gave a shuddering gasp and opened her eyes, collapsing forward. She gripped Kiria's shoulder to hold her up.

"You did it," Kiria said, struggling with her weight. Finally, she had to lay Chetana down on the bed. It was odd to see someone weak who usually held herself as straight as a queen. "You killed him."

Chetana didn't reply.

Hot tears stung her eyes. She had to tell someone. She had to tell everyone. Without Master Belik's leadership, their way back onto the throne was clear.

After checking Chetana's pulse and breathing, Kiria left her on the bed, eyes closed as if sleeping. Drawing back the tent flap, she caught the attention of the nearest Tanyuin guard. "He's dead," she said. "Belik's dead. Tell the Tanyu. All of them."

Surprise and a curt nod followed her words.

It's almost over.

She went back inside the tent to check on Chetana, who was trying to sit up. Kiria gently took her hands and helped her.

"It was for Daelon," came her first words, an excuse for committing a crime.

Kiria nodded and rubbed Chetana's back like her own mother had done so many times. This should have been a moment of celebration, but Chetana drew her hands over her face and her back shuddered. Kiria hugged her tighter and spoke soothing words in her ear as she cried.

83

BARD

BARD WATCHED Jori writhe in the grip of his captor. His shoulder wasn't right, and the Tanyu twisted his arm cruelly. Panic showed in the whites of Jori's eyes. Belik's face was a calm mask of concentration as the other Tanyu in the room waited for his demonstration. Bard's bowels turned to ice. This wasn't supposed to happen. He remembered the Torithian who escaped the night Firian came back from the war. He had screamed, writhed, and fallen a broken man with blood seeping from his eyes and ears. It was awful to watch, and now Jori had the same edge of confusion and terror.

Down the line, Firian screamed, a bone-chilling sound. Never before had Bard heard such a raw noise. Bard trembled as he looked just in time to see Firian go limp. His head lolled back, mouth open. Multiple Tanyu held him, even with his arm and leg restraints, and they pitched as he fell as though unsure whether to hold him up or lay him down.

"Fir." The word was a breath. Bard couldn't manage any more.

Was Firian breathing? Bard stared at his chest. He couldn't tell. It didn't look like it.

Belik's ability had worked. On Firian. Time stretched and blurred.

A servant cried. Beside Bard, Daelon's steady voice chanted prayers under his breath.

Jori's eyes tore away from Firian's unmoving body—Bard couldn't think the other word—and lighted on Bard in a question, a plea for help. He didn't grow up trained as a warrior, bred to resist the fear of death.

It's okay, Bard wanted to say, but the words stuck in his throat. It wasn't. In seconds, the same thing would happen to Jori. Bard could hardly see him through his tears. There was nothing he could do at this moment but comfort him.

He cleared his raw throat. "Thank you... for running out. You would make... such a... such a good Keeper, yeah?" His voice kept breaking, so he paused.

Jori paused too. He heaved a deep breath that sounded almost like relief.

Bard shot a glance at Belik. His eyes were still closed, and the empty quiet went on a beat too long.

Jori still looked scared but no longer panicked. Had... had Firian broken through the Sentry? Impossible. It couldn't be done, and even if Firian had tried again, the attempt, or Belik's secret ability, had killed him.

Still, something had distracted Belik. If the other Tanyu hadn't noticed, then Bard didn't want to draw attention to it.

"Glad you think so," Jori croaked, attempting to smile. The result was horribly lopsided. "Took three people to give me the tattoo. I think they just wanted a look. It hurt so bad." He grimaced, apparently reminded of the greater pain he was in at the moment.

The Tanyu behind Jori looked uncertainly at Belik, who hadn't moved, or even changed his expression. An unspoken question hung in the air.

Bard ran through options in his head though he knew it was like looking over a lost Indisfate board, more to see how he could have won than to make a difference now. All his allies in the room were bound and hopelessly outnumbered. No one, that he knew of, was coming. It would take a miracle to restore the Western Kingdom to its rightful owners.

Daelon still prayed in the background. That might be something. Divine intervention. But it wasn't something one could count on.

The Tanyu grew more restless. What was happening? Even Royce looked at Bard as though he wanted direction. But Bard's throat was dry as chalk, and he was out of ideas. His plan hadn't gone at all the way he'd hoped. And now Firian was...

Belik fell hard to the ground. A deep stain spread through the front of his black shirt, just over his heart.

Bard stared in disbelief. Tanyu leapt forward to revive him.

"Is he...?" Jori asked.

Bard coughed once to speak. "Charäkhnem is coming!" he said as loudly as he could. His voice sounded odd. "You heard him. There are thousands coming this way. Belik is... dead." His face and fingers felt numb, but he kept going. "If you help us, maybe they won't kill you. We can tell them you helped us." He stopped, out of breath as though he'd been swimming for hours.

Two Tanyu still bent over Belik, trying to staunch the wound.

The same care wasn't given to Firian, but they did lay him down. Bard didn't see a stain growing over his skin, no blood, but he wasn't moving. His roommate. His friend. His enemy. His brother.

He swallowed against the lump in his throat, trying to keep his thoughts clear. He couldn't lose sight of the chance Belik's sudden death provided. Maybe the game wasn't lost yet.

"Yes, we'll tell them what you did," Jori agreed.

"You'll have no hope if you kill us," Bard added.

Their glances met, a secret between them. Jori's eager trust was enough to get Bard to the next moment, and the next. It probably would get him through many moments, if he lived so long.

Belik and Firian lay on the ground a body-length apart. The two acting Tanyuin Heads. Tanyu didn't stay leaderless for long, but their uncertainty told Bard that neither had clearly appointed an heir to take his place.

"We can't listen to this," wheezed Shiro by the door. "Who's a traitor to the Tanyu in this room?"

"You wouldn't be a traitor if you help us," said Bard, though he knew his word was as good as dirt to Shiro. "Tanyu are warriors, not murderers. I don't want you all to die."

"Do we have more coming?" one asked his neighbor in a gruff undertone.

"Not in time," Bard answered.

"Shut up. Do we?"

Shiro lifted his chin defiantly. "You think we can't hold this city? The new army isn't even inside the gates."

"But they have more than ten thousand. And Tanyu. Suicide isn't glorious."

"It isn't suicide. To win we just need to kill him"—Shiro stabbed a finger at Jori—"and the princess." Apparently, Shiro had taken his position as Belik's new protégé seriously.

"And we have backups," Jori said. "Mine's Haved Ganesha."

Bard clicked his teeth together. There were so many reasons why he shouldn't have said that.

"Princess of Charäkhnem," Jori pressed on. "I'm reasonably certain they'd send more soldiers if their princess were in danger."

Actually, it wasn't the worst plan. Putting a target on Haved just wasn't a particularly good one.

"Kiria listens to me," Bard said.

"And me, of course." Jori winked and immediately twitched as though the movement pained him.

"We'll ask her to show you mercy."

Shiro's face was red now. "Tanyu don't need mercy. They don't show mercy." His angry stare flicked once to Firian's unmoving body and then concentrated on Jori.

A knife was in his hand before Bard understood where it had come from or what Shiro was doing. Shiro flew at Jori. Royce yanked his body sideways to block the blow but only managed to knock Jori off balance. The armor clacked into the back of Bard's wooden chair.

Two large Tanyu held Shiro by the arms. A quick fight left three more Tanyu with their limbs bound. No one had let go of Jori or the others, but obviously the majority saw the sense in what Bard said.

Shiro spit in Bard's face.

Bard blinked the warm saliva away. "Call off the attack," he said. They all knew what he meant. If the Tanyu killed Kiria, they doomed themselves. All the Tanyu went vacant for a moment. The servants looked at each other in confused astonishment, still clutching their plates of food.

It was working. Bard's plan was actually working. The Tanyu were calling off the attack on Kiria. Lightheadedness took him for a moment and he swayed in his chair.

"Let them come back one at a time, or go back to the Academy," said Bard, righting himself again. He didn't need the confusion of angry Tanyu coming all at once. "And let Jori announce what happened."

"Before we have any terms?" someone asked, incredulous.

"We need something that benefits us both," said another.

"*Life* benefits you," Jori said.

Bard tried to raise his eyebrows in agreement but his face didn't work that way at the moment.

The argument went on for a long time. Bard negotiated with Kiria, who talked to the Charäkhni forces, promising no killing of Tanyu until a proper investigation had been done. Tanyu would wait until their judgment could be pronounced, and Kiria promised to show leniency to anyone who helped her cause and protected her people. The Tanyu had to promise afterward to be escorted from the city. Bard knew there were many who would rather run back to the Academy than stand trial under Kiria. Positions of power were there for the taking, and the guilty could prevent execution. They would deal with that later.

Finally, there was a tentative agreement, a truce strong enough to untie their bonds. Shiro and Enktuya were taken down to the dungeons. The bodies of Firian and Belik were carried from the room.

At sunrise, in a makeshift sling, Jori stepped onto the same balcony where Belik had been crowned, and he announced their victory.

84

JORI

Jori stepped back from the balcony as winded and flushed as if he'd just been thoroughly kissed.

From that height, he could actually see Kiria's troops marching toward the palace. An uncomfortable stab of apprehension lanced him before he could remind himself that this wasn't an attack. These people weren't coming to murder but to help. He strained to look for Kiria but she was so small, she could have been heading the column and still been invisible. A helpless little smile crept onto his lips. He felt nearly hysterical.

As he turned back to Bard, Royce, Daelon, and a few Tanyu, his shoulder throbbed. Bard's poor face, all smudged from beatings and crying. And still he'd managed to come up with a way to get the Tanyu to surrender.

"Could you change out of black, please?" he said, looking at the others. "You can see how that would make me uncomfortable." Personally, Jori doubted he would ever wear black again.

"We need to get ready to greet the troops outside," Royce suggested, completely ignoring the comment.

Together, still on guard, they all made their way to the palace's main entrance. Jori hardly ever used that entrance. The door always struck him as more of a decoration than something functional.

As they stepped outside into the morning sunlight, his stamp as the black sheep of the Calthwaite family took him with tremendous force. He hadn't even fought. He'd just struggled to stay alive, and that alone would inevitably leave him with suffocating nightmares of being pulled apart from the inside. Kiria should be here to do this. But she led the other side of this meeting.

The sun climbed as the army made its torturous way. Jori's life was an eternal wait, apparently. The rising sun gilded the stone houses and courtyards and side streets. He should have felt elated, but he only felt... lots of other things. He wanted to say something to the others but all his thoughts were half-formed sentences.

Bard gently touched his arm, his good arm, to bring him back to reality. Reliable, that one. Responsible and tender in a way Jori feared he would never be. Well, while there was life, he could still try. He gave Bard a crooked smile that felt weaker than what he deserved for his efforts today. Bard's cheek crinkled back, a mirror image of his own expression.

Up the long walk from the street below, Kiria was coming, with Haved, a couple friendly Tanyu, and members of the Kingdom guard. An un-Keeper-like sob escaped his mouth before he could stop it. He cleared his throat to cover it up, but no one would believe he was only coughing.

Kiria was a vision, Beautiful and tired. They both still wore armor, he realized. It felt like he had put his on a week ago. And Haved beside her looked nearly as lovely, with some of his brother's love reflected in her eyes. Others were there, but, compared to his girls, they didn't matter.

It wasn't diplomatic, but then, neither was he. Jori crushed Kiria and then Haved in the best one-armed hug he could manage, kissing their temples as something warm slid down his cheeks. Haved gently pushed him from her. "It was a close one," he said once he released them. "We've got the palace under control now though. Finally."

Just behind his eyelids were the bodies of Viktor and Belik and Firian and even that Tanyu who made to stab him and got cut through the neck. Did Jori still have blood on his face? He raised his good hand—even that motion earned him a stab of pain in his other shoulder—and surreptitiously rubbed his cheek.

"I heard," Kiria replied. "We'll get the final casualties soon."

Jori could have done without the numbness in her tone. "You, my dear, are Keeper again."

She mustered a smile that seemed to give her enough energy to grace the others with it too. "I was always the Keeper," she teased. "You're the one who's new at it." She lowered her voice so the people behind them couldn't hear. "And not forever. Haved just told me—"

Jori's mouth dropped.

"—she's pregnant."

"No!" His fist flew to his mouth. "Jorrim the Second! No, wait. Atael the Second!" He looked at Haved to see if he'd guessed right. A nephew! An heir! His brother's heir!

She smiled in that self-possessed way of hers.

"Atty the Second." Jori cast his eyes upward. *Are you seeing this?* So he only had to rule for sixteen or seventeen years. He could live with that. He could do more than live with it. It was perfect.

"I have the terms listed here," Kiria said, reaching behind her for a short stack of papers. "Shall we head to the Main?"

Right, they still had war things to discuss. Jori flashed a smile at Haved before looking at the paper.

"Obviously, they're basic now," Kiria explained, "but enough to call an official end to the war. I'll sign it." She nodded to someone over his shoulder. "One of the Tanyuin Masters has to sign it next."

"Please, I know all that," said Jori, handing the paper back to Kiria. He caught a glimpse of citizens coming out of their houses, tentatively looking at the palace steps. He gave them a regal wave before going inside.

"I'm glad you're all right," Bard said to Kiria, his comment oddly pointed. "You seem all right."

She was looking up at the ceiling. Jori tipped his head back too. Artwork, verses, and architectural features now spread unevenly across the vaulted interior. What had been uniform now was smudged or emphasized, based on the whim of the fire.

Kiria's expression was somber and thoughtful, alive with memory. "I will be," she replied.

Bard whispered something into another Tanyu's ear and the warrior ran off.

Jori asked for information with a look.

Bard just whispered, "Firian."

Formalities took place in the Main, with Kiria and Jori standing on the dais amid the improbable configuration of chairs. Haved, Bard, and others, including Amir freed from their cells, Parohim among them, stood as witness. A Tanyuin Master Bard told him was named Ardal filled the role of surrendering party. The Tanyu lost none of their gravitas during the exchange, almost as though many of them thought that the whole exercise of taking over the capital was below their dignity, and they just wanted to return home.

When all was done, terms read, marks written, and prayers said, Jori handed the paper back to Kiria. She acted distant, but positively regal. Battle did that to a person, he supposed.

"Charäkhnem has agreed to stay for a few weeks to begin escorting Tanyu out of the city," she said.

"Sporting of them."

"And I will stay here as well," said Haved in her low, measured voice.

"Even better!" He observed the sea of Tanyuin and Kingdom and Charäkhni people dispersing, several under guard, and turned tentatively to Kiria. "Is that all then? Can I have a drink now? I believe Bard owes me a bottle."

Bard nodded in that way of his.

"Let's have a toast," Kiria suggested, finally lightening around the edges. "*May it rain hope always.* And then off to bed."

85

KIRIA

FIRIAN HADN'T WOKEN UP. Three days had passed since Belik's death. Every day, Kiria and Bard called to him in the Unreal, but they were running out of time. What else could they do?

Even though the Sentry had finally been found and dismissed, Firian hadn't shown himself. None of the Tanyu understood the Second Level well enough to explain what was happening. Maybe the First Level was nothing but pain. Maybe he was trapped. Maybe he didn't want to wake up.

Bard had taken a break to rest, leaving Kiria and her guards alone with Firian. She had much to do to reestablish the Kingdom under her protection—new coronations to prepare for, judgments to pass on traitors, alliances to make and dissolve, building restoration projects to oversee... Yet here she was, with every spare minute, and even a few that weren't spares.

Firian's face looked gray, his lips cracked and parched. He couldn't survive much longer like this. His dark brows stayed slightly furrowed as though he were having a bad dream.

Come on, Firian.

Kiria would have to judge him, as she had judged other high-ranking Tanyu. Shiro had been executed, along with Enktuya,

Belik's other enforcer. Some, as expected, had fled—another day's problem. She didn't know how she would judge Firian, but she knew she wanted him to wake up.

She brushed his hair away from his forehead. His skin felt feverish. Not long now. Closing her eyes, she went into the Unreal again. If their *katah* didn't save him, nothing would. Enveloped in darkness, she called his name. Again. Again.

Nothing.

The pit of her stomach roiled. Was there nothing more she could do?

When she came back to the cool medical room, her hand held his. She and Bard would keep trying, but maybe this was it. He was dying in his effort to kill Belik and restore her throne. A beautiful crack of light.

She threaded her fingers through his. It was a fitting end, if it had to be the end.

His chest rose and fell more quickly, his eyes moving behind the lids. Kiria caught her breath and shot a look at the guard. "Get the doctor." She turned back to Firian's sleeping form. "Firian," she whispered. "Are you awake? Open your eyes." Remembering herself, she raised her voice so another guard could hear. "Get Bard too!"

Firian's throat moved as he swallowed. His lips parted sleepily.

"Firian, can you hear me?"

Squinting up at her, he gained his bearings, trying to angle up on his elbow. The blanket covering him fell, exposing his bare chest and revealing a thick bandage on his lower back. As he moved, his hand caught his attention, entwined with Kiria's. He looked confused more than pleased, as though he were seeing an illusion.

"I didn't get him. I didn't get Belik," he said quickly, in a voice husky with disuse. "I don't think he's dead."

"We got him," she replied. "Chetana stabbed him through the heart." Chetana had also been bedridden the past few days, but she was sitting up and eating now. She needed her strength to fill the place she'd earned as regent until Kader came of age. Her *katah*, even so many years removed, had made her pay a high price for executing Belik.

Firian squeezed her fingers gently, almost tentatively. She squeezed back. "So the Kingdom's yours again?" he asked, easing himself back down on the bed.

"It is. We won." She was still getting used to the idea, but she smiled.

His expression turned to a frown. "You came back for me."

She nodded.

"Why didn't you leave me there?"

The arrival of Bard and the doctor saved her from answering. She pulled her hand from his.

"Ah, he's awake," said the doctor, a good-natured Hinterlander, taking Kiria's place on the seat and easing his arm behind Firian's back to help him up.

"Fir!" It looked like Bard wanted nothing better than to hurl himself forward in a hug. Bard's broken nose looked purple and his hair, as usual, was wild. "You're up! You're out of the Unreal."

The effort of sitting took all of Firian's concentration. Even his eyes were shut tight in pain.

"Kiria and I called and called. I didn't know if you'd come out of it, mate. I thought..." He scrubbed his face with a knuckle, careful to avoid the splotchy bruises.

Kiria could only nod again.

The doctor pressed his thumb to Firian's wrist. "Dehydration."

"I'm okay," he replied, more to Bard than the doctor. "I heard..." He took a deep breath and hunched over, as though gathering his thoughts. With one hand on his forehead, he continued. "I heard you. Both of you." He didn't give more details. His pain seemed too powerful for him to focus.

The doctor ushered over some water. "And a stab wound."

"You heard us?" Bard came to stand next to Kiria.

"Yeah." He couldn't speak for a few more seconds. The doctor pressed a cup into his hand. "We won?"

Something in his tone gave Kiria pause. "You'll live, Firian."

"Yes," the doctor confirmed. "Liquids and rest will get you up in a couple days."

"Jori's alive too?"

"Yeah. Yeah, he's fine," answered Bard.

"Kader's on his way too," Kiria added. "We'll be all right."

"All right," Firian repeated, half-delirious. Small pangs distorted his face at intervals, as though he were bracing for a blow.

"Jori told me what you did, how you kept him safe. That's pretty amazing." Bard gave Kiria a glance as he said it. "And Kiria's army was ambushed right after sunset."

Kiria cut off his praises, which were inevitably coming. She deserved little praise. The people around her had made victory possible. "Without Bard, none of this would have happened. He negotiated the surrender."

Dimples appeared in Firian's slow grin. "Ah," he said, "I can't believe it. You're like..." He looked at Kiria. "You could take down a mountain ghost, couldn't you?"

She smiled, delighted by the compliment. Firian rarely gave them, so they were all the more precious. *Be dangerous. Be brave.*

"You too," said Bard.

"And you"—he looked at Bard—"your plan worked."

"Don't be surprised."

Kiria couldn't tell if Firian's response was a cough or a laugh. Then he hummed softly, disbelief and thoughtfulness echoing through the sound. The same question ran through Kiria's mind: What next?

As soon as Firian was up, she'd have to decide whether would she lock him up indefinitely, exile him, consign him to physical punishment, execute him... His ability to kill others with his mind made him a dangerous prospect for a prisoner. She relished none of the possibilities. Somehow, though, she sensed he'd bow to her wishes. It was an odd feeling. He'd found a cause and he'd stuck to it, to his own hurt. He'd always been extreme, but now he seemed to have found an outlet for his focus. And he chose to help her.

"You should probably leave him alone," said the doctor, startling her out of her reverie.

She looked up to find Firian already looking at her. They both looked away. She cleared her throat. "Of course. We can go."

"Just—" Firian caught her hand.

She pulled it away swiftly, but stopped to hear what he had to say. Her fingers felt warm.

He pinned her with his bloodshot gaze and his voice dropped, low and earnest. "I never should have..." His throat worked as he forced out the words. "You deserve more... than me."

She regarded him, his sovereign but also one of his only friends. The moment stretched between them, his words echoing like crashes in an empty room. She felt the presence of Bard and the doctor. Firian, on the other hand, seemed completely oblivious to them. Firian had had opportunities to apologize before, and she never thought she'd hear the words.

"I know," she said. "Get some rest."

Bard joined her near the door.

Jori met them outside, looking fresher than any of them,

despite a few scrapes and his dislocated shoulder. "He's alive, I take it."

"He opened his eyes. He's talking!" Bard exclaimed.

Jori shot Kiria a look, almost wary, and adjusted his sling. It looked like it was made from a tapestry, it was so elaborate. "Does he remember his heroics or is he back to his insufferable self?" He said it teasingly, as though he couldn't decide whether to take himself seriously.

Kiria and Bard just gave wry smiles.

"You're not in love with him, are you?"

Kiria dropped her eyes, but the question was directed at Bard.

"No," Bard said firmly.

Relief crossed Jori's face. A barely perceptible smile flickered in and out. "Shows good judgment. Although you didn't see him fight those other Tanyu."

When Kiria raised her eyes again, Jori met them, sparkling laughter in his look. He was teasing, not criticizing. He hugged her sideways. "Keeper business is so serious."

She hugged him back. The first few days after the battle had worn her out. Justice was slowly being done, as much as she and Daelon, her new advisor, could reckon. But joy was yet to come.

"We all look dreadful," Jori said, wobbling his broken arm.

He wasn't wrong. Bard's hand flitted toward his face before he dropped it again. Kiria had almost forgotten about the scars on her own face. The reactions she got as she sat on her makeshift throne in the ruined Main hadn't substantially changed. Now she had not only Beauty, but Beauty that had overcome.

"I've come to a decision," Jori said suddenly.

"What is it?"

"My official coronation is... soon. Whenever we can finally get a good party going. So I've chosen my advisor."

Kiria had a feeling she already knew who he'd choose.

"Bard," he confirmed. "Has to be."

One person, at least, was surprised by this news. Bard raised both eyebrows so high they almost disappeared in his hairline.

"He's a Tanyu," Kiria pointed out, not because she disapproved—Bard was an excellent choice—but to goad him. "He'll have to learn the Scroll."

Jori held out his arm toward Bard and pushed up the sleeve. "What does this say, love?"

"*May it rain hope always.*"

Jori replaced his sleeve and gave her his most self-satisfied expression. *There,* he seemed to say. *No need for discussion.*

"I'm happy to take lessons," Bard said. "You know, if... if that's your decision. I've always been kind of curious. And I've read some of it. Firian's copy, remember?"

A Tanyuin advisor. An Amiran regent. Times were changing, but not for the worse.

"I think that's a great idea. I'd love to have you as our advisor —Jori's advisor." Truthfully, she'd like having Bard close by. Judging by the way Jori had started to look at him, that was likely one way or another.

"It could be good for relations between Amir and Tanyu," Bard added eagerly.

"Absolutely," Jori said, winking at Kiria.

And it would be. Kiria had big plans, ones that involved years of careful reconciliation between the two groups. Bard, with his Tanyuin training and Amiran spirit, would be the perfect ambassador.

86

KIRIA

Two days later, Kiria sat on the dais in a black dress edged in silvery blue. Beside her sat Jori, looking almost too pleased to be wearing that crown. On her right, the throne was empty. Kader, whose throne that would eventually become, would return shortly from Hinter, where he'd been in hiding. She couldn't wait to see him and get more involved in his life than she'd been before. In the absence of Cúron, Chetana was regent, voting with the other Keepers and advising in the Main, but she wouldn't occupy the throne. Instead, she sat in her usual seat at the foot of the short steps alongside Bard and Daelon. A Tanyu and an Amir. Who would have thought they could co-exist so peacefully?

Royce had requested to attend the final round of judgments as well. For all his help, Kiria agreed to his request. He sat a few rows behind, holding the hand of his wife and one of his daughters. After some of the dust had settled, Kiria found out that all but one of his children had survived the battle. The mix of joy and grief on his face when she told him nearly broke her heart.

Bard's brother Jac had survived too, though he was currently helping with the effort to escort pardoned Tanyu out of the city.

"Bring him in," Kiria commanded, and two Charäkhni soldiers opened the carved double doors. They were partially burned now, but she planned to have them reinforced with metal as soon as possible to preserve what was left.

Firian appeared, bound, flanked by six Kingdom guards and a new Sentry. Someone had given him clean clothes—tan and deep purple instead of his customary black. He walked with a straight back and a grim expression until the group reached the foot of the platform. He knelt down before her.

Jori shot her a furtive look. Kiria hadn't told him what she was planning to do. Even now, looking at Firian, she knew she could change her decision and no one would argue, not even Bard, the only one she'd told.

"Firian Kess," she said, "it's time to pronounce your judgment." Why was her stomach in knots? She had lost nights of sleep over this decision. Finally, she believed she came to the right one.

He looked up at her with resolve in his blue eyes. There were still shadows under them from his recent coma. Almost imperceptibly, he nodded. *It's all right.* She could almost hear his thoughts, despite the Sentry. *Go ahead. It's all right.*

She blinked before continuing. "You took me hostage, threatened the Kingdom, are responsible for conquering innocent towns, blackmailed your Keeper, and led an army of Tanyu to our walls."

He didn't look away as she recited his crimes.

"But, for your assistance in the last battle, I am commuting the death sentence which, in the past, you deserved."

His lips parted with relief and hope, and his gaze intensified with the obvious question. What, then, were they going to do with him?

"You are hereby banished, body and mind, from the Western Kingdom, all of its lands south of the Charúnin Thôr, for a span of three years. During that time, and for the rest of your natural life, you will work on behalf of the thrones, starting by gathering those who have committed crimes against the Western Kingdom. The first will be the former bodyguard to the King of Charäkhnem. Master Tanery will give you details. He is the only one you are allowed to have any contact with inside the area from which you are exiled. Should you enter our lands during that time or fail to continue your work for us then or afterward unless released by word of a Keeper, the punishment will be death."

His chest rose and fell in deep breaths. His lashes fluttered as he looked down for a moment. When he turned his attention to her again, his look was bright and intense.

"You will be escorted from Brithnem immediately," she continued, her tone automatic. "Then you will have seven days to get to the mountains."

She saw Firian's throat work as though he were trying to swallow.

"Plenty of time for someone like you," Jori added, rubbing two fingers together as though they had something sticky on them. He didn't look at Firian. "And Bard will be in touch."

There was something knowing in Firian's gaze when he looked back at her. He knew this was mercy. This was thanks.

She raised her chin and nodded back at him—the tiniest movement, like his had been. Then the guards turned him around and she watched him march out of the Main.

87
——

EPILOGUE

Firian knew he was born in the last cold stretch before spring, so that meant he had just turned twenty-three. When he had first come to the Academy, they told him he would have to work until he was twenty-four before he became a Tanyuin Master. Even with his exile, he beat their estimate.

It had been almost three and a half years—eighteen missions—since he received his judgment.

Everyone called it the Autumn War now. He'd heard his sister and her husband call it that more than once. Giving the battle a name made it sound like it should be written down in the Scroll. But his memory of the pain and cold and death couldn't congeal into a simple fact to be memorized. It was the life in his veins, more wholesome than the pure fiery liquor of the Tanyuin Academy. He belonged nowhere, but pieces of himself had slowly started to come back together, creating someone he liked more than the desperate boy he once was.

Before, breath had stuck tight in his chest. Always, he lived braced, tense, ready to fight. He still had that grace, that poise, but he could breathe again. Strange, for someone called the Ghost.

He'd hunted criminals, assassinated warmongers, protected innocents, stolen plans for weapons, and even encountered creatures that in the past he would have called monsters.

He was everything the Kingdom needed him to be—a one-man force taking care of the northern borders. Still a weapon, but now a weapon in a just hand. Most of the time, he didn't mind traveling by himself. He had always enjoyed being alone.

Last year, Bard and Jori had visited the Academy—Bard on official business as the liaison between the Kingdom and Tanyu, and Jori for the sheer joy of it. At least, that's what it seemed. The Third Keeper acted as though he could barely stay in his skin. Firian caught glimpses of them after their meetings and time at the pub looking at every detail of the fortress and the town beyond.

The Academy's power had diminished. Tanyu had returned to find the treasure stores looted and curious folk harassing those in Tánuil. The strangers were quickly dealt with, but the bigger change was the new integration with the Kingdom. Patrols of silver and blue soldiers were a common sight now.

On their trip, Bard was delighted to explain everything and Jori asked questions, hanging on every word. Bard brought the new Indisfate set his oldest brother Edom had hand carved for them. The woodwork was impressive, but Jori kept saying he looked like a hunchback compared to Kiria, who looked beautiful and fierce, holding a sword aloft.

"You're running," Bard had explained.

"No one runs like that. Why can't I hold a sword?" Jori tried out the pose.

Bard laughed.

Today was different. Technically, today's visit was for the Second Keeper to meet face to face with Master Erron, the new Tanyuin Head, to talk about integrating parts of the Tanyuin and Amiran Academies. Three years of work with the public had convinced the people of Brithnem to consider the idea. At least, that was what Firian had heard.

He'd kept his word, hadn't looked in on Kiria in the Unreal, though there had been nights in the first year when he couldn't sleep for the ache in his chest.

Of course, he listened eagerly any time someone brought news from Brithnem. The Main had been rebuilt, roads had been repaired, new statues crafted by the best artists. Much of the news, however, wasn't as positive. Events surrounding the Autumn War rent the Western Kingdom along many lines. Unrest filled the streets of Brithnem. Every report of Kiria and the other Keepers showed them handling the difficult situation the best they could.

The Charäkhni princess Haved lived in the palace with her little boy, who would inherit the throne from his father Atael, taking Jori's place when he came of age. Amrit Ganesha, heir to the throne of Charäkhnem, felt sympathetic toward Kiria and the others, so their official alliance with the neighboring kingdom would be reestablished sooner or later.

Kiria had made her good start. He felt her presence with every positive advance the Kingdom made. She ruled with compassion, but didn't hesitate to protect her own. She could be fiercely just, and it made Firian admire her more.

No one ever brought more than the thinnest rumors that she met a partner. The entire kingdom would know if she were engaged, would flame with the news faster than a wildfire.

He imagined her happier now. How could she not be? Bard certainly was. He was meant for Brithnem, not the Academy. Sometimes Firian suspected that it was Bard's happiness bolstering him on days when he would have felt sullen. In a strange way, Firian felt more satisfaction too. A veneer of regret slicked over him like sweat, but the spikes of anxiety and the black rush of rage were less common. He could sleep.

Except for last night.

Kiria was coming to the Academy for the first time. *The first time!* That didn't seem possible. After all they'd been through, all the times she had seen it through his eyes...

But first, a required meeting with Bard about another mission. When Firian slept at the Academy, he stayed in a small room at the end of the second-story hallway. Past the washroom, the corridor curled deeper into the fortress, like the curve of a shell. Firian spent only a small fraction of his time here, so it didn't make sense to reserve a better room for him. His was practically a closet, even smaller than the one he'd shared with Bard. Here, he sat cross-legged on the floor, Watchman-like, to ground himself. All day he'd barely heard a word. His ears had piqued only for Kiria.

"Master Kess."

"Master Tanery."

They began every session that way, partly because it reminded them of the seriousness of what they were doing and partly because it was funny, for some reason.

"Hey, Fir," Bard greeted again, grinning. He wore a light beard now, along with finer clothes, and his nose looked a little crooked from the break. His hair was still crazy. "Shifra, please."

Firian, who'd been there far more often than Bard, created the swampland around them with its great, mossy trees and wooden walkways, like endless docks, zigzagging through.

"The edge," Bard clarified.

Yellow grasses from outside the jungle became visible through the trees. Sunlight filtering down looked more yellow and less green. "Good?" Firian asked.

"Good. There's a little village near here—I don't know if you've heard of it. Probably, but it's small. Honesowel?"

The odd name sounded even weirder in Bard's accent. Firian's lips twitched. "Yeah, I've heard of it."

"We've gotten reports that a man is hiding there. He attacked several of Kiria's personal guards during a diplomatic visit to nearby towns, but he fled before anyone could get him. We need you to bring him in."

Pretty typical target, then. They discussed more details—names, faces, times, dangers.

"Has she arrived yet?" Bard asked after their official business was done.

"Hm? No."

"Should be today, yeah?"

"I know."

There was mischief in Bard's look. "It'll be all right, mate. You've done good work. I tell them everything."

Firian knew that. What he didn't know was why he felt so nervous. "I've got to go," Firian said, unable to wait any longer. The trees poofed into colored smoke.

"Tell me how it goes."

His heart beat thickly as he nodded and left, striding down the long hallway, then taking the stairs down to the main floors three at a time. Was she here? How many would be with her? Would they get a chance to talk?

As Firian jogged down the resident hall, he felt the shifted atmosphere. Down in the fountain courtyard, Learners, Defenders, and Masters all moved more quickly, though Kingdom soldiers in their silver and blue armor stood at their customary posts. Part of the deal Kiria had cut with the Academy was that they would have to endure oversight, and that any attack on her soldiers would be tantamount to a declaration of war. Firian had watched from this vantage point so many times that the change, though small, was unmistakable. Daily disputes among warriors vanished in a concert of motion. This was one thing the divided Academy could agree on—preparing for the arrival of the Keeper.

Running a hand over his face, he wished he could look out a window. *Breathe. Maybe she doesn't care to see you.* He forced himself to calm down. The next steps he took one at a time. What was he running toward? Her? After all that had happened, her heart probably didn't beat faster at the mention of *his* name. Three years was a long time.

The soldier guarding the right side of the wooden double doors at the entrance peeled away from his post to approach him. The armor gleamed dully in the light of the single chandelier.

"Master Kess?"

Firian pulled his shoulders back, evaluating what to expect. "Yes?"

"The Second Keeper requests your presence after her meeting," he announced.

Firian tensed. He'd half expected her to leave without seeing him. "When?"

"She should finish soon."

"Then I'll come immediately."

The guard led Firian through his own Academy as though he knew its halls and secrets better. But the small indignity was swallowed up by the magnitude of what was happening. *Requests your presence?* For what? Was there a second judgment she would hand down? Did she want to say hello? None of that would match what they had been to each other.

The guard led Firian to the Head's office. He avoided this hallway when he didn't have official business. The memories rankled. His pulse pounded as he crossed the threshold into the familiar space. Two Kingdom guards, Master Erron, and a person taking notes filled the small room.

Behind the desk sat Kiria. Beautiful, perhaps even more so with the long scars that ran across her lips and cheek. The wound had healed into dark lines that proved she could outlast storms. Her face and posture showed she was a few years older, settled into her role as the most influential Keeper of the Western Kingdom. She wore a new crown of metal and glass, like something shattered that had been pieced together into something more beautiful. Little of that uncertainty he remembered from their first meeting remained. As he entered, Kiria's amber eyes fixed on him.

He'd forgotten—he always forgot—how much her Beauty affected him. It wasn't something he could imagine the right way, even in the Unreal. His throat worked as they locked eyes, deep recognition sparking there.

"My Keeper," he managed, and bowed. His voice sounded steady and professional. Years of practice kept his face even too.

"Master Kess," she replied. She seemed much more composed than he was. "How have the missions been going? Are they successful?"

Why did she even ask? She got updates from Bard regularly. "They've gone very well." One side of his mouth crinkled in a proud smirk.

"The assignment seems to suit you."

In the past, he would have taken the comment to mean that it suited him better than being the Tanyuin Head, and he would have bristled at it, but she was right. He was more effective than he had ever been, finally using his skills in a way that mattered. The job was dangerous, but he'd always liked the cold snap of danger. Now, he didn't have to ask himself if the danger was needless. His purpose was clear, and he sliced his way toward it like a bird through the air.

She had known him better than he knew himself. Was that still true? The buzz of her mind rested against his like white noise in the room.

"Would you be open to a change in position?"

He raised an eyebrow. She could simply command him, and yet she asked his opinion. "I might be."

"I need a new bodyguard. Mine's about to retire."

Firian's stomach flipped, a chaos of emotion running through him. He flexed his hands open and closed to retain feeling in them. He met Kiria's gaze, but words didn't come for several labored breaths.

Even with several years as Keeper, she was still a new leader. Firian was a legend, and more recently the ghost visiting justice on fled Tanyu and criminals. Everyone knew who he was, and what he had done. Well, no one knew the whole story. An eleven-year-old boy he'd met near Enderin said he thought Firian was the good guy, because he did the coolest stuff and killed the bad guys. But only his most infamous deeds were agreed upon by his few admirers and many critics. If he became her bodyguard, it could make other nations trust her less.

"My Keeper," he began, unsure of where his response was going, "what about your reputation?"

At that, Kiria beamed, stretching the scar across her lip.

For a moment, he couldn't think. She was so lovely. All that existed was Kiria and her smile.

"It's been worse," she laughed. "I know you wouldn't allow anyone to harm me." She gestured vaguely to her head. Their *katah*. Harm to Kiria would mean harm to himself too.

Was this real? This felt too much like dreams he'd had on the road. "Of course I wouldn't." The words came out more breathless than he'd wanted. He cleared his throat. "If that's what you want."

"You've proven yourself loyal these past three years. You have the chance to prove it again. Or do you know someone who would be better for the job?"

There was a slight challenge in her eyes, amusement on her lips. They both knew what he would say.

"No one, My Keeper." His insides burned. This was actually happening. Then he remembered. "I have a mission that will keep me away for a week."

"The transition doesn't need to happen immediately. I'll still send you on missions periodically, even after you are my official bodyguard. No one has been as effective as you have in catching fugitives and carrying out the will of the Kingdom in... difficult situations. When you're finished with your work here, come to Brithnem. I'll tell the palace guards to look for you."

"Thank you." He gave another small bow from the waist. Everything felt familiar and new. Even the tug he sensed in the Unreal. His skin prickled, but he didn't respond. She couldn't be waiting for him there. He already had enough of his dreams come true for one day.

"That's all for now," she said. "I'm leaving tomorrow. If I need you again, I'll let you know."

Her words were kind, but he felt the distance in them. After three years without communication, though, this proximity felt like floating interminably in the ocean and finally seeing land.

As he exited, the Unreal beckoned again. It was the matter of a thought to get there. Still, he hesitated. A true *katah* never went away, but that didn't mean that she wanted him inside her head. It was too dangerous to undo all that carefully cultivated self-denial. As her bodyguard... He smiled. Her bodyguard! He would have to continue keeping his feelings in check. It was worth it to be near her, to protect her, to do something worth doing.

"Firian."

This time there was no mistaking her voice from the Unreal. Heart thundering, he answered.

They stood far apart in a replica of the fountain courtyard. Kiria had recreated it almost perfectly. He blinked. Her skill had improved tremendously.

She no longer used her Ability, and stood as he knew her best—simple but breathtaking, the girl he had known and protected and betrayed.

There was something archetypal about Kiria, especially this way, as though other people were patterned after her. She made everything more real. Seeing her felt more like coming home than going back to the Academy did after a mission. It was a sense of rightness, of belonging, like the way he fit into his own body, even when it was in pain, just because it was his.

For a moment they stood in silence, the weight of all their history surging between them. Then, slowly, Kiria smiled, her look full of memories. His chest suddenly ached with them. God, he loved her. Without her, he wouldn't have become the man he was. A man he could finally be proud of.

She looked younger this way, with such raw thanks on her face, a mirror of some of his own feelings. In her gaze, there was a touch of the wonder he'd seen when they'd gone to Shifra. An evaluating kind of gladness, one that invited him to share in it. Since meeting her, he had seen her grow more determined, confident. Maybe he'd had a hand in that too.

Neither moved toward the other, but there was understanding and there was hope. Despite everything, despite how their story should have ended, they had made each other better.

And he smiled back.

ACKNOWLEDGMENTS

I have the usual suspects to thank for this book. Seriously, my heart is full of gratitude for the way these people have supported me and these books.

Readers first. I'm blown away by the reviews and art, the gifted copies and words of encouragement. I hope this final installment of the series gives you joy.

Family. You all thought I could be an author even after I'd given up on the dream. You are worth more to me than all my other readers put together (sorry, guys). Your tough love, constant presence, medical explanations, and excitement when I got one more favorable review means more to me than I can say.

School. I teach English at a high school, if you didn't already know. Teachers and students like Hannah K. have provided me with ideas, names, insight, and general enthusiasm that make me happy.

Beta readers. Now, I really, really couldn't put out books without you guys. Giving feedback on a chunky novel is not a small thing, and yet you all helped make the Tanyuin Academy series better than I ever could have made it on my own.

More books in the Tanyuin world are on the way. I want them not only to provide you an escape and characters to love, but also to show that God always provides hope, even in the darkest of places.

ALSO BY CARLY STEVENS

Firian Rising

Into the Unreal

Tanyuin Academy Stories

ABOUT THE AUTHOR

Carly Stevens lives and works as an English teacher in Colorado.
She plans to keep writing adventure-filled fantasy novels about
courage and hope.

To find out more about upcoming projects, check out her
website: https://carly-stevens.com
Her author newsletter is the best place to get an exclusive,
behind-the-scenes look at the world of the Tanyuin Academy.
You might even win free books for signing up!